I0760175

BOOK XIX IN THE RAIDING FORCES SERIES

STAND TO!

PHIL WARD

A RAIDING FORCES SERIES NOVEL

This book is a work of fiction. Names, characters, businesses, organizations, places, events and incidents are either a product of the author's imagination or are used fictitiously. Any resemblance to actual persons, living or dead, events or locales is entirely coincidental.

Published and distributed by Military Publishers, LLC
Austin, Texas
www.philwardauthor.com

ISBN: 979-8-9920645-5-1

Cover design by Stewart Williams
Maps: Tom Houlihan
Color by Maddie Kleinwachter
Social Media Management: The Social Butterfly,
https://socialbutterflytx.com

For ordering information or special discounts for bulk purchases, contact
Military Publishers LLC
3616 Far West Blvd., Suite 117, Box 215 Austin, TX 78731

~~

The Raiding Forces series continues all the way to VE Day.
Be the first to get updates and know about upcoming releases.
To be on our notification list, scan the QR below and sign up.

Visit the Raiding Forces Series Facebook page at
https://www.facebook.com/raidingforces
phil@philward.com

GETTING THE MOST FROM THE RAIDING FORCES SERIES

The Raiding Forces WWII Series is written like a continuous WWII special operations campaign. It unfolds raid by raid. Missions are high intensity, rapid tempo of short duration, characterized by surprise, speed and violence of action. Characters rotate based on tasking and operational necessity while command relationships and strategic objectives remain fixed – win the war. Raiding Forces, the unit, is constantly being reconfigured to meet the demands of different theaters and mission profiles as the conflict develops.

These books are designed to be read in sequence with tempo, reach and lethality escalating as the war progresses.

Jump in and hang on. It's a wild ride.

Phil

Phil Ward
RLTW

PS: I recommend researching even the minor characters. Many are real people with amazing tales of their own. You may be surprised at some of the famous names that show up in the story from time to time.

DEDICATION

STAND TO! is dedicated to Charles Barnett aka Charlie.

I met Charlie in the first grade. His father was our Scout Master and I always credited him with saving my life when I was bleeding out from a face wound in Vietnam. My two medics could not figure out where to put the tourniquet – my neck being the only option. Suddenly I remembered the diagram of pressure points Charlie's father, a decorated WWII Marine, had taught our Boy Scout troop. I reached up, pressed it, the bleeding stopped like flicking off a light switch and now I'm sitting here writing Charlie's dedication, not KIA in the Mekong Delta.

It did not have to work out like that.

We went all the way through school together. But life took us in different directions when we got out of high school. Charlie graduated from the University of Texas. After college he joined the Bureau of Alcohol, Tobacco and Firearms (TABC).

When Charlie got married I was his best man at the wedding – (events leading up to the ceremony remain classified.)

Charlie had a colorful career in law enforcement. He transferred out to the West Coast. From time to time he would come home to Austin and we always got together. The last time I saw him he described the six agent-involved shootings he had been in. That has to be some kind of record. Not sure he told very many people.

As you go through life, you do not have a lot of friends like Charles Barnett – I wish I weren't writing this.

RANDAL'S RULES FOR RAIDING

RULE 1: The first rule is there ain't no rules.

RULE 2: Keep it short and simple.

RULE 3: It never hurts to cheat.

RULE 4: Right man, right job.

RULE 5: Plan missions backward (know how to get home).

RULE 6. It's good to have a Plan B.

~~RULE 7. Expect the unexpected~~.*INACTIVE*

RANKS, DECORATIONS AND NICKNAMES

RANK PROTOCOL:
The first time a person is named in a chapter or after a chapter break their full rank and name is given. Addressing military personnel by their rank is a mark of respect. At all levels rank is earned and those who have it from a corporal to a four star general are proud of it.

DECORATIONS:
In the British military officers are authorized to put the initials of their decorations after their name. In the Raiding Forces Series the protocol is the first time an officer is introduced in a book the initials of his decorations are listed following his name. After that for the rest of the book they are not.

In the U.S. military officers do not have the same privilege.

NICKNAMES:
In the British military nicknames are endemic. Radio operators are called Sparks, red heads are called Ginger, tall people are called Lofty but sometimes short people are called that too etc.

In the U.S. military there are a lot of nicknames but nothing like the British.

ONGOING OPERATIONS

OPERATION BODYGUARD – A comprehensive deception campaign covering the D-Day invasion– a bodyguard of lies, code named "BODYGUARD."

OPERATION FINDERS KEEPERS – Leave an auger in plain sight on every beach in France.

OPERATION FLIPPER – Kill or capture Field Marshal Erwin Rommel, commander of the German Afrika Korps. The target was believed to be Rommel's headquarters villa. Militarily: a failure.

OPERATION FORTITUDE – A deception plan to convince the Germans that the D-Day landing would occur in Pas-de-Calais instead of Normandy.

OPERATION FORTITUDE NORTH – An Allied deception plan designed to convince Nazi Germany that the Allies intended to invade Norway.

OPERATION FORTITUDE SOUTH – A subset of FORTITUDE is aimed at presenting *Pas-de-Calais* as the target for the invasion.

OPERATION LONG NECK –
(previously OPERATION LEAF EATER)
Diamond interdiction program / Eliminate diamond smugglers.

Command and Control team – code name **CARD GAME**, consisting of Col. Randal, Major the Lady Jane Seaborn, Captain "Geronimo" Joe McKoy, Captain Billy Jack Jaxx, Waldo Treywick, Captain Pamala Plum-Martin, Mandy Paige, Beverly Blackwell, King, Captain Roy Kidd, MSgt. Mack Beckwith

OPERATION OVERLORD – The eventual invasion of enemy-occupied France being marshalled in Great Britain.

OPERATION RED INDIAN
Cover name for OPERATION GOLDEN FLEECE.

OPERATION REVERSE MUSKET
The semi-true plan to deliver Liberator pistols to the French Underground.

OPERATION STEINBOCK – A German bombing campaign against southern England. The operation was largely considered a failure. It did not significantly disrupt Britain's war effort and further weakened Germany's already strained air force just months before the Allied invasion of Normandy.

Calais – Cap Gris Nez Sector

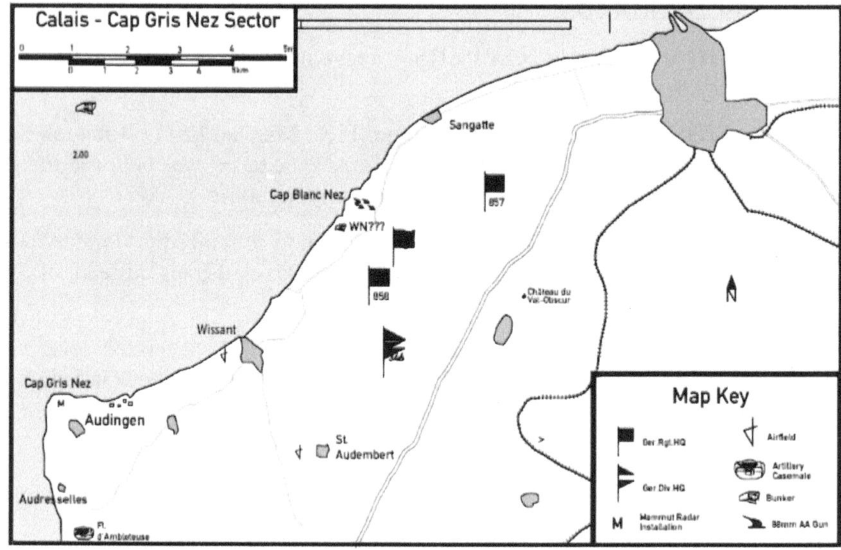

1

BURN AFTER READING

From: Lieutenant Colonel John Henry Bevan, Chief, London Controlling Section
To: General Dwight D. Eisenhower, Supreme Allied Commander
Subject: Strategic Purpose of OPERATION FORTITUDE SOUTH
Classification: MOST SECRET/TOP SECRET- EYES ONLY

The object of Fortitude South is not merely to mislead the enemy as to the place of our initial landing, but to compel him to retain his principal mobile and reserve forces in the Pas-de-Calais area in anticipation of a decisive assault that will never occur.

The operation is designed to create and sustain the enemy's conviction that any landing in Normandy constitutes a preliminary or subsidiary effort, and that the true main blow, delivered by a powerful U.S.-led force assembled opposite the Dover- Calais axis - remains pending.

Our measure of success will lie not in the enemy's reaction on D-Day, but in his failure to release and commit his Calais-based formations against our forces in Normandy during the critical period of consolidation.

FORTITUDE SOUTH must accordingly be maintained *after* the landings with sufficient plausibility to justify continued German inaction. The deception is intended to fix enemy forces in place, delay their decision-making, and deny them the freedom of maneuver at the decisive moment.

In short, we seek not to surprise alone, but to cause hesitation - and to make that hesitation decisive.

NOT TO BE RETAINED - BURN AFTER READING

2230 HRS. 25 DEC 43 BLETCHLEY PARK (GC&CS): INTERCEPTION AND DECRYPTION

A CODED GERMAN ABWEHR MESSAGE INTERCEPTED BY A British Y-station was dispatched to Hut 6 for decryption then passed to Hut 3 for intelligence analysis. Since the content of the message related to Abwehr suspicion about the reliability of certain German spies operating in the United Kingdom, it was flagged ULTRA – indicating MOST SECRET/TOP SECRET signals intelligence. Because the codename ULTRA itself was classified it was blacked out and the Bletchley Park intercepts/decryptions were stamped in red ink: MOST SECRET SOURCE (MSS). The classification was the highest Allied Forces' personnel not cleared for ULTRA were authorized to see.

Protocol for any MSS decrypt involving the Security Service (MI-5) required it to be routed "with utmost urgency" to Group Captain Eric Jones, the officer-in-charge of Hut 3, who sent it up the chain-of-command to Commander Edward Travis, Director of the Government Code & Cypher School (GC&CS). From there the decrypt was hand-delivered to Major General Sir Stewart Menzies aka "C", DSO, MC, Chief of the Secret Intelligence Service (MI-6) by a Special Liaison Unit (SLU) courier who had been ULTRA "indoctrinated" – SLU was an MI-6 asset. Since the contents concerned domestic security and were time-critical, "C" had it forwarded by the SLU officer to Major General Sir David Petrie, KCB, OBE, Director General of MI-5 at his personal residence.

Maj. Gen. Petrie scanned the message. Then he instructed the SLU – who was under strict orders to remain in the room while he read the decrypt – then take it back. "Pass this on to Lieutenant Colonel Robertson, Chief of Section B1-A."

Lt. Col. Robertson was responsible for handling German spies captured in Britain and playing them back against the Nazis. The SLU officer was then to hand-carry the message on to the London Controlling Section (LCS). This slowed the notification process but ensured security.

There was only the single copy to safeguard. No others were made.

A surprisingly small number of officers within MI-5 were cleared for ULTRA. Lt. Col. Robertson was not one of them. Where ULTRA was blacked out on the cover sheet next to MSS, Maj. Gen. Petrie wrote "Expedite" and initialed it. The general also ordered a senior officers conference at MI-5 same night and made plans to return to his office.

Within the hour after Maj. Gen. Petrie read the "Boniface" – the informal nickname used by those individuals cleared for ULTRA to obscure an ULTRA decrypt – a King's Messenger arrived at Major the Lady Jane Seaborn's Christmas party. He delivered a dispatch to Colonel John Randal.

> PLACE RAIDING FORCES ON ALERT FOR AN IMMINENT MISSION FORTHWITH.

This was not the typical directive Col. Randal had come to expect from King's Messenger (KM) conveyed messages – an order to "Stand To." Raiding Forces had three levels of alerts. 1) Standby Alert, 2) Standby Ready and 3) Red Alert. The unit was always on Standby Alert. In order to elevate the status to Standby Ready – meaning with weapons, ammunition *and* mission-specific gear – there had to be a mission statement, however brief, that defined the objective. That was necessary for him to form an estimate of the situation – who, what, when, where, in order to know how to brief the strike team leader to prepare for load out.

None was specified.

Since the dispatch had been delivered by a King's Messenger it was not only TOP SECRET it was TOP PRIORITY. At least someone with enough pull to have it conveyed by KM thought so. That meant expedite now.

Who ordered the alert was not indicated – but then it never was. The source of Raiding Forces' KM directives was a mystery. There were not many people in government or the military who had the authority to order one dispatched. When a KM arrived it meant stop what you are doing and execute, execute, execute.

"Forthwith."

Col. Randal glanced at the flimsy and then placed it in the inside pocket of his tailored U.S. Army Class A uniform blouse. The missive required no action on his part. Raiding Forces *was* on alert. Whoever dispatched the KM should have known that.

Col. Randal and Lady Jane were at her Christmas party sitting at a table with her godfather Lieutenant Colonel John Henry Bevan, MC and his wife, Lady Barbara. They were engaged in a convivial conversation when the KM arrived. The Controller of London Controlling Section was regaling them with a story about his passion – fly fishing. The Chief of Deception could not ignore that Col. Randal had received a dispatch delivered by the most discreet and reliable armed courier service in the realm.

But he did not act surprised or inquire about the contents.

Soon after the King's Messenger departed Squadron Leader Dennis Wheatly, the author of *Jump on Bela,* appeared. He had been summoned from his home on Christmas night to the War Office where the LCS maintained a secretive suite of subterranean rooms close to the center of power. The night duty officer alerted him to return to the office to be on hand to receive a MOST SECRET Source message.

Downstairs in the suite – with the SLU physically present to retain the original copy and ensure no duplicates were made, it only took seconds for Sqn. Ldr. Wheatly to scan the contents. It was clear the Most Secret Source intelligence outlined in the decryption constituted exigent circumstances for MI-5, B1-A, the XX Committee and LCS.

The implication of what was contained in the GC&CS-decrypted intelligence was earth-shattering. The most priceless asset LCS, XX Committee and MI-5 B1-A possessed was imperiled. The cover story for the D-Day invasion was at risk. Sqn. Ldr. Wheatly realized he needed to bring the matter to the immediate attention of his boss, Lt. Col. Bevan, in person.

The colonel was attending a party at the Brandford Hotel thrown by his goddaughter. The SLU was instructed to remain in the suite in control of the ULTRA document while he personally went to find the Controller of LCS to break the news.

When the Squadron Leader discreetly whispered in Lt. Col. Bevan's ear the Chief-of-Deception said, "Sorry, Jane, duty calls."

After making arrangements for Lady Barbara to be driven to their quarters he and Sqn. Ldr. Wheatly departed the hotel in a rush.

While this was taking place, the Security Service night watch officer walked in. He spoke to Lieutenant Colonel Thomas Argyll "Tar" Robertson. The Head of Section B1-A also made his apologies and left with his wife.

Upon arriving at MI-5 and reading the MOST SECRET SOURCE plain language decryption, Lt. Col. Robertson instructed the SLU courier to deliver it to Lieutenant Colonel John Cecil "J.C." Masterman. He also phoned ahead to notify him a message was en route and of the meeting Maj. Gen. Petrie had called.

Not long after Lt. Col. Robertson's departure, one of the Vulnerable Points Wing security operators came to inform James "Baldie" Taylor of a priority phone message waiting at the front desk. He excused himself to take the call. And did not return.

As these developments were playing out across the room Lieutenant General "Geronimo" Joe McKoy was staring holes in Col. Randal. As was Captain Billy Jack Jaxx at another table. Both officers had dates with showgirls. "Geronimo" Joe was with a "stationary nude" from the infamous Windmill Theatre and Jack Cool with one of Bob Hope's Gypsy Dancers. The two female entertainers had transitioned from the center of attention to being ignored in a heartbeat. An experience neither woman was used to.

What just happened?

Major General William "Wild Bill" Donovan was seated with Veronica Paige, OBE, Major General Sam Houston Blackwell, friends called him "Bronc," and Brandy Seaborn, GC, OBE at another table. The Director of the Office of Strategic Services was observing the events taking place wondering what it might be that OSS was being left out of.

Dealing with the British intelligence services was a constant battle for inclusion – they wanted to maintain their monopoly on the European continent.

Col. Randal was sitting perfectly still. Outwardly calm. Lady Jane knew that was a tell – he was clicked on. Just when things were going so swimmingly. Now they were never going to hear the end of her godfather's fish story.

Lady Jane noticed Col. Randal had turned his champagne glass upside down. Around the room Raiding Forces' officers took notice. One by one they tossed down the last of their bubbly then turned their own glass upside down.

No one made any comment.

MAJOR GENERAL SIR DAVID PETRIE, DIRECTOR GENERAL MI-5, Lieutenant Colonel John Cecil Masterman, Chairman of the XX Committee who preferred the title Professor instead of his military rank, Lieutenant

Colonel John Henry Bevan, Chief of the London Controlling Section, Lieutenant Colonel Thomas Argyll "Tar" Robertson who held the dual titles of Head of Section B1-A and Controller of the Double Cross System (operational control of the turned German agents) which was different from the Double Cross Committee, and James "Baldie" Taylor gathered at 58 St. James Street. This was an emergency meeting to address the MOST SECRET SOURCE message's implications for the Double Cross System, Twenty Committee, the London Controlling Section and the upcoming D-Day invasion of France.

Only Maj. Gen. Petrie and Lt. Col. Bevan were cleared to know the MSS message was an ULTRA decrypt.

Maj. Gen. Petrie produced a transcript. He had transcribed it from memory having had to surrender the original decrypt back to the SLU officer per protocol. Fortunately, MI-5 was full of officers with photographic memories. The general was one of those.

```
TELEX-BERLIN HQ-12 DEC 43-URGENT
      ABWEHR OFFICER MAJOR HANNS VON REISEN
   CALAIS DISTRICT REPORTS CONCERN REGARDING
   AGENT RELIABILITY IN ENGLAND
      STOP
      SIGNS BRITISH MAY HAVE COMPROMISED OR
   TURNED ONE OR MORE OPERATIVES STOP REQUEST
   IMMEDIATE VERIFICATION OF CODED REPORTS AND
   NETWORK STATUS
      STOP
```

Only Jim was learning of this development for the first time. He immediately realized the gravity of the situation. If the Germans learned that their spies in England were under MI-5 control, the deception codenamed OPERATION FORTITUDE SOUTH, designed to cover the actual site of the D-Day landing, could and likely would be compromised – a disaster.

FORTITUDE SOUTH was designed to convince the Nazis the invasion would take place across the narrowest part of the English Channel–the Dover Strait. Equally important, the deception plan called for the cover story to deceive the Germans into believing the landing at Normandy, when it came, was a feint. The real invasion would be later in Pas-de-Calais – a classic double bluff.

The second part of the deception was imperative. There were two German armies in France. The 15th in the Calais region and the 7th in Normandy. FORTITUDE SOUTH was tasked with two missions: 1) covering the actual invasion site – Normandy, and 2) pinning the 15th Army in Calais in anticipation of the "real" invasion landing there later – which was never going to happen.

General Dwight D. Eisenhower had asked Maj. Gen. Petrie, Director General MI-5, to "Hold the 15th Army in place for at least fourteen days after the initial landings in Normandy to prevent our 21st Army Group from being defeated by sheer weight of numbers."

The likelihood of being able to accomplish the Supreme Allied Commander's request was now in question.

Maj. Gen. Petrie said, "What to do, gentlemen?"

Lt. Col. Robertson said, "We have to remove von Reisen – whoever he is. Take him off the board, sir. If he goes away the impetus to follow through on an investigation into the German spies in England will be stymied if not eliminated. We need to buy time until the invasion.

"We shall most likely be forced to sacrifice one or possibly more of our double agents to make it appear to the Abwehr the problem is solved."

Prof. Masterman said, "A pity."

Lt. Col. Robertson said, "Actually not. We can sacrifice notional agents. Since they never ever existed, no great loss."

Maj. Gen. Petrie said, "Mr. Taylor, check in with MI-6 to see if they have a dossier on this von Reisen fellow. Also, launch an effort to pin down where he is located."

"Sir!"

Maj. Gen. Petrie said, "You are a military analyst. In your professional opinion what would an operation to eliminate this threat look like?"

Jim said, "Three possibilities immediately come to mind, General. Assassinate von Reisen by employing a long-range sniper, kidnap him, or locate his headquarters and have it bombed when he is on the premises."

Professor Masterman said, "All three of those three options would appear to require our dependence on Special Operations Executive to carry out all or part of the operation – one pales at the thought."

Jim said, "Possibly not."

BOXING DAY THE DAY AFTER CHRISTMAS IN GREAT BRITAIN – was a long-time tradition going back to the 17th Century. It originally referred to "boxes" or gifts of money given out by the wealthy upper class to their servants, tradespeople, or the poor. Now it mostly consisted of bonuses for employees. And it was a way to keep the holidays going for one more day.

Captain Billy Jack Jaxx said, "I thought it was a day for boxing matches."

Beverly Blackwell added, "I thought it was for boxing up all the Christmas presents.

Colonel John Randal said, "I had never heard of it before enlisting in the Rangers Regiment when I first arrived in London."

Mandy Paige laughed, "Now you know – we like to keep the party rolling."

Major the Lady Jane Seaborn, LG, OBE, RM, was going around the hotel with the manager and Happy passing out envelopes containing cash bonuses to the staff. When she was finished there was a get-together in the small Penthouse Lounge for Raiding Forces and noted other personnel, such as Major General William "Wild Bill" Donovan and Major General Sam Houston "Bronc" Blackwell.

Earlier when General Dwight D. Eisenhower and his staff were having lunch in the restaurant, Lady Jane presented him with a seal brown Jacket, Flying, Type A-2 with an oversized Supreme Headquarters Allied Expeditionary Forces (SHAEF) insignia painted on the left breast and four gleaming stars on the epaulettes.

Lady Jane invited the general up to the Penthouse Floor in the private elevator – others in the hotel did not have access to the top level. Lady Jane showed him a suite built out for him by combining two rooms. The "Supreme Commander Room" was for his use when the general was in London. It was located adjacent to those of the exiled heads of state and deposed royalty staying in the hotel – fit for a king.

Just not in the Raiding Forces' Section.

Lady Jane was a strategic gift-giver – she knew about the Smiling Jack bandit affair. Gen. Eisenhower was pleased with the unexpected Supreme Commander Room and leather bomber jacket. Normally cautious about accepting presents because they created an implied obligation to return the favor he did not feel threatened by accepting her gifts.

Gen. Eisenhower could not think of one thing Lady Jane could ask of him in return and that made her generosity all the more appreciated.

He might have been wrong about that.

WHEN EVERYONE INVITED WAS ASSEMBLED IN THE PENTHOUSE Lounge, Major the Lady Jane Seaborn passed out the presents she had been accumulating for months in anticipation of the Christmas season. She had not expected to celebrate it in England which was especially nice for her.

Lady Jane became so excited about giving the gifts she sat on the floor next to the recipient and helped rip the wrappings off. She was a one-of-a-kind original. Everyone loved her for it. The presents, while not wildly expensive, were not cheap. Each was selected with a great deal of thought.

Colonel John Randal received the bespoke Turkish walnut pistol grips for his 1911 Colt.38 Supers and 22 High Standard Military Model D – with the fine, almost imperceptible cross-hatch checkering she had ordered handcrafted for him months earlier in Cairo.

Lieutenant General "Geronimo" Joe McKoy was given a Wilkinson's Sword Ltd. drop point folding knife with creamy mammoth ivory stocks to match his pistols.

Major General William "Wild Bill" Donovan and Major General Sam Houston "Bronc" Blackwell both were gifted 1911 Colt.38 Super service automatics. Lieutenant General "Geronimo" Joe McKoy had them tuned for her to the exact same specifications he, Col. Randal and Captain Billy Jack Jaxx had on their fighting pistols. Trigger job, polished feed ramp and higher profile sights with a gold bead on the front blade – basic modifications to improve reliability and performance.

The grips on Wild Bill's handgun were high-figure Bastogne walnut. Bronc's were ivory. Both sported a pair of silver stars inlaid on the right grip panel denoting their rank. From their reaction, it was clear both generals were delighted–they knew weapons.

Neither man had ever owned a .38 Super caliber handgun.

Waldo Treywick was given a Damask steel cigar cutter with his initials WT engraved – an appropriate present considering his passion for passing out custom hand-rolled panatela cigars.

Capt. Jaxx was gifted two pairs of grips for his 1911 Colt 38 Super pistol. Ivory for rear area dress wear. Gaboon ebony known as black ivory, for night operations. Both sets had a slim sterling silver Raiding Forces' scroll inlaid on the right grip panel the same as Col. Randal's.

Lady Jane said, "I want the ivory set I loaned you back, Jack."

In fact, the stocks she wanted returned were a pair of Col. Randal's carved ivory grips from his Abyssinian "Big Shot" days she had appropriated. There was a long list of items of his that Lady Jane had commandeered for her own… to include Happy.

Lieutenant Colonel Sir Terry "Zorro" Stone, KBE, DSO, MC, received a Jacket, Flying, Type A-2 with an oversized regimental crest of his family regiment – the Lancelot Lancers aka Lounge Lizards painted on the left breast.

King was presented a silver cigarette case created by Asprey's of London – a nice contrast in gifts only Lady Jane would have thought of… hardcore soldier of fortune, elegant cigarette case.

Lieutenant Ted Hamilton aka "The Great Teddy", OBE, was given a Savile Row Lock & Company silk top hat, a trick vanishing cane and a 1st edition of *Greater Magic* by John Northern Hillard, widely known in certain circles as the "Magician's Bible."

Each of the women, to include Red, received a small green velvet-lined case containing a silver Cartier compact with their initials monogrammed on the lid under a RAIDING FORCES flash – an exquisite gift they would use every day.

Col. Randal gave Lady Jane a bottle of Chanel No. 5, the only fragrance she would wear. He liked to tease her it smelled like Vanilla extract. Brandy Seaborn obtained the perfume for him. Not easy in wartime London.

Brandy was impressed Col. Randal knew the name of the brand Lady Jane wore.

Happy got a big bone from the hotel kitchen.

The Boxing Day gathering was a small affair. Even though they were away from home everyone enjoyed being there. For some present it was the closest thing to a family they had.

No mention was made of certain aspects of last night's Christmas dinner. That did not mean anyone had forgotten about the sudden departures of select guests in the middle of the evening's festivities.

James "Baldie" Taylor was still absent.

A FOLLOW-UP MEETING ON BOXING DAY FOR THE TOP MI-5 personnel was called by Major General Sir David Petrie, Director General of the Security Service. There had been a mad flurry of activity relating to the MSS intelligence regarding Major Hanns von Reisen – the Abwehr officer who was questioning if the German spies in England were a reliable source. The major posed a significant threat to the Double Cross System– meaning the network of turned German spies now working as double agents for the Allies.

And that, in turn put FORTITUDE SOUTH, the cover story for the D-Day invasion, at risk.

OPERATION BODYGUARD, so named after a Churchill quote, "In wartime the truth is so precious it should be attended by a bodyguard of lies" – was the overall Allied deception strategy for D-Day. The plan included subsets of multiple subordinate operations.

The most important was OPERATION FORTITUDE SOUTH, the cover for the invasion that would take place in Normandy. The plan was to convince the Nazis the Allies would land in Pas-de-Calais. Selling FORTITUDE SOUTH to the Germans was the primary focus of Lieutenant Colonel Thomas Argyll "Tar" Robertson's MI-5, Section B1-A – the team responsible for handling turned Nazi spies.

If the fact the entire German spy network in England was under British control was ever learned by the Abwehr, the deception campaign to mislead the Nazis about the actual whereabouts of the D-Day invasion site would be blown. The London Controlling Section and XX Committee would be out of business. And the possibility of a forced entry of the European continent via France might well be compromised.

Amphibious assaults are most vulnerable at the point of attack and for some days after landing. They remain so until a strong enough beachhead can be established ashore to fight off counterattacks. Until that time the numbers work in the defender's favor.

For the Allies to have any hope of succeeding they had to go in where the Germans were least expecting them. By luck of the draw the actual landing would be taking place in a section of France commanded by Field Marshal Erwin Rommel aka "The Desert Fox." He knew full well that the time and place to defeat an invading army was on the beach on the first day at the water's edge.

FM Rommel was a formidable opponent.

The handful of men who were meeting today with the Director General of MI-5 were responsible for making that deception, FORTITUDE SOUTH – the "bodyguard of lies" Prime Minister Churchill had described, a reality. Present were Lieutenant Colonel John Henry Bevan, Professor John C. Masterman, Lt. Col. Robertson and James "Baldie" Taylor. With the exception of Jim these were the best minds in the counterintelligence business – he was there in his capacity of being their liaison officer to various intelligence services.

The war could be won or lost in this room on this day by relatively junior officers – Maj. Gen. Petrie's military rank was an honorary title – he was a former policeman. If the meeting were a war movie or a novel, no one would believe this part of the plot.

Maj. Gen. Petrie said, "Anyone have any change of thoughts since last night?"

Lt. Col. Bevan said, "We cannot risk having this Abwehr officer, Major von Reisen, uncover the fact that every single German agent in England is under our control."

Lt. Col. Robertson said, "Agreed."

Maj. Gen. Petrie said, "Professor?"

"Quite right!"

Maj. Gen. Petrie said, "Any additional ideas on how to go about accomplishing that – no?"

Jim said, "MI-6 has a small dossier on von Reisen. Nothing of much to know except he is a highly experienced Abwehr officer. Joined the Nazi

Party shortly after it was formed. A diehard fanatic who must be taken seriously – he presents a significant threat.

"While SIS has assets in place in Calais, they do not have anyone in or around Major Reisen's headquarters – no help there.

Maj. Gen. Petrie said, "As our resident military analyst what is your recommendation?"

Jim said, "I have two people standing by to brief you on their thoughts about removing von Reisen from the equation. Neither one has any idea *why*. They are only here to provide input on the *how*."

Maj. Gen. Petrie said, "Excellent, have them in Mr. Taylor."

First up was Wing Commander Alastair "Mac" Macrae, DFC. He commanded a wing of Hawker Typhoon single-seat fighter-bombers–the deadliest low-altitude ground-attack aircraft of the war. He had no idea why he was at MI-5 today.

Jim said, "You have been advised of the Official Secrets Act. You were never here, we never had this meeting, none of this ever happened. I need a Wilco."

"Wilco!"

"There is a château located somewhere in the countryside of an undisclosed enemy-occupied country. A certain individual resides there. You have been ordered to eliminate this person with extreme prejudice. How would you go about it?"

Wng. Cdr. Macrae said, "Employing the RAF would be using a sledgehammer to swat a gnat. Tiny winged insects are difficult to hit with a heavy object. The Hawker Typhoon is a powerful engine of war – but if you are asking me to slot a specific Jerry, there is no guarantee we can take out a single man with absolute certainty.

"We can destroy the target provided. It's a specific point – no trouble there. Bomb it, pound it with rockets and strafe it with our 20 mm cannons but there is no guarantee of getting your man or confirming it if we did.

"Afraid that requires an on-site bomb damage assessment."

Maj. Gen. Petrie said, "Thank you, Wing Commander. That shall be all."

Next in was Major Peter Wilkinson, a prewar MI-6 officer and diplomat. He was seconded to SOE when it formed to plan and oversee special operations. The major was a professional intelligence officer whose record spoke for itself.

No one mentioned the Official Secrets Act.

Jim said, "Major, we have an individual who poses a national security threat in an undisclosed location in an enemy-occupied country. We need to eliminate this threat – a time-sensitive operation. How would you go about it?"

Maj. Wilkinson said, "If this were 1941 I would say send in the Small Scale Raiding Force. They pulled off some amazing stunts early in the war. Unfortunately, the men were audacious amateurs. The SSRF never made the next step up professionally. The senior command was virtually all killed. The unit disbanded. There is more to small-scale raiding than raw courage.

"Nowadays SOE is virtually out of the direct action special operations business. It prefers to send in advisers to raise guerrilla bands and let them do the dirty work – sabotage, resistance and subversion. If this is an important mission I recommend against using the local underground."

Lt. Col. Bevan said, "How would you go about it, Major?"

Maj. Wilkinson said, "Sending in a sniper team would be my preferred course of action, sir – minimum of two men. However, that requires significant advanced planning, forward reconnaissance, infiltrating the team to the target and the ability for it to remain in the area without discovery until the right opportunity to take the shot presents itself. And that requires a photograph of the individual to identify our mark prior to.

"Long-range sniping of a dedicated target is a lot more complicated than simply dispatching a marksman to go shoot someone."

Maj. Gen. Petrie said, "We need a recommendation, Major."

Maj. Wilkerson said, "I was with Section D at MI-6 under Lawrence Grand before SOE was formed, sir. There was an MO-9 officer we used for our direct action missions. If it were me, I would bring him in, give him the assignment, all the support he asks for and stand back out of the way."

Maj. Gen. Petrie said, "What's this officer's name?"

"Randal."

COLONEL JOHN RANDAL AND MAJOR THE LADY JANE SEABORN were in their suite. She was barefoot, curled up on the couch in a pair of faded blue jeans winding down from the excitement of the last two days.

Lady Jane loved giving presents. Strangely enough as a general rule she did not particularly enjoy getting them. She preferred to pick out things for herself – having her own personal style.

There were exceptions like the Sheba Diamond.

However, in general, Lady Jane did not much care for surprises she was expected to like.

Happy was on the floor next to the couch with his head down on his paws hoping for her to reach down and scratch him between the ears.

Col. Randal had his pistols lying on a towel on the coffee table. Lady Jane was watching him install the new grips she had given him for his 1911 Colt 38 Super. The Turkish walnut panels had a depth to them. Black figure in the dark wood created a 3-D effect against the slim sterling silver RAIDING FORCES scroll inlay – understated elegance.

There was a knock on the door. Lieutenant General "Geronimo" Joe McKoy, Major General Sam Houston "Bronc" Blackwell and Beverly Blackwell came in. They were not unexpected. Beverly was carrying a manila envelope.

There was a pink elephant in the room Lady Jane and Col. Randal had been doing their best to ignore. Now she went on Red Alert. Was this going to be the big reveal – why her godfather was yanked out of the Christmas party along with James "Baldie" Taylor and Lieutenant Colonel Thomas Argyll "Tar" Robertson?

Visiting room to room was rare on the Penthouse Floor. People's suites were their sanctuary – which was not the same thing as saying they never had guests. Lady Jane accused Captain Billy Jack Jaxx of his girlfriends wearing out the hall carpet traipsing in at all hours.

Chances were this visit was not good news.

Maj. Gen. Blackwell was already wearing his Colt 38 Super Boxing Day gift in a chest holster – he loved it.

Bronc said, "A while back Joe and Beverly were talking to John about your plan to breed palominos like his show horse, Slick, after the war. John brought up Appaloosas. They wondered if you might have an interest."

Lt. Gen. McKoy said, "I told him the breed might have some appeal bein' real colorful – you bein' an artist and all."

Lady Jane said, "Appaloosa?"

Maj. Gen. Blackwell said, "We'll get around to that in a minute, Lady Jane. So, Beverly mentioned the conversation to me. Last time I was in the States I flew out to Moro, Oregon. Met with a Mr. Claude Thompson, the founder of the Appaloosa Horse Club, a brand new organization set up in 1938.

"We did a little horse trading – cut a deal."

Lady Jane's curiosity was piqued, "An Appaloosa is a horse?"

Lt. Gen. McKoy said, "The Nez Perce tribe up in the Pacific Northwest were talented stockmen goin' back to the 1700s. Had 'em a selective horse breedin' program which was almost unheard of among Native tribes. The bloodline they created was a distinctive and visually strikin' animal known for its spotted coat. Has what they call a 'leopard gene.'

"In addition to their color pattern, Appaloosas are known for endurance, speed, intelligence and havin' a gentle disposition."

Beverly said, "During the Nez Perce War in 1877 the U.S. Army chased Chief Joseph, his tribe and all their horses for 1300 miles before running 'em to ground. After the tribe surrendered most of their horses were confiscated or slaughtered by the government. The cavalry didn't want to have to go chasin' 'em again – Appaloosas nearly went extinct."

Maj. Gen. Blackwell said, "A few of the ranchers in the area at the time bought some of the animals. The Nez Perce kept a small herd in secret. Working independently over the years the two groups managed to keep the Appaloosa breed alive. Then just before the war in 1938, Mr. Thompson formed the Appaloosa Horse Club – a registered horse breeders association. Knew all the contacts to find the best stock to put in the book.

"When Beverly heard I was checking 'em out she told me to buy one for you. So the three of us chipped in – John too, since it was his idea in the first place, and we did."

Beverly handed Lady Jane the envelope, "Merry Christmas a little late."

Lady Jane opened the packet to find an 8x10 photo of a foal no more than a day or two old lying on the ground, head up high, very alert. A cream-colored "blanket" ran across the colt's rump with spots the size of silver dollars on it. "Oh my!"

Lt. Gen. McKoy said, "Reckon you can find a pasture on one a' those big spreads you bought out in the Big Sur durin' the Jap Flap to run a string a' spotted ponies on, Lady Jane?"

"Oh my!" Lady Jane said again.

Maj. Gen. Blackwell said, "Meet your new breeding stallion, Lady Jane. Top-of-the-line pedigree, excellent conformation, sired by a champion, dams from an equally proven bloodline – Nez Perce pedigree. Your Appaloosa Horse Club life membership card is enclosed along with a registration form and a self-addressed envelope. You'll need to fill in the little fella's name when you get around to giving him one."

Lady Jane said, "Most beautiful colt I have ever seen."

THE PHONE RANG. COLONEL JOHN RANDAL PICKED UP.

James "Baldie" Taylor said, "I need to see you downstairs in the War Room – forthwith…"

Col. Randal was really beginning to dislike that imperative.

Jim added in typical Raiding Forces' fashion, "…if not sooner."

2

CLEAR AND PRESENT DANGER

AFTER ASKING MAJOR GENERAL SAM HOUSTON BLACKWELL to stand by in the suite with Major the Lady Jane Seaborn, Colonel John Randal and Beverly Blackwell went down to the War Room. James "Baldie" Taylor was waiting impatiently when they arrived.

Jim informed the staff on duty, "We need the room."

Already clicked on, Col. Randal transitioned into an even higher state of awareness.

Jim glanced at Beverly. Was the colonel taking her personal assistant role seriously? He knew better than to object to her being there. She was, at least on paper, OSS-X2 (Counterespionage) and the OSS liaison to the XX Committee – that last was an actual assignment.

Jim said, "Last night you received a directive delivered by King's Messenger to place Raiding Forces on a state of alert. There is the possibility of a mission in your future. Likely the most highly classified you have ever taken part in, Colonel. You will never be cleared to know the root cause of the operation.

"Not in this lifetime."

Jim was not wired in to OPERATION LONG NECK because of DeBeers Diamond Corporation's powerful political influence in the United

Kingdom. It was an Office of Strategic Services mission with a priority as high as classified operations can get. So it was not likely a hasty mission that just came up unexpectedly had a higher priority – but then it could happen.

Col. Randal kept that thought to himself.

LONG NECK's stated mission was to prevent the Nazis from purchasing industrial-grade diamonds – which was a cover story designed for Raiding Forces. The real objective, not known to Col. Randal, was to prevent Nazi diamond-buying agents in the Congo from being in a position to *also* purchase certain high-grade ore and send it back to Nazi Germany – by eliminating them.

OPERATION LONG NECK was a kill mission.

Col. Randal knew nothing about the ore or what it might be used for. There is a rule in intelligence. "You don't know what you don't know."

He *did* know that rule.

Jim said, "Understand, I am not at liberty to discuss the *why*. I can only provide you with the when and the where. Except that has not yet been nailed down.

"What I need today is to get your thoughts on whether an operation of the nature I am about to describe is feasible or not within the time constraints we have to work with."

Col. Randal and Jim had served together for most of the war. They knew what to expect from each other. Trust – both ways, had been earned. The MI-6 officer had never started out briefing an operation the way he was now.

Tentative.

Jim said, "There is a certain Abwehr officer, one Major Hanns von Reisen, who poses a clear and present danger to SHAEF's plans to invade the Continent of Europe. He has a small headquarters at a château located in the countryside somewhere outside of Calais approximately three and a half to four miles inland from the coast. Exact details of the site are being acquired as we speak.

"What is wanted from you is to know if you can conduct a raid–kill or capture this man von Reisen. I need a preliminary response now."

Col. Randal said, "Be specific – *kill* or *capture*?"

Jim said, "Capture is the preferred executive outcome. We need to interrogate him. The major presents a serious threat to future Allied operations. Strictly between us you can interpret that to mean the D-Day invasion."

Col. Randal said, "I see."

Jim said, "Not able to elaborate further. That was more information than I should have disclosed. I am trying to provide you as much detail as I can, Colonel."

"When?"

"Yesterday would have been preferable. Not a possibility, of course, but you get the picture. What you need to know is we are facing a full-blown catastrophe of epic proportions. We have a situation here, Colonel – understand, this is a mission worth doing."

Col. Randal said, "Show me on the map the general area where this château is located."

They walked over to the wall map. Jim pointed. There was nothing on the mosaic to indicate anything about the objective.

It was a blank space.

Beverly said, "That's a problem."

While sounding simple enough – take a team, go kill or capture a certain high-value target and return, the logistics alone for a mission of the nature Jim laid out were staggering.

Advance reconnaissance/surveillance would have to be conducted – could take days. Transport to and from the French Coast would have to be organized. Covertly travel to the objective, kill or capture the target, then move the prisoner to an extraction point 3-4 miles away through enemy territory – with the possibility the objective and or the surrounding countryside would be heavily guarded. All that had to be determined. It was not the typical land ashore, carry out a recon or pinprick raid just off the beach and return to base type mission of short duration – which are never as simple as they might sound.

Prisoner snatches are the most complex of all special operations.

Col. Randal said, "I have to know where the targeted individual is located at a certain time and a certain place – down to the split second. And I need the number and type of enemy forces in the immediate vicinity. You get me that intel and I'll go get your man."

Jim said, "I will provide what I can, Colonel. Missions do not get any hastier than this. There are a lot of unknowns – which, as you know means high risk."

Beverly said, "Who ordered this operation – what hat are you wearing, MI-6, MI-5 or LCS?"

Not a question she should have asked because Jim most likely could not answer it – but one that needed to be if you were planning to go on it.

Jim said, "I have no idea where this mission originated."

Which was not entirely true – he had an opinion.

Major General Sir David Petrie could order the operation, subject to approval from the Joint Intelligence Committee (JIC), or pass it to Lieutenant Colonel John Henry Bevan at LCS – who reported directly to the Prime Minister. Lt. Col. Bevan did not need any approval to greenlight a mission. Most likely, if the raid was a go, who sanctioned it would never be known. Major General Sir Stewart Menzies aka "C," Chief of MI-6 could be behind it but he would have to go through the same approval process as MI-5.

Jim was as interested as anyone to pin down for certain who was behind the mission.

Col. Randal said, "I sign off on all Special Operations Executive activities up to five miles inland. So if the question comes up, I'm clearing this – no conflict with anything we have going. However, keep SOE out of it, Jim. Some of their assets in France likely have been compromised."

Jim said, "Baker Street will never be in the loop, Colonel. No one will. Not even the participating Raiding Forces' personnel.

"You are going to need to develop your own cover story for the strike team."

RAF BENSON, NO.1 PHOTOGRAPHIC RECONNAISSANCE UNIT (No.1 PRU) – a De Havilland Mosquito Photoreconnaissance Mk IX, the latest variant in the De Havilland line, scrambled for a highly classified, top-priority, cross-channel sortie. The unarmed plane was capable of 400 mph making it one of the fastest operational aircraft in the Royal Air Force inventory. Today it was equipped with an F52 camera in an oblique mount for high-resolution, high altitude photography – 30,000-plus feet. The resulting photographic images, when developed, would be 8.5x7 inches. The F52 was selected for its single-pass, high-resolution imagery, long range or off-the-line-of-flight capability. That allowed the pilot to avoid directly overflying the target to minimize detection of intent when a covert mission was called for. The camera had the ability to photograph point-type targets from 15-30 miles *sideways*.

Today's flight was classified MOST SECRET.

SPECIAL DUTIES
MOST IMMEDIATE INTERPRETATION REQUIRED
BY COMMAND OF THE AIR OFFICER COMMANDING

That would be Air Chief Marshal Sir Charles Portal, Marshal of the Royal Air Force. No. 1 PRU flew the most time-sensitive secret missions of the war. 'Most Immediate Interpretation Required' was an executive order that covered both flying the mission and having the film processed. While it sounded understated, the directive was the most urgent Sortie Order No.1 PRU had ever received.

Today, the pilot Flight Lieutenant Trevor Roper, DFC, had limited navigation data on his sortie sheet. There were the grid coordinates. And the notation "French country house."

That was it.

The coastline was the Initial Point (IP). There was no second checkpoint. That was the bad news. The good news was Flt. Lt. Roper did not have to hit his Recon Objective dead on. A miss by as much as 15 miles was close enough for military work today.

There was one other thing… an Allied aircraft making a single pass flying at 30,000 feet was not going to arouse any suspicions it was on a clandestine mission.

THE INITIAL INTERCEPT OF MAJOR HANNS VON REISEN'S message to Abwehrleitstelle Frankreich – the Abwehr Control Center headquartered in Paris, reporting a concern about the status of one or more of their spies in England, had been made by a team of Women's Royal Naval Service (WRNS) intercept and direction-finding operators located at the Royal Navy's Admiralty Wireless Station, Swingate. The Y-Station was concealed in an abandoned farmhouse on the cliffs of Dover overlooking the English Channel.

The signal emanated from a location just across on the other side.

The Swingate intercept was forwarded to GC&CS at Bletchley Park, codename Station X. Immediately upon being decrypted, two other Y-Stations, Beachy Head and Whitestable in the general vicinity of Swingate were alerted to assist with a priority HF/DF (High-Frequency Direction Finding) triangulation called "Huff-Duff." Normally this could take up to 3-6 days. However, GC&CS attached a FLASH – D/F NOW – ALL OTHER TRAFFIC STANDBY–MOST IMMEDIATE, OOI (Operational Order of Intercept). The highest priority assignment a Y-Station could receive. Now the time it was going to take to triangulate the target was reduced to six hours.

The WRNS pinpointed the source of Maj. von Reisen's transmission in record speed –margin of error less than 500 feet. That intelligence was forwarded through channels to No. 1 PRU.

Flight Lieutenant Trevor Roper had all the information he needed.

JAMES "BALDIE" TAYLOR DEPARTED THE WAR ROOM TO DELIVER Colonel John Randal's response to Major General Sir David Petrie at MI-5. He met with the Director General and Lieutenant Colonel Thomas Argyll "Tar" Robertson. The mood was tense.

Maj. Gen. Petrie asked, "How did Colonel Randal react?"

Jim said, "He told me exactly what I expected him to."

"What pray tell was that?"

"If we provide intel on where Major von Reisen will be at a certain time at a certain place he will go get him."

Lt. Col. Robertson said, "My information is the colonel is a reasonable man to work with. He does not fight the problem. At last, a positive development in this wretched affair."

Jim said, "Actually, Colonel Randal's response is a rejection."

Maj. Gen. Petrie said, "What makes you say that, Mr. Taylor?"

Jim said, "We have no way of complying. Obtaining the intelligence the colonel needs is not achievable in our narrow window of opportunity. We do not even know what von Reisen looks like.

"And Randal has an additional caveat. SOE is not to have any advance knowledge of the mission. He wants a guarantee of full operational security."

Maj. Gen. Petrie said, "One cannot fault him for that. What is our estimated time frame to work with, Tar?"

Lt. Col. Robertson said, "Major von Reisen is likely the officer in charge of Abwehr substation Calais. His chain of command would require him to report to the regional Abwehr station based in Paris commanded by Oberst Friedrich Rudolf. From there, provided Rudolf signs off on it, the message goes to OKW Berlin – Admiral Canaris.

"The Nazis tout their 'superior organization', but that has not always translated to the Abwehr. German intelligence is not the fine-tuned omnipotent machine it would have people believe. Paris station is likely buried in communications from all its outposts in France. For all we know Rudolf might not even get around to reading the message for a day or two. There is no guarantee he will forward it up the chain of command when he does.

"That stipulated, we need to act sometime in the next 72 hours. Our ability to affect the outcome in our favor diminishes exponentially after that time."

Jim said, "Not possible – no way to gather the required target data in that short time."

Maj. Gen. Petrie said, "Do you have a recommendation, Mr. Taylor?"

"Negative – not at the moment, sir."

Maj. Gen. Petrie said, "Stand by here at the Box. We shall have need of your services before this day is done. Thank you for your efforts to provide us a straightforward picture of what we can and cannot do."

"My pleasure, sir… regret I do not have something more positive to offer."

When Jim left the room Maj. Gen. Petrie said, "I have it on good authority Colonel Randal jump-started Mr. Taylor's stalled career at MI-6 as a result of an operation they ran out of the Gold Coast. Raided the island of Rio Bonita – a Portuguese Protectorate. From there the two moved to Abyssinia where they conducted a classic textbook guerrilla campaign against the Italians. Then transitioned to the desert running gun jeep patrols behind Rommel's lines, operating from a secret base.

"He may be too close to the colonel for a situation like this. We have to neutralize von Reisen *at all costs.* That means exactly what it says. Mr. Taylor may not view it the same way. I want you to personally take charge of this bloody shambles – covertly.

"Bring me the hard recommendation."

Lt. Col. Robertson said, "Understood, General."

Maj. Gen. Petrie said, "We are on the cusp of what has the potential to develop into a catastrophic crisis. Our Double Cross System is imperiled – D-Day is at risk. This situation cannot be allowed to stand."

"Sir!"

"Reports indicate you and Miss Blackwell have developed a good working relationship. At Donovan's promotion party I could not help but notice she and Randal have an obvious bond. See if you can capitalize on it."

Maj. Gen. Petrie had been the Inspector General of Police, Palestine prior to the war – he had clearly kept his policeman's eyes open at the party.

Lt. Col. Robertson said, "Not likely, sir. I cannot tell if I am playing Beverly or she is playing me. Not the dizzy blonde she allows one to see. Have to tread carefully with her."

Maj. Gen. Petrie said, "A pity – we could use leverage. What information have you been able to obtain from SIS?"

Lt. Col. Robertson said, "They have not been able to provide so much as a single photograph of von Reisen. All MI-6 has on him is one decidedly thin dossier. The major is a bloody shadow man. What we know is he's a prewar professional intelligence operative and a longtime member of the Nazi Party.

"Other than he is reputed to be a trusted personal friend of Canaris – which enhances the likelihood of our having a serious problem. We know virtually nothing about von Reisen."

Maj. Gen. Petrie said, "I have to present the Prime Minister an assessment on the current state of affairs by close of business today. I need an option at that time. Sniping and aerial bombing are off the table. One takes too long to organize and the other is uncertain."

"Yes, sir."

It was said of Maj. Gen. Petrie that he only possessed an average brain but was the best man manager anyone ever saw. In his typical low-key way he was demonstrating his leadership skills today – no panic. Composed at a time when it would have been justified to show alarm. The general was going to get the best out of his people by leading by example.

If only he knew which way to go.

FLIGHT LIEUTENANT TREVOR ROPER WAS AT 30,000 FEET WHEN he approached the IP. He turned on the cameras in his high-speed DeHavilland Mosquito PR MK IX just before crossing the beach. No. 1 PRU was employing six F52 cameras for this mission. The camera system was set to take one frame every 3 seconds. The film rolls held 125 exposures per camera using 9" wide film. However, this mission was designed to bring back photos of a point-type target – a "French farmhouse."

Only a handful of the 8.5"x7" pictures would be of any use for tactical planning – not that he knew anything about that.

Flt. Lt. Roper was holding at a steady 325 mph true air speed (TAS). The idea was to maintain a consistent frame overlap, minimize blurring due to motion and optimize fuel usage at the high altitude he was flying.

Not that fuel was a problem on this sortie. It was a short flight. He was ordered to make a single pass photo run on the target, kick the speed up to 400 mph maximum Indicated Airspeed (IAS) on his egress from the target area and return to base "With All Dispatch."

He cruised over at 30,000 feet ten miles west of the target. There was sporadic anti-aircraft fire. It was ineffective. The Germans were not really trying to hit a single reconnaissance plane at that altitude and speed. Flt. Lt. Roper made a wide sweeping circle completely passing around the town of Calais to throw off anyone who might be observing his flight path and headed back to RAF Benson – "Chop-Chop."

Normally live film would be sent to the Central Interpretation Unit (CIU) at RAF Medmenham for processing and interpretation. Not today. An armed officer courier was waiting on the airfield at RAF Benson to rush the film to be processed in the base Photographic Section before the Mosquito's engine stopped. There would be no photo analysis.

All highly irregular.

BEVERLY BLACKWELL AND KING WERE ALSO AT RAF BENSON sitting in a Westland Lysander with the engine ticking over. A U.S. Army Lend-Lease jeep sporting RAF rondel markings raced up. The base commander, Group Captain W.B. Murray in the passenger seat was clutching a large flat canvas map case containing the developed prints. He jumped out of the jeep and passed the satchel to Beverly through the Lysander's left side window.

She immediately began taxiing, raced down the strip, pulled back on the stick and zoomed almost straight up making an extremely short takeoff – the kind the Lysander was known for. A throwback to her teenage crop-dusting days in South Texas.

Then banked hard.

Beverly was en route to London – downtown London. It was 50 miles from RAF Benson to the city. It would take too long for a motorcycle dispatch rider to deliver the developed aerial photos – time being of the essence.

The Lysander could make it in a little less than fifteen minutes flying at war emergency power (WEP).

Beverly was heading for the skyline of the city straight ahead. She was on a tightly controlled Flash Special Duty Approved flight plan leading into London. The route was signed off on by the Air Ministry, Directorate of Operations (Home) – a flight plan never before authorized in the war.

King was attaching a 10-foot linen tape streamer to the canvas map case. The streamer was a method for dropping lightweight, time-critical packages. It offered enough drag to protect the payload and guide it to the DZ – a small parachute might drift and there was no time to go chasing this satchel through the streets of London.

Securing approval for the Special Duty flight plan had been critical. Behind the scenes, Lieutenant Colonel John Henry Bevan worked his magic expediting it – the Chief of the Air Staff (CAS) had to be involved. The city's airspace was tightly controlled. London air defenses tended to shoot first and ask questions later. No one in the know wanted this airplane shot down before it could deliver its package.

Beverly flew in at rooftop level, visually lining up on the Thames River. She followed it upstream – toward Westminster. Next came her checkpoints. She had them written on a pad and taped to the left leg of her flight suit–

Parliament Square, then Whitehall and finally Trafalgar Square. From there to the Bradford Hotel.

By the time she came over the hotel, Beverly had her airspeed down to 65 mph – barely above stalling. Major the Lady Jane Seaborn, Mandy Paige and Captain Billy Jack Jaxx were standing on the roof. King leaned out the window and tossed the dispatch case. They were so low the 10-foot streamer did not have time to fully deploy.

He nearly beaned Jack Cool.

COLONEL JOHN RANDAL ARRIVED IN THE PHONE ROOM ON THE Penthouse Floor of the hotel. He was not going to be able to use the War Room for mission planning. There was a small rotating team of FANYs from Special Operations Executive assigned to coordinate SOE missions taking place in the 5-mile zone he had to sign off on. The SOE FANY personnel were not cleared to have any advance knowledge of the assignment to kill or capture Major Hanns von Reisen until after the Raid Team launched.

The need for secrecy was nothing against the women personally. It was a given that these FANYs were going to be debriefed regularly by SOE to learn what was taking place in the War Room. That was something that was going to have to be resolved eventually but there was no time now.

There was a concern the French Resistance might have been penetrated. SOE advised, supplied and in some cases controlled the Underground. If Baker Street got wind of the mission any advance warning about the upcoming raid making its way back to France was a death sentence for the Raiding Forces' strike team. Every effort was going to be expended to make sure that did not happen.

Major the Lady Jane Seaborn, Captain Billy Jack Jaxx and Mandy were putting up the aerial photos of the objective. There were a lot of black and white 8.5"x7" photos to sort through. While only a few frames covered the objective, it was important to understand the surrounding terrain from the beach to the target. A big job.

Luckily there was one long wall in the Phone Room to use as a map board.

The stills were individually marked in pencil on the back with Frame Number, Compass Orientation and Mosaic Position Code. The markings were important in helping to correctly align overlapping images into a continuous visual photomap. On the front of each picture a tiny north Track arrow was drawn in the upper right-hand corner.

Lieutenant General "Geronimo" Joe McKoy arrived with Waldo Treywick. They stood with a couple of Waldo's cigars in their teeth watching the mosaic grow. Major General Sam Houston Blackwell walked in uninvited.

Waldo handed him a cigar.

One of the Vulnerable Points Security operators arrived. Col. Randal provided him with a short, very short list of people authorized to be allowed in the Phone Room. He went outside and took up a post in front of the door. Since the Phone Room was behind the partition blocking off the Raiding Forces' section from the rest of the penthouse floor, this was double security.

Brandy Seaborn and Captain Penelope "Legs" Honeycutt-Parker, GM, OBE, RM, arrived next. The Vargas Girl look-a-like, Captain Pamala Plum-Martin, was right behind them. The three women took over assembling the mosaic from Capt. Jaxx.

Lieutenant Chase Starrett walked in having been sent for. Col. Randal wanted him to observe planning for a complex high-priority mission with a tight time constraint. He had a long history of grooming his promising junior officers – mentoring them by inclusion for further leadership roles in Raiding Forces. Lt. Starrett being present was a sign he was on the fast track for bigger future assignments.

Typically commanders did not operate that way. Most preferred to work with a tight-knit inner circle of staff officers. The problem with that style of mission planning was it created a disconnect between planners and the officers and men who would execute the operation.

Very few commanding officers understood that.

Col. Randal left the Phone Room and walked down the hall to Major General William "Wild Bill" Donovan's suite. The general was having a meeting with three senior OSS officers from London Station. He came to the door but did not invite Col. Randal in. Wild Bill wanted to keep as much separation between Colonel David Bruce, London Station Chief, and Col. Randal as possible to avoid any rivalry between the two.

Even though the Office of Strategic Services officer had been promoted to full colonel recently Col. Randal had date of rank which could cause resentment. Maj. Gen. Donovan had his hands full doing battle with MI-6 and SOE. The last thing he needed was friction between his two top European Theatre of Operations officers.

Col. Randal said, "Raiding Forces have been placed on alert, sir. I've been informed it's a priority MOST SECRET/TOP SECRET code word, mission. I'm not cleared for the code word but Jim assures me this is no drill."

Maj. Gen. Donovan said, "What is it you need from me, Colonel?"

Col. Randal said, "I want you to come to the Phone Room and assume command, General."

"That would be because you intend to lead the operation yourself?"

"Affirmative, sir."

"Give me ten minutes."

CAPTAIN DICK COURTNEY WAS WAITING WHEN COLONEL JOHN Randal returned. The two moved to the back of the Phone Room out of the way. They needed a word alone.

Col. Randal said, "I have a top priority recon job, Captain. I want you to put eyes on the objective in anticipation of a raid. Establish wireless contact with Seaborn House via burst transmission. I need to be informed when a certain person is present on target."

"When do we go in, sir?"

"Tonight."

"Life always gets interesting when you turn up, Colonel."

"Get with Mrs. Seaborn. The two of you work out the details of her inserting you by PT boat. Or, and this is your call, Captain, you may choose to go in by parachute. Keep in mind, this operation is full-on covert. No one can know you're going. No one, meaning the Germans, can ever know you were there – even after the Raid Team's come and gone.

"If you jump in you'll have to bury your chutes."

"We can do that, sir."

Col. Randal said, "Go down to the VIP Section in the lobby. Brandy will meet you in a few minutes. If you decide to insert by PT I want you to slip away without anyone realizing you're gone until you make your commo check with the TOC at Seaborn House once you've set up your OP in the target area."

"Wilco."

"Are you taking Vanish and X-Ray?"

"Always, Colonel."

"Make it happen, stud."

ONE OF MAJOR THE LADY JANE SEABORN'S ROYAL MARINES said, "Sir, the front desk is calling – Colonel Robertson is in the lobby."

Colonel John Randal said, "Have one of the security people escort him up here."

He and Lady Jane were standing in front of the aerial photo montage of the château as it was being pieced together. The women were putting the finishing touches on the mosaic. Taping up the shots taken from the coastline running the three and a half miles to the target was like putting together a giant crossword puzzle. It was a team effort.

Everyone pitched in.

Lady Jane said, "Château du Val-Obscur – Dark Valley Castle – sounds ominous."

Col. Randal said, "It's not in a valley and it's not a castle."

Lady Jane laughed, "The French, what can one say?"

"What's on the sign in front of the main house?"

"I had to use a magnifying glass to read it – 'Feld Post'."

"Meaning?"

"Reich Post Office."

"That's a pretty thin cover for the local Abwehr HQ."

Lady Jane said, "Nazis are known for arrogance."

It looked like someone had simply stuck up a sign – any sign, in the front yard. Still…

Col. Randal had the uneasy feeling whoever originated this mission might have provided the wrong grid coordinates for the target. Considering the disastrous OPERATION FLIPPER in Libya dispatched to kill or capture Rommel, mistakes like that had happened before. The Desert Fox had never been in the building raided… he was not even in Africa – away in Rome on the night the raid took place. The Commandos had been wiped out except for two men.

One of them, Major General Robert Laycock, was now in command of Combined Operations.

Militarily the failed mission was a cautionary tale not to be discounted.

Lieutenant Colonel Thomas Argyll "Tar" Robertson came into the Phone Room. As usual "Passion Pants" was wearing his Seaforth Highlanders regimental trews. Beverly and King were with him. After landing, the two had raced to the hotel with an RAF police escort, siren blaring.

Lt. Col. Robertson said, "I shall be the in-house representative of MI-5 for the duration of your operation."

Col. Randal said, "There's a sign on the château that identifies it as a post office. That's a pretty flimsy cover. Are you confident this is the right target?"

Lt. Col. Robertson said, "I would bet my last shilling, Colonel."

"It's not your money we're betting."

"Quite right, sir. Three Y-Stations triangulated a radio transmission from that building. We are acting on a geographical location accurate to within 500 feet As you can see there is no other structure within that distance other than a barn and a small outbuilding – likely a tack shop and/or a workshop. In fact, there are no other estates within a mile of the château.

"I have come bearing topographical maps – '*cartes topographiques*' 1:50,000 of the area… you can see for yourself."

Major General William "Wild Bill" Donovan walked in.

LIEUTENANT GENERAL "GERONIMO" JOE MCKOY PULLED Colonel John Randal aside. "You plannin' on sendin' Dick over to put eyes on?"

Col. Randal said, "Affirmative."

Not much got past Lt. Gen. McKoy.

"What's his LD time?"

"As soon as it gets dark."

"How's he supposed to know how to identify von Reisen?"

"We're going to go when the major's staff car is parked outside the château."

Lt. Gen. McKoy said, "Ain't the best idea I ever heard, John."

Col. Randal said, "You have a better one?"

"This mission's gonna be a rip snorter with the hair on – a lot a' things can go sideways."

"That's why we're not going to tell anybody our entire plan – especially Lady Jane."

"Now *that*, young colonel, is a plan I can whole heartedly endorse."

BRANDY SEABORN WAS SITTING WITH CAPTAIN DICK COURTNEY in the VIP lounge. They had adjusted a pair of high-backed upholstered chairs. No one could overhear what they were discussing.

Capt. Courtney said, "You studied the aerial photos. Did you see a location where my team could put ashore?"

"I did not," Brandy said. "There are high cliffs off all the beaches in the area covered by the photographs. You would have to land and make a sheer 80 or 90-foot climb. Those chalk formations are notoriously unstable, Dick."

Capt. Courtney said, "Definitely."

Brandy added, "I do not recommend you attempt to climb them – even though a few of our teams have before. Chalk crags are dangerous. I have no idea how John is planning to bring a strike team in."

Capt. Courtney said, "Possibly by parachute?"

Brandy said, "Absolute deniability is a condition of mission planning – zero footprint Raiding Forces was ever there. An assault team would require ten to twelve men. Enough to present problems for a parachute insertion. If the jump is only slightly scattered or a chute entangled in a tree it could compromise the mission before it ever gets started.

"I have no idea how we intend to pull this one off."

Normally, Brandy was not this negative.

COLONEL JOHN RANDAL HAD A WORD WITH BEVERLY, "I HAVE a mission for you."

"I like missions."

"There are certain aspects of this operation we do not want to share– particularly with MI-5."

Beverly said, "Difficult with Tar here. I don't have the impression he's planning on leaving anytime soon. We can't underrate him – Passion Pants is pretty smart."

Col. Randal said, "Well, that's your job, Beverly. Keep him away from any planning that has to do with timelines or troop movements."

"How am I supposed to do that Johnny, you're giving me a lot more credit..."

"You've been tasked with a serious assignment at XX Committee – issued a TOP SECRET clearance. They don't pass those out to just anyone. I need your help. Why do you think I've been keeping you in the loop on everything?"

"I've been wondering about that."

"You've got this."

Beverly did not fail to note Col. Randal had not answered her question – exactly.

CAPTAIN DICK COURTNEY RETURNED TO THE PHONE ROOM while Brandy went downstairs to notify Seaborn House to have her crew prepare the PT boat for sea.

Upon arriving he spoke to Captain Penelope "Legs" Honeycutt-Parker, "Mrs. Seaborn would like you to join her in the War Room."

Colonel John Randal walked over after she departed, "Give me a report – my ears only."

Speaking under his breath while glancing around to make sure no one could overhear, Capt. Courtney said, "There's no good way to infiltrate the target area in a reasonable amount of time, sir."

"So what's your plan, Captain?"

"I am going to go with the best of the least desirable options, sir – my team will jump in."

"OK – pick a DZ."

"Already have one in mind, sir. The terrain is wooded in places along streams but open fields elsewhere. We will drop in a pasture a mile from the château. Bury our chutes in one of the hedgerows that mark the boundaries. Then move to a place of concealment and initiate observation of the objective."

Col. Randal said, "Signal the TOC when you take up position in your Observation Post."

"Wilco."

"When you determine the major's staff car is physically present send a burst signal to that effect. Then move to the road that runs past the château and set up a blocking position. Do not let that vehicle depart the area – suppressed weapons only. If it tries to leave take the car out and everyone in it."

"Understood, sir."

"Prior to Raid Team arriving close on the château, secure the front and back entrances, and stand ready to link up preparatory to our extraction – you'll come out with us."

"Yes, sir."

"Sorry, that's all I have, Dick – don't expect much more."

"No problem, sir. I have never actually understood what I have been doing for the last year or so. Go in by sea, escort a signals technician behind the lines, hide in the forest, provide security, stay a week or ten days then come out – turn around and do it all over again. No idea what that's about.

"Comparatively speaking, this mission is clear as a bell, Colonel."

Col. Randal looked across the room and made eye contact with Major General Sam Houston "Bronc" Blackwell. Then he turned and walked out into the hall. Beverly glanced at him as he came past.

Bronc waited a discreet amount of time then followed Col. Randal out. He made it into the hall in time to see him going into the suite he shared with Major the Lady Jane Seaborn.

Beverly was talking to Lieutenant Chase Starrett. She excused herself and trailed after her father. Col. Randal was holding the door to the room open when they arrived.

"Captain Courtney will be dropping in tonight with a recon team to place the château under observation. Can you arrange a C-47, General?"

"I'll fly the mission myself."

"Daddy, you're not supposed to fly over France – you're a BIGOT."

Meaning he was cleared to know all the secrets of D-Day.

"Can't blame me for trying, baby. I'll put my best crew on it, Colonel. Why all the secret squirrel stuff?"

Col. Randal said, "I don't want anyone to be aware of our movement schedule. It's pretty hard to keep a secret. If the Germans were to learn where and when…"

"Why take a chance?" Beverly said.

In Raiding Forces that was not really a question.

Col. Randal said, "General, I need you to link up with Captain Courtney in the War Room. You two quietly work out the details of the flight plan and select a DZ. Time on Target 2200 hrs."

Maj. Gen. Blackwell said, "From here on I'll handle logistics. Tell me what's needed. You concentrate on your mission.

"I'll take care of the rest."

MAJOR GENERAL WILLIAM "WILD BILL" DONOVAN AND Lieutenant Colonel Thomas Argyll "Tar" Robertson were in one corner of the Phone Room having a private conversation. Tar was surprised to see him there. The extent of Maj. Gen. Donovan's association with Raiding Forces had not been known to him.

It was now.

It did not escape Lt. Col. Robertson that the personnel present did not react to Wild Bill's presence as being that of a high-ranking senior officer looking over their shoulder – he was part of the team.

Lt. Col. Robertson was not sure what to make of what he was observing. He had never experienced three general officers being involved on a working level with a unit as small as Raiding Forces. They were present, ready to do their part – clearly committed to making this operation a reality.

What was striking about their involvement was that two of the three had no idea why this mission was important – they were not cleared 'Need To Know.' If MI-6 and MI-5 could have had their way Maj. Gen. Donovan would never have known either.

Maj. Gen. Donovan said, "What's the Security Service assessment in the event the Double-Cross System is blown?"

Not a question Lt. Col. Robertson wanted to have to answer, "Devastating – worst-case scenario D-Day has to be postponed, sir."

Maj. Gen. Donovan said, "If we do that it will cause our ground operations to be conducted in the dead of winter. French winters are known for harsh wet conditions. Ice and mud become a quagmire – slow down our armor.

"In addition, Stalin has been screaming for us to open a Second Front to take the pressure off his forces. A delay is sure to harm inter-Allied relations. The Russians might seek a separate peace with Nazi Germany."

Lt. Col. Robertson said, "Precisely our conclusion, General."

Maj. Gen. Donovan said, "What makes MI-5 believe eliminating this Major von Reisen will prevent exposure of the Double-Cross System?"

Lt. Col. Robertson said, "Security is taking countermeasures as we speak, sir. We shall be burning one or two of our double-agents – letting the Germans know they have been turned and are working for us. The implication being they are rotten apples and the rest of the Abwehr's spies are still loyal Nazis.

"If the major goes away there may not be anyone else in the Abwehr questioning the reliability of their spies – essentially we are stalling for time."

Maj. Gen. Donovan said, "Do you believe you can buy us six months' worth?"

"That is the burning question, General."

MAJOR THE LADY JANE SEABORN SAID, "JOHN, YOU HAVE A CALL from the main desk in the lobby that someone has arrived who claims my godfather sent him."

"Would you go check him out?"

"Love to."

She returned in a few minutes with a man in a suit who did not introduce himself and said, "Mr. Smith gave me the secret handshake."

Which Colonel John Randal took to mean he was MI-6. As far as he knew the SIS did not have a secret handshake. Lady Jane was trying not to laugh.

"What can I do for you Mr. Smith?"

"I am on loan to Military Intelligence, M-14(b) – the section charged with tracking and assessing the German Army in France. Colonel Bevan thought you might have need of my services."

Col. Randal waved Lieutenant Colonel Thomas Argyll "Tar" Robertson over, "Any chance you can vouch for Mr. Smith?"

"Absolutely. We cover the same region of Nazi-occupied France. I am aware of what Smith does. He does not know what I do."

Col. Randal said, "Works for me."

They walked over to the wall where Lt. Col. Robertson's maps were pinned up. Col. Randal pointed to the coordinates in the vicinity of the Château du Val-Obscur but not the estate itself. What kind of local security should we expect to find in this region?

Everyone in the room stopped what they were doing and gathered around to observe what was taking place. Mr. Smith glanced at the map. That was for show. He already knew the location in question and had his answers ready.

"This area of France is under the control of 15th Army, part of Army Group B, specifically the 711th Static Infantry Division. Typically in a rural area with no large beaches, main roads or anything of significant strategic value, as in this case, there will only be a light German military presence.

"The 711th has a number of Landesschützen, meaning Territorial Units, attached for guarding areas such as this. They consist of older, lower-quality troops, some in their sixties. The division also has low-grade Osttruppen or Hiwis – Auxiliary troops, often Soviet or Eastern European 'volunteers' it uses for guard duty in quieter sectors inland from the coast.

"They are what I anticipate you shall encounter in the region you are interested in – the lowest quality troops on the German Army list."

In fact, Mr. Smith could tell them exact details of the enemy forces down to the name of the Auxiliary unit commander in the area. How he knew was classified. And nothing would be gained by showing off to men who would shortly be traveling in harm's way with a high risk of capture.

"What are your questions gentlemen?"

Captain Billy Jack Jaxx said, "How will these Auxiliary troops be deployed?"

Mr. Smith said, "They are even more 'static' than the men in the 711th Static Division. No mobile patrols. You can expect small parties to establish roadblocks, two-man checkpoints at crossroads or coastal watch posts. The reason for the low troop density in the area you are inquiring about is because it is a dead zone militarily – no nearby potential landing beaches. There are only a few coastal batteries, radar stations or fuel dumps and no hard surface crossroads.

"Questions?"

Col. Randal said, "Good report, Mr. Smith… tell Colonel Bevan we appreciate his help."

That earned him one of Lady Jane's best grade heart-attack smiles.

Not rattled by his cover being blown Mr. Smith said, "The colonel will be by later today to check if there is anything else you might require."

CAPTAIN PAMALA PLUM-MARTIN DEPARTED IN ONE OF THE hotel limousines with Captain Dick Courtney and Captain Penelope "Legs" Honeycutt Parker to take them to the airfield where the Lysander was parked. She was going to fly to Seaborn House, then stand by there to fly Capt. Courtney, Vanish and X-Ray to whichever airbase Major General Sam Houston "Bronc" Blackwell designated as the Departure Airfield.

Capt. Honeycutt-Parker was along to supervise the preparation of the PT boats for sea. What role she and Brandy Seaborn would play in the mission had not been determined at this time. It was a given a boat or boats would be needed at some point.

COLONEL JOHN RANDAL SAID, "HAND OFF COLONEL PASSION Pants to Mandy. She knows the drill. Then make your way down to the Tea Room. I'll meet you there, Beverly."

"I'm on it."

Col. Randal made eye contact with Major the Lady Jane Seaborn. She came over. He reminded her, “Be ready to back up Mandy. Like we talked about.”

“Love to.”

A highly trained intelligence officer, since attaching herself to Raiding Forces Lady Jane rarely had an opportunity to ply her tradecraft – she liked to keep her hand in when the occasion arose.

Col. Randal said, “First, I’d like you to walk over and quietly ask General McKoy to make a big show of inviting me to go downstairs for a cup of coffee with him and Bronc. Then tell Jack to slip out and follow us.”

Lady Jane said, “A gathering of eagles may…”

“I need you to stay here with Colonel Robertson. Keep him out of trouble. Beverly will give you a full report when she gets back. Even though I’m going to tell her not to.”

Lady Jane laughed, “Anything you require from me besides playing Mata Hari?”

Col. Randal said, “When you have a chance sketch a small working diagram of the two outbuildings and the dirt road I can use – without making too big a production out of it.”

“Love to.”

“I’m also going to need a schematic of the interior of a typical French château – if there is such a thing. I doubt we’ll be lucky enough to find anything on Château du Val-Obscur. I just need something to go by. Maybe Tar can help with that – give him something to do.”

“I shall do my best, John.”

“We don’t want anyone outside this room to know we’re asking.”

Lady Jane said, “You are developing quite the taste for *private* enterprise.”

Col. Randal said, “I like it when you talk spy talk.”

Lady Jane laughed, “Haven’t had an opportunity to thank you for my Christmas present – you are the world’s best gift giver, ever.”

Col. Randal said, “Thank Beverly, Bronc and General McKoy. I just asked if they thought you might like a spotted pony. They did the rest.

Lady Jane said, “I love my spotted pony.”

She walked over to speak to Lieutenant General “Geronimo” Joe McKoy. In a moment right on cue, he called across the room, “Hey John, let’s go have a cup a’ joe with Bronc.”

"Can do."

Waldo Treywick fell in behind them on the way out. A few minutes later Captain Billy Jack Jaxx left the room. With people coming in and out no one paid attention.

In the Tea Room the group took a table in the back. Everyone ordered coffee. With more and more U.S. servicemen visiting the hotel it was fast becoming the beverage of choice. The Bradford offered a wide variety of premium blends. British officers would drink coffee but Americans were reluctant to drink tea.

Waldo passed around cigars, which could not be lit up in the Tea Room – Beverly declined.

Col. Randal said, "Situation…we have a target 3 to 4 miles inland. Enemy forces in the area are estimated to be negligible. If we go in by sea we have to land ashore, scale a 80 to 90-foot chalk cliff, make our way overland to the objective, carry out an assault on a point-type target, secure our prisoner, return to the beach, make it down the cliff, link up with a PT boat and come home."

Major General Sam Houston "Bronc" Blackwell said, "Sorta failed to mention the forward reconnaissance phase, Colonel. Being a prisoner snatch you've got to have a visual. And that means there's always the risk of your recon team being compromised. You might have the bad guys waiting when you come in."

Lt. Gen. McKoy said, "Yeah, and you also left out the part about the signal for us to launch bein' we go when the target's staff car is confirmed parked out in front a' the château. That could mean somethin' or nothin' at all."

Capt. Jaxx said, "Don't forget sir we evaluated scaling chalk cliffs on the last raid. They were a no-go then. What's changed?"

Col. Randal said, "Only the exigency of the operation."

Lt. Gen. McKoy said, "Has anyone explained exactly *why* this mission is such a barn-burning necessity all of a sudden?"

Col. Randal said, "Negative – not to me."

No detailed explanation had been forthcoming. Not even Beverly had any hint of an idea and she was the OSS liaison to the XX Committee. Anyone who knew was not talking.

Major General William "Wild Bill" Donovan had not even been aware of the operation until Col. Randal informed him.

Raiding Forces had never been assigned a mission without being read in on the purpose of the exercise – at least parts of it. Men going on a dangerous enterprise need to know the reason they are risking their lives. Col. Randal had a long-standing policy of giving his troops as much information prior to an operation as possible. All he had been told at this point was a certain individual posed a threat and needed to be killed or captured.

Usually Waldo sat back, observed and had little to contribute during pre-mission planning sessions. But he had amassed quite an extensive portfolio of behind-the-lines experience scouting the German light cruiser *Konigsberg* up the Rufiji River in German East Africa with PJ Pretorius during the last war, poaching Portuguese ivory in Mozambique, over a year spent with Force N in Abyssinia, operating out of Oasis X in the Great Sand Sea on jeep patrol and off Castelrozzo Island in the Aegean.

He said, "That right there's a leisurely unfoldin' raid you're describin', Colonel. You usually go in with guns blazin'."

Across the table Capt. Jaxx's eyes narrowed in agreement. He preferred his raids to be lightning-fast, high-intensity, hit-and-run affairs – heavy on violence of action.

Beverly said, "So what's the plan, Johnny? We all know what you described isn't what you're going to do."

Col. Randal said, "We may not have the option to insert by sea but we can have Brandy extract the raid team in one of the PT boats at end of mission."

Beverly said, "How do you intend to reach the objective?"

"Jump in."

Maj. Gen. Blackwell said, "Bad idea, Colonel – you got away with it once. Don't press your luck."

Lt. Gen. McKoy said, "Say you parachute in – how're you plannin' to travel over three miles to your extraction point with a prisoner in tow and maybe one or two a' your men WIA?

Maj. Gen. Blackwell said, "You've got a Standing' Order that stipulates, *Plan Raids Backwards. Know How to Get Home.* Yeah, I've memorized 'em like I told you before. You gotta' know how you're going get there before you can figger out how to get back – a jump that far inland..."

Capt. Jaxx was starting to like the sound of this better and better. Low-level drop. Go in fast, hit the target, come home – party's on.

How to conduct the exfil… he had a few ideas.

As if reading his mind, Col. Randal said, "So how're we going to travel to the ERP, Captain?"

Capt. Jaxx said, "Commandeer the truck parked out front, head down that dirt road to the coast, sir – shoot our way through any roadblock. I'll ride on the fender with a suppressed M3 Grease Gun."

Lt. Gen. McKoy said, "I don't know, John. Lot a' possibilities – all bad. The most likely bein' excessive winds on the drop zone which we all know are unpredictable that close to the coast. Scatter the jumpers and take too much time assemblin', bein' that far in… with the sun comin' up… it could all go south in a hurry."

Beverly said, "A red-line precondition of this operation is it has to be totally covert. The Germans can never know Raiding Forces carried out a raid on the Abwehr's Pas-de-Calais HQ."

Col. Randal said, "That is a fact."

Beverly said, "A parachute entangled in a tree you can't retrieve. A jumper loses a piece of equipment when he makes a hard PLF and can't find it in the dark… clandestine doesn't happen, Johnny."

That was met by icy silence. No one had a better option to offer. Ingress was the consistent unknown peculiar to this raid.

Maj. Gen. Blackwell said, "I'll supply the aircraft if you ask but I strongly recommend against the jumping-in idea, Colonel – don't do it."

Col. Randal said, "General McKoy, you and Mr. Treywick head back up to the Phone Room. I want both of you acting individually to pull Colonel Robertson aside and voice your reservations about this mission to him.

"Don't make too big of a show of it but tell Colonel Bevan as well ."

"General Blackwell, you do the same thing when you get there. Don't hold back. Lay it out the way you see it."

Beverly said, "You mean like this is totally insane?"

No one else had anything to add. There was no easy answer. Col. Randal must have his reasons for wanting them to tell Col. Bevan and Lt. Col. Robertson their reservations… he always did. They were wondering what it could be.

Not Jack Cool. He was thinking, "Dark of night, element of surprise, point type target, suppressed weapons, hit and run… *hell yes*!"

Col. Randal said, "We'll start drifting upstairs separately after you two leave."

When they were gone, Col. Randal said, "We're not having this conversation. I'll fill General McKoy in privately when I get upstairs. But right now what I'm about to say does not leave this table."

Maj. Gen. Blackwell said, "We're just drinking coffee."

Capt. Jaxx said, "Roger that, sir."

Beverly said, "You're making my heart beat fast, Johnny."

Col. Randal said, "We need to deliver a team of Rangers to a pinpoint target, behind enemy lines, with absolute precision, intact, in total silence, armed and equipped, ready to fight – leaving nothing behind to indicate to the Germans we were ever there when we withdraw.

"Here's how we're going to do it…"

3

ZONE OF DEATH

IT WAS AS IF SOMEONE HIT THE FAST-FORWARD BUTTON. THE order to Stand By Ready went out to Seaborn House. The estate went on lockdown. All personnel away on temporary duty or leave were recalled. A rash of auto thefts was reported to police stations throughout the countryside as Raiding Forces' operators made a mad dash to return to base with no time to wait for buses or trains.

Lieutenant Colonel John Henry Bevan arrived in the Phone Room. A military snob who did not trust anyone not in uniform, he got a jolt from the electric charge in the air the moment he walked in. The atmosphere, while tense, was humming with efficiency. What he saw was a disciplined team of professionals acting with intent working toward a common goal.

He liked it.

In a back corner, Brandy Seaborn, whom he had known most of her life, was in an intense conversation with Colonel John Randal and the big USAAF Major General, whom Lady Jane had informed him was Brandy's "friend" – a new development.

While drawing on her sketch pad, Major the Lady Jane Seaborn was talking with Beverly Blackwell and Mandy Paige. James "Baldie" Taylor and Lieutenant General "Geronimo" Joe McKoy were in deep conversation studying the patchwork aerial photo picto map of what Lt. Col. Bevan presumed was the target – Château du Val-Obscur. From the men's expressions neither was pleased with what he saw.

Lady Jane spotted him and came over. As did Lieutenant Colonel Thomas Argyll "Tar" Robertson and Major General William "Wild Bill" Donovan. Lt. Col. Bevan had not been expecting the Director of OSS to be present. He made a point of trying to avoid him whenever possible.

Maj. Gen. Donovan wanted to attach one of his OSS officers to the London Controlling Section. Lt. Col. Bevan had no intention of allowing that until he was absolutely forced to. The Director of the Office of Strategic Services was not a man who took no for an answer.

The seven-member LCS was a strictly British affair. He intended to keep the status quo for as long as possible. There was not going to be an American serving in the "Lie Factory", as the London Controlling Section was known, as long as he could help it.

The British clandestine services were rooted in discretion, secrecy and tradecraft. A business best left to gentlemen. Maj. Gen. Donovan was viewed as a politician in uniform who talked to the press – something simply not done in "the trade" – favored action-oriented, aggressive, paramilitary operations and posed a threat to the security and integrity of delicate wartime intelligence operations.

Yet here Lt. Col. Bevan was, the Controller of LCS, hat in hand to see Col. Randal – the recently appointed OSS Operational Group Branch (Europe) commander. Desperate for him to carry out a sensitive code word CROMWELL-level mission to save the LCS, the XX Committee and possibly the D-Day invasion of France. He was feeling more than slightly incongruous.

The London Controlling Section was not supposed to work this way.

Lady Jane said, "Hello Uncle, we understood you would be dropping by. John would like a word as soon as he finishes with Bronc and Brandy."

As they walked over, Brandy was saying, "Only you could dream up something like this, handsome. You are always entertaining. Do your part, Sam – Parker and I shall do ours."

Maj. Gen. Blackwell said, "I'm all in."

Col. Randal said, "Colonel Bevan, let's step over to the map."

He pointed to the château. There's our objective Château du Val-Obscur. Calais is five miles southeast. When we go in I'd like a diversion – a tactical distraction, between the village and the target."

Lt. Col. Bevan said, "What kind of diversion?"

Col. Randal said, "An air strike, a naval bombardment, or both."

"When?"

"Pilots sitting in their aircraft waiting for the order to scramble beginning from twenty-two hundred hours tonight. They may not get the green light – could be postponed a night or two. But they have to be ready to take off at an instant's notice. The air strike and or naval bombardment needs to be simultaneous with our hitting the château.

"When this goes down it'll happen fast."

Lt. Col. Bevan said, "The Royal Navy will protest it requires lead time to pre-position a ship for naval gunfire support. The Senior Service cannot be counted on in these circumstances. Let's not waste our time with the Navy.

"I shall coordinate with the RAF for a bombing mission."

Col. Randal said, "Can you arrange a second mission to bomb the château *after* we've withdrawn from the area?"

"Why would you want to do that?"

"Destroy the building. You don't want the Germans to know there's been a Commando raid. The idea is to make it look like an RAF bomber was forced to turn back from a mission with a full bomb load. Before trying to make it across the Channel, the pilot lightens his aircraft by jettisoning the payload and accidentally hits the house."

Lt. Col. Bevan said, "Now that is a plot worthy of an Academy Award, Colonel. Quite right! We absolutely do not want the Nazis to know Raiding Forces were ever on the ground.

"Timing not a problem?"

Col. Randal said, "As long as it goes in after we're away and before BMNT on the night of."

Lt. Col. Bevan said, "It shall likely require a bit of organization to create the desired illusion. Not that jettisoning a bombload over enemy-occupied France is any unique occurrence. Happens nightly, pilots trying to make it home aboard a crippled aircraft.

"We simply need to take care to make it appear that hitting the château is an unintended consequence."

Col. Randal said, "That is the idea."

Lt. Col. Bevan said, "One can see you have grasped the intent of the undertaking bang on, Colonel – commendable."

Lady Jane said, "You shall soon discover John is a gifted small-unit tactician."

"I can tell."

Beverly said, "Make sure the RAF uses incendiary bombs."

Lt. Col. Bevan said, "Very good, Miss Blackwell. I shall pass along your recommendation."

He was aware of who Beverly was because of her role as OSS liaison to the XX Committee – an assignment subject to much internal debate within the deception community.

Maj. Gen. Blackwell said, "You run into any trouble, Bevan, get back to me ASAP. I'm pretty sure I can get this done if you can't. My boys supply the head of RAF Bomber Command–Sir Arthur Harris, a C-47 for his personal transport."

Col. Randal worked to hold back a smile – typical Bronc.

Maj. Gen. Blackwell said, "We like to call him 'Bomber'."

Lt. Col. Bevan said, "As do we."

He was feeling slightly disoriented.

COLONEL JOHN RANDAL PULLED JAMES "BALDIE" TAYLOR, Lieutenant Colonel John Henry Bevan and Lieutenant Colonel Thomas Argyll "Tar" Robertson aside to have a conversation on another subject.

"Jim, is it possible for you to have SOE coordinate with the Resistance in the Calais district to blow up a rail bridge somewhere in the area without them knowing why?"

"When do you need it done, Colonel?"

Col. Randal said, "Same night they receive the Execution Order – possibly as early as tonight. I don't need perfect timing. As long as it's *after* we launch our raid… prior to sunrise. All that's required is for them to carry out an operation to confuse the situation after we egress."

"I can arrange that."

"How much drop-ahead time do the French require?"

Jim said, "Best case scenario – 5 plus hours."

"That fast?"

"SOE has its best communications with the Resistance in Calais of anywhere in enemy-occupied France because of its immediate proximity to England – direct voice in some cases. SOE will insert a coded "*action immediate*" order in the BBC 'Personal Messages' segment of the nightly Free French Services broadcast. This will alert the local resistance circuit leader to have his wireless operator stand by for a coded action message detailing a top priority assignment to be carried out.

"SOE HQ will then transmit detailed instructions by Morse specifying the sabotage to be conducted. The marquis leader will assemble a team of 4-6 resistance members. A small party will place the target under observation. The rest retrieve the necessary explosives from one of their pre-cached demolition dumps.

"Once SOE transmits the execution order a demolitions team will move into position, place their charges set to go off after they withdraw using a No.10 delayed time pencil. Then the Resistance fighters will disperse into the countryside in order to be long gone before the explosives detonate.

"Chances are it will take longer than five hours, but in the Calais district you can count on a mission such as you are requesting to be accomplished in well under twelve hours. Ever since the German occupation, France has operated on Central European Time, which makes it the same as our hostilities only British Double Summer Time. Sunrise occurs at 0830-0845 hrs – fits your timeline."

Col. Randal said, "Works for me – go ahead put that in place."

Jim said, "If a railroad bridge turns out to be too difficult a target to deliver on such short notice will blowing a stretch of tracks or knocking down a string of powerlines suffice?"

Col. Randal said, "That's fine – we just need the result to be noisy and noticeable the next day."

Lt. Col. Bevan and Lt. Col. Robertson traded glances, impressed by the attention to detail and the depth of the planning they were observing. Col. Randal was trying to cover every angle. Which was impossible.

Jim said, "What you are asking for the Underground can deliver. Those people have a thorough understanding of the 'P for Plenty' formula. You will have your big bang."

Col. Randal said, "SOE can't have any idea why the sabotage assignment has to be carried out – non-negotiable."

Lt. Col. Bevan said, "I can arrange for the orders to come directly from the Joint Intelligence Committee if it's helpful."

Jim said, "That would guarantee compliance. Gubbins will want to carry out the assignment to demonstrate SOE has the capability of delivering high-priority assignments on short notice. You can always count on organizational self-promotion.

"He won't ask questions."

Col. Randal said, "Good."

MAJOR GENERAL SAM HOUSTON "BRONC" BLACKWELL AND Lieutenant Ricky Mascuch flew to RAF Aldermaston, home to the 4th Troop Carrier Group (USAAF) assigned to Troop Transport Command. The 88th Glider Infantry Battalion(GIB) was stationed on the airfield.

It was the advance party of the 13th Airborne Division "Golden Unicorns" who would be arriving in country sometime in the next ninety days.

Lt. Mascuch, formerly of the U.S. 551 Parachute Infantry Regiment (Airborne) (Separate) was the most experienced glider man in Raiding Forces. He was traveling to Aldermaston to arrange for the installation of reinforcing metal skid shoes on a Waco CG-4A – a modification he had never even seen before. While widely acknowledged in Raiding Forces as the expert on all things related to U.S. military gliders, it was not by choice. Lt. Mascuch hated the canvas death traps – widely called "flying coffins" by paratroopers and glidermen alike.

And he never wanted to ride in another one ever again.

Maj. Gen. Blackwell was along to make sure the installation took place in a timely fashion – meaning posthaste or in Raiding Forces' speak, "As soon as possible if not sooner." With Bronc's personal interest there was a good chance an all-time record for the installation of the metal skid shoes would be set today.

When they landed, Maj. Gen. Blackwell had a word with the base commander then repaired to the 88th GIB to speak to the battalion commander, Lieutenant Colonel Elbridge G. Chapman. Bronc requested the name of the best glider pilot in IX Troop Carrier Command.

He did not say why.

Lt. Col. Chapman said, "That would be Warrant Officer George E. May, sir."

Maj. Gen. Blackwell said, "What makes him such a hot stick?"

Lt. Col. Chapman said, "Not only is May my best pilot, he's also an expert on glider retrieval from a forward area – aren't many of those around, sir."

Maj. Gen. Blackwell said, "I have a lieutenant along to supervise installation of metal skid shoes on a Waco CG-4A. As soon as the install is complete, move the glider to a remote section of the airfield. Have a squad of MPs establish a perimeter and cordon off that section of the runway. It's a black site – no one in or out.

"Is that clear?"

"Clear, sir."

"Have WO May stand by 'Ready Five' with his flight gear. I'll be flying in around 1400 hrs to brief him on the flight profile of a classified mission. Under no circumstances is he to be questioned about it."

'Ready Five' meant prepared to take off on five minutes' notice.

Maj. Gen. Blackwell said, "May is not to leave the base. He's not to have any communications with anyone other than you until I return, starting now – don't let him near alcohol.

"I need a Wilco, Colonel."

"Wilco, sir!"

Bronc had the ability to put the fear of God into even relatively senior officers when he wanted to.

He took off from RAF Aldermaston and flew to RAF Ramsbury, home of the advanced party of the 437 Troop Carrier Group. The remainder of the group would be arriving at the airfield in a few weeks. He went directly to the Glider Maintenance Detachment and spoke in private to Chief Warrant Officer Warren G. Davidson, the man in charge.

CWO Davidson said, "This what you're looking for, General?"

He was holding up a piece of equipment he had never been called on to install before.

"Roger that. Load it on my plane. A pleasure doing business with you, Chief. I was never here, we did not have this conversation, you did not supply me with any equipment."

CWO Davidson wondered what he was going to tell his CO when he came hot-footing it to the Glider Maintenance Detachment to welcome his boss's, boss's, boss to Ramsbury airfield.

Bronc was winging his way back to London in the Lysander before the Maintenance Detachment's commander arrived.

BRANDY SEABORN GOT ON THE HORN AND CONTACTED THE Inshore Patrol Flotilla (IPF) She spoke with the young Royal Navy Volunteer Reserve officer she had worked with previously, Sub-Lieutenant Jeffery Macomber. "A jeep and driver is on the way to pick you up, Jeffery. Report to the TOC at Seaborn House immediately. Bring your toothbrush. I have need of your services this night.

Sub-Lieutenant Jeffery Macomber said, "Yes, ma'am."

He wondered how he had become the go-to IPF officer for Raiding Forces.

LIEUTENANT COLONEL JOHN HENRY BEVAN PLACED A PHONE call to General Sir Hastings Ismay, Chief of Staff to the Minister of Defence – Winston Churchill served in the dual capacity of Minister of Defense as well as being the Prime Minister. Gen. Ismay then contacted the PM for approval of a code word CROMWELL (Urgent, Strategic) mission. Since the request came from the Chief of the London Controlling Section, there was no question it would be approved – that was automatic.

Lt. Col. Bevan could have called the PM directly for authorization had he chosen to.

When he received the message, acting in his capacity as Minister of Defense, the Prime Minister proceeded to phone the Air Ministry on the

Green Line (Classified, Highest-Level Voice Communications). He spoke to Air Chief Marshal Sir Charles Portal, Chief of the Air Staff (CAS). The PM/M O D informed him General Ismay was en route to his office with a code word CROMWELL mission to be laid on from that night forward until executed.

CROMWELL was the highest-level alert code word that could be sent to an operational unit. Only those with a direct operational Need-to-Know, senior commanders, key RAF squadrons, MI 5/MI-6/ and certain Special Operations units had access to its meaning – to anyone else it was just a word. For those cleared, CROMWELL signaled a mission of the "highest strategic urgency."

Receipt of a CROMWELL mission meant "all standing orders, administrative duties, and routine missions were to be abandoned forthwith."

The "Former Naval Person's" direct involvement was a rare event. It spoke to the exigency of the operation – elevating the highest mission designation to an even higher level in the minds of the recipients.

And it ensured one hundred percent compliance with no questions asked.

As soon as the PM hung up he proceeded to travel the half mile to Lieutenant Colonel John Henry Bevan's subterranean suite of offices at 2 Carlton Gardens for a briefing on the operation. The Prime Minister was apoplectic when he learned the details. The news was potentially as disastrous as any he had received up to this point in WWII.

Considering for the first two years England had been losing the war, Prime Minister Churchill knew bad news when he heard it.

ACM Portal ordered up a staff car and was driven the 30 miles to Air Chief Marshal Sir Arthur Harris's Bomber Command Headquarters at Naphill near High Wycombe, Buckinghamshire – Codename "SOUTHDOWN."

Following their meeting ACM Harris issued a verbal directive to the Air Ministry's Director of Bomber Operations, Air Vice Marshal Norman Bottomley.

AVM Bottomley sent a Flash code word "Z" (Overriding All Other Signal Traffic, Regardless of Origin or Destination) to the Air Officer Commanding (AOC) No.5 Group – Air Vice Marshal Ralph Cochrane, advising him of the mission.

AVM Cochrane contacted Wing Commander Leonard Cheshire, VC, DSO, DFC, the commander of 617 Squadron and ordered him to place his best pilot on Readiness Alert (Aircraft Fully Armed, Fueled, Ready to Take Off).

Wg. Cdr. Cheshire was one of the most highly decorated officers in the RAF. He opted to fly the mission himself. He was the most skilled pilot in the squadron for precision low-level flying – as low as 30 feet in a four-engine Avro Lancaster B Mk I (Special). Six Seventeen Squadron was famously known as the 'Dam Busters', which meant the Wing Commander was a very, very good bomber pilot.

THE ORIGINAL REQUEST FROM LIEUTENANT COLONEL JOHN Henry Bevan for a code word CROMWELL mission was in two parts. As a result, a pair of Flash-Z messages were immediately sent out. The first was an alert for Bomber Command. The second was an alert for Fighter Command.

It had been quickly determined a squadron of de Havilland Mosquito ground attack fighters would be required for the diversionary attack. The Mosquitos were armed with four 20mm Hispano Mk II cannon, eight .303 Browning machine guns and six 500-pound bombs – two per wing and two in the bomb bay.

Fighter Command ordering up a ground attack was a much simpler process than Bomber Command organizing the Lancaster bomber from 617 Squadron "accidentally" bombing Major Hanns von Reisen's Abwehr headquarters. It did not require precision bombing or subterfuge for the flight plan. All that was needed was a loud, violent air attack on German targets of opportunity located on the outskirts of Calais in the corridor between the village and Château du Val-Obscur. All that was needed was a diversionary air raid – a feint, timed to draw attention away from the Raiding Forces' strike taking place on the Abwehr HQ.

Only Fighter Command did not know any of the details.

In the request, Lt. Col. Bevan specified, "...the best special operations qualified Mosquito Squadron available to support a CROMWELL level Commando raid."

The CROMWELL order arrived at RAF Fighter Command Headquarters in Bentley Priory, Stanmore, Middlesex and was immediately brought to the attention of Air Chief Marshal Sir Trafford Leigh-Mallory. He bypassed the entire chain of command and personally contacted his best ground attack squadron commander on the Green Line and followed that up with a Flash message.

Wing Commander A.M. Murphy aka "Sticky", DSO, DSC, of 198 Squadron – the best night intruder ground attack unit in the RAF, took the call which was followed up by a teleprinter signal. He had not been expecting a mission since his squadron was in the process of deploying to the Mediterranean. He would need to improvise to put a full complement of pilots in the air.

```
RAF SIGNAL-OPERATIONAL ORDER
Date-Time-Group 261430ZDEC43
Priority: FLASH
Classification: MOST SECRET/TOP SECRET
To: Officer Commanding No. 198 Squadron RAF
VIA: RAF Manston Operations Room
BY ORDER: FIGHTER COMMAND
STAND TO: FULL OPERATIONS STATUS FROM 262000ZDEC43
OBJECTIVE: SUPPORT OF SPECIAL OPERATION-CALAIS DIST
TARGET ZONE: GRID REF TO FOLLOW VIA HAND CARRIER
ORDNANCE: LOAD OUT CONFIG B-1 - 2x500-POUND GP BOMBS
CALLSIGN: RAMROD 1
ESCORT COVER: NIL - LOW LEVEL STRIKE PROFILE
STRIKES: TO COMMENCE ON ARRIVAL OVER TARGET AREA AND
CONTINUE UNTIL ORDNANCE EXPENDED
PRIMARY OBJECTIVE: DISRUPT ENEMY MOBILE RESPONSE
SECONDARY OBJECTIVE: TARGETS OF OPPORTUNITY
NO RADIO TRANSMISSION UNTIL ENGAGEMENT
ACKNOWLEDGE VIA GREEN LINE - NO REBROADCAST
GROUP COMMANDING OFFICER HAS TACTICAL OVERRIDE
FURTHER INSTRUCTIONS TO FOLLOW VIA HAND OF OFFICER
```

The raid on Château du Val-Obscur was a national-level joint operation. It was to be conducted by the best men and equipment the United States and Great Britain had at their disposal. Anyone who thought a code word

CROMWELL small-scale raid in the European Theater of Operations (ETO) was simple to execute because of the limited number of boots on the ground had no concept of what had to take place behind the scenes to carry off a national-level strategic special operation.

CROMWELL meant failure was not an option. There were too many eyes on it in high places to allow that. Lt. Col. Bevan did not require a lot of men and women – he needed the right ones.

And he got them.

MAJOR GENERAL SAM HOUSTON "BRONC" BLACKWELL HAD ordered a VIP transport Beechcraft Model 17 Staggerwing biplane – the United States Army Air Force (USAAF) nomenclature was UC-43 Traveler, to be made available to Raiding Forces. Approximately 270 of the Beechcraft planes had been purchased by or impressed by the Army Air Force. The Traveler was a luxurious military transport normally reserved for generals, high-ranking staff officers or civilian dignitaries. Bronc temporarily assigned this one to Raiding Forces for in-country transport because of its short landing and take-off capability. The plane was fast – 200 mph. But it could only carry three passengers provided there was no co-pilot so it was not much in demand by the USAAF.

Which meant Raiding Forces might not have to give it back.

Major the Lady Jane Seaborn was impressed because it had carpeted floors, hand-polished wood trim and silver hardware – not the typical military transport. She and Colonel John Randal were sitting in the two seats behind Beverly, who was the pilot. Happy was in the right front seat next to her. The dog seemed to enjoy looking out the air screen as the UC-43 sped toward Seaborn House.

Col. Randal was studying the drawings Lady Jane had made of the interiors of three "typical" French country houses. She had delegated to her godfather the assignment responsibility for trying to find one of Château du Val-Obscur. He contacted his office and dispatched Squadron Leader Dennis Wheatly to the Royal Institute of British Architects (RIBA) library located at 66 Portland Place, London. It archived pre-war architectural journals and estate surveys with floor plans some of them in France. No joy.

Left with no other option, Sqn. Ldr. Wheatly gathered up the plans for three of the most common French designs to take to the Bradford Hotel. The librarian protested they were not to leave the premises. However, Sqn. Ldr. Wheatly was a famous bestselling author of occult thrillers and swashbuckling historical adventure novels, known to her (he did not claim *Jump on Bella* on his resume). He gave his solemn word to return the journals in the same condition they were borrowed.

A promise Sqn. Ldr. Wheatly hoped he could keep.

Lady Jane used the magazines to make her sketches for Col. Randal and briefed him on the flight to Seaborn House, "The typical Renaissance Period French château has two or three stories – our target has two. The ground floor, *rez-de-chaussée* is used for service areas, kitchens, pantries and other informal rooms.

"The first floor, *premier étage,* is where you shall find the main living area, salons, dining rooms, libraries and bedchambers.

"The second floor, le premier étage, is for family bedrooms – you shall find the master on this level, possibly a small office, guest rooms and/or nurseries."

Col. Randal said, "That's three floors. You said two stories."

Lady Jane laughed, "The French do not count the ground floor as a story."

Col. Randal said, Well, that's good to know. Bad idea to go in planning for two stories and find three."

Lady Jane laughed, "That is what you have me for, babe – clarification."

Col. Randal said, "Pick the one you believe to be most representative of a typical rural chateau. When we arrive at Seaborn House I'm going to need an enlarged schematic to brief the mission. Can you make that happen?"

Col. Randal knew this was the textbook example of how *not* to plan a mission but it was all he had.

"My pleasure – do not give it a second thought." She knew this was a desperate situation. Lady Jane was trying to project a sense of calm she did not feel. She had been involved with Raiding Forces long enough to know "poor prior planning produced poor results."

"Poor results" in this case would be a polite phrase for the entire Raid Team being lost.

The sun was starting to go down when Beverly rolled in over Seaborn House and landed on the drive.

COLONEL JOHN RANDAL IMMEDIATELY WENT INTO A MEETING with Captain Dick Courtney and Waldo Treywick. The former ivory poacher had informed Col. Randal he wanted to be on the Recon Team. Since Waldo was arguably the most experienced reconnaissance man in Raiding Forces and the fact most teams performed better when their members worked in pairs – the original plan being for Capt. Courtney and his two strikers, X-Ray and Vanish to go in alone – he was added to the team.

Col. Randal brought in X-Ray and Vanish and issued one of, if not the most barebones Operations Orders he had ever given for a mission of this complexity. No Warning Order. The only pre-mission preparation was going to be a radio check. Arms and equipment were part of every operator's "ready bag." Raiding Forces maintained a status of always being prepared to deploy on a moment's notice.

Recon Team's primary weapons and gear were good to go.

"This is Château du Val-Obscur, your point of interest. Immediately upon completion of this order Recon Team consisting of Capt. Courtney, Mr. Treywick, X-Ray and Vanish will be flown to a departure airfield where you will link up with a C-47 piloted by one of General Blackwell's Troop Transport Command pilots. From there you will be flown to a drop zone located in a pasture one mile northwest of the Château du Val-Obscur.

"Immediately upon landing recover your chutes. Bury them where they won't be found later. Leave nothing behind – I say again, nothing is to be left to indicate you were ever there.

"After getting rid of your parachutes, advance to a position of concealment where you can physically observe the château and set up an OP. What you're specifically looking for is an Opel Admiral model staff car parked outside the château. The one shown in the aerial photo is a four-door model.

"Once you spot the car, transmit the message, '*The dog is sleeping in the sun.*' The TOC will authenticate receipt of your message with '*The girl has a nice smile.*' Mrs. Seaborn will have established a radio relay station in the Channel aboard her PT boat to facilitate traffic. You may receive a double confirmation – not a problem.

"Then close on the target if you are not there already. However, stay well away from the front of the building. A team under my command will be arriving in the next fifteen minutes.

"Be advised we'll be coming in hot.

"There will probably be a sentry in front and one in the rear of the château – possibly even a roving guard to patrol around the perimeter. Captain Courtney, you and Vanish will be responsible for taking out the guard at the front of the house utilizing suppressed weapons.

"I say again, move away from the front of the château as soon as you take out the sentry.

"Mr. Treywick, you and X Ray are responsible for eliminating the security in back and the roving patrol utilizing suppressed weapons. Once that has been accomplished remain in place and secure the rear of the building.

"When Raid Team arrives, Captain Courtney you will affect link-up by identifying yourself with a blue-lensed flashlight. If someone challenges you the password is 'Rat Poison.' Report to Lieutenant Mascuch. He'll need your assistance.

"Mr. Treywick, you and X-Ray remain in position until you hear the command to rally. Then move around to the front of the château displaying a blue light. If anyone attempts to exit the back door prior to the signal to rally without shouting 'Ranger,' light 'em up.

"Once assembled we'll all come out together.

"Mission-specific equipment: Paraset Type 17 special operations wireless set. Suppressed M3 Grease Guns. Silenced pistols either .22 Colt Woodsman or.22 High Standard Military Model Ds – no unsuppressed weapons. Blue-lensed flashlights common to all.

"This is a code word TRIPLE-NINE mission. A classification reserved for operations so sensitive their existence is denied to Allied command channels outside of MI-6, MI-5, SOE, OSS or Raiding Forces."

Most of Capt. Courtney's missions for the Naval Intelligence Division (NID) were classified TRIPLE-NINE. He knew what it meant. No witnesses left behind.

"What are your questions?"

Immediately following the briefing, Captain Pamala Plum-Martin flew the Recon Team to RAF Manston on the Isle of Thanet in Kent aboard the UC-43 Traveler. It was a tight squeeze to get the extra passenger aboard. The base was the nearest airfield to Pas-de-Calais – 37 miles. Since the beginning of the war, the UK had been on British Double Summer Time

(BDST) – two hours ahead of Greenwich Mean Time (GMT). However, recently the British had reverted to GMT – which could be confusing and throw an operation off if not taken into account.

"Pitch Dark", defined as when astronomical twilight ends, was in full effect by 1800 hrs GMT. Recon Team immediately boarded one of Major General Sam Houston "Bronc" Blackwell's C-47s piloted tonight by a pilot Bronc personally handpicked.

Takeoff was at 1830 hrs.

The plane was airborne right on schedule. The only person other than Recon Team in the troop compartment was the USAAF loadmaster. It would be his responsibility to haul in the static lines and parachute deployment bags streaming behind the aircraft after the jumpers exited the aircraft.

No one talked during the flight. Every member of Recon Team had done this before. They knew what to expect, which was every parachute jump is different. They were all wearing full camo on their face and hands – even Vanish and X-Ray to cover the shine of their faces.

Waldo said, "X-Ray, you keep on smilin' I'm gonna put some camo on your gleamin' white teeth."

The flight to the drop zone was not a straight line. The flight plan called for the pilot to make his approach 8-10 miles down the coast from Calais Village, travel a short distance inland then loop around and fly back toward the English Channel. The jumpers would exit the aircraft at 500 feet – a low-level drop, and the plane would continue on headed back to Manston.

The German defense system in the Calais district was stacked in the vicinity of the large beaches where an invasion was likely to come ashore. That did not mean there were no anti-aircraft batteries in the area. There were. The C-47 could expect to take fire.

In areas where there were no suitable beach landing sites 711th Static Infantry Division troops were stationed at key points. On their flanks farther away, were the Hiwis auxiliaries composed of Russian, Ukrainian, Latvian and Estonian "volunteers" – sometimes styled as SS, but that was in name only. They were essentially an armed mob a grade or two below penal units such as the Dirlewanger Brigade in the Aegean.

In the immediate area around Château du Val-Obscur there were no key points such as road crossings or rail lines. The Hiwis located in the vicinity were even less mobile than the Static 711th – which was the beginning, the middle and the end of the intelligence on the troops stationed in the immediate vicinity of the objective Raiding Forces had.

If there were any auxiliaries in close proximity to the DZ tonight, they would not venture out even if they saw parachutes – their job was to observe and report. Follow up would wait for daylight when they could get support.

Searchlight and anti-aircraft batteries were scattered all along the coast. They were not densely packed in the target area but were randomly distributed in a wide checkerboard pattern that grew larger and larger the farther away from metropolitan areas like Calais Village. Typically German anti-aircraft batteries did not have ground troops assigned available to conduct search parties for bailed-out aircrew in the dark. They too would wait for daylight in the event parachutes were spotted.

No matter what Joseph Goebbels claimed, the Atlantic Wall aka Zone of Death was not defended wall-to-wall by elite first-line Wehrmacht "Field Divisions" backed up by mobile Panzer reserves. Not even in the heavily defended Calais district where the invasion was expected to land. The Germans simply did not have enough troops to guard every square inch of the coastline.

Provided the C-47 did not get shot down on the infil, Recon Team should not have any problem with getting on the ground. Once down, the four Rangers were fully capable of making themselves invisible.

Especially in the dark.

BRANDY SEABORN AND CAPTAIN PENELOPE "LEGS" HONEYCUTT Parker put to sea in her PT boat. Onboard was Lieutenant Westly Slade with a five-man team of OSS Special Warfare Operators aka Frogmen who would comprise the landing party. And Sub-Lieutenant Jeffery Macomber of the Inshore Patrol Flotilla. There was one other passenger – Major the Lady Jane Seaborn. She was wearing Colonel John Randal's A-2 Bomber jacket with the 575 Ranger Regiment scroll painted on the front – a little large for her. Her ivory-gripped 9mm Browning P-35 was in a chest holster under it.

The PT boat was outbound to take up station five miles off the French Coast on a three-part mission. Initially it was to relay messages from Captain Dick Courtney's Recon Team to the TOC at Seaborn House. Once that assignment was completed, the second task for the boat was to close on a tiny crescent-shaped pocket beach located at the base of a tall chalk cliff. It was located not far from where the dirt road from Château du Val-Obscur dead-ended at the top – the missions Extraction Rally Point (ERP). Last but not least was a task that had never been attempted before. Not even in training…probably because no one ever thought of the idea.

It might work.

COLONEL JOHN RANDAL AND THE THIRTEEN RAIDING FORCES' personnel – heavily weighted toward officers, who would make up Raid Team were flown to RAF Manston where they linked up with Major General Sam Houston "Bronc" Blackwell and Lieutenant Ricky Mascuch who had flown in from RAF Aldermaston. Beverly Blackwell, Mandy Paige and Jim Taylor accompanied them on the flight down in the C-47.

Immediately following the Raid Order, Captain Pamala Plum-Martin was to fly Jim and Lieutenant Colonel John Henry Bevan back to London for a conference at MI-5 aboard the UC-43 Traveler. Major General William "Wild Bill" Donovan would also be on the plane.

Wild Bill needed to be present when Lieutenant Colonel Thomas Argyll "Tar" Robertson broke the news to General Dwight D. Eisenhower, Supreme Commander Allied Expeditionary Force Europe, about the possibility the Double-Cross System and OPERATION FORTITUDE were at risk of being exposed to the Nazis.

Maj. Gen. Donovan was to brief Gen. Eisenhower on the status of the Raiding Forces' mission to eliminate the source of the potential compromise of the double agents.

Lt. Col. Bevan was beginning to realize he was not going to be able to avoid the Director of the Office of Strategic Services forever. Not with the war transitioning into the pre-D-Day preparation phase. Both officers were slated to be heavily involved with OPERATION FORTITUDE SOUTH.

There was a reason Col. Randal had such a high concentration of officers on the Raid Team tonight. The key players for future Seaborn House operations had been flown in to Seaborn House to be the advance parties of their teams as the troops were shuttled in from Castelrozzo. The NCOs had been left behind to supervise the loadout of the men and gear staging for redeployment to the UK.

Col. Randal decided to use the mission as an opportunity to introduce his new in-theatre officers to small-scale raiding on the French coast, which was different from island raiding in the Aegean. For this raid the best-qualified individual would lead regardless of rank. There would be one team led by a lieutenant with a captain acting as a private.

Having a mostly officer team was a good plan for a number of reasons, the most significant being it placed his most experienced decision makers at the initial point of contact. The downside was if the mission failed, OSS Operational Group (Europe) – meaning Raiding Forces, would be out of business. Considering the raids' code word TRIPLE-NINE classification, it was a risk worth taking.

Given any other option Col. Randal would have never done things this way.

On the plane to the airfield, Col. Randal huddled in the tail with Lieutenant General "Geronimo" Joe McKoy, Captain Billy Jack Jaxx, Lieutenant Chase Starrett and King.

"You men are my Raid Team leaders. I have a list of names. I'll pass it around. Each of you pick a man. No team will have more than three operators, counting yourself.

"Capt. Jaxx, go first you may have the toughest assignment. Captain Coogan and Lieutenant Mascuch will be on the operation but they're are not available for team assignments – both have other commitments."

"I'll take Horn Dog, sir."

"King?"

"Jake-the-Snake – Captain Novak."

"General?"

"I'll take Ferguson. You take Fenwick."

Col. Randal said, "Done – Lieutenant Starrett?"

"I'll take Captain Bonham."

"Capt. Jaxx, pick another man."

"Wildman Terrell – he and Hanson'll work pretty well together as long as there's not any women on the target."

"King?"

"Captain Hays."

"Lieutenant Starrett?"

"Captain Morgan, sir."

"General?"

"I'll take Major Dance."

Col. Randal said, "OK, Lance Corporal Karlsson is on me."

The men laughed. They all knew Tank liked working with the colonel. Raid Team had picked his operators for him. Leaving the U.S. Marine Special Warfare Operator until last was their way of taking care of their commanding officer.

Little details like that are how soldiers demonstrate respect. It might not seem like much. But it was a lot.

It is said in the U.S. Army, "You salute the rank, not the man." Raiding Forces was the exact opposite. Any officer the men did not salute because they respected him was out of a job –period.

Quite a few had come and gone.

Organizing the teams was Right Man, Right Job – not a popularity contest. Team leaders made their choices based on how well they thought their selections would function together. At this point they had no idea what their individual assignments were going to be. They did not even know what the mission was. But it was crystal clear – in order to accomplish what lay ahead, teamwork would be critical. It always was.

Not a single raid any man present had ever been on was task organized this way – like a sandlot football game.

4

GODSPEED THE BUTTERFLY

ROYAL AIR FORCE MANSTON AIR BASE

COLONEL JOHN RANDAL BRIEFED THE MISSION IN AN aircraft hangar prior to takeoff.

Col. Randal said, "*Situation*: I don't know what the situation is. We may never find out. This operation is strategic – all that's ever going to be said about it. Tonight, for reasons of security, we'll be operating as a team from the 575th Ranger Regiment.

"*Enemy forces*: The target is an Abwehr HQ located in a French château five miles outside of Calais. Typical nighttime staff is expected to consist of the officer-in-charge – in permanent residence according to reports, a duty officer, two-four security personnel guarding the entrances with possibly of one guard patrolling the perimeter – the guards will be eliminated by the time we arrive, a radio operator, cook, an orderly, six to eight additional guards to rotate the duty, drivers, support personnel etc. No intel on how many officers to expect quartered in the main house. Some may be commuting from Calais and not be at the château when we arrive. The enlisted men are anticipated to be housed in the horse stables adjacent to the main building.

"This is all an estimate. It's not based on any actionable intelligence. Best guess is not more than 15 Germans total on the target. Most should be off duty at the time we arrive.

"*Friendly Forces*: Captain Courtney is on site with Recon Team consisting of Mr. Treywick, X-Ray and Vanish.

"*Mission*: Conduct a raid on an enemy headquarters, capture the officer in charge – Major Hanns von Reisen, and return to base.

"*Execution*: The purpose of the exercise is to capture or kill Major von Reisen – priority is to capture. Otherwise, this is a kill mission. I say again, this is a kill mission. No one can be left behind alive to report we were ever there. Shoot anyone not wearing the same uniform we are.

"*Concept of the Operation*: Conduct a night airborne infiltration, assault the château and the two out buildings…"

Mandy and Beverly came forward and placed a large schematic of the objective on a wooden tripod. Beverly handed Col. Randal a pointer. Then the two girls returned to stand behind the Raid Team operators who were down on one knee on the concrete floor of the aircraft hangar.

"*Scheme of Maneuver*: Assault elements Team King, Team Randal and Team McKoy breach through the main entrance in that order of march. Team Jaxx attacks the barn and Team Starrett attacks the smaller outbuilding.

"The château is three stories tall. Team King, consisting of Captain Novak and Captain Hays, will make the initial assault and clear the ground floor. Mr. King will secure a prisoner who he will encourage to supply him with the whereabouts of Major von Reisen – French châteaus typically have the master bedroom on the second floor where it is expected we'll find him.

"Once Mr. King has ascertained the major's location he will immediately have the prisoner lead him to where he's located. Once King departs, the remainder of his team will continue to clear the ground floor which will likely consist of offices and the night duty personnel.

"Team Randal will follow Team King into the objective, flow through and proceed to the second floor to clear it. The likelihood is Mr. King will join on the second floor with his prisoner to lead the team to the target – Major von Reisen.

"Team McKoy will follow on the first and second teams and continue to the third floor as they peel off. Captain Coogan will accompany Team

McKoy and make entry to the attic where he will place incendiary devices with a 45-minute delayed fuse.

"Team Randal and/or Team McKoy will be prepared to assist Mr. King on whichever floor Major von Reisen is to be found – unless by chance he is on the ground floor when we breach.

"Team Jaxx will be responsible for assaulting the troop barracks in the barn. As soon as it is secure the team will repair to the château and stand by to provide support for the teams clearing the building as needed.

"Team Starrett will assault the second smaller outbuilding. Once that building is secured the team will first go to assist Team Jaxx then proceed to this location…" Col. Randal tapped the map with the pointer, "…and set up a blocking position on the road leading to Calais Village."

"Both Team Jaxx and Team Starrett will place a prepared incendiary device with a delayed fuse on the roof of their targets before continuing on to their secondary objectives.

"Captain Courtney's Recon Team is going to be on the ground in close proximity to the target when we go in, keeping it under observation. The team will be responsible for eliminating outside security. Be advised the four men composing the team will signal their presence with blue-lensed flashlights.

"As soon as Raid Team is on the ground Recon Team will join and serve as an additional reserve element. In addition, they will assist Lieutenant Mascuch with making preparations for our withdrawal.

"Signal: Do not engage anyone showing a blue light. Anyone exiting the château after the assault must identify themselves by shouting 'Ranger'. An element of Recon Team will be in place providing rear security with orders to engage anyone not doing so.

"Extraction: Raid Team will withdraw utilizing the Opel Admiral Type 39 staff car and/or the Ford V3000 3-ton truck parked at the château. We'll travel the three miles to the coast, rappel down to a shelf that will serve as the Extraction Rally Point where we'll be met by Team Slade to ferry us to Mrs. Seaborn's PT boat.

"Then we return home and never discuss this operation – it never happened."

Col. Randal had skipped over a lot of items normally found in an Operations/Raid Order –a fact not lost on any of the operators.

"What are your questions?"

Capt. Jaxx said, “Do we have a photograph of Major von Reisen, sir?”

“Negative.”

Standing in the back with Beverly and Mandy, Lieutenant Colonel John Henry Bevan knew he was going to have to give a report on Col. Randal’s mission statement to those in attendance at the MI-5 high-level crisis conference he would be attending later tonight. Then, after that meeting he was scheduled to brief Prime Minister Churchill. Under his breath, almost as if talking to himself he said, “Most brazen proposition ever put before me – extraordinary.”

Lt. Col. Bevan sounded like a man who might be experiencing a twinge of misgivings about what he had helped set in motion.

Beverly said, “Johnny’s never been big on the indirect approach.”

RECON TEAM WAS ON THE GROUND OBSERVING CHÂTEAU DU Val-Obscur. They had dropped in a mile from the target. Immediately upon landing the men recovered their parachutes, stuffed them in their lightweight kit bags and slung them over their heads like a backpack on the webbing straps designed to allow jumpers to keep their hands free for their weapons. The chutes could not be left behind.

It was a nice night. The moon was perfect for a clandestine op under. A waning crescent. According to the meteorology report only about 11 percent illumination. Some Commando units would not have felt that way, preferring a full moon. Not Recon Team. They did not need the light to see by. Everyone on Captain Dick Courtney’s team was highly experienced at operating under cover of darkness.

What they wanted was cover and concealment.

The team shook out into a simple file formation. Capt. Courtney had an azimuth pre-dialed in on his Mark III Prismatic Marching Compass. He led off on point, X-Ray and Vanish were close behind with Waldo Treywick pulling rear security. They ghosted across the fields toward the objective. It was good going over level ground.

When the patrol came to a hedge row they crawled inside and buried the kit bags containing their parachutes. No one would ever find them. In

France, hedgerows were like fences. People did not force their way through them. They had gates.

Once that was accomplished Recon Team moved out again. The fact the team was three miles behind the lines having just invaded France all alone did not occur to them in any way other than they were "on mission." Traveling at night in enemy territory was business as usual. The patrol was entirely focused on fieldcraft.

And reaching their objective undetected.

"Black Regulations," as the Germans called blackout, meant good land navigation was a must. There would not be any lights showing at the château to guide by. There were no discernible terrain features in the flat farmland. Capt. Courtney did have one checkpoint he was looking for –the dirt track running past the target and continuing on toward the coast. When they hit the road then he would be able to vector in on the target.

They were on it in minutes. This was not a major highway. It was an occasionally used country lane. And it was not easy to distinguish in the dark.

Standing in the middle of the track Capt. Courtney knew which way the Channel was. He went the other direction.

There was no guarantee it was the right call. Land navigation at night on perfectly featureless terrain is trial and error. Dirt roads were sometimes hard to discern – what they looked like on a map and what they looked like on the ground at night in the dark were often two different things. There was the possibility what they were on was simply a path some farmer had used for years to move from one pasture to another.

Staying on azimuth and knowing your pace count will not always get you to where you want to go. It only indicates how far you have traveled on that line of march, which is helpful but does not tell you where you are. Or where your target is in relation to which direction you need to move to find it. Besides, the patrol did not know exactly where they landed to start the count from. All they knew was where they were *supposed* to have landed. There are a lot of ins and outs, ifs and maybes when it came to map reading – hope was not a course of action you have to do it.

However, Capt. Courtney was making an educated guess – which is what skilled land navigators do best.

Moving at night, creeping up on an unsuspecting armed and dangerous enemy is a sensation that has to be experienced to fully appreciate. You feel like a big hunting cat – aware. You seem to be floating. And you feel very, very alive.

Which can be a false read of the situation. Get it wrong and you can be very, very dead – fast.

Though he had not said anything at the time, Capt. Courtney had been reluctant to bring Mr. Treywick along on the mission – he did not really know the man.

X-Ray and Vanish had been his strikers for years. As a result, a lot of their communication was telepathic. And the two had the ability to appear and disappear at will right in front of your eyes like phantoms.

As it turned out, so did Waldo. When moving, the old ivory poacher never made the slightest sound. Capt. Courtney realized he should have known the former sidekick of the legendary P.J. Pretorious would be skilled in bushcraft.

Up ahead a dim smudge seemed to appear in the distance. Simmering like a mirage. Maybe he was imagining it. There are no mirages at night. The sensation is not uncommon when observing fixed objects in the dark. The trick was not to stare directly at them – look off to one side. That helps a little.

The closer the team approached the more the object steadied down until finally becoming clearly defined.

Château du Val-Obscur.

Capt. Courtney halted the patrol. Waldo moved forward to confer. Vanish and X-Ray went to the prone to provide security.

Nothing could be learned about the objective from this distance, which was only 50 yards, maybe less. It was difficult to determine distance with barely a sliver of moon. There is no trick for that.

Capt. Courtney and Waldo were so close together they were physically touching. Nevertheless, they did not speak or even whisper. Capt. Courtney pointed his finger at the château. Waldo nodded with an exaggerated movement of his head.

The patrol moved up. Very slowly. Walking in exaggerated slow motion, placing every foot carefully to avoid breaking a stick, kicking a rock or anything else that might make a hint of a sound. This was the final movement to contact, and now their moves did mimic that of big cats.

Armed enemy were ahead.

They moved and paused. Moved and paused – stalking – or more accurately, still hunting. Listening hard. Straining to penetrate the sea of darkness by sight or sound. Studying the layout of the château grounds. Looking and listening before moving again. Reconnaissance is the purest form of warfare.

Not everyone has the patience for it.

When they reached a position within 15 yards of the house, Recon Team went to ground. At this point the operators had a sense of being fully in control of the situation. They were relaxed, but not in a laid-back way – everyone was dialed in, focused on the tasks at hand.

At this point the team had to examine the target in detail. They needed to determine if the Opel Admiral staff car was present. It was. They had to pinpoint the sentries. And they had to decide the best way to silently take them out.

Once the Go-Code phrase was transmitted, Raid Team would be landing in fifteen minutes – no guard could be alive when it arrived. There was no rush now. Capt. Courtney was in control of the timing for the raid to commence.

The operators could see a guard standing his post in front of the main entrance. After watching for a while the glow of a cigarette appeared moving around the left side of the château. A roving sentry was walking his post around the perimeter of the house, making their job easier by smoking as he made his rounds.

Capt. Courtney timed it. He came past every seven minutes. There would almost certainly be a fixed sentry stationed at the rear of the building standing his post.

Waldo and X-Ray were responsible for taking care of the roving guard and the sentry in back. Capt. Courtney and Vanish would eliminate the Nazi at the front door. However, there was a problem.

Parked out front, the Opel Admiral was standing next to a pair of Ford V3000 all-purpose trucks – Capt. Courtney wondered if Hitler was paying Ford Motor Company their licensing fees. Strange the thoughts that flashed across your mind at moments like this. There were *two* trucks when he was expecting only one.

What did that mean, if anything?

Capt. Courtney pointed at the château and held up five fingers indicating five minutes. Waldo nodded. He and X-Ray slipped out of the position and moved off in the dark a fair distance away from the target. They were moving to circle around and approach the house from the back. The sentry standing his post behind the building would be silently eliminated. Then the perimeter guard when he came around.

Waldo and X-Ray were going to have to time it carefully.

Capt. Courtney would wait five minutes after the two disappeared in the dark. Then he would send the Go-Code then take down the sentry in front. Once that was done he and Vanish would move to a safe location to wait for the cavalry to arrive.

The clock was ticking. However, time seemed to stand still. It was a long five minutes.

While he was standing by waiting impatiently for the hands on his Army Trade Pattern standard-issue wristwatch to advance, Capt. Courtney set up the Whaddon Mark VII aka Paraset transmitter. It was simple to operate. He was an accomplished Wireless Telegraphy (W/T) operator by necessity. All of his classified NID patrol communications were in Morse.

At the appropriate time Capt. Courtney transmitted '*The dog is sleeping in the sun.*'

Now there was another wait for the acknowledgement. That could take up to ten minutes. Not tonight. With a pre-arranged message, a pre-determined response and a W/T operator at Seaborn House monitoring the frequency, confirmation came right back.

'The girl has a nice smile.'

Around back of the château, Waldo and X-Ray were in position. They waited for the perimeter guard to come by. Then Waldo moved along the box hedge that ran past the château to the front yard while staying on the far side away from the back porch. The sentry on it was also smoking a cigarette. Generally, guards are not supposed to do that when standing their post.

Discipline at Château du Val-Obscur was clearly lax.

At a range of about 10 feet Waldo raised up over the top of the waist-high shrubbery with his 9mm M3 Grease Gun to his shoulder… *SSSSS*

The sentry dropped.

So fast if Waldo had blinked he would have missed it. He moved around the hedge, dragged the dead Nazi off the porch up against the wall into the shadow cast by the house. And put the German's billed hat on.

Then he assumed the guard's post.

There was a little time left before the roving sentry came back around so he took out the stub of one of his Cairo custom-rolled panatela cigars and lit up, smoking apparently not being forbidden when pulling guard duty at this station. If it was the order was being ignored this night.

Waldo was enjoying his cigar when the perimeter guard came around the corner and walked by... *SSSSS*

X-Ray appeared out of the dark and helped drag the body up against the wall in the shadow of the building next to the other dead Nazi. Then they pulled back a few yards and took up a prone position facing the rear door. If the timeline laid out in their briefing was followed they did not have long to wait.

Waldo put out his cigar

Capt. Courtney waited nearly the entire fifteen minutes before walking down the sidewalk to where the German was standing his post. The soldier had his 8x57mm Karabiner 98 rifle at sling arms. It took the guard a few seconds to realize he was not being approached by the sergeant-of-the-guard pulling a surprise inspection. Before the sentry could get the K-98 unslung… *SSSSS*

The Nazi fell off the porch landing behind an Azalea bush. Capt. Courtney leaned around the plant and gave him another short burst… *SSS.*

Then he moved back, linked up with Vanish and they retreated to what was hoped to be a safe distance away.

RAF HAWKINGE: RAIDING FORCES DEPARTURE AIRFIELD

THE RAID TEAM BRIEFING WAS CONCLUDED. THE BRASS HATS were gone. Now came the wait. It was commonly said in Raiding Forces the waiting was worse than the mission. That might not be so in this case. This raid was unlike any other the veteran team had ever gone on – there was a sense of unreality about it. Were they really going to do this? However to an extent that was true for all of their missions.

Colonel John Randal had his Rangers assembled around the Waco CG-4A. There was no heavy equipment to be loaded though there was some lightweight specialty gear aboard. This was going to be a high-speed, low-drag, hit-and-run operation. Only suppressed individual weapons were being carried – stealth was paramount.

A supply of incendiary devices was being taken – Lewes Bombs. Developed by Captain Jock Lewes of Special Air Service fame. The fire bombs had been invented by SAS to use to destroy enemy aircraft during their desert airfield raiding days. The small, lightweight devices delivered maximum effect with minimal weight.

Captain Richard "Dynamite Dick" Coogan had a dozen in a Bag, Musette, M1936 designed for U.S. Army airborne troops. He also had several damaged nose cones from RAF incendiary bombs. The idea was to leave those behind scattered in an obvious place for the Germans to find the next day.

Like Beverly said, "You don't want to make it too hard for the bad guys to figure out what you want 'em to." At the time, she was talking about XX Committee deceptions intentionally planted to mislead the Nazis. Her logic worked just as well for tonight's raid. The purpose of the exercise was to leave no evidence behind the team of 575th Rangers had ever been there and make it look like something else had taken place.

The idea was to blame the burning château and outbuildings on being hit by errant incendiary bombs dropped by an RAF pilot aboard a damaged Lancaster who salvoed his bomb load to lighten his aircraft.

Nothing to see here, just a coincidence.

Capt. Coogan assured Col. Randal he could make it look like the buildings were struck by incendiary bombs even if the bomber pilot missed the mansion or was shot down before he could fly his part of the raid. The Lewes bombs were a contingency plan. Raiding Forces' Rules stipulated, 'It's Good to Have a Plan B.'

That was true, but the only Plan B tonight was Capt. Coogan's incendiary devices – it was not always possible to do things by the book.

The Rangers going on this raid were all old hands. Mature operators. There was not a lot of horseplay as they assembled around the Waco CG-4A. Most stretched out on the ground conserving their energy. The men were in the zone. Mentally going over their individual assignments, visualizing their moves once the glider went in.

Waiting to get the word.

Everyone was calm. They had sweated out missions before. But none like this – time was standing still.

Col. Randal thought it might be the best team he ever put together. Experience is priceless on an operation as strategically important and technically challenging as this one. This raid was going to require split-second timing, violent execution and zero mistakes.

Zero mistakes is impossible.

Tonight, acting as individuals in some cases was going to be as important as teamwork. The operators all needed to carry out their assignments with flawless precision. Each man would have to perform his individual task at peak performance in concert with the other Rangers spread out over the objective who were all operating to the same skill level. Success depended on individuals acting as one knowing without any doubt they could count on the other Raid Team members to be performing with the same proficiency they were.

That synergy creates a force-on-force high-intensity team effort.

Col. Randal was expecting – demanding – a degree of execution that could only be achieved by dedication, long hard training, and experience of operating against an armed and hostile enemy in places where failure can and will result in death or capture.

Raid Team was composed of veteran Rangers who met the criteria.

Suddenly, unexpectedly, the specially designed low-light flare path on the airstrip lit up for an incoming aircraft. The lights were not very bright. They looked like a string of glowing cigarettes laid out in a row. Because RAF Hawkinge was right on the coast, normal airfield lighting could not be employed so as not to attract the attention of a passing Kriegsmarine E-boat or Luftwaffe night fighter.

The UC-42 piloted by Captain Pamala Plum-Martin dropped in out of the dark and touched down. The subdued landing lights were extinguished before the plane rolled to a stop. A figure disembarked. Capt. Plum-Martin was already taking off again before whoever it was that deplaned made it off the strip.

Lieutenant Ted Hamilton aka "The Great Teddy" came jogging over to where Raid Team was assembled.

Col. Randal said, "What are you doing here, Lieutenant?"

"I thought you might need help, sir."

"How in the world did you manage to convince Pam to fly you to Hawkinge?

"I FROGSPAWNED her, sir." Which was not true. Capt. Plum-Martin had known The Great Teddy since Habbaniya. They shared a bond as did everyone in Raiding Forces who had been there during the siege. The snow-blonde, Vargas Girl look-alike pilot flew Lt. Hamilton to join up with Col. Randal because he asked her to.

"We're maxed out on weight for the glider."

"I am pretty light, sir."

"Where's your weapon?"

"All I have is my Colt.38 Super, Colonel."

"OK, go find Lieutenant Mascuch. Tell him I said to give you his suppressed M3. He's not going to need it. You stick with me when we land – get Captain Jaxx to brief you on the mission."

"Yes, sir!"

A jeep driven by Beverly Blackwell came racing up. Two of Major General Sam Houston "Bronc" Blackwell's military policemen were with her. The MPs knew she was Bronc's daughter. They were prepared to carry out her orders. Even though what she had instructed them to do did not make much sense.

Beverly said, "Dick Courtney just confirmed the Opel staff car is at the château – it's a Go, Johnny."

Col. Randal ordered, "Saddle up."

The Rangers stood up, shook out their weapons, adjusted their gear, and made ready to board the Waco CG-4A.

Maj. Gen. Blackwell was sitting in the cockpit of the C-47 Dakota tow plane. The aircraft's left engine coughed to life with a sharp backfire, wheezing as it slowly turned over, sounding rough then smoothing out into a loud roar. The right engine followed suit. In no time both engines were running with a steady roar.

The Dakota was straining to taxi.

Col. Randal was by the side door of the Waco CG-4A. He saw each Ranger aboard. Loading was smooth and orderly, only taking a few minutes.

There was no pep talk or bravado.

Captain Billy Jack Jaxx was last. He wanted to be seated next to the canvas half screen that separated the troop compartment from the cockpit.

Waco CG-4As did not have an internal intercom. Jack Cool wanted to be in a position to communicate with Col. Randal who would be sitting in the co-pilot's seat during the flight.

"All right, Jack – let's do this."

"Roger that, sir!"

Around at the front of the plane out of sight of the loading in progress, Beverly pulled the jeep up next to Warrant Officer George E. May – the pilot, who was making one last safety check of the tow line nose connection. He wanted to make double sure the assemblage did not come loose prematurely in flight.

Beverly said, "Mr. May, these two MPs would like a word with you."

WO May looked up in surprise. "What?"

"They'd like you to come with them."

"Are you crazy?"

"That's what they said – have you paid all your parking tickets, George?"

The two burly MPs escorted the protesting glider pilot to the jeep.

Beverly took out a long-billed baseball cap, tucked her blonde ponytail under it and put the cover on. Then she climbed into the pilot's seat of the glider and put on the headset to be able to receive instructions for takeoff from her father in the C-47 tow plane.

Communications between the two planes would be kept to a bare minimum. She was planning not to transmit at all until reaching the point of no return.

Maj. Gen. Blackwell radioed, "Prepare for takeoff."

Beverly clicked the push-to-talk switch twice to break squelch on the improvised phone system – the predetermined signal for "Wilco."

After seeing all his men aboard Col. Randal climbed into the pitch dark cockpit and took the co-pilot's seat – no co-pilot tonight. He fastened his seat belt. This ship was going to crash.

Beverly – in the dark Col. Randal was not aware it was her – was standing on the brake of the CG4-A to prevent slack in the towline during takeoff. The stick on a glider was a steering wheel just like in a car. There were two of them. One for the pilot and one for the co-pilot– he was not about to touch the one in front of him.

Bronc transmitted over the line, "Rolling now."

Beverly waited a fraction of a second after the C-47 started moving then eased off the brakes to avoid a violent jerk on the tow rope. Nevertheless, it pulled taut with a sharp crack. The Rangers in the troop compartment had to brace themselves to prevent being thrown off the bench seats.

Maj. Gen. Blackwell proceeded down the grass runway. The glider's canvas wings rattled in the wind as the Waco CG-4A rolled along behind the tug. Not a reassuring sound to those on board – were they going to fall off?

As speed increased past 45-50 mph the tail on the C-47 started to lift. In the dark that was difficult to see – the tow rope was 350 feet long. The slipstream from the C-47's Pratt & Whitney engines buffeted the glider's nose until Beverly eased the stick back slightly to let the lift build under the wings.

The Waco CG-4A left the ground at about 55 mph – before the C-47 did. It floated above the runway a few feet in the air, skimming over the tarmac while the tow plane lumbered down the strip picking up flying speed. At this point Beverly had to keep to a gentle climb to avoid overtaking the tug.

Once the Dakota lifted off she eased the Waco CG-4A into the high tow position slightly above the tug's tail – where the airflow was smoother. Back in the tiny troop compartment the Rangers were sitting on bench seats running down each side of the aisle, crammed in like sardines. The canvas fuselage was flapping from the C-47's prop wash which was not comforting for those leaning back against it. It felt flimsy.

Like maybe it was going to rip apart.

As the Waco CG-4A moved into the tail high position, the ride became smoother but the compartment still vibrated. Raid Team consisted of hardened paratroopers but this ride was worse than jumping out of an aircraft in flight. The Rangers felt trapped… and they were.

There was no way to get out and they were not wearing parachutes if there was.

The troop compartment was loud and noisy. The constant roar of the Dakota's Pratt & Whitney "Twin Wasp" radial engines never let up. A deep vibrating hum was coming from the tow rope under strain sounding at times like a giant guitar string being plucked. Air was rushing through the canvas skin. Creaks and groans came from the wooden frame under stress – that was really discomfiting. The plywood floorboards rattled and the metal fittings clanged with every bump of turbulence.

Conversation was reduced to shouting but no one much felt like talking.

Col. Randal said, "Nice job on the takeoff."

"Thanks, Johnny."

"Beverly… what the hell! Where's WO May?"

"He got detained."

"Do you even know how to land a glider?"

Beverly laughed, "You've seen my Glider Wings… so yes, I can land one. Did you know the average U.S. Army glider pilot qualifies after only about a dozen touch-downs? Flight training is 100 hours – total..."

No, Col. Randal had not been aware of that.

"…it's almost criminal to send them out to ferry troops."

Col. Randal hated gliders. Now he really hated them. It did not make him feel any better knowing that, acting on his orders, Capt. Coogan had placed demolition charges aboard this one before takeoff. They would not go off prematurely, but still, it was a flying bomb.

Beverly said, "After we came back from Camp Mackall in North Carolina, every chance we've had Daddy and I shoot landings in gliders assigned to the units TTC tows – I've made over fifty."

"Really."

"I'm pretty good."

"Does Bronc know you're flying tonight?"

"He's about to find out."

"Do you have any idea what's going to happen when we get back – between MI-5, Wild Bill, your Dad – and maybe Eisenhower…"

Beverly said, "I don't want to think about it."

MAJOR GENERAL SAM HOUSTON "BRONC" BLACKWELL WAS flying down the length of the English Channel at an altitude of 3,000 feet. He was three miles off the French Coastline. Bronc was prohibited from flying over enemy-held territory because of the classified information he possessed as the SHAEF Air Transportation Officer. He was a BIGOT – meaning he was cleared to know the when and where of the D-Day invasion once the timing was settled on – the where had already been determined. The Allies were going to land in Normandy – a secret as highly classified as ULTRA.

Flying overhead providing top cover was the top-scoring night-fighter unit in the Royal Air Force, No. 85 Squadron. Bronc could not see them but they were up there in their de Havilland Mosquito Mk XIIs armed with four 20mm Hispano Mk II cannon and four.303 Browning machine guns. Bronc might not see them but they could see him on their Airborne Interception AI Mk VIII radar.

Not part of the original air support package – after Colonel John Randal's briefing, Lieutenant Colonel John Henry Bevan placed a phone call and No. 85 magically appeared at RAF Hawkinge.

Another call resulted in a second de Havilland Mosquito squadron being added to the Calais diversion – now it was to be a full-on air attack. Both 23 Squadron and 406 Squadron were airborne at this time en route to conduct low-level bomb and cannon strikes on targets of opportunity in and around the port city. There had not been enough time to develop a formal Strike List. Not a problem. This was the kind of mission the intruder ground attack pilots loved best.

Targets of opportunity.

While technically in compliance with his orders not to fly over enemy territory until after D-Day, Maj. Gen. Blackwell was clearly violating the spirit of them. His plan was to release the CG-4A Waco he was towing over the Channel. He would never actually be over German-held territory.

Bronc was almost at the point of ordering the release. At this altitude a glider could travel 6.8 miles before having to land. That gave the pilot almost a mile's margin of safety to reach the target.

There were no guarantees on that.

In addition to being a storied lady killer, international playboy and former football hero, Maj. Gen. Blackwell was a semi-reformed hellraiser at heart. He was pretty sure this was the craziest stunt he had ever participated in or even heard of. Bronc was on record having said when he learned Col. Randal's plan, "Jumping on Château du Val-Obscur was dangerous but a glider air assault… insane."

That was why Maj. Gen. Blackwell was flying the tow plane tonight. To make sure the job was done right. In addition to all his other sterling qualities, he was the best pilot in Troop Transport Command (TTC) – maybe the entire USAAF.

Bronc did not know how to quantify this mission. Once released, the canvas "dead stick taxi," as gliders were called by power pilots, would be on its own flying into enemy-occupied France through some of the heaviest defended airspace on the planet – a one-way trip guaranteed to end in a crash.

Glider pilots liked to say, "There's no turning back."

What could possibly go wrong?

Everything.

On a positive note was CG-4As had virtually no radar signature. The Germans would never know it was coming. The bad news – glider troops who rode in them called the Waco CG-4A a "canvas casket."

Normally there was no voice communications between a tow pilot and the glider pilot. Waco CG 4As did not carry organic radios. The idea was to sacrifice communications for payload. Gliders were designed for one thing only… to carry men and equipment into battle. Visual signals from the two aircraft would have to make do.

Tonight in order to eliminate any possible confusion, acting on Maj. Gen. Blackwell's orders, a phone line was strung down the length of the tow rope to the glider's cockpit. It was a crude field expedient means of communication… not intended for casual conversation.

Bronc had been concerned standard operating procedure (SOP) for signaling the command to slip the tow – rocking his C-47's wings – might not be easily recognizable tonight with virtually no moon out. There was no room for even a moment's uncertainty. To have any chance to land on the pinpoint-sized target, the mission had to be flown with absolute precision.

"Stand by to cast off… CAST OFF."

Beverly acknowledged, "Roger that, Daddy."

Bronc froze. He had handpicked a glider pilot to fly this mission and it was not his daughter. What just happened?

MAJOR GENERAL WILLIAM "WILD BILL" DONOVAN ARRIVED at General Dwight D. Eisenhower's new suite on the Penthouse Floor of the Bradford Hotel. This was a SECRET SOURCE code word TRIPLE-NINE, TOP SECRET briefing. The topic was on a level with ULTRA as far as secrecy classification was concerned. However, nothing to be covered was signals intelligence therefore it was not code word ULTRA.

Even so, most of SHAEF staff were not present because they were not cleared for what was to be discussed.

Present were Gen. Eisenhower, Major General Walter Bedell Smith aka Beetle, Chief of Staff – widely known as "Ike's hatchet man", Major General Harold R. Bull aka "Pinky", G-3 (Operations) and Major General Sir Kenneth Strong, SHAEF G-2 (Intelligence).

Lieutenant Colonel Thomas Argyll "Tar" Robertson, who was to give the initial part of the briefing, was the last to appear. He had delayed departing MI-5 hoping for any glimmer of late-breaking news that might have a positive effect on developments before coming to the Bradford –no joy. The Security Service was in full meltdown panic mode over the possibility of its network of B1-A double agents being blown. It was the single worst crisis Tar had experienced in his time with MI-5.

Gen. Eisenhower had no idea what the topic of tonight's meeting was to be other than a top-level emergency required his attention. It had been decided not to bother him with the details until a plan of action had been established. In the U.S. Army it was long a tradition when you took your senior officer a problem, you also took him a proposed solution – do not burden him with a problem until you had the answer for how to fix it.

It was thought by British Intelligence that might be a good policy to adhere to when dealing with the new Supreme Commander Allied Expeditionary Forces. There was still some adjusting to having an American officer named to the post.

The development resulted in more than a few hurt feelings coupled with quite a bit of deep-seated resentment – the UK had been at war for over two years before the U.S. joined the fight. The British tended to think of the Americans as rank amateurs.

The plan was for Lt. Col. Robertson to brief the problem… an Abwehr officer was beginning to suspect one or more of the German spies in England had been turned and was working for the Allies. In fact, known only to a handful of intelligence officials, it was all of them. When Tar concluded laying out the problem, Maj. Gen. Donovan was going to brief the steps OSS Operational Group Branch (Europe) was taking to rectify the situation.

Wild Bill had seen more actual combat than all the other officers in the room combined – the men present primarily had staff-oriented backgrounds.

They were more war managers than commanders. Maj. Gen. Donovan knew the raid on Château du Val-Obscur was an extremely complex operation.

The plan he observed Colonel John Randal brief Raid Team on was one not even a madman would have come up with. Maj. Gen. Donovan was not looking forward to explaining it. The nuances were going to be difficult to articulate to men who had never done anything like this before.

Wild Bill knew with absolute certainty he would not be able to sound confident. Not if asked to give the operations' probability of success. Which he would be.

That was a given.

It would not have made Maj. Gen. Donovan feel any better to know that at MI-5 only moments before when pressed, James "Baldie" Taylor had estimated the mission's odds at 80-20 against. And that might have been optimistic.

Nevertheless Maj. Gen. Donovan made his best effort to lay out the details in simple bullet points, absent tone or facial expression to reveal his personal misgivings. When his brief concluded there was absolute silence in the suite as the weight of what had just been brought to the attention of SHAEF's top-tier officers was settling in.

They were shaken. None of them asked for a more detailed explanation. The implications were crystal clear. This development with Major Hanns von Reisen had the potential to be catastrophic for the next phase of the war in Europe.

The mission to put things right seemed like a forlorn hope.

A breach of the Double-Cross System would compromise OPERATION FORTITUDE SOUTH. And that meant the D-Day invasion would have to be completely rethought. It was like a string of dominoes being toppled over or a real-life version of the age-old military poem "For Want of a Nail." All because one relatively junior Abwehr officer was voicing concerns about the reliability of Germany's spies in the UK.

The overriding question – was anybody listening to him?

The fate of the Free World rested on the Allies storming ashore in France on D-Day and marching on Berlin. Without the element of surprise that was a military impossibility – amphibious invasions being the most difficult of all large-scale operations to carry off successfully. It did not seem possible a single enemy intelligence officer in a relatively minor post could pose such a threat – but there it was.

Gen. Eisenhower was sitting composed, not saying anything, quietly analyzing the situation – having his worst day in the service when a knock came at the door.

An armed sentry was posted outside with strict orders the meeting was not to be disturbed. Under any circumstances. What could this be?

Maj. Gen. Smith went to the door intending to sink his teeth into somebody. He came back with a Special Liaison Unit (SLU) officer in tow. The SLU officer produced an envelope out of his briefcase for Maj. Gen. Strong, the G-2, and asked him to sign for it.

When the courier was gone, the brigadier opened the dispatch, "This is a FLASH message from the Tactical Operations Center at Seaborn House, sir.

```
Colonel Randal and team have
departed RAF Hawkinge. The Château
du Val-Obscur operation is underway
at this time.
```

"It's on, General."

Gen. Eisenhower said, "Godspeed the Butterfly."

5

LIGHTEN UP, WESTLY

BRANDY'S RADIO OPERATOR RELAYED THE MESSAGE '*THE GIRL has a pretty smile*' to Recon Team. That meant Raid Team was airborne en route. At RAF Hawkinge Colonel John Randal and Raid Team had launched on receiving the message confirming the Opel Admiral staff car was present at Château du Val-Obscur.

On the PT boat Major the Lady Jane Seaborn said, "That's the signal we are all waiting for."

Brandy ordered, "Full Ahead Together."

The coxswain complied instantly. The PT boat exploded into motion powered by three Packard V-12 engines. Now it was time for Captain Penelope "Legs" Honeycutt Parker to do what she did best – navigate. It was not going to be easy. They were sailing to a pocket beach below shale cliffs on the French Coast where a spur of the dirt track that led past the château dead-ended. The strand was tiny.

The pinpoint was going to be difficult to find.

Lieutenant Westly Slade had his Special Warfare Operators come topside and assemble on the bow. The four Life Boat Service Men who were going to man the Goatley dories were already there. Both parties were armed to the teeth with suppressed weapons. Tension ratcheted up.

Everyone going ashore made a point of acting calm and cool – business as usual, which it was.

The teams were highly experienced. They had done this before. The Life Boat Service Men (LBSM) had been carrying out these small boat-type operations for Raiding Forces from the day Lady Jane arrived in the unit and now the OSS Maritime Unit Frogmen fresh in from the Aegean brought firsthand island raiding experience.

When the PT boat was within three miles of the French Coast, Brandy ordered speed reduced to 6 knots with only one of the three Packard engines powering the boat. It decreased the boat's tell-tale wake. And on the 80-foot Elco it was virtual silent running. No German manning a sound detection station was going to hear them approaching.

Brandy also ordered the masts lowered to further reduce the PT boat's radar signature.

Legs Parker hit her target dead on.

Brandy drifted the PT in close to shore. It was tricky work. Pocket beaches are protected on both sides by either giant rocks or cliff faces. Two of her sailors were on the bow taking soundings port and starboard.

"All engines stop" – the traditional command, however, at this point there was only the one Packard V12 running. The boat was within less than half a cable's distance to the shore when it hove to.

Brandy restarted the center engine but kept the RPM low… only enough to maintain station.

Lady Jane went forward to check on *her* Special Warfare Operators. When the LBSM put the two Goatley dories over the side, she climbed down in one of them. That was not part of any plan.

The distance to shore was around 200 feet. The length of that gap had been specified by Col. Randal. Brandy was pretty sure it had something to do with why Sub-Lieutenant Jeffery Macomber was aboard. Only now he, too, was in one of the Goatleys heading toward the strand, so she could not ask.

The "pocket" beach, being protected on both sides, was almost like a grotto. It was the perfect terrain feature for a covert operation of this nature. The cliff would mask the PT boat from radar if an E-boat came past. No one would be guarding a place so remote, difficult to reach and of no military significance. More importantly, no one would come strolling along the shoreline and discover the landing party.

The strand was only accessible from the open water of the Channel or by climbing down the chalk cliffs enclosing it.

As soon as the dories landed they were hauled up on the beach. Being double-ended, the Goatleys did not have to be turned around for a fast getaway. The LBSM set up a defensive perimeter while the Frogmen prepared to scale the cliff. They were responsible for extending the FRP to the top and securing lines for Recon/Raid Team to rappel down.

There was a flaw in this part of the plan. If they were not able to find something to attach the ropes to at the top then iron stakes would have to be driven into the ground. The problem was those stakes could not be left behind. It was not clear to the Frogs how that would be resolved.

When Lt. Slade discovered Lady Jane on the beach in his perimeter he was nearly apoplectic, "Do you have any idea what Colonel Randal will do to me if you get killed on my watch?"

Lady Jane said, "Lighten up, Westly."

She might have been hanging around with Beverly too much.

LIEUTENANT WESTLY SLADE AND ONE OF HIS SPECIAL WARFARE Operators started working their way up the cliff. Each of them had a coil of rope over one shoulder. The climb was fairly high but it was not technically difficult. The feature was more of a bluff than a cliff face. It was not as bad as it looked in the aerial photos.

The OSS Maritime Unit training program had included climbing. A lot of beaches around the world are backed by heights. Scaling cliffs was one of their skill sets.

The two Frogmen found they could work their way up the incline fairly easily. There were numerous handholds. And it was not straight up. The problem, as expected, was chalk is not stable and tends to break off.

They had to be careful.

Lt. Slade was a proficient climber. That did not mean he enjoyed it. During his training he thought mountaineering was the toughest physical challenge of the Maritime Unit program. He could not imagine doing it for sport.

While the climb was not overly taxing, coming back down without a rope would be close to impossible. Particularly if bringing out injured men. Or any captured equipment worthy of the trouble to take back to Seaborn House.

The plan was to install rappel lines down to the strand for the Recon/Raid Teams to use when they arrived. It was hoped – and in Raiding Forces it is understood that "hope is not a course of action" – to find something to use as an anchor point at the top.

No joy.

Anticipating that possibility, Lt. Slade carried two steel pitons in his pack and a rock hammer – which was a plan of action. He broke them out and hammered the stakes into the ground. They would do nicely to secure the ropes.

One point stressed repeatedly during the short time to prepare for the mission was this was a covert operation. Nothing could be left behind to indicate a raid had ever taken place. How Colonel John Randal intended to get the pitons down the cliff after the team extracted was a mystery – they were a dead giveaway.

The ropes were anchored and dropped down to the beach.

The ERP was now in place open for business. Major the Lady Jane Seaborn came over the top of the cliff climbing up the rope. Lt. Slade thought he was going to have a heart attack when he saw her but before he could protest…

Lady Jane said, "I shall go right back down, Lieutenant, and leave you to get on with setting up the ERP – my only desire was to be able to say I made the climb."

Lt. Slade said, "Please be careful, Lady Seaborn. I do not want you hurt, ma'am. When we get back I'll inform the colonel you personally scaled the cliff to inspect my work."

"I should like that."

An unusual conversation for two people to be having in enemy-occupied territory at the onset of an operation – but then there was nothing normal about this night.

Lt. Slade was proud to have been selected for the raid, being a fairly recent arrival in Raiding Forces. Col. Randal could have picked a more experienced officer. He wanted to do his best.

Having Lady Jane get killed on his watch would likely have a chilling effect on his future in Raiding Forces.

SEARCHLIGHTS CAME ON IN THE DISTANCE. ANTI-AIRCRAFT guns commenced booming. Tracers arched into the night from the ground. From the sky tracers slammed straight back down. No. 406 Squadron Royal Canadian Air Force whose motto was "*We kill by night,*" was putting in a low-level fighter-bomber strike on the outskirts of Calais. No. 23 Squadron RAF the "Red Eagles," known for their aggressive night raids – their slogan was *"Semper Aggressus"* (Always attacking), was orbiting out over the Channel almost skimming the water waiting their chance. The plan was for them to follow the Canadians in and attack the town proper.

There were twelve de Havilland Mosquito Mk IIs in each squadron. All of them were present tonight. Each aircraft was armed with four 20mm Hispano Mk II cannon, four.303 Browning machine guns and carried four 500-pound bombs.

The squadrons were formed up in flights of two for the attack. The first wave came in at hedge-top level to avoid German radar and flak. Approaching the village the pilots climbed slightly then rolled in on their gun run.

The Strike Order called for the squadrons to string out the attack for as long as possible – to draw attention away from the glider landing. The Mosquitos were going after targets of opportunity. It was the kind of air raid the pilots described as a "night intruder op."

Their mission of choice.

After making several passes to saturate the target area with 20mm cannon and .303 machine gun fire to suppress anti-aircraft fire the Mosquitos race tracked and came back around to make their bomb runs. A 500-pound. bomb is loud – tonight both squadrons were dropping them one at a time. Nearly one hundred bombs dropped in singles, one after the other from a low-level night fighter screaming overhead made for a lot of diversion.

In the distance the explosions could be heard by Recon Team at Château du Val-Obscur, onboard the PT boat and at the ERP. The flash of the bombs detonating lit up the sky like a distant electrical storm.

First the flash. Then approximately 15 seconds later the sound – a rolling boom – came in. Raiding Forces' personnel hearing the air raid were impressed. The Germans in and around Calais Village on the receiving end of the attack were even more impressed.

The 409's Mosquitos were blitzing the target area like a swarm of angry yellow jackets. It was a violent, deadly strike. The pilots had been ordered not to return to base with any ordnance unexpended. Tracers crisscrossed the sky, 500-pound bombs detonated shaking the ground creating mini-earthquakes and a few secondary explosions erupted.

Then 23 Squadron's daredevil pilots rolled in from an entirely different direction and the Red Eagles did it all over again. For Raiding Forces small-scale raid this was the mother of all diversions. When the sun came up in Pas-de-Calais there was not going to be any question an air raid had taken place.

No one would be thinking Commandos or Rangers.

Low-level night fighter-bomber intruder ops against ground targets in and around Calais – which was more heavily defended by AA flak batteries than anywhere else in German territory other than Berlin – were dangerous.

Three planes were lost. A higher number than anticipated. More were winging their way home battle-damaged.

It was a costly mission.

OUT THE WINDSCREEN, COLONEL JOHN RANDAL AND BEVERLY Blackwell could see the air raid off in the distance to their right. They could hear the bombs cruuuuump. He asked for a feint. This was more than imagined.

Captain Billy Jack Jaxx was leaning over the divider, watching.

"Wow!"

That summed it up.

Col. Randal said, "Where's Teddy?"

"Sitting right here next to me, sir, so I could brief him."

Lieutenant Ted Hamilton stuck his head in the cockpit, "You asking for me, sir?"

Col. Randal said, "Change II, Lieutenant – when we land you stay with the glider. Your job is to provide security for Lieutenant Mascuch's team and guard Beverly. If she tries to leave your side for any reason until we reach the ERP – shoot her. Try to hit someplace that doesn't leave a visible scar."

"Beverly, sir?"

"Yeah, who do you think's flying this glider?"

Beverly said, "You do, Theodore Hamilton, I won't fix you up with any of the debutants who work at MI-5."

Which pretty much guaranteed she was not going to get shot – at least not by The Great Teddy.

Major General Sam Houston "Bronc' Blackwell rocked the wings of his C-47 tow plane, simultaneously giving the verbal command "Cast Off."

"Here we go, Johnny."

Beverly pulled the yellow-painted release handle mounted on the instrument panel. This tripped the tow-rope hook on the nose of the Waco CG-4A. The rope streamed back beneath the tug.

In that instant, the constant noise inside the glider went dead quiet. The roar of the C-47's Pratt & Whitney engines stopped like a switch had been thrown, leaving only the sound of the canvas flapping, the occasional creak of straining wood and the wind flowing over the wings. There was no longer turbulence from the prop blast.

Now the Waco CG-4A was flying in almost total silence and the glide was very smooth – eerie. At that point gallows humor among glider troops stipulated the canvas coffin had, "No visible means of support."

The sensation on release felt like having gone over a cliff.

The Waco CG-4A's nose dipped. However Beverly was anticipating that happening and trimmed the glide to steady the aircraft. Now Col. Randal and his men were on their own headed toward the target – Château du Val-Obscur. The trick was going to be to get there.

In the troop compartment there was no longer any need to shout. The glider was sailing along silently at close to 100 mph. Headed into the great unknown with a crash guaranteed at the end of the flight.

This was the long-anticipated run-in to target.

The Waco CG-4A was established on final. Adrenalin was pumping. Unlike combat parachute drops when the one-minute warning was given no one was shouting "GO, GO, GO and rattling their static line. Everyone on board was dead silent.

Raid Team would be touching down in less than four minutes – it seemed a lifetime.

AT MI-5 THE CRISIS MEETING WAS INTERRUPTED BY A MESSAGE from Seaborn House stating Major General Sam Houston "Bronc" Blackwell had reported the Raid Team glider successfully released. The announcement was met by a heavy silence. Realization set in that they would know shortly if the mission was going to be a success or not.

Failure was an unthinkable prospect.

Then a harsh dose of reality slammed them in the face when J.C. Masterman, Chairman of the XX Committee, an Oxford don – one of only two men present who did not have a military background said, "Explain to me how a team of Commandos crash landing on the lawn of Château du Val-Obscur is a covert operation? One would believe leaving an American-made Waco CG-4A glider behind on the property to be an obvious giveaway."

It was a bombshell.

Major General Sir David Petrie, Director General of MI-5 said, "Surely that would have been cleared in advance?"

James "Baldie" Taylor, the liaison officer from MI-5 to the Office of Strategic Services and Raiding Forces' liaison to the London Controlling Section said, "Colonel Randal's Raid Team briefing was the first I learned about a glider assault."

Lieutenant Colonel John Henry Bevan said, "No one authorized the use of gliders. The plan is suicidal. We were so shocked by the audacity of the raid and events were moving so swiftly the details were not questioned at the time.

"Mr. Taylor and I flew here to attend this meeting immediately upon conclusion of Randal's briefing…"

Jim said, "I have worked with the colonel for virtually the entire war. He does not take on suicide missions. That said, he did not inform me of his plans prior to. It was my belief Colonel Randal intended to drop by parachute."

J.C. Masterman said, "Why do you suppose that was, Mr. Taylor?"

Jim said, "The colonel has been known to keep his own counsel when he does not want outside interference with his intentions."

Maj. Gen. Petrie said, "For Five's purposes, we must consider the raid on Château du Val-Obscur fatally flawed from inception. J.C., I want you to get with Colonel Robertson and organize a working party. Begin developing a contingency plan for what we intend to do when our entire stable of B1-A double agents is blown."

Professor Masterman said, "Yes, sir."

Maj. Gen. Petrie said, "We may well find ourselves back to square one when it comes to executing time and place deceptions to cover D-Day. FORTITUDE SOUTH is up in smoke – two years of brilliant counter-intelligence work squandered by a bloody rogue American cowboy."

Jim said, "There is one other development of note I should mention. Lady Seaborn is reported missing. It is believed she attached herself to the mission in some way."

This announcement was met by stunned silence. If anything happened to Major the Lady Jane Seaborn there were going to be repercussions. The people in the room were at the top of the list to be blamed. A bad night now spiraled out of control, crashed, burned and blew up.

Lt. Col. Bevan was scheduled to brief Prime Minister Churchill on the status of Raiding Forces' operation immediately following the MI-5 meeting. He was dreading it. Lady Jane was known to the PM – a friend of his daughter Mary.

Because of the disastrous Gallipoli amphibious landing in the last war that took place on Churchill's watch when he was First Lord of the Admiralty – failure blamed on lax security, he obsessed over protecting the current D-Day deception campaign, particularly FORTITUDE SOUTH.

The Prime Minister was not going to be pleased.

The news Lady Jane might be on the raid came as a shock. Lt. Col. Bevan was made almost physically ill when he heard it. There were a lot of unanswered questions. Had Col. Randal authorized her to go? What could the man have been thinking to insert by glider? Could he have possibly believed a Lancaster bomber dumping a few incendiaries on Château du Val-Obscur would obliterate all evidence of a raid?

Now Lt. Col. Bevan had to add bad judgment, loose cannon *and* placing his goddaughter at risk to the negative side of Col. Randal's ledger.

Before departing MI-5 to brief the Prime Minister, Lt. Col. Bevan placed a call from a secure phone using the code word CROMWELL. The recipient on the other end of the line said, "Right, straight away."

The Air Marshal he spoke to was not thrilled by his orders.

6

COME HELL OR HIGH WATER

THE WACO CG-4A WAS COMING IN WITH A FULL COMPLEMENT of troops. Possibly overloaded. The lack of heavy equipment or packs, the Rangers only carrying their suppressed M3 Grease Guns, a triple basic load of ammunition per man, four grenades, and not much else, might make up for squeezing in Lieutenant Ted Hamilton aka "The Great Teddy" at the last minute.

Beverly had studied the aerial photos of Château du Val-Obscur. The estate was set back from the lane that ran past it down a long tree-lined cobblestone drive leading to it. Not much could be learned about the trees other than it was thought they were "plane trees" – typically planted along French lanes and boulevards.

Beverly had never heard of a plane tree before. They did not have those in South Texas. What she did not know was that the species could grow over 80 feet tall. A detail that might have been discovered had there been more time to plan the mission. The trees tended to be an impediment to a glider landing on the château's front lawn.

There were open fields on all sides of the objective. Excellent landing zones. However, those were not satisfactory tonight. Raid Team needed to be put down close to the target. The Rangers wanted to disembark and launch an immediate attack to improve their odds of achieving the element of surprise.

The plane trees were a problem.

According to the book landing speed of a Waco CG-4A was supposed to be 45-50 mph. The glider was traveling at close to 100 mph. There were no air brakes. The only way Beverly had to slow down was by sideslipping or making S-turns.

Knowing it was the more effective way to reduce her air speed, Beverly put the glider into a sideslip. When she did the Waco CG-4A kept going straight forward but the aircraft skewed hard to port with the fuselage slightly angled to the airflow instead of flying straight.

Not normal flight attitude

In the back the Rangers did not like that one bit. With no intercom to give warning it felt like the glider had suddenly gone into a high-speed skid and might start tumbling. The maneuver caused the canvas wings to start flapping again as if they were going to tear away. Centrifugal force nearly threw the operators off their seats. Men instinctively grabbed at the bench but that was not going to do them any good. Whatever they held on to would be going down too – that's the problem in air crashes.

Suddenly, the floor tilted creating the sensation of riding in an elevator when the cable snapped.

The passengers had the impression the pilot had lost control of the aircraft. Raid Team was composed of seasoned paratroopers. A lot of unpleasant things had happened to them on board airplanes en route to bad places.

This was the worst.

And to make things more ominous, everything was taking place in almost total silence – except for the flapping, which did nothing for anyone's morale though admittedly the sound was better than ripping.

The sideslipping did not accomplish much in the way of reducing air speed. Next, Beverly tried S-turns. For the Rangers in the troop compartment the sensation was less violent but more disorienting. The glider was swaying back and forth hypnotically.

Raid Team had been advised landing in a glider was a controlled crash. Tonight, crammed in tight, experiencing borderline claustrophobia, not able to see anything ahead or out the side windows because of the dark and everything on the ground being blacked out in compliance with Wehrmacht Verdunkelung regulations, it felt like the crash was already in progress – no 'controlled' to it.

Sitting in the co-pilot's seat being able to see out the windscreen, Colonel John Randal was not affected as much by the maneuvers. However, this being only his second time in a glider – his first landing he had jumped on his first flight, the impression he had was the Waco CG-4A was diving almost straight down like a pile driver. While not the case, Beverly had the ship on a steep glide path which was typical for combat air assaults, the idea being to flare up just before touching down.

As a novice glider rider he did not know that. The shadow of the château swam into sight ahead. "How're we doing, Beverly?"

"Target coming up – stand by, we're going in hot."

"I've got confidence in you, kid."

"Tell the boys in back to brace themselves, Johnny."

Col. Randal gave the order over his shoulder, "Stand by for landing."

He did not have to shout. The glider was minuscule. The Rangers were packed in.

Events had not been going slow except for the hands on their watches, but now they hit double fast forward. Beverly was not able to get the air speed down to anywhere near normal range. Landing attitude for a Waco CG-4A is to make the approach in a steep glide then pull up before touching down. That was for coming in on a runway or a pasture, not on the lawn of a French château covered in trees.

Beverly may have been a sorority girl, beauty queen, high-maintenance type or looked like one. She was also a skilled pilot. And knew quite a bit about small unit tactics. The Rangers needed to get on the ground and hit the target in a hurry – surprise, speed, violence of action.

She was going to make that happen – as they said in Texas, "come hell or high water."

Time from touching down to assaulting the target was critical. It needed to be measured in seconds. Col. Randal had elected to make a glider assault to maximize the shock effect of arriving unexpected and unannounced out of the sky, in the dark of night with his team *intact*.

A glider assault eliminated the need for assembling – as was necessary after a parachute drop.

Beverly knew there was no time to land in one of the nearby pastures, disembark, form up and move on the objective the way typically taught on glider assault training exercises. Tonight, in this situation when nothing taking place was by the book, she brought the glider down in a steep 10-degree glide, flared before crashing and slammed it down hard, pancaking just short of the two stately plane trees at the entry to the drive.

Dead center.

Wingspan on a Waco CG-4A is just a few inches over 83 feet. The cobblestone driveway was not that wide. This controlled crash landing was actually going to be more of a full-on airplane crash.

There was a large disparity in how far a Waco CG-4A would travel on its skids once it landed – 600 to 1600 feet. And that was at 40-50 mph. They were doing almost twice that. The drive at Château du Val-Obscur was only about 150 feet long.

That could be a problem.

Col. Randal saw the two giant trees coming straight at him. They were monsters. He was glad it was dark in the cockpit so Beverly was not able to see the expression on his face. Sheer terror is not the image a mission commander wants to project at the start of a raid.

There was a tremendous crash. Beverly nailed it. The fuselage shot between the two massive trees but the wings did not. There was a deep, vicious *THOMPH* as the wings ripped off – an ugly sound. Both panels sheared away at the wing roots – catastrophic failure. Canvas was shredding, spars splintering. The Waco CG-4A shuddered violently from the impact but kept going straight ahead.

As hard as it hit, the glider should have slowed considerably.

However, acting on Col. Randal's instructions, Major General Sam Houston "Bronc" Blackwell had ordered metal skid shoes be affixed to the Waco CG-4A's skids to make it easier to slide over hard ground – that was for the extraction not the landing. However, Beverly had no knowledge of the modification. There was no reason for her to. She was not supposed to be flying the glider tonight. Warrant Officer George E. May was.

And while having five times more landing experience than the average USAAF glider pilot, Beverly had never put down a Waco CG-4A wearing skid shoes. The metal on the cobblestone was like coming in on a banana peel. The Waco CG-4A kept traveling straight ahead at a high rate of speed, shot past the end of the drive, sliced through part of the hedge at the front of the lawn, skidded down the sidewalk and slammed into the main entry of the château – constructed out of locally quarried limestone blocks where it came to an abrupt stop. After knocking down the massive double doors.

Fortune favors the brave from time to time… skill helps.

The Rangers were thrown forward from inertia when the wings ripped off. Then before they could fully recover, the Waco CG-4A hit the house and they were thrown forward again – hard. The only thing that saved them was the fact that they were wearing safety belts. Those men choosing not to buckle up when the Waco first took off soon thought better of the decision in flight and put their seat belts on. Fortunately, everyone was strapped in when the glider hit the building.

Even so, the Rangers experienced double whiplash.

In the cockpit Col. Randal had watched as the château was coming at him until it grew so large it covered the entire windscreen. Then the Waco CG-4A slammed into it. Surprised to find himself alive, he shouted, "GO, GO, GO!"

The Rangers untangled themselves and started exiting out both of the Waco CG-4A's side doors. Noise discipline had been emphasized so there were no blood-curdling rebel yells or team leaders shouting orders. The idea being to preserve the element of surprise as long as possible and not to let anyone know there were Allied troops on the ground.

To those inside the château – built like a castle, the crash could have been anything – but it was definitely unexpected. The Germans would not know what caused it. The last thing they would be expecting was a glider full of Rangers to come calling at their front door.

Col. Randal said, "You OK Beverly?"

"Terrific." Which might not have been completely true. "Go get 'em, Johnny."

Because both exits were clogged with Rangers disembarking, Col. Randal was last out. Lance Corporal Ray "Tank" Karlsson and Lovat

Scout Lionel Fenwick, both somewhat dazed, were waiting by the starboard side exit when he stumbled through.

The operators were shaking off the rough landing on the move. The assault was underway. The raid was unfolding, not at a dead run, berserker style – it was fluid. Operators were moving with a purpose, weapons to their shoulders. Slow is smooth, smooth is fast – teams in synch. Rangers spread out surging over the target. Moving on their team objectives, each evolution being conducted with absolute precision.

A deadly ballet – choreographed with evil intent.

High-level execution like this is achieved only by soldiers with experience, training, acting with premeditation and a will to win – determined to drive the attack home. But even more important was the Rangers' ability to improvise and adapt to the changing situation on the move without losing momentum.

Not as easy as it sounds.

Team King stormed the mansion in the lead, making a forced entry which was made easier by Beverly having knocked the doors down. Their suppressed 9mm M3 Grease Guns were hissing as they breached… *SSSSS, SSSSS, SSSSS.* Col. Randal's team managed to catch up as the Merc's Rangers went in.

By the time Team Randal came through the door, three Germans were already dead on the ground. King had the night duty officer bent over a desk sticking the needle-point tip of his Fairbairn knife in his ear, shouting at him in German.

It must have hurt.

"Master bedroom, second floor, Chief – he's volunteered to escort us."

Col. Randal said, "Nice of the man."

Team Randal moved up the giant central staircase with King and the prisoner leading the way.

As Team Randal proceeded up the stairs, Team King's Captain Clint Hays and Captain Jake Novak, aka Jake the Snake, continued to clear the ground-floor rooms. Their suppressed M3 Grease Guns hissing… *SSSSS,SSSSS,SSSSS,SSSSS*

When Team Randal peeled off on the second landing, Team McKoy, consisting of Lieutenant General "Geronimo" Joe McKoy, Major Jack

Dance, and Lovat Scout Munro Ferguson continued up the stairs to the third floor.

Captain Richard "Dynamite Dick" Coogan was trailing behind lugging his pack of Lewes Bombs. He needed to find a way to get into the attic. His assignment was to burn the main house. He would start by placing timed incendiary devices in the ceiling then work his way back down to the first floor strategically putting additional firebombs on interior support beams as he went.

From the moment he set the first charges in the attic, the three teams inside the château would have forty-five minutes to carry out their tasks and exit the premises. There was nothing unusual about that. The clock was always ticking on Col. Randal's raids. He did not believe in standing around on an objective once it had been secured.

"Hit and run – everyone who goes in comes out."

OUTSIDE, TEAM JAXX MADE UP OF CAPTAIN BILLY JACK Jaxx, Private First Class Norvel "Horn Dog" Hansen and Private First Class James "Wildman" Terrell was approaching the barn where it was believed the enlisted Abwehr troops were barracked. The problem was there had not been enough intelligence to adequately plan out each action on the objective down to the last detail like Raiding Forces would have normally done for an operation of this importance.

Barns typically have a large double door. Tall and wide to accommodate hauling in wagon loads of hay and other heavy farm equipment, with a smaller set of double doors over the top to hoist hay up into the loft. Some have a regular-sized door immediately adjacent to the big doors for people to use rather than always having to open the heavy double doors to get in and out. However, it was known that some barns in France also had other points of access besides those two. The question was if and where.

Team Jaxx had to immediately seize control of all the exits in the barn.

Capt. Jaxx could not risk any of the Nazis escaping. His team only consisted of three Rangers, including himself. It was believed there would be six or possibly eight Germans with their sleeping quarters in the barn.

Some would be on duty, so they were not all expected to be there when his team arrived. Colonel John Randal was not exaggerating when he said it might be the raid's toughest target. Capt. Jaxx was going to have to make his estimate of the situation, adjust his tactics and execute the takedown on the move.

Thinking about it onboard the glider en route to the target, Capt. Jaxx had ordered PFC Terrell to immediately circle the perimeter of the barn when they arrived to see if there was any other way in or out – which is not the optimal way to gather intel to plan your 'actions on the objective.'

If there was another exit, Wildman was to set up a hasty near ambush to prevent any Germans from escaping.

If not, he would rejoin the team.

TEAM STARRETT, CONSISTING OF LIEUTENANT CHASE Starrett, Captain Dan Bonham and Captain Dan Morgan was trailing Team Jaxx. When Jack Cool peeled off to go to the barn, they kept moving in the direction of the smaller outbuilding. There was no information on what to expect at that location.

There was some thinking it might not be occupied.

OUTSIDE IN FRONT OF THE CHÂTEAU CAPTAIN DICK Courtney and X-Ray linked up with Lieutenant Ricky Mascuch blue filtered lights in hand. A mad rush was underway to recover the wings from the Waco CG-4A that were ripped off on landing. The force of the impact had sheared them at the joints where they attached to the fuselage.

The panels were found at the entrance to the drive. A single wing weighed in excess of 500 pounds. Everyone, including Beverly, pitched in and helped drag them back to the glider one at a time. Lt. Mascuch entered the Waco CG-4A and came out with a series of canvas straps.

The next step was to secure the wings flat against the side of the fuselage. When that was accomplished, Lt. Mascuch's party was temporarily on stand down. Their next task was going to require a lot more reinforcements. No longer needed, Capt. Courtney and X-Ray went to the door of the château and stood by to be available on call if needed.

Beverly started to go with them.

Lieutenant Ted Hamilton said, "Do not make me do it."

Beverly laughed, "You *would*, too!"

WHEN TEAM KING, CONSISTING OF THE MERC, CAPTAIN Jake Novak aka Jake the Snake and Captain Clint Hays had gone in the front door of the château they immediately encountered the skeleton crew of the night duty staff – confused by the commotion outside but not overly alarmed at this point. Had a drunk driver crashed a vehicle into the building?

The château was dark inside but not totally. Lights were on in several rooms. They were helpful for the Rangers.

Heavy ceiling-to-floor blackout curtains hung from field expedient wooden rods installed above all the windows effectively preventing any interior light from being seen outside. The effect was oppressive – smothering.

The heavy-duty curtains not only prevented any light from escaping, but they also muffled sound. That last was a good thing. In the event any of the Nazis managed to get off a round it would not be heard outside. If it was at least not far away. And it would be muffled not sounding like a gunshot.

King shot the Abwehr clerk sitting at his desk in the foyer with his suppressed 9mm M3 Grease Gun… *SSSS* The short point-blank burst blew the German out of his chair. He probably should have taken the man prisoner to gain information per his orders. However, even a hardened professional soldier of fortune as experienced as the Merc could be keyed up on initial contact after such a dramatic forced entry.

Alerted by the crash, the night duty officer, a lieutenant, was just coming out of his office to investigate. King threw him over the dead clerk's desk and jammed the razor-sharp needle tip of his Fairbairn Fighting Knife in his ear.

The Nazi was trying to scream but making a bad job of it – happened so fast.

Capt. Novak and Capt. Hays stepped past King and proceeded to start clearing the downstairs rooms. Before they made it more than a few steps, the duty NCO and a radio operator came out of an adjoining room, alerted that something was up… but what? They were carrying cups of coffee.

SSSSS,SSSSS,SSSSS,SSSSS

The two went down hard. Coffee spilled on the floor.

Behind them Colonel John Randal followed by Lance Corporal Ray "Tank" Karlsson and Lovat Scout Lionel Fenwick burst into the château. King jerked his prisoner off the desk and forced him to lead the way up the main staircase.

That left Capt. Novak and Capt. Hays alone to finish working their way room-to-room clearing the first floor on their own. They came to a dimly lit room with a cot and a sleeping soldier on it. Likely the duty driver. The German must have been a sound sleeper. He raised up when Jake the Snake came in… *SSSSS*

Team King(-) continued methodically clearing the downstairs floor. They had already taken out more Germans than had been estimated to be inside the château.

So much for pre-mission intelligence.

BECAUSE KING HAD HIS HANDS FULL WITH THE PRISONER when Team Randal reached the top of the landing, Colonel John Randal moved forward and took the lead. He had been briefed by Major the Lady Jane Seaborn that this floor was called the *premier étage.* It would likely have the master bedroom, a small private study/office adjoining the master, a main reception hall for entertaining, guest chambers for important visitors, a formal dining room and possibly one or two other bedrooms for immediate family members.

The second level was going to be difficult to clear because of being chopped up. Large rooms were interspersed with smaller ones. The task was made harder because Raid Team did not have a floor plan of Château du Val-Obscur to study in advance. From this point on, as far as securing the main building, the Rangers were winging it.

Col. Randal stepped off the stairs into an antechamber. Just to the left were ornate double doors – to the master bedroom?

King said, "Go left, Chief."

Then he handed off the traumatized German Night Duty Officer to Lance Corporal Ray "Tank" Karlsson. The big Frogman hammered him with a blow that would have felled an ox. The Nazi went down without a sound. Lovat Scout Lionel Fenwick knelt down with his knee on the man's chest and covered the long corridor leading to the other rooms with his suppressed 9mm M3 SMG.

In response to a hand signal from Col. Randal, Tank came past and kicked the double doors so hard they shattered.

Col. Randal stepped into the room. There was a man in silk pajamas sitting up in a gigantic four-poster bed with a canopy. He was not alone. A slinky blonde in a black silk negligée raised up drowsily on one elbow. Whoever the woman was she was in the wrong place at the wrong time, keeping the wrong company.

Col. Randal shot her… *SSSSS*

Blood spattered on the man, whom Col. Randal felt pretty sure was Major Hanns von Reisen – their target. Seeing his paramour killed in front of him had a sobering effect. Instead of reaching for the Walther PP 7.65 pistol – favored by Abwehr officers, on the bedstand – the man started babbling incoherently, "*Bitte töte mich nicht.! Bitte töte mich nicht.! Bitte töte mich nicht.!*"

King barked at him in German. The only word Col. Randal understood was "Reisen."

"*Ja, ja, ja.*"

Col. Randal ordered, "Tank, secure the major. Take him outside to the glider and don't let him out of your sight. Clear?"

"Yes, sir!"

King walked back into the hallway and shot the Nazi Scout Fenwick was kneeling on.

Col. Randal said, "What does Bitte töte mich nicht mean?"

"Please don't kill me."

TEAM MCKOY KEPT GOING UP THE STAIRS WHEN TEAM Randal peeled off on the second floor. The third level was a more utilitarian space. The Rangers found a warren of narrow rooms, servants' quarters, and guest chambers – for the less important visitors.

There was access to the attic. Captain Richard "Dynamite Dick" Coogan spotted stairs leading to it. He proceeded up them to place his demolitions.

Down below on the second floor a barrage of muffled pistol shots erupted. Faint shouting in German could be heard. It sounded like Team Randal had kicked over a hornet's nest.

A head poked out from a door. Lieutenant General "Geronimo" Joe McKoy snapped off a crisp burst with his 9mm M3… *SSS*. The general was a trick shot artist who loved to put on shooting exhibitions and had incredible reflexes – he was very quick.

Lt. Gen. McKoy was not one to believe in wasting ammunition though famously known to advise, "Ain't no such thing as overkill."

The burst caught the Nazi full in the face. He fell dead halfway out into the hallway. Now with the unsuppressed gunfire on the second floor, the element of surprise inside the château was lost.

The fight was on.

The guests, or whoever it was staying at the château overnight, were not combat infantrymen. They did not come armed and equipped for battle. In fact, most rear echelon military, like the Abwehr, which translated to Defense Bureau – meaning it was an organization consisting mainly of staff officers, analysts, case officers and clerical personnel, seldom fired their weapons.

Most were not particularly proficient. There was no need for them to be. It does not require an expert marksman to place a bullet in the back of a prisoner's head.

The only weapons kept in the château were sidearms. Wehrmacht SOP called for the P-08 Luger to be carried with an empty chamber – making it an 8-shot handgun. P-38s and Walther PPs had modern decocking levers so they could be carried with a live round in the chamber. However, not many rear echelon staff types went to the trouble to load a magazine, rack a round in the chamber, then take out the magazine, top it off with a loose round and reinsert it – effectively making the pistols 7-shot and 8-shot weapons respectively as well.

When sleeping, some but not all of the Germans could be expected to keep their sidearm close by. What did they need weapons for? Guards were downstairs and patrolling the grounds outside.

Pistol belts with their spare magazine pouch might be left anywhere in the bedroom from hanging on a clothes hook to lying on a chair. Which meant the only ammunition readily available in a late-night emergency was the rounds in the magazine in their weapons – provided they were not left in their holsters.

Little details like that are important to know in a close-range encounter such as clearing a house. Nevertheless, with the Germans in the estate alerted – now the three teams were going to have to clear every single room, every closet, look under every bed. When fight or flight kicked in some of the Germans might be opting to hide.

That was not going to be allowed to happen. No one could be left behind alive to tell the tale about the raid, including any French locals pressed into service as servants. Those were strict orders.

Raid Team was not capable of taking prisoners tonight other than their target, Major von Reisen. There was no way to transport them to England without the possibility of escape en route to the ERP. That could not be risked.

Why take a chance.

Lt. Gen. McKoy, Major Jack Dance and Lovat Scout Munro Ferguson started working their way down the hall, leapfrogging each other, clearing the floor room by room. None of them were carrying standard issue US Mk II "Pineapple" fragmentation grenades tonight.

However, each man had four British No.69 Mk I concussion grenades, with the simple "All Ways Fuses," carried in the billow pockets of their M-42 Jump Jackets. The grenades were designed for missions like this – eliminating resistance in confined spaces.

Team McKoy set up a relay. They stacked on a door. The lead man kicked it in then stood aside. The number two man tossed in a concussion grenade. When it went off the number three man rushed in with his suppressed 9mm M3 Grease Gun while the other two Rangers shone their hook-nosed GI flashlights – with red lenses attached to protect night vision – around the room from the hall to give the designated shooter enough light to acquire a target.

Then the Rangers rotated duties. Having trained for this kind of room-to-room work – and done it before on raids, they quickly got into a rhythm. Most of the quarters were empty.

But not all of them.

WHEN TEAM JAXX ARRIVED IN THE VICINITY OF ITS target Captain Billy Jack Jaxx signaled a halt. He wanted to pause long enough for Private First Class James "Wildman" Terrell to work his way around the massive barn. He did not intend to give him much time to do it. Besides Capt. Jaxx had to work out a plan to drive on without PFC Terrell. In the event Wildman found an exit, he would not be coming back.

The Nazis quartered in the barn would have their primary weapons which were likely rifles but might include a submachine gun or two. Capt. Jaxx did not want them to be wide awake and alert when he and Private First Class Norvel "Horn Dog" Hansen came calling. He had his own personal rule: "Never fight fair."

Team Jaxx needed to get in and take the Germans down before they could react. This was an assignment for a shootist. One of the reasons Jack Cool got the nod from Colonel John Randal – 'Right Man, Right Job'.

That and the fact he could always be relied on to make the right decision in a fluid situation.

Watching the second hand on his Rolex, Capt. Jaxx gave Wildman exactly two minutes to carry out his task. Probably not enough time. However, the bigger risk was to wait. It was imperative for Capt. Jaxx to put in his assault before anything could alert the Germans a raid was in progress.

It was a good call. PFC Terrell discovered a door near the far end on the opposite side of the barn. He dropped down in the prone position no more than 10 feet away a one man near ambush as per his orders. No one was making it out that door alive.

When it was time, Capt. Jaxx and PFC Hansen closed on the barn. Almost to it they spotted a regular-sized entry called a "pass door" next to the giant double doors.

It was open.

TEAM STARRETT ARRIVED AT THE SMALL OUTBUILDING. There was no time to waste. The Rangers needed to clear the building then get back to reinforce Team Jaxx at the barn. The target was a small structure. There were no windows. However, the door was standing open.

To catch the breeze?

Lieutenant Chase Starrett took that to indicate there were people inside. He flattened against the wall on one side of the door. Captain Dan Bonham did the same on the opposite side. Lt. Starrett signaled the go-ahead to Captain Dan Morgan. He tossed in a No. 69 grenade. In the close quarters of the small building it would likely have a demoralizing effect on anyone inside.

It did.

WHOOOOOPH! The concussion grenade created a massive "blast effect" in the enclosed space – incredibly loud inside. Outside the sound was a muffled *COUGH*.

A concussion grenade works on a different principle than a fragmentation grenade. They are designed to create a pressure wave that engulfs a room or a bunker, incapacitating the occupants. There is no good way to hide from one.

In an enclosed space the blast can kill. It may rupture eardrums, lungs and/or other internal organs. Temporary hearing loss is guaranteed. Survivors are rendered unconscious or at best severely disoriented.

Lt. Starrett immediately rushed in. Capt. Bonham and Capt. Morgan had their red-lensed lights out shining them around the room from the door. He found four Germans inside – NCO quarters. Three were stunned or unconscious on their cots. One was sprawled on the floor bleeding from the ears.

SSSSS, SSSSS, SSSSS, SSSSS. Lt. Starrett shot all four. Those Nazis would not be telling any tales about what happened.

Out front Capt. Morgan stood on Capt. Bonham's shoulders and put a Lewes Bomb under the eave of the roof. Inside, Lt. Starrett was placing two more of the incendiaries in corners at opposite ends of the room – per "Dynamite" Dick's instructions.

Take downs of targets are rarely surgical affairs – this one was.

TEAM JAXX(-) PRESSED UP AGAINST THE WALL OF THE BARN on both sides of the smaller "pass door." They were getting ready to make entry. Private First Class James "Wildman" Terrell had not returned, which indicated there was another exit somewhere. So it was only going to be Captain Billy Jack Jaxx and Private First Class Norvel "Horn Dog" Hansen going in. How many Germans were inside was not known.

To complicate matters they had no idea of the layout of the barn which had been described as a horse stable. All Capt. Jaxx had to go on was there had not been any livestock in the aerial photos and none were present outside tonight. If it were a horse stable then it would be chopped up into stalls. Were the stalls walled or simply railed off? Horse barns come in different sizes and configurations. There's "partitioning" where the stalls are open-air divided by railings. "Walled" on one or two sides – rarely on all four. And "frontage," where the front is a solid wall with rails on the sides.

Walls were a concern. They would lessen the effect of the No. 69 concussion grenades. And provide the Germans with cover and concealment.

Capt. Jaxx knew quite a lot about barns. He was mentally running down a checklist of the probabilities. Making an on-scene tactical estimate of the situation prior to making the assault.

It did not look good.

Walls could work for or against them. A wall in front with side rails might provide cover for him and Horn Dog to leapfrog from stall to stall. The open side rails would provide the Nazis no protection at all from the No. 69 grenades.

Capt. Jaxx immediately rejected the idea of the walls being helpful as wishful thinking – 'hope' not being an option in Raiding Forces. At times like this, unit mottos, which might seem sophomoric to a civilian, were extremely helpful for a leader having to make snap decisions under intense pressure in a situation when getting it wrong was not an option.

Partially walled stalls would provide the Germans with concealment. The last thing Capt. Jaxx wanted to do was to try to dig out enemy soldiers armed and ready to fight. The advantage of the element of surprise in a structure this large was only going to be momentary.

It was pitch dark outside. Inside was going to be worse. If used to search for the Germans, Team Jaxx's red-lensed flashlights would give them a point of aim to shoot at. And a search was a given. The Germans were going to be spread out – it was a big barn.

Seconds away from breaching to make forced entry was no time for a team leader to question if his concept of the operation was going to work. A critical moment had arrived. What Capt. Jaxx did next could well decide the success or failure of the entire raid.

The primary reason Colonel John Randal had tapped Jack Cool for the assignment was should conditions on the ground dictate a change of plans, he trusted Jack Cool to make the right decision. There is no higher compliment a commander can pay a junior officer.

It was incumbent upon Capt. Jaxx to make a call. Stick to the plan or come up with another prior to breaching. There were no good options.

Before taking off from RAF Hawkinge, Col. Randal had pulled Capt. Jaxx aside and authorized him to exercise his initiative at his discretion in the event conditions at his objective warranted.

A sign of Col. Randal's trust. And that he was concerned about the barn turning out to be a problem – it had.

There were not enough Rangers on the ground to go around tonight.

Jack Cool was nothing if not decisive. He signaled Horn Dog to stand down. Team Jaxx(-) needed to regroup. The two moved back a few yards to a new position to rethink keeping the barn doors in their field of fire.

Should any of the Germans exit they would be walking straight into the killing zone of a two man ambush.

Team Starrett arrived while Capt. Jaxx was working through his options for the next move and not liking any of them. Every Ranger on Raid Team had been issued Lewes bombs. Lieutenant Chase Starrett reported his people had two left.

That meant Capt. Jaxx now had six incendiary devices and ten No. 69 Concussion Grenades to work with. Barns are highly flammable. How to light this one off from all angles simultaneously – that was the question.

There was a catch. Raid Team had not been issued any explosives other than the Lewes bombs. It was a covert raid and the Rangers were not supposed to be blowing things up. Which meant no blasting caps, detonation cord or time pencils – what are known as initiators.

Necessary to start the explosive chain.

The Lewes bombs had been prepared by Captain Richard "Dynamite Dick" Coogan with 45-minute fuses. There was no easy way to alter them. Even if there were, it would take time – which Capt. Jaxx did not have.

The plan for all teams was to place their charges and be outside and away from the buildings on Château du Val-Obscur when the incendiaries went off – 45 minutes from the time the first one was set. Since not all of the Lewes bombs would be put in place at the same time, their going off simultaneously was not going to take place. Not that that was necessary.

Capt. Jaxx now had five one-pound Lewes bombs. More than enough to burn the barn. What he could not do was put the incendiaries in place, set the fuses, then wait 45 minutes for them to go off. That plan only worked *after* an assault eliminated all the Germans.

If Capt. Jaxx waited 45 minutes for the Lewes bombs to detonate, Raid Team would be on the way home *before* he could confirm he had accomplished his mission – meaning eliminating everyone inside.

For his new plan, almost instantaneous detonation was a must. Anything short of that and some of the Germans might escape. Not even one could be allowed to get away.

Discretion on that outcome was not authorized.

The Special Air Service had informed Raiding Forces an incendiary round fired from a rifle or SMG might detonate one of their Lewes bombs. Or it might also destroy the bomb's firing mechanism causing it to be a dud.

Not that it mattered tonight.

The suppressed U.S. 9mm M3 Grease Guns were new arrivals. Raiding Forces had yet to test them with various types of ammunition. While British Forces did have 9mm incendiary rounds, they were rarely issued and their reliability in the American M3 SMG was unproven – meaning never tried. Tonight the only ammunition carried by Raid Team was 9mm Ball.

Shooting the Lewes bombs to detonate them was not an option.

Capt. Jack whispered, "OK boys here's the plan – we're going to make field-expedient firebombs. I'll walk you through it. Do what I show you step by step. First, place a grenade, Hand, No. 69 in the canvas Lewes bomb satchel with the fuse end pressed flat against the charge.

"Then tape the grenade to the satchel using the handy universal duct tape we all never leave home without. Make sure everything's taped down tight. No movement. That's important.

"Leave the safety pin in. Upon reaching your assigned position stand ready to pull it on my signal. Then throw your bomb at the spot I'll designate for each of you. The 'All Ways Fuse' will do the rest.

"Rally straight back here on the double and link up with me."

The process of assembling the improvised incendiary devices was simple. It took less than a minute. The Rangers thought this plan was a lot better. Getting to see their handiwork – they liked to watch stuff blow up.

If it burned even better

Capt. Jaxx whispered, “We’re going to detonate these firebombs on either side of the barn’s door frame and at the two corner beams we can reach without going behind the far side of the barn. Wildman’s back there somewhere with orders to shoot anything that moves – questions?”

None of the Rangers had any. They were keyed up. Ready.

Capt. Jaxx whispered, “Any of you football quarterbacks or shot put men?”

Captain Dan Morgan whispered, “I was a pitcher on the junior varsity at Florida State for a year before Pearl Harbor.”

“Think you can toss one of these satchels up on the roof?”

“No problem, Jack.”

Lt. Starrett whispered, “Did you notice what the barn's roof is constructed out of, sir?

Capt. Jaxx whispered, “Negative.”

“Slate – somebody spent a ton of money when they built these outbuildings.”

Capt. Jaxx whispered, “That’s not going to work. Dan, can you throw your Lewes bomb at the top of the wall? As close as possible to the eve of the roof?”

“Can do – I’ll get it close enough for military work.”

Capt. Jaxx whispered, “Chase, you and Dan take the support beams on the corners at the far end. Horn Dog and I’ll be responsible for the heavy timber beams on both sides of the barn’s double doors.

“Now listen up – don’t stand too close when you throw your bomb. These babies are going to explode big time the minute they hit. They’ll rain fire.

“My satchel detonating is the signal to Execute, Execute, Execute. Then like I said, rally back here locked and loaded. When the barn goes up in flames those Nazis are going to try to shoot their way out the door.

“Stay frosty boys.”

CAPTAIN BILLY JACK JAXX AND PRIVATE FIRST CLASS Norvel “Horn Dog” Hansen worked their way up toward the big double doors by edging along the barn's wall. As they neared it Capt. Jaxx almost bumped into a small 8x6 three-sided shed made out of rough-cut stone with a sloping slate half-roof about 6 feet tall. It was standing next to the barn near the double doors.

In the dark they had failed to notice it previously. The open side faced the barn. The small lean-to-like structure was the kind found at a château or big country estate designed to conceal something unsightly.

Capt. Jaxx shone his red lensed flashlight inside. Resting upright in a neat row on a flagged stone floor stood rows of 4-foot-tall 100-pound steel cylinders. Eight of them. Growing up on a ranch in Texas he knew instantly what they were – propane bottles. The type used to fuel kitchen ranges and lamps. There were no gas lines this far out in the country.

The open side was designed to prevent gas buildup and for easy access.

It was frequently said in Raiding Forces, "…improvise, adapt, overcome."

Capt. Jaxx took one look and immediately modified his plan of action – for the third time. He knew propane was highly flammable, which is different from combustible. It ignites easily and burns rapidly when exposed to a spark or flame.

Want to burn down a barn? Propane would do the job.

Capt. Jaxx whispered, "Horn Dog, you move up to the doors and stand by ready. When I throw my bomb inside this shed, you throw yours against the timber support beam on the near side of the door frame – up high. We need to try to bring it down as much as possible to inhibit escape."

PFC Hansen whispered, "Wilco."

Capt. Jaxx waited a few seconds until Horn Dog was in place. Then He took the best angle he could on the open side of the shed, pulled the pin on the No. 69 grenade taped to the Lewes bomb in its canvas satchel then threw it inside against the steel canisters as hard as he could. Then he ran as fast as he ever had on a football field at UT.

The No. 69 grenade's "All Ways" fuse made an instantaneous *CRAAAAACK!*

Capt. Jaxx throwing the firebomb initiated a sequence of events – one, two, three. First, the grenade went off. Followed by a loud ringing sound from the steel cylinders. Then the Lewes bomb detonated. *BOOOOOM!*

The resulting explosion was a sudden flat blast – louder than a Mark II "Pineapple" fragmentation grenade but not as heavy as a 60mm mortar round.

The explosion was semi-contained by the limestone walls and slate roof. It was forced out of the open side against the wall of the barn, similar to a shape charge. The blast caused the incendiary mix to spray burning shards against the steel bottles. At least one cylinder split from the concussion. A jet of propane escaped at high pressure. It shot out the open side of the shed spraying against the barn wall.

Then the flaming residue from the Lewes bomb ignited the gas. A ribbon of copper-blue fire streamed against the barn's wall – "flame impingement." Then as the other propane bottles split from the heat, the ribbon of flame became a giant blowtorch engulfing the other bottles resulting in a chain failure.

From PFC Hansen's position came a loud *CRAAAAACK!*

Then *CRAAAACK, CRAAAAACK, CRAAAAACK…* from the Team Jaxx team members throwing their improvised firebombs.

Had Capt. Jaxx known more about demolitions he would have anticipated the result of his throwing a Lewes bomb into a stack of propane bottles. The U.S. Army engineer term for it was a BLEVE burst – Boiling Liquid Expanding Vapor Explosion. It took a few seconds to come to full maturation as the other bottles cooked off.

When they did, the result was apocalyptic.

A blazing fifty-foot fireball erupted from the shed about the time Capt. Jaxx linked up with PFC Hansen. The two took up a position close to the barn doors and watched in awe. The ball of fire was forced out the open side of the hut plastering against the barn wall, then rising up and over the roof. It formed a luminescent mushroom-shaped cloud.

The spectacular ball of fire vaporized in an instant. When it blinked out, the barn was engulfed in flames. As if it were one of The Great Teddy's illusions – Hey, Presto! The building was an inferno and now the roar of the raging fire was louder than the initial explosion.

This part of the raid on Château du Val-Obscur was no longer covert – Capt. Jaxx might have some explaining to do

Lieutenant Chase Starrett and his two Team Starrett operators double-timed up and dropped down into the prone to help cover the barn doors. Horn Dog's Lewes bomb had caved in part of the frame at the top. When it exploded at least one beam to the hayloft collapsed. Hay, some possibly so old it was put there before the war, cascaded down, caught fire and partially blocked the doorway from the inside.

It was not going to be easy for the Nazis trapped inside to exit through the double doors.

Lt. Starrett said, "What the hell did you do, Captain?"

No need to whisper now.

Capt. Jaxx said, "I was trying to catch the barn on fire."

Captain Dan Morgan said, "Mission accomplished."

From inside, terrorized men could be heard shouting. One minute asleep. The next engulfed in smoke and flames. Many of the Germans' clothes were burning. The fire had reached full involvement seemingly from the moment of detonation.

Flames were dancing high into the sky. Smoke poured out of every crack in the building. More panicked shouting came from inside as additional hayloft beams caught fire, collapsed and burning debris started raining down.

Then a single Nazi looking like a stick figure engulfed in flames broke from the door.

The Rangers were so startled by the sight they lay there staring over the top of their M3's sights, not doing anything.

Then… *SSSSS,SSSSS,SSSSS*

Every man gave him a burst. More to put the Nazi out of his misery than because of any perceived threat. As battle-hardened as they were, the Rangers were shocked by this horror show.

The suppressed M3 Grease Guns could not be heard at all with the fire roaring. The Germans inside had no idea there was a raid in progress or that an ambush team was waiting outside. They had no idea what had happened.

A group of men, consisting of more Germans than they had been briefed to expect at the objective, stumbled out together in desperation trying to escape the flames – most were on fire. Those in the back were fighting to push past the ones in front. Some men were knocked down where they lay on the ground, desperately trying to stop the flames from burning them alive. A few not on fire were slapping at the blaze engulfing the others, trying unsuccessfully to put them out.

All of the Nazis were screaming.

Capt. Jaxx commanded, "Hold your fire… wait."

He wanted to let the Germans get clear of the building. The fire silhouetted them as they came out of the doors. Some were down on the ground trying to extinguish the flames. Others dropped to their knees coughing, overwhelmed by the smoke. Crazed men in the back were fighting to claw their way over the top of the mob in front in a frantic effort to escape. Full-blown terror had set in.

"Commence fire!"

SSSSS,SSSSS,SSSSS,SSSSS..... The Rangers ran their magazines. The Nazis were panicked, they were suffering from smoke inhalation, they were burning and they were channelized. Right into Capt. Jaxx's "killing zone" where they were mowed down silently – not realizing what was taking place.

A perfectly executed ambush.

Then a second smaller group fought their way out the doors. These Germans, coming from deeper in the barn, were in worse shape than the first bunch. All of the Nazis were on fire – screaming.

SSSSS,SSSSS,SSSSS,SSSSS...

Around back of the barn Private First Class James "Wildman" Terrell was lying in wait in the dark. A standard-issue-sized door was in his line of sight. He was set up in a "near ambush" about 10 feet away with his suppressed 9mm M3 Grease Gun at the ready.

One second nothing was going on. Then a series of detonations started popping like a string of firecrackers on the far side. Suddenly a brilliant ball of fire appeared over the top of the roof. Then poof – it was gone, snuffed out. Almost like he had imagined it.

PFC Terrell would not have wanted anyone to know how bad it scared him.

He could hear Nazis trapped inside the burning barn shouting. The door he was watching started rattling. Was it locked? Surely it would have been to prevent the local French Resistance fighters in the neighborhood from being able to walk in undetected during the middle of the night and shoot up the place.

Wildman could hear people kicking at it – screaming. He could see the door opened from the inside. That was going to make it hard to kick down.

Nevertheless, the desperate Germans managed to get enough of the door open by knocking it partway off its hinges to squeeze out one at a time. PFC Terrell opened as soon as the first Nazi cleared the door… *SSSSS*

Short bursts. The Germans fighting to force their way out were not aware a Ranger was outside in the dark cutting them down one by one as they came. He was careful to conserve ammo. Counting his rounds as any well-trained Raiding Forces' operator did in an engagement.

This was not the time to be changing magazines.

Five Nazis made it through only to be shot dead – silently. Then no more appeared. And the screaming gradually stopped. The flames inside the barn fueled by all the hay stored in the loft had turned the building into a rampaging fire. The roof started caving in.

PFC Terrell was forced to pull back a few yards to get away from the intense heat.

LIEUTENANT GENERAL "GERONIMO" JOE MCKOY AND HIS team consisting of Major Jack Dance and Lovat Scout Munro Ferguson finished clearing the third floor of the château. Captain Richard "Dynamite" Dick Coogan rejoined after placing his Lewes bomb incendiary devices in the ceiling and in specially selected places on the top floor next to support beams. Team McKoy made their way downstairs to the second level where a furious gun battle was taking place.

Team Randal had driven the Germans back across the open space into the family bedrooms area. Nazis were firing their pistols out the doors and down the hallway. Colonel John Randal and Lovet Scout Lionel Fenwick were dropping them when they made the mistake of exposing themselves to take aim.

Contrary to popular belief, volume of fire is not the important factor in a close-quarters contact. Placing the first round on target is what counts. The Germans were outclassed. They were blazing away wildly – sticking their pistols out around doors, often firing without aiming.

Col. Randal and Scout Fenwick were calling their shots, hitting what they fired at. The floor was littered with dead Nazis who had made the mistake of showing themselves. There were more Germans on the second floor than the total number of Abwehr personnel projected to be at Château du Val-Obscur – that part of their limited intel was wrong.

Lt. Gen. McKoy shouted, "Need a hand, John?"

Col. Randal said, "We've got this, General. Take your team outside and report to Lt. Mascuch. If we still haven't cleared this floor by the time you get through assisting him, come back and bail us out."

"Can do."

"Leave your spare magazines and concussion grenades."

"Wilco."

Capt. Coogan said, "I'll go place my charges on the first floor then be back up to set them here when you give me the all clear, sir."

Col. Randal said, "King, you stick with us."

7

WICKED DEADLY

OUTSIDE, LIEUTENANT RICKY MASCUCH WAS DISCUSSING THE situation with Beverly Blackwell and Lieutenant Ted “The Great Teddy” Hamilton. Captain Dick Courtney, X-Ray, Lance Corporal Ray “Tank” Karlsson and his prisoner Major Hanns von Reisen were standing nearby. They could hear the muffled sound of gunshots from inside the château. Then they heard the string of explosions from Captain Billy Jack Jaxx’s objective. And saw the golden orange fireball rise above the trees.

None of which was part of the plan.

Lieutenant General “Geronimo” Joe McKoy, Major Jack Dance and Lovat Scout Munro Furgeson came out of the mansion. “John told me to report to you, Lieutenant.”

Lt. Mascuch said, “We can use a hand, sir.”

“We’re here, son – doin’ what?”

“We’ve got to get this glider turned around in the other direction, General.”

“How much does this crate weigh?”

“Without the wings about a ton and a half, sir.”

“Well, you’ve got ‘em strapped on, Ricky.”

“Make that 4,000 pounds plus, sir.”

Lt. Gen. McKoy said, "Sure didn't seem that heavy – dancin' around on the end a' that string when we was sittin' in the back ridin' in it."

"That is a fact, General."

Lt. Gen. McKoy said, "OK, boys, let's do this. Put a little elbow grease in it."

Even Maj. von Risen assisted… with a certain amount of gentle prodding from Tank.

CAPTAIN BILLY JACK JAXX HAD A PROBLEM. THE BARN WAS blazing. The structure was in the final stage before total structural collapse. There was a pile of dead Germans outside the big double doors. Each of them had numerous 9mm bullet wounds. He could not leave the bodies where they lay. Tomorrow when the Abwehr main office in Pas-de-Calais sent someone to check on their outpost at Château du Val-Obscur after it failed to respond to phone calls, they would be found – shot to death.

What to do?

Capt. Jaxx said, "Horn Dog, go recover Wildman. The rest of you start heaving those dead guys back inside the barn. Has to look like the Germans died in the fire. When they're found, no trace of gunshot wounds can be visible to arouse suspicion."

Private First Class Norvel "Horn Dog" Hansen said, "On the way, Captain."

Capt. Jaxx said, "Chase, as soon as you're finished take your people and move out to establish the blocking force on the road per Colonel Randal's orders."

Lieutenant Chase Starrett said, "Yes, sir."

Throwing dead Nazis into a burning building… not a problem. They were already KIA. That said, it was arguably the most gruesome assignment any of the Rangers had ever been tasked with.

Theirs was not to reason why. They knew the answer. This raid never happened. Raiding Forces were never here. Any sign they might have been had to be completely obliterated.

Orders were orders.

As for post-mission operational security, it was guaranteed. No one on Team Jaxx or Team Starrett was going to tell this story.

Ever.

COLONEL JOHN RANDAL SAID, "TIME FOR A CHANGE OF PLAN, FENWICK."

"Sir!"

"They've got to be running low on ammo," Col. Randal observed. "I'll cover you while you throw three concussion grenades down the hall. When the last one goes off we'll move up and secure the entrance. From there we can take out the first two rooms. Then we'll move down the hallway, getting grenades inside the other rooms – one at a time.

"King, you cover us."

Lovat Scout Lionel Fenwick said, "Ready when you are, sir."

Col. Randal said, "Do it!"

He started firing his 1911 Colt.38 Super as fast as he could work the trigger, laying down covering fire. Col. Randal was firing across the large living room at the hallway on the other side leading to the family and important guests' bedrooms – not trying to hit anything.

The reason for using his handgun to deliver covering fire was because he wanted the Germans to know they were being shot at and keep their heads down. Which they might not realize with his suppressed 9mm M3 SMG.

A few more unsuppressed pistol shots inside the main building were not going to make any difference at this point.

Scout Fenwick stood up and threw the three No. 69 grenades as fast as he could, one after the other. They detonated on contact. *WHUUUUUMP, WHUUUUUUMP, WHUUUUUMP*

Col. Randal charged across the grand salon as soon as the third grenade went off, dodging coffee tables and couches. The idea was to make the Nazis keep down not knowing how many grenades had been thrown. The No. 69 grenades exploding in the hallway were noisy and caused the walls and the windows behind their blackout curtains to rattle but were not going to kill or incapacitate anyone. The Germans did not know that.

No one was about to peek out.

Scout Fenwick followed by King came right behind Col. Randal as soon as he was in position. Their rubber-soled raiding boots made virtually no sound. The Germans never heard them. On arriving at the entrance to the hall the three slammed flat against the wall on either side. Col. Randal and King to the right, Scout Fenwick to the left. From this point on it was going to be a matter of clearing the rooms one at a time – carefully.

Col. Randal and Scout Fenwick had worked together since the first days of Raiding Forces when it was still called the Small-Scale Raiding Company (SSRC). King was a master at conducting military operations in urban terrain. This type of house-clearing drill was second nature. The team moved as if they were gliding – very smooth. No wasted effort. A deadly military ballet bringing heat.

Col. Randal knelt down and pointed at the open door on his side of the hall. Scout Fenwick nodded. Then he threw in a No. 69 grenade.

WHUUUUUMP

Col. Randal was crouched with his 9mm M3 Grease Gun at his shoulder to cover the hallway while keeping an eye on the room immediately opposite. King remained standing and provided overwatch around the corner.

Col. Randal moved into the hall then entered the room while the dust from the grenade's blast was still billowing out.

There was a German Hauptmann sprawled on the floor with a 7.65mm Walther PP lying nearby. He was unconscious. Col. Randal gave him a short burst… *SSS.*

Then he turned back to the door, looked out and made eye contact with Scout Fenwick. Col. Randal pointed across the hall at the room opposite. The Lovat Scout nodded.

Col. Randal threw a No. 69 grenade, waited for it to explode then leaned out in the hall to cover Scout Fenwick who was already going through the door to clear the room. King was above him at the start of the hall with his 9mm M3 at the ready.

When operators work together with flawless execution as the three did, it is a thing of beauty. They kept it up, leapfrogging their way down the hall room by room. There were four bedrooms on each side of the hall. An Abwehr officer was found in each one.

Not one round was fired back at Team Randal from the time they started clearing the guest bedrooms. The Nazis were paralyzed by terror, frozen into inaction unable to defend themselves. Not trained or experienced in this kind of house fighting, they could hear the grenades going off but nothing else. One German foolishly stuck his head out a door and was immediately shot dead. The rest cowered in their rooms and died.

Suppressed 9mm M-3 Grease Guns were wicked deadly in that environment.

"Second floor secure."

CAPTAIN JAKE NOVAK AKA "JAKE THE SNAKE" WENT TO THE back door and opened it carefully. He knew Waldo Treywick was out there in the dark lying in wait with murderous intent. Care had to be taken. That old smuggler would light him up in a heartbeat and then say he was sorry for the confusion later at the funeral.

"Ranger, Ranger, Ranger… stand down Mr. Treywick, we're clear in here."

"That you, Jake?"

"Roger, come on in, sir."

Waldo and Vanish came up on the porch but had difficulty opening the door all the way. There was a dead German blocking it. He had come running out to escape Jake the Snake and Captain Clint Hays.

Waldo and Vanish both shot him with their suppressed 9mm M3s.

Capt. Novak said, "That the only one?"

"Negative, two more in the bushes."

"OK, let's drag 'em inside… can't leave anyone sporting bullet holes out here."

LIEUTENANT CHASE STARRETT LED HIS TEAM TO THE LANE that ran from Calais to Château du Val-Obscur. His orders were to set up a blocking force to keep anyone from arriving from the village. He was hoping he would not see any more action. If Team Starrett ambushed a German column of any size coming down the dirt road to investigate, they did not have the firepower to sustain a prolonged contact.

If a firefight did develop the chances of Raid Team being able to exfiltrate to the ERP on the coast and extract by PT boat would be less than ideal – a lot less.

Lt. Starrett had made plans to go out with Beverly tonight before the raid came along and put a crimp in that plan. He was hoping to get back in time to make it a late date.

According to Captain Billy Jack Jaxx, the concept of hope not being a course of action did not apply when it came to women.

He would know.

CAPTAIN BILLY JACK JAXX ORDERED PRIVATE FIRST CLASS Norvel "Horn Dog" Hansen and Private First Class James "Wildman" Terrell to return to the château. They reported they had thrown the Nazis Wildman had shot into the burning barn. He decided to remain in place to make absolutely certain there were no living Germans left in the area – 100%.

Capt. Jaxx had no idea why it was important. All he knew was Colonel John Randal had ordered him not to leave anyone alive. He had never been given those type orders before.

There had to be a reason.

The burning barn was on the verge of total structural failure. It did not resemble the building Capt. Jaxx found when he first arrived on the scene. The bodies of the Germans inside would be burned beyond recognition – reduced to charred remains. No one would be able to determine the exact cause of death or even be suspicious as to what it might have been.

The fire might be written off as a result of smoking in bed – could happen sleeping in a barn.

Part of the structure groaned, twisted, then collapsed. Sparks shot high in the sky before falling back down to earth. Now the fire was mostly a giant bed of glowing red coals.

Team Jaxx: Mission accomplished.

OUT IN FRONT OF THE CHÂTEAU LIEUTENANT RICKY MASCUCH was busy connecting a 15-foot tow line to the nose of the Waco CG-4A. The nose hook had been damaged when the glider hit the front door of the château. He took a hammer from the glider's tool kit and managed to make it work.

Colonel John Randal arrived. "You good to go, Lieutenant Mascuch?'

"Roger that, sir."

Col. Randal said, "Major Dance, have Capt. Courtney standing by to send code word *Eskimo Pie* as soon as we roll out." The signal was confirmation to Seaborn House Major Hanns von Reisen had been captured and that Raid Team had departed Château du Val-Obscur en route to the extraction rally point on the coast.

The TOC would forward the message to RAF Hawkinge to clear the 617 Squadron Lancaster bomber standing by with its motor ticking over on "Cockpit Readiness Alert" to take off. Its mission was to dump a bomb load of incendiaries on Château du Val-Obscur. And make it look like an accident.

Col. Randal said, "I'm going to go pull in Captain Jaxx and Team Starrett. Have everybody loaded up ready to move when I get back."

"Yes, sir."

"General McKoy, you going to be able to handle the tow?"

Lieutenant General "Geronimo" Joe McKoy said, "No problem, John – I been haulin' cattle rigs since I was twelve years old."

Beverly said, "Me too. Why don't you let me drive?"

Lt. Gen. McKoy said, "You've had all the time behind the wheel you're gonna get for one night missy."

It was not difficult to locate Captain Billy Jack Jaxx. All he had to do was walk in the direction of the glowing timbers twenty yards away. A fire this early in the mission had not been in the plan.

Capt. Jaxx barked, "Halt!"

"Ranger."

"Come on in, Colonel."

"What happened here, Jack?"

From the size of the bed of coals, Col. Randal was beginning to realize he had underestimated the difficulty factor of Team Jaxx's target.

Capt. Jaxx said, "More Germans were quartered in the barn than we were anticipating, sir. No way we were going to be able to clear a place that big in the dark, not take any causalities and ensure no one escaped.

"I didn't see another option but to light it up."

Col. Randal said, "A burning building in wartime Calais isn't going to arouse suspicions. We were planning to set fire to it anyway. Good job, stud.

"Any problems?"

"None we couldn't handle, sir."

"Let's go pull in Lieutenant Starrett."

BY THE TIME COLONEL JOHN RANDAL, CAPTAIN BILLY JACK Jaxx and Team Starrett arrived back at the château, Major Jack Dance had Raid Team assembled, ready to move. Lieutenant General "Geronimo" Joe McKoy was in one of the Wehrmacht Ford V3000 model trucks backed up to the wingless Waco CG-4A. Lieutenant Ricky Mascuch had hooked up the 15-foot tow rope Col. Randal had ordered brought along on the raid for just this purpose.

Everyone was anxious to be away.

Col. Randal ordered, "Captain Courtney, stand by to transmit *Eskimo Pie* when I give you the word."

"With pleasure, sir."

This was a pre-arranged code word in two parts to inform Raiding Forces' Tactical Operations Center at Seaborn House the mission's objective had been accomplished. *Eskimo* indicated Major Hanns von Reisman was in custody. *Pie* signaled Raid Team was leaving or had left the objective en route to the ERP on the coast.

The second part of the message alerted the TOC to inform RAF Bomber Command it was cleared to send in the Lancaster from 617 Squadron to drop its payload of incendiary bombs on Château du Val-Obscur.

Col. Randal said, "Give me a head count."

Maj. Dance said, "Good count, sir."

Raid Team climbed in the back of the truck with Lance Corporal Ray "Tank" Karlsson guarding the prisoner. King was riding on the Ford's left fender and Capt. Jaxx was on the right. In the event a roadblock was encountered they were to immediately engage.

Lt. Gen. McKoy would make a split-second decision whether to crash through the block or halt and let the rest of the Rangers dismount and maneuver on the Germans while King and Jack Cool pinned them down with their suppressed 9mm M3 Grease Guns.

This plan was simply a precaution. Civilian traffic in the Pas-de-Calais region was under curfew from 2000 hrs to 0600 hrs. Anyone moving after dark was subject to being fired on. There would be no good reason for the Germans to set up a roadblock in the middle of the night on a remote dirt track that did not lead anywhere.

Nevertheless, when planning a raid it is imperative to think the operation through to the end per Raiding Forces' Rule 5: Plan missions backward (know how to get home). Nothing was taken for granted or left to chance.

Col. Randal stood by the truck with Lieutenant Ted "The Great Teddy" Hamilton and Beverly Blackwell waiting for everyone to board.

Major Jack Dance walked up to report, "Ready to move out, sir – the prisoner is secured."

At that moment a series of muffled detonations came from the château. The Lewes bombs Captain Richard "Dynamite Dick" Coogan had placed were beginning to cook off.

Time to go.

Col. Randal said, "We're moving now, Major. Load up – let's roll."

Beverly hopped in the cab then Col. Randal climbed in. Lt. Hamilton stood on the running board. He was Col. Randal's self-appointed bodyguard for the three-mile run to the coast.

Col. Randal tapped on the rear window of the troop compartment, "Send your message, Captain Courtney."

Lt. Gen. McKoy rolled out slow and easy, being careful to take up the slack in the tow rope. Waco CG-4As were never intended to be towed very far. Certainly not three miles. They were designed for short hauls around airfields. The metal skid shoes would help. That was the reason Col. Randal asked Major General Sam Houston "Bronc" Blackwell to have them installed.

If they hit rough patches of road or hard curves Lt. Mascuch was ready to dismount with a team to make sure the glider kept traveling in the right attitude and did not skid off the lane. Top speed was going to be 10 mph or less.

If they could go that fast, the movement to the ERP would take approximately twenty minutes.

The Rangers wished it were faster. At the beginning of a raid they were always raring to go. At the end of one they were always more impatient to go home.

For all they knew there were one million Germans preparing to descend on Château du Val-Obscur and kill them all.

Extractions can be more high-stress than insertions.

WING COMMANDER LEONARD CHESHIRE, THE COMMANDER OF 617 Squadron "The Dam Busters" was sitting in his Avro Lancaster B Mk I (Special) at RAF Hawkinge having flown in for the CROMWELL mission. He had the engines ticking over waiting for the GO-order. His instructions were to dump a full bombload of incendiary bombs on Château du Val-Obscur. Tonight a full bombload meant 3,000 4-pound Incendiary Bombs (IB) in Small Bomb Units (SBU).

"Victor Leader you are cleared for take-off." RAF Call signs changed on a daily basis. Tonight Wg. Cdr. Cheshire's personal designator was 'Victor Leader.'

Usually the command sequence was longer. Not tonight. The Luftwaffe had radio intercept stations all along the enemy coast on the far side of the Channel listening in. The RAF was not taking any chances. In the interest of operational security, communications were kept to a bare minimum. For this flight it was imperative to prevent the Germans from discovering a CROMWELL priority single plane mission was taking off from RAF Hawkinge.

Or had flown anywhere near Raiding Forces target.

Wg. Cdr. Cheshire's run on Château du Val-Obscur had to appear accidental – a battle-damaged bomber jettisoning its load to lighten the aircraft, not a top priority CROMWELL mission. The Lancaster was rolling down the runway almost immediately. Since RAF Hawkinge was a fighter base it had a short runway not normally suitable for bombers. Because flight time was approximately 20 minutes, the plane was carrying a minimal load of fuel – one hour's endurance to lighten the load.

Take-off for a pilot as skilled as the Wing Commander was not a problem.

The flight plan was simple. Fly in at 1000 feet hedge hopping. Climb to 1500 feet to mimic a damaged aircraft aborting its flight plan and turning back to England. Then Wg. Cdr. Cheshire would drop back down to 800 feet to set up the approach to target flying at a speed of 180-190 mph.

The bomb run was equally simple. As he approached the target Wg. Cdr. Cheshire was to begin releasing his bombs. The idea was to saturate the chateau and its immediate grounds with incendiaries – burn everything.

Navigation was made easier because Wg. Cdr. Cheshire could see a large fire on the target while he was still over the Channel. The Lancaster flashed over the enemy coast. He flew inland for some distance then came back around to line up on the target, flying toward the coast and home.

Directly ahead the roof of the château burst into flames. Wg. Cdr. Cheshire flew straight toward it. On his command the bombardier started toggling the 4-pound IBs. Then dumped the bulk of the bomb load directly on the already burning château as the Lancaster started climbing to head back to England.

Thousands of 4-pound IBs smothered the château.

Precision imprecision. The tightest concentration of bombs drenched the main building with the tail of the pattern coming down across the glowing coals of the barn and shed.

The bombs' impact matched the footprint of an accidental salvo rather than a calculated strike. Mission accomplished. The shortest and simplest Wg. Cdr. Cheshire had ever flown. While not as glamorous as busting dams, at this stage of the war tonight's air raid was arguably more important strategically than flooding the Ruhr Valley.

That was classified – Wg. Cdr. Cheshire did not possess the Need-to-Know why he was bombing a solitary château in the country. Or the reason it had to look accidental.

He never would.

ESKIMO PIE WAS HAND-CARRIED BY AN SLU ARMED MESSENGER to the MI-5 Director-General's office – attn: Major General Sir David Petrie with copies to B Division, Mr. Guy Liddell, Director of B Division Counter Espionage, Lieutenant Colonel Thomas Argyll "Tar" Robertson, B1-A, and

Professor John Cecil (J.C.) Masterman, XX Committee. The three were holding a late-night vigil to determine what steps had to be taken now that the Double-Cross System was at risk of being compromised – a disaster of the utmost magnitude.

The senior counterintelligence officers understood the code word indicated that Major Hanns von Risen had been captured – had he been killed the second word would have been *Sandwich,* and that the Raiding Forces' party had departed Château du Val-Obscur. Normally that would have been cause for celebration.

Not tonight.

The Raiding Forces' team had gone in aboard a U.S. Army Waco CG-4A. The Germans would find it tomorrow. The Abwehr would realize Commandos had kidnapped Maj. von Reisen.

They would want to know why.

It would not take long for them to read through all of the major's recent communications with his higher headquarters and discover his concerns about German spies in England possibly being turned. If Maj. von Reisen had not been taken seriously prior to he would be now.

Worst-case scenario – FORTIUDE SOUTH was exposed as a deception.

D-Day would have to be postponed. Possibly cancelled. At the very least, a new site to land on the Continent would have to be selected and due to operational exigency it might not even be in France. Changing the plan would increase the war by at least six months and maybe longer.

What the MI-5 senior officers – the best minds in the business – were now faced with was an implosion of their entire deception campaign. One minute MI-5 was the most brilliant intelligence organization in the world even more highly regarded than the British Secret Intelligence Service, MI-6. Suddenly, through no fault of their own, the Security Service found itself teetering on the brink of becoming the laughing stock of both the Allied and Axis camps.

No one had a suggestion for the next course of action.

LIEUTENANT COLONEL JOHN HENRY BEVAN WAS IN HIS LONDON Controlling Section office at Norfolk House, St. James Square, London where he was monitoring Raiding Forces' operation when the *Eskimo Pie* message arrived.

He had to sign for it, read the message, then return it to the Special Liaison Unit armed courier that delivered it. It was a good news, bad news situation.

The good news was the snatch mission to capture Major Hanns von Reisen had been a success. The bad news was Colonel John Randal's recklessness would in all probability result in the Double Cross System being compromised and all of LCS's carefully laid deceptions exposed for what they were – theatre.

Lt. Col. Bevan had a duty driver run him the three-quarters of a mile to the Cabinet War Rooms beneath Whitehall where the Prime Minister was also monitoring the raid – pacing back and forth, chomping on a big Cuban cigar. Incoming signals from MI-5, MI-6, and the armed services were logged in and briefed to him immediately as they arrived.

The PM would have seen the *Eskimo Pie* by the time he could arrive and interpret the developments for him. He would likely be celebrating the raid as a success at this point – Churchill loved victories. Lt. Col. Bevan was about to rain on his parade.

While the Prime Minister did not punish subordinates for reporting failure, given the opportunity, Lt. Col. Bevan would have cheerfully throttled Lady Jane's "gentleman friend" for putting him in this position.

JAMES "BALDIE" TAYLOR WAS AT MI-5 WHEN THE *ESKIMO PIE* signal came in. He immediately hailed a taxi and was driven to the Bradford Hotel. Once there Jim proceeded to the Penthouse Floor and went to the Supreme Commander, Allied Expeditionary Force, General Dwight D. Eisenhower's new suite.

Gen. Eisenhower had been alerted there was a crisis brewing but was not aware of the details at this point. He was in a Bradford Hotel bathrobe with the "B" monogrammed on it chain-smoking cigarettes when Jim arrived.

The general listened carefully to what Jim reported. The Supreme Commander was very composed for a man who was hearing what was possibly the worst news of his military career.

He had been selected for the most prestigious assignment of WWII only to be learning his new command had turned into a nightmare – marooned in England with no way to get at the Germans if the D-Day landing had to be canceled because the deception campaign designed to cover the Normandy invasion was compromised.

If it was the case, D-Day would be an ambush – the biggest in history.

As he briefed Gen. Eisenhower, Jim had the impression someone else was in another room of the suite. Possibly a woman? A skilled intelligence officer who had long survived by relying on his highly refined sixth sense, he had an idea who she might be.

"What does this signal indicate, Mr. Taylor?"

"It is a two-part message, General. *Eskimo* means the extraction phase of the operation is underway. *Pie* confirms Colonel Randal has captured the Abwehr officer who voiced suspicions about the loyalty of certain German spies in England.

"Once the exfiltration is carried out and the Rangers are onboard the PT boat en route home, *Appaloosa* will be transmitted.

Gen. Eisenhower said, "In that case, why do you appear so concerned, Mr. Taylor?"

Jim said, "Colonel Randal landed by glider at the Château du Val-Obscur where the target, Major von Reisen, had his headquarters. While a Lancaster bomber will be dropping incendiaries to cover up evidence of the raid it is not believed the bombs can completely destroy all signs of the Waco CG-4A left behind on the grounds of the château.

"The Germans will discover Major von Reisen has disappeared and that an abandoned USAAF glider is present at his HQ. The Abwehr will then launch an investigation into what it was von Reisen had been working on to merit a raiding party being dispatched to kidnap him."

Gen. Eisenhower said, "What is your assessment of the situation, Mr. Taylor?"

Jim said, "Essentially, sir, we shined a light on a problem German intelligence may not have even been paying any attention to, General."

Gen. Eisenhower said, "Why would we do that?"

Jim said, "Strictly off the record, sir, for your ears only – I feel MI-5 and the LCS may have overreacted. Middle-level counterintelligence officers suspect things all the time. Major von Reisen was simply doing his duty by reporting his concerns.

"Organizations like the Abwehr do not become overly alarmed by one of their people having suspicions. They are supposed to have doubts. When they do, higher headquarters demands verifiable proof before taking any action."

Gen. Eisenhower said, "That makes sense."

Jim said, "When our counterintelligence people realized the Double Cross System, the foundation of OPERATION FORTITUDE SOUTH… linchpin of the entire deception plan covering D-Day, might be blown – their lives passed in front of their eyes."

Gen. Eisenhower said, "I can appreciate how it would."

Jim said, "MI-5 was and still is desperate to interrogate Major von Reisen. They need to find out what he advised Abwehr HQ Berlin about the German spy network in the UK. And more importantly what the reaction to his suspicions have been, if any.

"Colonel Randal was informed a top-level, highest priority, MOST SECRET/TOP SECRET mission needed to be undertaken to bring a certain German officer from his headquarters in the Pas-de-Calais District to England for interrogation. He was given the location of the target and the name of the individual to be snatched."

Gen. Eisenhower said, "That is all the colonel knows?"

"It is sir."

"Then what is the problem?"

Jim said, "Operations proposed by MI-5, MI-6 and/or LCS are usually talked to death prior to. Not this time, General – no one involved had ever worked directly with Raiding Forces previously. Give Colonel Randal a mission and he carries it out.

"The Colonel coordinated with General Blackwell to provide air support. Gathered as much intelligence on the target as he could. Then went straight over to France and snatched von Reisen – same night."

Gen. Eisenhower said, "Was Randal fully briefed about the importance of not tipping our hand to the Germans?"

Jim said, "He was, sir."

Gen. Eisenhower said, "How do you account for him landing by glider knowing he would have to leave it behind following his raid?"

"I have no explanation, General."

"Is there any way to retrieve the glider?"

"Negative – not that anyone has been able to come up with sir."

"Has General Donovan been updated on this development?"

"My next stop."

"I appreciate you keeping me informed, Mr. Taylor… and for your candid assessment of the situation. It shall not leave this room."

Gen. Eisenhower could not help thinking for a man he had never spoken to, Randal had been a pain in his neck for a long time. If, in fact, the colonel had compromised FORTITUDE SOUTH, he intended to have him reduced to his permanent grade in the U.S. Army – lieutenant.

Then ship him home to the States.

RIDING ON THE RUNNING BOARD OF THE WEHRMACHT FORD truck, Lieutenant Ted "The Great Teddy" Hamilton said, "Bombs away."

The Lancaster bomber had flown directly overhead at low level on its way back to base with its four Rolls-Royce Merlin V12 piston engines thundering as Raid Team was approaching the ERP. They had been traveling away from Château du Val-Obscur for about as long as Wing Commander Leonard Cheshire had been flying toward it.

This kind of coordination was only possible because of the short distances and the high level of professionalism of all parties involved. Tonight was a classic Combined Operation – on a small scale.

Colonel John Randal leaned out the window to look back. He saw impact flashes – thousands of them. Château du Val-Obscur speckled with flickering points of light resembling the sparks thrown off by children's sparklers on the 4th of July.

The result of this part of the plan exceeded anything he had expected.

Excellent air support. Perfectly executed. What Col. Randal did not know was there was more to come.

Lieutenant Colonel John Henry Bevan had ordered up a full RAF Lancaster wing to divert their return flight to support the raid. Now the bombers would egress Château du Val-Obscur over the Calias Village region after hitting their primary target. If any of the aircraft were flying home with bombs still on board they were to attempt to delay lightening their load until they reached the vicinity of Château du Val-Obscur.

The purpose of the exercise was to have sixty-plus Lancasters flying home independently passing over the general vicinity of the château. The idea was to make Wg. Cdr. Cheshire jettisoning his bombs not seem like anything out of the ordinary. Additional bombs falling at various places throughout the area would be icing on the cake for that deception.

Bomber Command had not been thrilled with the directive. However, CROMWELL meant snap to. Comply with your orders. Do not ask questions. The returning Lancasters would now be diverted through the heaviest concentration of anti-aircraft defenses anywhere in Europe outside of Berlin.

Brave men would die tonight in an attempt to deceive the Nazis about the Raiding Forces' operation.

THE FORD V3000 3-TON TRUCK WAS GETTING CLOSE TO THE coast. A red light up ahead blinked three times. Captain Billy Jack Jaxx flashed his hook-nosed red filtered light back two times. It was the proper challenge and response. Raid Team had arrived at the ERP.

As Colonel John Randal dismounted the truck, Lieutenant Ted "The Great Teddy" Hamilton said, "How are you planning to get rid of this fuselage, sir?"

Col. Randal said, "I thought I'd have you wave your magic wand at it and say 'Hey, Presto!'"

Beverly Blackwell said, "That's all you've got?"

Col. Randal said, "Seems like a plan to me."

"Johnny, did you hit your head when we crash landed?"

"Hide and watch."

Lieutenant Westly Slade approached. "Rappel lines are in place, sir. The Lifeboat Service Men are standing by down below. We're good to go when you are."

Col. Randal said, "Stand ready, Lieutenant – you bring what I asked?"

"Roger that, sir."

"Give it to Captain Coogan."

The Rangers dismounted from the back of the truck. They gathered round Col. Randal. The euphoria from successfully carrying out the mission was beginning to wear off. The men were ready to return to base – time to go.

Col. Randal said, "Major Dance, take charge of the team. Turn the glider around. As soon as that's done push it to the edge of the cliff. Leave six people here and have the rest start rappelling down to the beach.

"When they get there, the Lifeboat Service Men will ferry them out to the PT boat then return and stand close in offshore.

"Questions?"

"Negative, sir."

As Major Jack Dance went about those tasks, Lieutenant General "Geronimo" Joe McKoy was turning the 3-ton truck around. While Lieutenant Ricky Mascuch was waiting for the Ford to get into position, he unhooked the tow rope from the glider and retrieved a 100 ft. 2 in. manila rope from inside and attached it to the Waco CG-4A nose hook.

At the edge of the cliff Rangers started going down the rappel lines.

Lt. Mascuch hooked the tow rope up to the truck. When the last man had gone down the ropes, Col. Randal ordered, "Major Dance, have your men push the glider over the edge."

As they shoved the Waco CG-4A, Lt. Gen. McKoy slowly backed up giving the Rangers enough slack to slide it. When the glider went over the edge he kept backing to lower it down to the sliver of beach.

When the glider completed the trip to the bottom Sub-Lieutenant Jeffery Macomber and a team of sailors fell to and started working. Maj. Dance unhooked the tow rope and dropped it down the cliff where it was recovered.

Captain Richard "Dynamite Dick" Coogan said, "Lieutenant Slade gave me a 50-pound pack of Composition C. That's enough explosive to bring down Hoover Dam. What do you want me to do with it, sir?"

Col. Randal said, "Run that truck back up the road a quarter of a mile or so. Drive in a ditch to appear as if the driver ran off the road and got stuck. Then blow it. I want it to look like the truck took a direct hit from a bomb.

"Can do?"

Capt. Coogan said, "No problem, sir. I'll blow the truck to smithereens. No one will ever be able to tell what happened to it."

Col. Randal said, "Make it fast. I'll be waiting for you here."

"On the way, Colonel."

When Col. Randal went to the edge of the cliff to check on progress down below he found Beverly standing there with Lt. Hamilton.

"Why haven't you rappelled down?"

"You ordered me to stick in your back pocket, Johnny."

"What's your excuse, Lieutenant?"

"You ordered me to guard Beverly, sir."

Col. Randal said, "OK, you can go down when I do. Stay right here. Don't wander off that's an order."

Lt. Hamilton said, "I am still trying to figure out what you intend to do with the Waco, sir. The Germans will find it down there at the base of the cliff. It's just a matter of time."

Col. Randal said, "Maybe not."-

Down below Brandy Seaborn was standing 200-feet off the beach. One of the Goatley Dories was being rowed to the PT boat. S/Lt. Macomber's sailors were working around the front of the fuselage of the glider. From the top of the cliff in the dark it was difficult to see what was taking place.

King came over to stand with Col. Randal.

"You going to be able to pull out those pitons?"

"Affirmative, Chief."

In the distance behind them a massive explosion went off. Capt. Coogan had not wasted any time. He set his charges with a short delay fuse, waited at a safe distance for them to detonate and now came double-timing back to the ERP.

"Mission accomplished, sir – in spades. I stuck around to check. The body's shredded into a million pieces spread out all over the countryside. Frame's broke… the axels sheared.

"And it's on fire, Colonel."

Col. Randal ordered. "Major Dance, get the rest of the people down the ropes."

Lt. Slade and King stood by the two rappel lines assisting people going over the edge. The first step was tricky. They were not using a snap link rope rappel harness tonight. It was a body rappel with the line over one shoulder running across a slung M3 Grease Gun to prevent rope burn. The method was more painful but tonight, no one minded the hurt.

Finally only Col. Randal, Maj. Dance, King, Capt. Coogan, Lt. Slade, Beverly and Lt. Hamilton were left on the top with Capt. Jaxx providing security.

Maj. Dance said, "Good count, sir."

Col. Randal said, "You and Coogan take off – make sure it's organized down there."

"Yes, sir."

They were followed by Lt. Slade and Lt. Hamilton. Then Beverly – King gave her his M3 to sling perpendicular across her back for the rappel line to run across. He was not going to need it. Now it was only Col. Randal, Capt. Jaxx and King remaining.

Col. Randal said, "Let's go, Jack."

When Col. Randal reached the bottom he checked with S/Lt. Macomber, "Are we good to go?"

Affirmative, sir.

On the cliff King was making a risky free-climb descent. Coming down fast. The Merc was like a human fly.

Col. Randal said, "Get your men back to the PT boat, Lieutenant Macomber."

"With all due speed, sir."

"Captain Coogan, time for your final act."

"Roger that – on your command."

Now it was only Col. Randal, King and Beverly standing on the shale – Capt. Coogan ducked inside the Waco CG-4A momentarily then came back and joined them.

"Fire in the hole."

Col. Randal said, "OK, Beverly… you've earned the right this night – give the order."

Beverly's Ten Most beauty pageant smile flashed white in the dark, "Let's get the hell out of Dodge – always wanted to be the one to say that."

The Life Boat Service Men put everything they had into reaching the PT boat in record time – a hundred-yard dash over water. When the Goatley Dory pulled alongside and they climbed up on deck, Major the Lady Jane Seaborn was there to greet them.

Col. Randal was not expecting her to be there.

"Hard night, John?"

"Had its moments."

Now was not the time to take her to task for being on the PT boat.

Lady Jane said, "You rather overachieved on this one, babe."

At the stern, Brandy was consulting with S/Lt. Macomber.

"Ready on your command, ma'am."

Brandy gave the order, "Stand by the towline – easy ahead."

The PT boat gradually made way, carefully taking up the slack in a 300-foot tow line attached to the nose hook of the Waco CG 4A. When the line went taut, the glider slid into the water. It was not pretty but the fuselage stayed afloat as it wallowed along.

Brandy gradually increased speed. The PT boat stood out into open water making around 9 knots. This may have been a military operational first – a boat towing a glider.

Lt. Hamilton said, "No one would have ever thought of this, Colonel. And it's working – might be a future for you as an illusionist, sir."

Beverly said, "Do you believe the glider's going to make it all the way home, Johnny?"

"Negative."

Waldo Treywick handed Col. Randal one of his cigars. He stuck it between his teeth. The glider was porpoising on its tow rope, still making headway behind the PT boat. It was not designed for anything like this.

Three-quarters of a mile out in the Channel, Capt. Coogan was watching the luminous dial of his watch.

"Any time now, sir."

POP, POP, POP… A rapid-fire staccato of blocks of Composition C onboard the glider started cooking off like a long string of giant-sized firecrackers. The tow line went slack. The Waco CG-4A was gone – it simply vanished. What was not destroyed sank.

The Germans were never going to find this glider.

Just to make sure 15th MGB Flotilla would have a gunboat standing by at sunrise to recover any small pieces of debris that might have floated up. Not that it would be any problem if they did. The Channel was full of wreckage from boats being blown up and aircraft crashing.

Why take a chance?

Everyone on deck watched in awe – it was like… magic.

The Great Teddy said, "Hey, presto!"

Capt. Jaxx said, “Never saw that coming.”

Lady Jane said, “Extraordinary.”

Lt. Gen. McKoy said, “Whatever they’re payin’ you, John, it ain’t enough.”

Brandy ordered, “Full speed ahead.”

Col. Randal said, “Have your radio operator transmit *Appaloosa.*”

8

S&M

0330 HOURS

RAID TEAM ARRIVED BACK AT THE TACTICAL OPERATIONS Center (TOC) at Seaborn house. There were a handful of top-tier counterintelligence officials in from London waiting when they arrived. Those present included Colonel Valentine Patrick Vivian former head of Section V Counter-Espionage now serving as Vice-Chief MI-6, Lieutenant Colonel John Henry Bevan, Chief of the London Controlling Section, Professor J.C. Masterman, Chairman of the XX Committee, Lieutenant Colonel Thomas Argyll "Tar" Robertson, Section Chief B1-A, MI-5, James "Baldie" Taylor, and Colonel Benjamin H. "Monk" Dickinson, Chief of Counterintelligence, X-2, SHAEF.

Major General Sam Houston Blackwell was there as a member of the team that conducted the raid – not Troop Transport Command's Commanding Officer.

Major General William "Wild Bill" Donovan was also there. Initially he had not been invited by the members of the British intelligence community. When Major the Lady Jane Seaborn radioed from the PT boat during the exfil to confirm their arrival time and learned he was not on the list to be read into the debriefing, she ordered Seaborn House to contact the general at the Bradford Hotel and have him brought down to the TOC in one of the limousines.

When Bronc discovered Maj. Gen. Donovan was being frozen out of the debriefing he cancelled Lady Jane's instructions and had a TTC aircraft fly Wild Bill to Seaborn House.

All of the intelligence officers in attendance were entrusted with power that far exceeded their military rank. As a group they were seething with barely controlled rage, more distraught than angry. This was a night when the balance of the war in the European Theatre of Operations was balanced on a razor's edge. And they were powerless to do anything about it.

But they would be blamed if it went wrong.

No FORTITUDE SOUTH – no D-Day. No D-Day – the Russians might make a separate peace with the Nazis. No Russia in the war and the full might of the German Army fighting on the Eastern Front – approximately 200 divisions – could and probably would be rushed west to reinforce the Atlantic Wall.

The visiting officers had every reason to be alarmed. Not even the most optimistic of them believed the Allies could defeat an additional 200 German divisions guarding the beaches on D-Day – 3,000,000 enemy troops.

Not by launching an amphibious assault on France across the Channel.

Colonel John Randal had no knowledge of that. When the Rangers composing Recon Team/Raid Team filed in they found the atmosphere in the TOC was highly charged. Not in a good way.

Long-established protocol for Raiding Forces was a short debriefing held immediately upon return from every mission while the events of the operation were still fresh in the participants' minds. A debrief was for the people who went on the raid. Not armchair commando-type strap hangers no matter how important they might be.

Additional chairs were brought in to accommodate the visitors. They sat behind Recon Team/Raid Team. A seating arrangement that did nothing to appease some of those in attendance who were already not happy.

None of the out-of-town observers applauded or congratulated the Rangers on the success of their raid when they entered the room. Normally when a team came home from a mission it was SOP for everyone to make a point of welcoming them back. Not tonight. Most of the senior officer visitors stayed in their seats when the Raiding Forces' personnel present who had not gone on the raid stood up and greeted Recon Team/Raid Team home.

Lady Jane made note of who had remained seated. She was quietly furious. Those officers – one of whom was her godfather, would answer for their rude behavior at a later time and place of her choosing.

That was guaranteed.

Col. Randal debriefed. He could read a room. The undercurrent among the visitors was tense and decidedly unfriendly. In compliance with Raiding Forces' Rule #2: Keep it Short and Simple… he kept it short and simple.

There was a ripple of disapproval among the guests when Col. Randal reported prior to taking off, Beverly Blackwell "replaced" the USAAF glider pilot. Clearly the glider was a bone of contention, possibly it was because Beverly had exposed herself to capture or the fact a female flew the mission. The audience listened noncommittally as he described how she sheared the wings off by landing between two trees to slow down the overloaded Waco CG-4A, when it was coming in for landing at double the normal speed.

Then deliberately crashed the glider against Château du Val-Obscur's main entryway.

The visitors listened in silence as Col. Randal walked them through the Actions On the Objective. It was an impressive tour de force. However, they were not there to hear how the raid was conducted no matter how brilliantly executed it may have been.

Interest perked up somewhat when Col. Randal described towing the Waco CG-4A to the ERP. Made possible by the skid shoes specially fitted prior to the mission. Both developments were unexpected and there was no way to get around it… impressive feats of drop ahead planning.

Still, nothing Col. Randal said gave anyone reason to believe the XX System and Lt. Col. Robertson's stable of double agents had not been compromised. The Germans would eventually find the glider no matter how far the Rangers towed it from the chateau or how well hidden it might be… and that would be that.

A hush gradually came over the audience as Col. Randal described lowering the Waco CG4A over the cliff, down to the beach, then hauling it out into the channel with the PT boat. Possibly a first-ever in military history event – a glider towed by a boat. The officers respected the unorthodox creativity – but to what end? Canvas gliders float. With the sun coming up it would be seen bobbing in the Channel – a dead giveaway.

However, now the audience was dialed in on what Col. Randal was saying. The best minds in the United States Army Air Force, Royal Air Force and Combined Operations had been working frantically to find a solution to the glider problem from the moment it was learned Raiding Forces made an assault landing aboard a Waco CG-4A. Not one scenario any of them came up with envisioned something as ingenious as towing the glider out to sea by PT boat.

Col. Randal said, "Just short of a mile offshore, prepared explosives placed aboard the Waco prior to departure from RAF Hawkinge were detonated. Everything not blown up sank – without a trace.

"15th MGB Flotilla will have a gunboat on station over the site at daybreak to make sure there is nothing left."

It was like a bomb had detonated. The news electrified the room. The dignitaries from the intelligence services stood up and rushed Col. Randal, violating military decorum. The briefing was not concluded until he said it was. The exact phrase being, "This concludes my briefing…"

The Allies' top counterintelligence and deception planners in England gathered around peppering him with rapid-fire questions unable to constrain their excitement. They were talking over each other. Having heard what Col. Randal said, now everyone wanted to confirm what they heard was, in fact, what he said.

It sounded too good to be true.

And Col. Randal's opinion was sought on whether or not the Germans would be able to determine if a raid had taken place. A sea change in attitude among the VIPs – they were in a state of near delirium.

Not one had anticipated this turn of events.

Col. Randal summed up the raid again in rapid-fire bullet points. "The glider was silent and produced no radar signature larger than a seagull going in. Every Nazi and/or anyone else at the château except for von Reisen was eliminated. Incendiaries were placed on each building to simulate them being burned by aerial bombs. To ensure that perception, a bombload of over 3,000 No. 4 magnesium incendiary bomblets dropped by the RAF blanketed the main house, outbuildings and the grounds. The Ford V3000 used to haul the glider to the ERP was blown up utilizing 50 pounds of Composition C brought along specifically for that purpose – and it burned. The Waco CG-4A was towed out in the Channel and sunk with prepared demolitions, eliminating any trace it had ever landed on the target.

"I'll leave it to you gentlemen to evaluate how effective we were at sanitizing the operation."

Col. Randal was unaware of the additional bombing mission on the château Lt. Col. Bevan had ordered up – which was icing on the cake.

Anger dissipated in a flash as the atmosphere turned jubilant. There were some very important very relieved people standing around Col. Randal. It remained to be determined if von Reisen had managed to convince his superiors of his suspicions that some of the German spies in England had been turned. Nevertheless, now MI-5 had him in custody and would find that out soon enough and could take countermeasures.

If it chose, MI-5 might leak a story to the effect Major von Reisen had defected complete with a photo of him sitting in the Bradford Hotel holding up a copy of the London Times with the date on it. The Abwehr would be forced to discount everything he had ever reported on anything. Any suspicion he might have aroused about the German spy network in England controlled by MI-5's Section B1-A would be checkmated.

Or MI-5 could take a wait-and-see approach – though that was not likely.

Lt. Col. Bevan, Prof. Masterman and Lt. Col. Robertson, the top Allied deception experts, men entrusted with safeguarding one of the two or three most closely guarded secrets of the war – were already running through possibilities in their minds.

The good news. And it was *really* good news. Now they had options.

As the intelligence officers discussed the dramatic reversal of fortune, Colonel Benjamin H. "Monk" Dickinson pulled Col. Randal aside, "General Eisenhower ordered me to escort you to his suite in the Bradford Hotel immediately following your debriefing. He wants a verbal first-person account of the raid ASAP.

"I can tell you Ike's going to be pleased when he hears the outcome of your operation, Colonel. No one's been anticipating the result you laid out. Frankly, we feared the worst-case scenario – FORTITUDE SOUTH compromised."

This slip was a breach of security likely produced by euphoria – Col. Randal was not cleared to know OPERATION FORTITUDE SOUTH existed.

Lady Jane was standing beside Col. Randal so close that they were physically touching. With Happy heeled at her side, she said, "John shall be riding with me, Colonel… you may follow my limousine to the hotel if you wish."

Monk had not stood up to welcome Raid Team/Recon Team home – payback was starting posthaste.

Col. Dickinson said, "It will be my pleasure, Lady Seaborn."

He went in search of a landline to place a call to General Dwight D. Eisenhower's suite. "We're departing Seaborn House now, sir – I bring good news."

Gen. Eisenhower was up and fully dressed. He had been pacing his suite chain-smoking Camel cigarettes non-stop ever since Jim Taylor had departed.

Monk's phone call brought a flood of relief.

LIEUTENANT COLONEL THOMAS ARGYLL "TAR" ROBERTSON and 'Professor', as he preferred to be called, J.C. Masterman pulled Beverly Blackwell aside. She had been dreading this moment.

Prof. Masterman said, "Miss Blackwell, you serve as the Office of Strategic Services liaison to XX Committee. That makes you read in to secrets 99.9% of the officers in Allied Forces Europe are not cleared for. Taking part in a Commando raid behind enemy lines was a highly irresponsible act on your part. And a direct violation of your standing order not to do anything to expose yourself to risk of capture.

"You should thank your lucky stars we do not have you arrested for compromising security, young lady."

Lt. Col. Robertson said, "That would be deuced awkward considering if you were not an American we would be recommending you for the Victoria Cross."

Beverly said, "I knew how important the mission was. The pilot selected to fly the glider was the best available but nowhere near as experienced as me. Won't happen again."

Prof. Masterman said, "In the future, Miss Blackwell, should another mission this vital to the war effort come up and you feel your services enhance the probability of success… come see me straightaway. We shall work something out."

"I promise, J.C."

Beverly felt like she had dodged a bullet.

Before departing Seaborn house Colonel John Randal ordered, "Major Dance, give the men a chance to get cleaned up. Then bring them to the Bradford Hotel. Lady Jane has arranged a breakfast at 0700 hrs – make sure Brandy, Parker and Lieutenant Macomber are there."

"Yes, sir."

Prior to the mission Major the Lady Jane Seaborn had been driven to Seaborn house in the Bradford Hotel's Rolls Royce Phantom III reserved for her personal use when in residence. It would comfortably seat six – actually seven with the fold-down jump seat. When they departed Seaborn House those were Col. Randal, Lady Jane, Captain Billy Jack Jaxx, Beverly Blackwell and King.

Since Lieutenant Chase Starrett had missed his highly anticipated night out on the town with Beverly he was given the sixth seat as a poor substitute for not being able to go on his hot date. Being invited to ride with key players in Raiding Forces in the Rolls-Royce almost made up for it. The operative word being "almost."

The two had their date sitting up front with the chauffeur.

Lady Jane whispered in Col. Randal's ear, "Always looking after the welfare of your troops."

Col. Randal was wondering when he was going to need to have the talk with Lt. Starrett. Not that Beverly needed the big brother act. There was a pistol on or about her person at all times

Still…

COLONEL JOHN RANDAL CONDUCTED GENERAL DWIGHT D. Eisenhower's briefing in the Phone Room on the Penthouse floor of the Bradford Hotel. Present were Major General Sir Kenneth Strong, SHAEF G-2 Intelligence; Colonel Benjamin H. "Monk" Dickinson, X-2 SHAEF Counterintelligence; Lieutenant Colonel John Henry Bevan, LCS; and Commander Ian Fleming, RNVR, NID. Major General William "Wild Bill" Donovan, OSS, and Major General Sam Houston "Bronc" Blackwell, TTC, were also in the group.

No one else was on the short list to attend.

Major the Lady Jane Seaborn was sitting with Gen. Eisenhower. Before the briefing started she took the opportunity to discuss with him her idea of walling off his suite at the end of the hall and putting in a security desk with a phone. Her thought was an added layer of security would be prudent. There was a need to prevent visitors from being able to walk right up to his door unannounced.

She also offered to augment his protective detail with Raiding Forces' Vulnerable Points Wing personnel – elite British security operators. He accepted both suggestions. Gen. Eisenhower tried to achieve a mixed US/UK SHAEF headquarters staff.

As the commander of both countries' armies he was fully cognizant that coalition politics were always in the background of every decision he made. Particularly when it came to personnel assignments. One of the more tiresome aspects of coalition command.

"Lady Seaborn, you are certainly going out of your way to make my stay at the Bradford an agreeable experience."

"My pleasure, General."

"Is it true Prime Minister Churchill brings his senior staff to the hotel for lunch once a week?"

"It is – English roast beef carved at the table."

Col. Randal walked in with Lieutenant General "Geronimo" Joe McKoy, Captain Billy Jack Jaxx, Beverly and King. It was his briefing and Lady Jane's Phone Room so he had the prerogative to invite whoever he wanted.

Gen. Eisenhower said, "Is that Bronc's daughter?"

"Yes... she and the colonel are inseparable.

"Good thing you're not the jealous type."

Lady Jane laughed, “Oh, I am… always. Just not of Beverly. She is the beautiful little sister I never had, love her.

“Next to Beverly is Captain Jaxx – our most peerless small-unit leader and my great favorite. A true Texas gunfighter straight out of Hollywood central casting.

“General McKoy – our old lion… sets the tone for Raiding Forces, extraordinarily high standards.

“Then there is King… slightly harder to explain – Swiss mercenary.”

Gen. Eisenhower said, “Quite the colorful cast of characters.”

Col. Randal had not had time to change. He was wearing battledress to include sidearms. This gave the briefing an edgy ‘just back from the raid’ feel. He started step-by-step from alert to end of mission.

“Raiding Forces was ordered to Stand To…”

This was a briefing – different from a debriefing. The purpose was to inform those present how the operation was planned, organized and executed in detail.

A debrief, like the one at Seaborn House, was always conducted immediately upon return from a mission for the benefit of the people who went on it. The idea is for those on the ground actively engaged in carrying out their individual assignments to learn what had taken place with the other teams on the objective – while the raid was fresh in their minds.

The idea was to develop lessons learned.

A briefing is for people who did not go on the mission. Most of the top brass in the room this morning, composed mostly of career staff officers, had never been on a raid or planned one. Two of those present had not even been aware Raiding Forces existed before last night.

Special Operations were practically non-existent in the U.S. Army – had been since the Civil War. By this stage of the war the British Commandos' role as small-scale raiders had largely been discontinued by Combined Operations. The focus now was on larger brigade-sized units to be used as assault troops on D-Day – like the U.S. Marines out in the Pacific.

What those in attendance learned was fascinating. Especially the insight into the thought process of the mission commander, meaning Col. Randal, prior to and during the operation. Not something most of these officers had the opportunity to hear every day – if ever.

When Col. Randal concluded before asking the obligatory, "What are your questions?" he said, "For those who have not already met her, I'd like to introduce you to Beverly Blackwell – General Blackwell's daughter.

"Acting on her own initiative Beverly replaced the glider pilot assigned to fly the mission because of being the more experienced flyer. Without the daring landing she performed… intentionally shearing off the wings of the Waco CG-4A glider to put us down at the door of the château, this mission might have failed at the onset.

"The most time-sensitive phase of the raid was the movement to and assault on the main house. That had to take place lightning fast to achieve the element of surprise, creating shock and awe. Thanks to Beverly's incredible flying skill we could do it from the porch of the chateau– step off the glider and go – she knocked down the front door for us.

"Next is Lieutenant General "Geronimo" Joe McKoy – my military advisor. He has been with Raiding Forces almost from day one. General McKoy, a Medal of Honor recipient, was responsible for fighting his way to the third story of the château and clearing it of enemy personnel. That allowed our demolitions expert to gain access to the attic, while the house was still in the process of being secured.

"The intent was to burn the main house and outbuildings in advance of an RAF Lancaster salvoing a full load of incendiary bombs on the château to eliminate any signs we had ever been there.

"This is Captain Billy Jack Jaxx – we call him Jack Cool. He was responsible for taking down the German troops housed in what turned out to be one of the biggest barns anyone has ever seen. The toughest objective on the raid.

"Captain Jaxx led a team of three Rangers which was later reinforced by a second team of three. Realizing circumstances were not favorable to his being able to execute the assignment with so few troops – at the very point of making entry, mere seconds before going in, he paused the breach in order to improvise a new plan.

"As a result of Captain Jaxx's quick thinking, the barn was destroyed. The Nazis quartered in it were eliminated. Important to note… had a single German soldier escaped the raid would have been deemed a failure.

"At the main house on the initial entry with a firefight in progress, Mr. King led the assault, conducted an on-scene field interrogation of a prisoner, obtained intel on our target's location, then tracked down and captured our target – von Reisen.

"Mr. King was all over the place tonight… always where needed.

"During the exfil after Raid Team went down the rappel lines at the ERP, Mr. King removed the ropes and pitons at the top of the cliff erasing the last signs we had ever been there. Then he free-climbed down to the beach – a one-man army.

"Last, not wanting to be left behind, Lady Jane stowed away on the PT boat dispatched to extract Raid Team. Without informing anyone of her intentions she then went ashore with the OSS Maritime Unit's Special Warfare Operators. Not content to remain on the beach Lady Jane scaled a nearly 100-foot cliff to inspect the ERP to ensure it had been laid in to her personal satisfaction.

"These people are representative of the type of men and women you have serving in General Donovan's Operational Group Branch, Raiding Forces – what are your questions, gentlemen?"

This time the people in the room did stand up and applaud.

LIEUTENANT GENERAL "GERONIMO" JOE MCKOY SAID, "PRETTY smart a' you John."

"What was?"

"Describin' Raidin' Forces as OSS Operational Group Branch givin' Wild Bill a plug."

"Well that's who we are…at least on paper."

"You're gettin' pretty good at the art a' military politickin'."

AS THE PRIVATE BREAKFAST FOR RAID TEAM WAS WINDING down, Major the Lady Jane Seaborn slipped out and phoned General Dwight D. Eisenhower's suite. He had requested permission to visit the Rangers after their meal. Gen. Eisenhower may not have ever commanded as much as a platoon in combat, but he knew a thing or two about leadership.

Raiding Forces' personnel were not impressed with rank for rank's sake. They were used to having Vice Admiral Sir Randolph "Razor" Ransom, VC, KCB, DSO, OBE, DSC, RN officing in the TOC on Castelrozzo. And Lieutenant General "Geronimo" Joe McKoy was a member of the unit in good standing. He had gone on more operations than nearly anyone.

Nevertheless, having the Supreme Allied Commander drop in was well received.

The general made a point of working the room. Like a politician. Which some of his longtime associates, like Lieutenant General George S. Patton, suspected he was becoming. A judgment possibly motivated in part by jealousy at his stratospheric rise at the tail end of what could only be described as a mediocre army career. He had bypassed over 30 U.S. Army generals senior to him – some of whom were now on his staff or would be commanding divisions under his command.

No one had foreseen that… especially Ike.

Gen. Eisenhower spoke to everyone – took his time and did not get in a hurry.

When he came to Col. Randal he said, "Bronc tells me you'll be replacing Jim Gavin as our Airborne Advisor."

Col. Randal said, "That's what he tells me too, sir."

"Look forward to working with you Colonel – vertical envelopment constitutes a major element of the D-Day plan."

As he turned to go, Gen. Eisenhower said, "We can never discuss your mission publicly so awards pose a problem. However, there is a new valor decoration in the works that will be authorized in the next month or so – the Bronze Star. It can be backdated to 7 December 41. The day Pearl Harbor was attacked.

"When the decoration is approved I want Bronze Stars awarded to every man and woman who went on the operation last night. Submit a list of those you feel merit a higher decoration. I'll personally approve them – we just can't risk a public ceremony."

"Yes, sir."

"There is this other matter I would like to discuss with you privately, Colonel..."

GENERAL DWIGHT D. EISENHOWER WAS RETURNING TO HIS suite on the Penthouse Floor when he ran into Major General Sam Houston "Bronc" Blackwell walking through the lobby of the hotel.

"Ride up with me Bronc?"

Maj. Gen. Blackwell had not been going upstairs but he said, "Yes sir, Ike."

When the doors on the private elevator to the Penthouse Floor closed Gen. Eisenhower said, "You have a very beautiful and very brave daughter, Bronc – how did she become a pilot?"

"Beverly was flying before she could drive a car, Ike. Less chance of running into something on the ranch. Didn't want her crashing into one of our oil wells."

"I have been informed you are quite close to Colonel Randal. I'm still trying to wrap my mind around how he managed to pull this operation off. No one believed it possible. My people advised me once the glider landed, the mission was compromised.

"Was it a fluke?"

Maj. Gen. Blackwell pulled a folded piece of paper out of the inside pocket of his Class A uniform blouse and handed it to Gen. Eisenhower.

```
Rules for Raiding
Rule #1: The first rule is there ain't no rules
Rule #2: Keep it short and simple
Rule #3: It never hurts to cheat
Rule #4: Right man, right job
Rule #5: Plan missions backward (know how to get
         home)
Rule #6: It's good to have a Plan B
```
~~Rule #7: Expect the unexpected.~~ INACTIVE

"Take a look at Number 5 – that sound like a fluke to you, Ike?"

"No it doesn't – what are these?

"Randal's standing orders – carry a copy in my pocket. Every officer and NCO in Troop Transport Command has one. I'd claim authorship except Beverly would murder me if I did."

"So, you are of the opinion Randal is that capable?"

"Check out Rule #4: Right man, right job – that's what I believe, General."

"High praise – mind if I keep this?"

It was not really a question.

MAJOR THE LADY JANE SEABORN WAS SITTING IN THE Raiding Forces' VIP section of the lobby in the Bradford Hotel with her godfather, Lieutenant Colonel John Henry Bevan. They had more or less patched up their differences. However, Lady Jane was still less than pleased about the way he treated Colonel John Randal in days past.

She was defensive about him – very.

Lt. Col. Bevan said, "Your boyfriend came to town at my request for Christmas leave. Primarily because I wanted to spend the holidays with you and knew you would not come alone. Straightaway he managed to earn the regard of some of the most influential people in Allied Forces."

"How is John doing with you, Uncle?"

"As of the debrief this morning I am making my way to the head of the queue as Randal's biggest fan. While you are not cleared for the details about the why of the raid I believe it is safe for me to say I regard it as one of, if not *the* most unparalleled small-unit actions of the war. A masterpiece of planning, split-second timing, flawless execution and extraordinary teamwork – brilliant leadership.

"No one believed such a mission possible – absolutely no one."

Lady Jane laughed, "I have never heard you speak about anyone in such glowing terms."

Lt. Col. Bevan said, "Your colonel snatched victory from the jaws of defeat. At least what those of us in the intelligence community perceived as a potential reversal of fortune of biblical proportions. It is not clear what our next move would have been had not Randal stepped in as he did.

"I should have trusted your judgement, Jane."

"Then we have your blessing?"

"You do now."

MAJOR GENERAL WILLIAM "WILD BILL" DONOVAN SPIED Lieutenant Colonel John Henry Bevan and Major the Lady Jane Seaborn sitting together in the VIP section. He walked over to where the two were having a conversation. Wild Bill could not help noticing Lady Jane seemed particularly vivacious today, which was worth noting because she was almost always smiling. Had she received good news?

If so, he was about to rain on her parade.

"May I have a word with you in private, Lady Jane?"

Maj. Gen. Donovan was well aware of Lt. Col. Bevan's low opinion of U.S. Army officers – particularly OSS. Only recently had the Chief of Deception bowed to pressure and allowed an American to be attached to the London Controlling Section as liaison to SHAEF – Lt. Col. William H Baumer.

There were two reasons Lt. Col. Bevan had accepted Lt. Col. Baumer…LCS had to have an American onboard, and he was not OSS.

What Maj. Gen. Donovan wanted to discuss with Lady Jane was classified, but nothing Lt. Col. Bevan was not cleared to hear. He could have had the conversation with her godfather present. However, providing her this piece of intelligence in private was Wild Bill's chance to put a stick in the Chief of Deception's eye by excluding him.

And he took it.

After they moved over to a more private section of the VIP area Maj. Gen. Donovan said, "What I'm about to tell you is based on signals intelligence classified far above any clearance you have. You can reveal parts of what we're about to discuss but not that it's SIGINT."

Lady Jane said, "Understood."

Maj. Gen. Donovan said, "The purpose of our having this conversation is for you to begin making preparations for a future event – I'm giving you a heads up."

Not quite sure what the expression meant, Lady Jane said, "Well, you certainly have my attention, General."

Maj. Gen. Donovan said, "In the next few weeks the Luftwaffe is going to launch OPERATION STEINBOCK – named after the Alpine Ibex for some reason. A second Blitz is about to commence aimed at southern England to include London."

Lady Jane said, "That is dreadful!"

She knew in 1940-1941 period during the eight months the Blitz lasted, some 30,000 plus Londoners had been killed and approximately another 50,000 more were seriously wounded. Maj. Gen. Donovan's news could hardly have been worse.

"Do you understand why I'm telling you this?"

"I do – consider arrangements underway, General."

Maj. Gen. Donovan said, "Hate to be the bearer of bad news, especially on a day when celebrations are in order. Speaks well of you to have landed ashore and scaled that cliff, Lady Jane… if a bit reckless.

"Try to stay on the boat in the future. In fact, do me a personal favor – don't even get on the boat."

Wishing to deflect the direction the conversation was going Lady Jane said, "I appreciate the 'heads up" – still not sure what the Americanism meant, exactly. But she got the idea.

Maj. Gen. Donovan said, "The only sure thing in this war is it never stands still – not for a second."

JAMES "BALDIE" TAYLOR CAME OVER TO WHERE COLONEL John Randal was sitting with Beverly Blackwell. He was carrying a thin folder. Col. Randal had dispatched him on a mission and now he was reporting back.

Since Beverly was the liaison officer from OSS to the XX Committee and therefore read in on highly classified information Jim did not question if she should be included in the conversation. Not that it mattered nothing in the file mentioned MI-5, OSS or XX Committee.

Jim said, "You asked about MI-9 Escape and Evasion. I thought you might like to start with its chain of command. Knowing how it's structured might be constructive for any interest you might have in the organization.

"Currently MI-9 Escape and Evasion's total strength across all ranks is approximately 100 personnel. The agency is almost an afterthought.

Col. Randal studied the single typed page in the file.

OVERVIEW
MI-9 (Military Intelligence, Section 9)
Created: December 1939

MISSION: To assist Allied personnel to evade capture when cut off behind enemy lines, to facilitate the escape of those held as prisoners of war, and to train Allied aircrew and other personnel in escape and evasion techniques.

PARENT ORGANIZATION: *Directorate of Military Intelligence (DMI)* under the War Office

CHAIN OF COMMAND
Director of Military Intelligence (DMI)
Major General Sir Stewart Menzies (Chief SIS, MI-6)
Brigadier Norman H. Crockatt (Director MI-9)

COORDINATION LINKS
MI-6
Special Operations Executive
RAF Directorate of Air Intelligence (DAI)

Col. Randal said, "That's it?"

Jim said, "I am wired into every major intelligence agency except MI-9. It's a bastard outfit – underfunded, understaffed and not respected within the intelligence establishment. People only pay Escape & Evasion lip service."

Col. Randal glanced over to where Lieutenant General "Geronimo" Joe McKoy was sitting with Major General Sam Houston "Bronc" Blackwell and Brandy Seaborn. Lady Jane was briefing them about her plans for the hotel.

He made eye contact.

Lady Jane was saying, "I want to put in an Olympic-sized pool for my Marines to swim laps in."

As Lt. Gen. McKoy was standing up to go talk to Col. Randal he said, “Billy Jack and I are of the opinion we could use a pistol range down there, Lady Jane.”

Lady Jane laughed, “I have that on my list.”

Lt. Gen. McKoy excused himself, strolled over and pulled up a chair. Col. Randal handed him the folder. “Notice anything missing, General?”

Lt. Gen. McKoy studied the single sheet of paper. “Yeah, I do, John.”

“What might that be?”

“No mention of OSS.”

Jim shook his head… there was no way to get one by the old Arizona Ranger.

Col. Randal said, “Why is that, Jim?”

“MI-9 may be small, understaffed and underfunded but like all the other intelligence services – it’s very territorial. We British own Escape & Evasion – part of our monopoly on intelligence. And we intend to keep it that way enough so as to turn down money and offers of help if it comes with the caveat of U.S. participation at the decision-making level.”

Col. Randal said, “Relax, Jim I’m not going to ask you to get involved with MI-9 any more than to seek your advice from time to time.”

Jim said, “Thanks, Colonel. That is a relief. I hate my job. If I could get out of the commitments I have already made and go back to cruising the Great Sand Sea in a gun jeep I would in a heartbeat. Big mistake, me taking on these liaison duties. I need to be going on operations with you.”

Col. Randal said, “Glad to have you any time but you’re a lot more valuable doing what you’re doing.”

“Appreciate you saying that, Colonel… I do not feel great about the work.”

AFTER JAMES “BALDIE” TAYLOR DEPARTED, LIEUTENANT General “Geronimo” Joe McKoy said, “You takin’ a look at a new project, John?”

“I am.”

“Anythin’ I can do to help?”

“Maybe – if we can work it in with your other responsibilities.”

"I spent quite a bit a' time studyin' Veronica's E&E operation. Even sailed with 'March or Die' Mikkalis aboard the *Santa Claus* to bring out a sailor washed up on a island from a ship that got sunk."

Col. Randal said, "I wasn't aware of that."

Lt. Gen. McKoy said, "Escape's a good mission, John. More to the job than meets the eye. Whatever you need you can count on me down to the ground."

Col. Randal said, "I know that, General. For now it's best we act like we never had this conversation. Sometimes our friends can be foes."

Lt. Gen. McKoy said, "Roger that – good talk."

MAJOR THE LADY JANE SEABORN WENT IN SEARCH OF MAJOR General Sam Houston "Bronc" Blackwell. She found him having coffee with Brandy Seaborn – she was drinking tea.

Lady Jane said, "Would you care to have a London-based Troop Transport Command Headquarters here in the hotel, General?"

Maj. Gen. Blackwell looked up, surprised, "Hell yes!"

He had viewed a number of potential locations for his headquarters but with the war on, space in the Westminster District was at a premium – practically nonexistent. Nothing offered TTC was even remotely satisfactory.

Brandy studied Lady Jane closely. She knew her cousin. What brought this about?

Lady Jane said, "Do not ask me questions I am not at liberty to answer, Bronc – let's simply work out the details."

Maj. Gen. Blackwell said, "I won't ask you anything except how and when."

Lady Jane said, "Several of the hotels in the Westminster District house military and government agencies. The Metropole has the Air Ministry. The Savoy and Dorchester have subterranean suites for diplomatic personnel.

"The Bradford has six floors underground. We are only using one as a bomb shelter and now sharing it with Raiding Forces for our Rear HQ as well. The other five floors have never been built out.

"If you can arrange for the construction we can give TTC its own floor – you shall have the most exclusive address of any government agency in London.

Maj. Gen. Blackwell said, "Engineer support is not a problem. Now tell me the part you're not telling me without getting into the details I promised not to ask. Helps to be able to see over the hill so I can make plans."

Lady Jane said, "There are indications the Luftwaffe is preparing another aerial attack on London like the 1940-41 Blitz. In anticipation of that taking place, I want to move Raiding Forces Rear HQ to its own private floor and expand the bomb shelter for the guests – increase its amenities.

"You can have a floor for Troop Transport Command. I am thinking we shall require a Medical aid post and at least one floor needs to be converted to bachelor quarters for Raiding Forces and your duty personnel on 24-hour rotation. And for both our units' people to stay in when they are in town for business or on a weekend pass.

"I want to turn one level into a subterranean ballroom."

Maj. Gen. Blackwell said, "I'll have Army Engineers in this afternoon. What kind of time frame are we looking at for buildout, Lady Jane?"

"Three weeks."

Maj. Gen. Blackwell said, "For my own TTC headquarters floor I'll have work crews here 24-7 till it's done – handle the whole project. We might not get everything completed in that time. You may have to do some of the finish out of your nightclub a little later."

Lady Jane said, "The Bradford shall reimburse the Army for the expense of the club construction and there shall not be any charge for TTC's rent."

Maj. Gen. Blackwell said, "Not a chance, Lady Jane. Consider it a tradeoff for allowing TTC the use of your hotel. You have no idea how much I like the idea – thank you for letting me be a part of it."

Brandy said, "What do you plan to call the ballroom, Jane?"

Lady Jane laughed, "Secrets."

CAPTAIN BILLY JACK JAXX, MANDY PAIGE AND BEVERLY Blackwell were standing at the bar in the Bradford Hotel. It was packed. As more and more American troops were arriving for the buildup to D-Day, their commanding officers were discovering the Bradford to be a social Mecca. A lot of seeing and being seen, connections cultivated, military and political business transacted in a convivial atmosphere.

A stunning girl with razored cheekbones and a magnificent mane of feathered black hair stopped by to speak to Mandy and Beverly.

Mandy said, "Jack, allow me to introduce you to Sloan Marlow."

Capt. Jaxx said, "Hi."

Studying him like she was sizing up her prey, Sloan said, "I have seen you in the hotel… what do you do, Jack?"

Capt. Jaxx said, "I'm OSS, but don't tell anybody – that's classified."

Mandy and Beverly froze.

Sloan produced a card out of her shoulder bag, took out a pen, struck something out then wrote on it.

"I have always wanted to meet a real-life secret agent – ring me if you can ever tear yourself away from these two."

Then she was gone.

Capt. Jaxx said, "You girls make good wingmen. We need to do this more."

Beverly said, "Jack… you idiot."

Mandy said, "Sloan's working the bar tonight."

Capt. Jaxx said, "She's a hooker?"

Mandy said, "Internal Security… flirtation agent. Flags breaches of security by men who divulge sensitive information – to impress her. Around MI-5, Sloan's known as S&M because it's said she makes men submit. She's quite the legend."

Beverly said, "Disclosing you're OSS – you just stepped in her honey trap."

Capt. Jaxx said, "You're kidding."

Mandy was studying Sloan's card, "Doubt you have much to be concerned about. She scratched out the dedicated MI-5 number set up for targets to call. This is her private line."

Beverly said, "Don't do it, Jack."

Capt. Jaxx said, "I'm not OSS, at least I don't think I am. We just pull missions for General Donovan – it was a joke."

Mandy said, "Fairly sure Sloan knows that."

9

NOT IN KANSAS ANYMORE

COLONEL JOHN RANDAL WAS SITTING ON A COUCH IN THE VIP Section of the Bradford Hotel with Brandy Seaborn. She had her arm draped across his shoulder. They were enjoying the chance to spend time together. It had been a while since the two of them had the opportunity to talk.

They were watching Major the Lady Jane Seaborn standing in the lobby with Happy heeled at her side. She was in conversation with Major General Sam Houston "Bronc" Blackwell and two generals neither of whom Col. Randal nor Brandy had ever seen before. The group was joined by the Bradford Hotel manager and a civilian with what looked like a large roll of building plans under one arm.

Col. Randal said, "Do you know those people?"

Brandy said, "I know Jane, Sam, the manager – and Happy."

"What do you think they're doing?"

"Jane is planning to remodel the six underground floors of the hotel that have never been built out."

"Really… there's that many floors down there?"

"Even back when the Bradford was being built before the turn of the century space in the Westminster District was in such short supply basement floors were laid to use for expansion at some later date in the event the space was ever needed."

Col. Randal said, "And it is now?"

Brandy said, "Jane is planning to move Raiding Forces' Rear to its own separate floor with a pistol range and an Olympic-sized swimming pool for Rocky to conduct her swimming training. She's giving Sam one floor for his London TTC Headquarters – he is wildly excited at the prospect. There will be a level consisting of quarters for Raiding Forces and TTC duty personnel.

"And Jane wants a subterranean ballroom where people can dance the night away while bombs rain down."

Col. Randal made eye contact with James "Baldie" Taylor sitting with Lieutenant Colonel Thomas Argyll "Tar" Robertson. Jim came over. "Do you know those generals talking to Lady Jane?"

"Major General Cecil R. Moore, the Chief Engineer, U.S. European Theatre of Operations, and Brigadier General James J. O'Connor, Commanding Officer, Engineer Command Europe. Is there something going on I need to be aware of, Colonel?"

"Jane's decided to do a little remodeling."

"Must be some project. Those are the two top U.S. Army Engineers in England."

Col. Randal said, "There's five basement floors below the hotel – she's planning on building 'em out."

A lieutenant general entered the hotel wearing a highly-polished helmet liner with three shiny stars on the front and three on the back so there could be no mistaking who he was, coming or going. Six stars on his headgear – something not even the flamboyant commander of the phantom First U.S. Army Group (FUSAG), Lieutenant General George S. Patton, had the nerve to do.

The general walked over and spoke to Lady Jane.

Col. Randal said, "Who might that be, Jim?"

"Lieutenant General J.C.H. Lee. His troops say the initials stand for "Jesus Christ Himself" – commands the U.S. Services of Supply. His magnificence has his own private train."

Col. Randal said, "Really?"

Jim said, "Churchill does not have a private train. Eisenhower does not have a private train. My guess is McArthur out in Australia does not have a private train. Get the picture?"

Col. Randal said, "I do."

Brandy laughed, "General Lee's helmet could use additional stars on the sides. One would not wish for anybody to fail to recognize his exalted rank from any direction. Possibly on top as well.

"Do not tell Jane I said that or the next thing we know she shall be presenting J.C.H. with one."

Col. Randal wondered, "What was Lt. Gen. Lee doing here?"

As if reading his mind Jim said, "Building out five sub-level floors will require a substantial amount of construction materials. Those are rationed. U.S. Services of Supply controls them – looks like Lady Jane has the problem solved."

Actually Bronc had swung into action on the building project with his usual take-no-prisoners style. Lt. Gen. Lee may have had a private train, but did he have an airplane? If not there was likely one in his future."

Lady Jane glanced across the lobby at Col. Randal and winked.

COLONEL JOHN RANDAL AND BEVERLY BLACKWELL WERE IN the VIP area. She was just back from her OSS/MI-5 liaison duties at the weekly Thursday morning meeting of the XX Committee. Since Major the Lady Jane Seaborn had her driven to the Security Service in a hotel limousine that waited at the curb until the Double Cross conference was over to drive her back to Bradford, Beverly's arrival and departure at MI-5 always made a splash.

No one else in the meeting had a limo parked outside.

Beverly's daring performance on the raid to capture Major Hanns von Reisen was known to the officers of Twenty though not spoken of in her presence. She no longer had to prove herself to anyone. Nevertheless, she was sticking strictly to Lady Jane's game plan: beautifully tailored uniform, hair in a severe French twist, walk in right to the minute the meeting was to start, leave immediately afterwards – no small talk.

Col. Randal had advised her to use her looks to her advantage as a weapon – she knew how to do that.

Beverly had studied art and drama at the University of Texas and knew how play a role. Which is what she felt like she was doing every time she sat in the XX Committee meetings – so highly classified there were armed guards at the door. She was a Tri-Delta party girl. How did this happen? The line from the hit musical *The Wizard of Oz,* "We're not in Kansas anymore," came to mind every Thursday when she walked in.

That said, something was happening Beverly had not anticipated. The more Double Cross meetings she attended, the easier it was for her to understand the purpose of the exercise. Deceiving the Nazis was turning out not to be as complicated as those who practiced the art would have people believe. All the XX Committee was doing was determining what fiction to disseminate next.

Now back at the Bradford she was entertaining Col. Randal with anecdotes from the meeting she was not supposed to tell anyone.

Beverly said, "Tar developed intel that a certain German counter-intelligence agent was attempting to infiltrate a Resistance network somewhere in France. The Nazi was out of MI-5's reach. So Tommy sent him a package containing 1,000 pounds Sterling with a thank-you note for his excellent work as a British double agent – then made sure the Abwehr intercepted it."

Col. Randal said, "Why would Tar do that?"

"To trick the Nazis into shooting him. MI-5 couldn't do it – no retribution against the Resistance members either."

Col. Randal said, "Nice."

Beverly laughed, "Tommy's got some moves."

"Sounds like."

"Ian Fleming managed to land himself in a little hot water recently."

Col. Randal said, "What's new about that?"

Beverly said, "Since he speaks fluent German, the Naval Intelligence Division asked him to interrogate two captured *U-Boatwaffe* officers to find out how their U-boats avoided minefields. So Ian came up with a plan. Instead of breaking out a rubber hose to work them over with he brought the Nazis here to the Bradford for cocktails. The idea was to get the two drunk, then pump them for the details."

Col. Randal said, "How'd that work out?"

Beverly laughed, "The waiters overheard them speaking German and called the police."

Col. Randal said, "Typical Fleming."

Beverly said, "I have a follow-up to the carrier pigeon story we've talked about. As you know, civilian pigeon fanciers donate their birds to the National Pigeon Service – a civilian organization formed at the start of the war by MI-5. Each of the birds is issued its own individual serial number.

"They're in the Army, but they still fly back to their old homes. The owners have to bring the birds to PGS immediately when they return from a mission. And promise not to read the messages they're carrying."

Col. Randal said, "I have a hard time believing pigeons are a reliable means of communication."

Beverly said, "Agreed, but they're in big demand. Every RAF bomber carries two birds so if the plane goes down and the radio's damaged they can be released by the crew with the coordinates of their location. Coastal Command relies on pigeons too since radio silence is common practice when its boats are at sea. SOE uses the birds for one-way communications France to England from the resistance groups it supports."

Col. Randal said, "I've heard there's problems with that program."

Beverly laughed, "SOE dropped 16,000 birds to the French Resistance. They ate most of 'em. Oh, well.

"One pigeon that had been captured by the Germans returned to England. The note in the capsule attached to its leg read, "You can have your bird back. We have enough food."

Col. Randal said, "Did you do any actual work at your meeting today?"

Beverly laughed, "Not really, Johnny. Everyone was so excited about the success of our raid it was basically a celebration. Still no one's filled me in yet on why the mission was so important – big time classified."

Col. Randal said, "You ever find out I want to know."

Beverly said, "On a more pressing matter. I'm a little worried about Jack. We may have a problem."

"Why might that be?"

"He's being stalked by a female MI-5 maneater the staff at Five call S&M."

"Really?"

She told Col. Randal what took place in the bar.

He had a hard time trying not to laugh and would have, except Beverly was telling the story with a straight face, no laugh, no smile – dead serious.

Col. Randal wondered, "Who's Sloan Marlow?"

CAPTAIN ROY KIDD, CAPTAIN MIKE "MAD DOG" REUPART, MC, Chief Warrant Officer Hank Rawlston and Master Sergeant Mack Beckwith arrived at the hotel. They had just flown in from Castelrozzo. Colonel John Randal was getting his key people assembled. The new arrivals, with the exception of Capt. Kidd, would be moving on to Seaborn House.

A major reorganization of Raiding Forces Europe was in the works. OSS Operational Group Branch (England) and 575th Ranger Regiment – formerly the 575th Parachute Infantry Regiment (-) (Separate)(Special) aka "Rangers" needed to be amalgamated into it. The plan was to form a SHAEF-level, small-scale, combined operations, raiding task force capable of carrying out strategic missions – some of which were deceptions.

One of the deceptions was that there was a 575th Parachute Infantry Regiment(-) (Separate) (Special) – meaning a single battalion 1/575 Abn, now redesignated the 575th Ranger Regiment. There were not enough troops in Raiding Forces (Europe) for there to be a Ranger or any other kind of regiment. The unit was semi-notional – one understrength company which was only going to exist as a regiment on paper.

Raiding Forces was being formed into teams.

Col. Randal had orders from Major General William "Wild Bill" Donovan to keep Operational Group Branch a U.S. organization as much as possible. A rotation was in progress transferring British personnel to Castelrozzo and the U.S. personnel on the island to Seaborn House. From inception Raiding Forces had been continually evolving to adapt to changing operational demands in different theatres. While it was not clear at this point exactly what the new TO&E would look like change was coming. The troops were used to it.

And they were ready.

Col. Randal said, “Beverly, see if you can locate Major Dance. Have him link up with his people. We’ll be in the Tea Room. These men look like they could use a meal.”

“I’m on it, Johnny.”

Lieutenant General “Geronimo” Joe McKoy spotted the group of arrivals when it came in. He walked over to welcome them. Raiding Forces was that kind of outfit – glad to see each other.

Col. Randal pulled Capt. Kidd aside for a word as they were moving toward the Tea Room, “Now that you’re here Roy, we need a CARD GAME set up ASAP – get with Lady Jane.”

“Yes, sir.”

Captain Billy Jack Jaxx was talking to Major the Lady Jane Seaborn by the concierge’s desk. They both stopped what they were doing and came to greet everyone. Happy was dancing around demanding attention from his old friends.

Col. Randal said, “Captain Kidd’s going to need a place to stay for the next couple of days.”

“He can bunk in with me, sir,” Capt. Jaxx said.

Lady Jane said, “Perfect – the Penthouse Floor is running out of space. I would not want to put Roy somewhere else in the hotel. We shall work out a permanent place for him.”

Col. Randal said, “I was telling Captain Kidd we haven’t had a CARD GAME in a while.”

CARD GAME was classified. Only the members knew they did not actually play cards.

Lady Jane said, “I shall have Mandy organize one in our suite for early this evening.”

King and Captain Pamala Plum-Martin stepped off the private elevator. They spotted the group and immediately changed directions to come say hello.

Major Jack Dance and Beverly arrived. The former commander of the 10th Ranger Battalion was not sure why Col. Randal had described the men transferring in from Castelrozzo to Beverly as “his people.”

He had already informed Col. Randal of his preference to remain in the Aegean.

CAPTAIN BILLY JACK JAXX ARRIVED ON THE PENTHOUSE FLOOR for CARD GAME. The Vulnerable Points Wing security operator sitting at the desk guarding the private entry to the hall leading to the section that housed Major the Lady Jane Seaborn's family, friends and Raiding Forces' officers, grinned when he saw him.

"There was a real scorcher up here a few minutes ago looking for you, Captain."

One of the responsibilities of the Vulnerable Points Wing (VPW) security personnel on the Penthouse Floor was to make sure Jack Cool's girlfriends did not run into each other coming and going.

"Who?"

"Never saw this one before, sir. Said you would find her in the bar."

"That's it?"

"Asked me to inform you she is not on duty tonight."

COLONEL JOHN RANDAL AND MAJOR THE LADY JANE SEABORN were the last to arrive for CARD GAME. Major General William "Wild Bill" Donovan was with them at Col. Randal's invitation. He had never sat in on one of the CARD GAME/LONG NECK meetings. Waiting were Lieutenant General "Geronimo" Joe McKoy, Captain Billy Jack Jaxx, Captain Roy Kidd, Mandy Paige, Beverly Blackwell, Waldo Treywick and Master Sergeant Mack Beckwith.

Col. Randal said, "I'm sure you all have other things you'd like to do this evening so we'll keep this brief. One administrative announcement – General Donovan is not here. He did not attend this meeting. If you believe you saw him… you didn't."

Maj. Gen. Donovan had authorized Raiding Forces to carry out LONG NECK then informed Col. Randal he never wanted to hear about the diamond interdiction program again. It was not, he claimed, an OSS operation. However, Maj. Gen. Donovan was unable to resist the opportunity to be brought up to speed on how a program he was *not* interested in was progressing.

Col. Randal had mentioned there was going to be a classified briefing the general might like to attend, or maybe not, since it was about an ongoing Raiding Forces' operation code name LONG NECK.

Maj. Gen. Donovan jumped at the invitation. He seemed to be aware of what LONG NECK stood for. Which was somewhat suspicious considering the name had been changed twice from the time he had given the assignment to Col. Randal. Long after he denied any OSS connection to the mission.

Col. Randal said, "Before Lady Jane and I departed Castelrozzo for London, General McKoy and I decided he and Mr. Treywick would accompany our party. Then after Christmas, they would fly to the Congo to inspect Frank's team operating against Nazi diamond buyers in the colony.

That plan is still green-lighted. However, there's been a change that'll affect LONG NECK'S TO&E. Captain Butterfield's services are required at Seaborn House. We'll need a replacement to take over his duties as gun jeep patrol commander interdicting smuggler's caravans out of Cairo.

"Suggestions?"

Lt. Gen. McKoy said, "Waldo could handle that pretty easy."

Lady Jane said, "Mr. Treywick's presence is required here. He has a classified assignment that takes precedence over his participation in LONG NECK – so secret he does not even know what it is."

Which might not be true as far as taking precedence over his involvement in LONG NECK was concerned. Lady Jane, or for that matter no one, to include Col. Randal, had any idea *why* Raiding Forces was conducting an off-the-books campaign to stop diamond smuggling.

CARD GAME would have been incredulous to learn LONG NECK was of more strategic importance to the war effort than D-Day – they would not have believed it.

Strange considering no Allied military or intelligence organization was actively/ knowingly on record supporting LONG NECK. It was a stand-alone Raiding Forces' operation. Only the handful of people in the Phone Room knew the details of what they were involved with. And to be clear, not even CARD GAME understood the purpose of the exercise.

Mandy said, "Does whoever we select need to be read in on LONG NECK?"

Col. Randal said, "Partially… but they don't have to be a voting member of CARD GAME – Preston's not."

Capt. Jaxx said, "I'd nominate Chase Starrett but I need him."

Col. Randal said, "Sergeant Major, how would you feel about taking over Captain Butterfield's assignment?"

MSgt. Beckwith said, "I don't know, sir. Independent command. Never done anything like that, Colonel – not having anybody to report to."

Col. Randal said, "Somebody has to keep General McKoy's dancer friends at the Kit-Kat Club company while he's stationed here in London."

Lt. Gen. McKoy said, "Yeah, Right Man, Right Job – I'll give you a few names, Mack. First you need to fly down to the Congo with me n' Waldo. See Frank's operation up close and personal. We'll make a good team."

MSgt. Beckwith said, "If you say so, General."

Col. Randal said, "That's settled then – anything else to discuss?"

Lt. Gen. McKoy said, "Yeah, I do... Waldo's gonna be travelin' back n' forth to Cairo pretty regular. He needs to keep up appearances with the Three. Mandy, that gonna pose any problem for your Double Cross work with Rocky?"

Apparently, Lt. Gen. McKoy knew more about what Rikke Runborg was doing than MI-5 was aware of.

Mandy said, "Nothing we shall not be able to work around, General."

Capt. Kidd said, "So, I should consider this trip to London a permanent change of duty station, sir?"

Col. Randal said, "Affirmative... at least until the invasion."

Lady Jane said, "You need to send for the pistol collection you have stockpiled, Roy. I am in need of German and Italian handguns to use as gifts for the armchair commandos we have to deal with locally. Most shall never get anywhere near a live German combatant but would dearly love a war souvenir."

Capt. Kidd said, "Not a problem, Lady Jane. Anticipating how you operate I brought a small arsenal with me. I can have the rest flown in with the incoming contingents of troops. You can be generous.

"We have plenty of pocket pistols – mostly Italian Berettas. "

Lady Jane said, "Perfect."

Col. Randal said, "If there's nothing else people... enjoy your evening."

COLONEL JOHN RANDAL WALKED MAJOR GENERAL WILLIAM "Wild Bill" Donovan back to his suite.

Col. Randal said, "I understand the USAAF is requesting U.S. involvement in Escape & Evasion for its downed aircrew."

Maj. Gen. Donovan said, "That is correct. Currently MI-9 handles Escape out of Room 900 – Section 9d run by a Major Airey Neave. It is also the Escape training establishment – "Intelligence School 9d. It puts on classes in escaping and evading for air crew flying combat missions. You can surmise from the major's rank the priority Escape has – not very high.

"Not only is Major Neave responsible for setting up E&E training, he has the operational brief to establish escape lines in enemy-occupied countries. It's the most convoluted mission statement I've ever heard of for a tiny section run by a junior field grade officer in a standalone War Office-level organization.

Col. Randal said, "A section of MI-9 handles training and coordinates running escape lines out of France?"

Maj. Gen. Donovan said, "E&E training is high profile. Actual escaping and evading is more of an afterthought. Major Neave is responsible for both."

Col. Randal said, "What section of OSS is involved with E&E, sir?"

Maj. Gen. Donovan said, "We're a worse embarrassment than the British. Escape is not an OSS branch or even a section. We have what is called the MIS-X Detachment, OSS London. Its stated purpose is to handle E&E on the Continent – it's not staffed."

Col. Randal said, "Would you like some help with that, sir?"

Maj. Gen. Donovan said, "Where are you going with this, Colonel?"

Col. Randal said, "As you are aware, Raiding Forces was tasked with Escape in the Aegean. Veronica Paige runs it out of Castelrozzo. So we know something about how the program operates.

"I have an officer who lived in Paris before the war. He served in the Foreign Legion. Speaks fluent French. Has contacts in France. If you have any interest, General, I might be able to assist OSS in setting up an escape line."

Maj. Gen. Donovan wondered where Col. Randal was getting his information. The fact USAAF was demanding an OSS Escape program to retrieve downed aircrew was not widely known. But it could not be kept quiet forever – then there would be a scandal.

Why, at a time when Raiding Forces was understrength and overtasked, with all the commitments Raiding Forces had, would Col. Randal be volunteering to get involved with Escape & Evasion (E&E)?

Maj. Gen. Donovan said, "OSS, London Office is overwhelmed getting Secret Intelligence and Special Operations up and running. We're years behind playing catch-up to MI-6 and SOE. It doesn't help that they are fighting us every step of the way. We simply do not have the time or manpower to take on MIS-X duties.

"Not proud of it, Colonel. But there it is."

Col. Randal said, "Captain Preston Butterfield III is the officer Sergeant Major Beckwith will be replacing in Cairo, sir. I believe he can help with Escape. With your permission, sir, I'd like to fly in Mrs. Paige and the captain to take a look at the problem.

Maj. Gen. Donovan's law firm represented the Butterfield family in New York. Preston Butterfield was exactly the kind of officer the Office of Strategic Services liked to recruit... a New England blueblood. Around Washington it was widely claimed the acronym OSS stood for 'Oh So Social'.

The fact he had run off and joined the Foreign Legion made him an even more attractive candidate – Wild Bill had a weakness for officers with foreign service backgrounds.

What Col. Randal said was true. USAAF generals were screaming for help getting their downed aircrews brought out of France. While not quite at the level of a cover-up, the lack of OSS support was not widely advertised. If the news media found out downed USAAF aircrew on the run were on their own for making it home the story would not play well with the public in the States.

The lack of E&E support had worked its way up the chain of command. SHAEF G2 was voicing concerns. Did Randal know? If so, how?"

Maj. Gen. Donovan was not a man who liked to admit he could not tackle any assignment, anytime, anywhere, worldwide. He was a problem solver. But there was no question OSS had swept this one under the carpet. Or more accurately, only provided E&E token support by attaching a handful of OSS personnel to Major Neave's Section 9d.

In reality they were little more than observers.

There was one other factor that had to be taken into consideration. The MI part of the acronym MI-9 denoted 'Military Intelligence'. The British were not about to allow the upstart OSS to have more than perfunctory involvement in any intelligence mission if they could avoid it.

Having to pick his fights with the British intelligence community, E&E was one battle Maj. Gen. Donovan elected not to take on. As an attorney and a former politician as well as a soldier he thought along legal, political and military lines. Wild Bill had well-honed survival instincts.

As Director of Strategic Services he was always cognizant of the repercussions from his actions. Not only in theatre but how they would play in Washington. The OSS, meaning the United States, not having a fully functioning Escape operation in place to help their boys get home would not be something easily explained to the American public.

Maj. Gen. Donovan wanted to know what Col. Randal knew, when did he learn it and *how* was his information obtained. The main question in Wild Bill's mind was why the colonel would volunteer to take on added responsibility during the run-up to opening the Second Front? Raiding Forces was going to be strained to the breaking point. It did not make sense.

"I'll take any help with E&E I can get, Colonel."

COLONEL JOHN RANDAL AND MAJOR THE LADY JANE SEABORN were riding down in the private elevator. They intended to drop by the bar. From time to time the two would stop in and have a drink with any of the Raiding Forces' personnel who happened to be there. Afterward they were planning on going to dinner at the Dorchester. Then drop by the Ritz.

Col. Randal needed to be seen around town wearing his Jacket, Flying, Type A-2 with the big bold 575th Ranger Regiment scroll painted on the front. For all practical purposes it was a notional unit. Though made up in part by the remnants of the 1st Battalion, 575 Parachute Infantry Regiment (Airborne)(Separate) and the 10th Ranger Battalion (Airborne) (Provisional) and elements of Raiding Forces.

The details of the plausible story designed to create the fiction of the 575th Ranger Regiment having arrived in England were not completely worked out yet. The 575th Ranger Regiment was either assigned to the ghost

First United States Army Group (FUSAG) commanded by the very real bigger-than-life Lieutenant General George S. Patton or they were the Supreme Headquarters Allied Expeditionary Force's dedicated special operations unit.

At least those were the two stories being put out. Both could be true. Which made the 575th Ranger Regiment such a viable notional unit. Because if the Rangers were known to be operating against targets in the Pas-de-Calais District that reinforced the OPERATION FORTITUDE SOUTH deception that the Allies would attack across the Channel at the narrowest point, Calais. Something Hitler already believed, according to ULTRA intercepts coming out of Bletchley Park. Certainly the Allies would use their best Special Operations unit to prepare the battlefield.

The best deception is one the enemy tells himself.

On paper the picture being disseminated of the 575th Ranger Regiment was a classic textbook deception. It was simple. The German High Command would believe it. Rangers were known to them because of their operations in North Africa, Sicily and Italy. Col. Randal was a known commander of special forces. The critically acclaimed author Squadron Leader Dennis Wheatly had written a book about one of his operations. Hollywood was making an A-list movie out of it.

XX Committee made sure those facts were known to the Germans.

The Nazis would never suspect the legendary Colonel John Randal was commanding a special force about the size of a reinforced rifle infantry company any more than they would believe the Allies best fighting general, Lt. Gen. Patton, was commanding a make-believe army made up of inflatable tanks and cardboard trucks.

Col. Randal was not cleared to know the details about where the landing was going to take place. He was supposed to believe D-Day would take place somewhere in the Calais District because he had been intentionally led to that conclusion. There was a reason.

Because the type of small-scale missions Raiding Forces conducted had a high probability of capture, it was thought best Col. Randal not know the true location. And in the cold-blooded assessment of the deception planners, if he believed the invasion would take place in Calais and was captured, the best thing that could happen was he would break under interrogation and give up what he believed to be true.

However, privately, unknown to each other, both Lieutenant Ted Hamilton aka "The Great Teddy" and Beverly Blackwell advised Col. Randal Calais was not the target. It is hard to keep a secret. Especially from an officer as respected as he was.

Col. Randal wore his 575th Ranger Regiment leather jacket every chance he had.

Lady Jane was wearing an elegant black dress with a long slit up one toned leg. Her taste in evening wear ran to simple classic designs in black or white. She believed a woman should wear the dress and not the other way around.

Lady Jane definitely wore the dress.

Col. Randal always wondered how she could breathe in them – they fit like a snake skin.

Lady Jane said, "I offered General Eisenhower the use of a few of our Vulnerable Points Wing operators to add to his personal security detail."

Col. Randal said, "Good – they'll enjoy the assignment."

"I would like your permission to have Major Chatterhorn fly in with Captain Butterfield. The general has agreed to allow him to interview for the job as his chief of security. Provided that is acceptable to you."

"Works for me."

Col. Randal was amused at the way Lady Jane was cultivating access to General Eisenhower's circle of social contacts – akin to infiltrating it. He knew what she was doing… taking care of *her* troops. Repayment in full would be extracted for all generosities extended the SHAEF commander at some later date.

Lady Jane said, "I intend to ask Dr. Milam to return to England and run the hotel Aid Station – a small fully equipped operating theatre, we shall be putting in."

Col. Randal said, "Now that's an outstanding idea."

She added, "General Lee balked at building out my ballroom."

Col. Randal said, "No kidding."

Lady Jane laughed, "Until I informed him one level would be SHAEF's London Headquarters."

"And when did you add that to your dream sheet?"

"The instant General Lee objected to my nightclub. Improvise, adapt, overcome. Exactly the way you taught me."

Col. Randal said, “How did that work out?”

Lady Jane laughed, “Like a charm.”

Col. Randal asked, “Does General Eisenhower know about his new digs?”

“Not yet.”

“Oh, that’s great.”

Lady Jane said, “Has Beverly voiced her concerns Jack may be in the cross-hairs of a female MI-5 hush-hush officer?”

“Affirmative – she has.”

“What is your take, John?”

Col. Randal said, “I don’t think the Gestapo could make Jack give up his name, rank or serial number, much less reveal sensitive intelligence to some girl he’s trying to pick up in a bar.”

Lady Jane nodded, “Agreed… still, Beverly is worried. Apparently this woman is one of MI-5’s top ‘flirtation agents’ – a femme fatale. Apparently she gave Jack her private phone number.”

“So I heard.”

“Not standard operating procedure, John.”

Col. Randal said, “There is that.”

Lady Jane said, “Do you believe Jack may actually be at risk or is Beverly being overprotective – possibly slightly jealous?”

“I don’t see how she could be jealous considering Jack's track record with women,” Col. Randal said. “Beverly knew him back in his panty raiding days at UT. Her grandfather was the judge who gave him the choice of jail or the paratroops after he was arrested by campus police for scaling her sorority house.”

Lady Jane laughed, “One has to love Billy Jack – he can really get the girls.”

They walked into the bar. It was packed. Colonels and generals rubbed shoulders with Lords and MPs from Parliament, MI-5 and MI-6 agents in mufti, entertainers from USO shows, Senators and Congressmen in from the States. Women wearing evening dress, WAAFs, WRENS, FANY’S and Lady Jane’s Royal Marines in uniform all mingled in the crowd.

Lady Jane said, “Oh no!”

Captain Billy Jack Jaxx was at a small table in one corner with a spectacular black-haired girl. They were absorbed in conversation, oblivious to everything taking place around them – she was a knockout.

Lady Jane laughed, “Beverly’s right… Jack’s a dead man.”

Col. Randal said, “Sloan Marlow, I presume – S&M?”

Lady Jane said, “That would be my guess.

Beverly came over, “Does the Tower of London let you post bail?”

Lieutenant General “Geronimo” Joe McKoy was standing at the bar with Waldo Treywick and Rikke Runborg. He spotted Col. Randal and Lady Jane talking to Beverly. He came over.

Beverly was saying, “…like a moth to a flame.”

Col. Randal said, “Never gives up – I'll give him that.”

Lady Jane said, “Jack's always exhibited exquisite taste in women, but this time...”

Col. Randal said, “Exquisite?”

Lady Jane laughed, “Disregard my last… make that demonstrates reasonably good taste in girls from time to time.”

Lt. Gen. McKoy said, “She the one they call S&M?”

Col. Randal answered, “That would be her.”

Lt. Gen. McKoy said, “Jack's punchin' above his weight class with that one. But at the end a' the day if a man can't look back on his life and say 'I was an idiot'… he still is. What's the worst could happen?”

Beverly said, “Prison.”

ONE OF THE VULNERABLE POINTS WING SECURITY OFFICERS walked into the bar, “Sir, there is a gentleman who would like to speak to you in the lobby.”

A King's Messenger.

10

GOOD NAME FOR A STUD

COLONEL JOHN RANDAL AND BEVERLY BLACKWELL WERE sitting together in the VIP Section of the lobby of the Bradford Hotel. They pulled two of the tall-backed chairs close together facing each other for a private conversation. Beverly had been studying MI-5 Counterintelligence means and methods. She was taking her job as the OSS liaison officer to the XX Committee aka Double Cross Committee, known to insiders as *Twenty*, seriously. Now she was briefing Col. Randal on what she was learning.

"The success of MI-5 is dependent on three TOP SECRET operations. Signals intelligence, Double Cross and Deception, plus the application of the principles of offensive counterintelligence such as deterrence, detection, neutralization and deception."

Col. Randal said, "That's more than three things."

Beverly laughed, "You kind of have to combine 'em together then sort 'em out again."

Col. Randal said, "I see."

Beverly said, "So, how it works is we manipulate the intelligence flowing to the Abwehr by controlling the German spy system in the United Kingdom. The concept of the operation is to make the Germans act in a way calculated to assist our plans on D-Day – we're basically tricking 'em, Johnny. The idea is to make the Nazis believe we'll attack in the Pas-de-Calais region. The best deception is one the bad guys tell themselves.

"Pretty neat, huh."

Col. Randal said, "I don't think I'm cleared for that."

Beverly laughed, "I don't think I am either."

Col. Randal said, "Yeah, probably not."

Beverly said, "Here's where we come in. A strategic deception operation called OPERATION BODYGUARD has been stood up that covers two other deceptions. OPERATION FORTITUDE and a subset of it, the one Raiding Forces is concerned with, OPERATION FORTITUDE SOUTH – designed to keep the Germans away from wherever it is we do intend to invade."

Col. Randal said, "Make sure you don't talk in your sleep."

"So, who do you think I'm sleeping with?"

Col. Randal said, "That's more information than I need to know, Beverly."

"OK... Do you understand the difference between Counter-intelligence and Counterespionage?"

"Why don't you lay it out for me again?"

Beverly said, "Counterintelligence is the hunting down, capturing or killing of German spies. Raiding Forces doesn't do that. Though we probably could if someone asked us to."

Col. Randal said, "No one's going to ask. We wouldn't be good at that."

Beverly said, "General McKoy's a U.S. Marshal... he could show us how. Jack was a reserve deputy sheriff when he was in high school. Might be fun kicking in doors."

Col. Randal said, "I don't think Raiding Forces' operators are cut out for the job. Catching spies won't work for Jack. You need 'em alive to interrogate or turn. He's more of a 'take the place by storm, arrive unannounced and unexpected in the enemy's midst then shoot everybody inside' type operator."

Beverly laughed, "That's what they say about you, Johnny."

Col. Randal said, "Who…."

Quoting, almost word for word, from MI-5's restricted, internal issue-only Handbook for New Officers Beverly said, "Counterespionage is the offensive use of counterintelligence. It's characterized by employing a succession of complex strategies deliberately made known to the bad guys with the intent of confusing and disrupting their operations."

"Pretty sure the MI-5 manual did not say 'bad guys'," Col. Randal said. "How's that work?"

Beverly said, "A perfect example is the series of seemingly meaningless small-scale operations we've been carrying out ever since coming to town. Turns out they're not so pointless after all.

"Raiding Forces is being used to craft a visual narrative that's leading the Nazis to draw the wrong conclusion about Allied intentions based on our telling them what they already believe."

Col. Randal said, "And what might that be?"

Beverly said, "That we're conducting preparatory operations for SHAEF in the Calais Military District, which we're not."

Col. Randal said, "You've been doing your homework."

Beverly laughed, "Not sure OSS did theirs. Counterintelligence Branch is misnamed Counterespionage Branch. I don't believe Wild Bill's people understand the difference."

"I'm impressed," Col. Randal said, "You're taking away a lot more than you bring to the table at those XX Committee meetings – good for you."

Beverly said, "Don't tell Tar. He only recommended me for the assignment in the first place because he thought I was a bimbo."

"That's because you are."

"Too true."

COLONEL JOHN RANDAL AND MAJOR THE LADY JANE Seaborn were in their suite on the Penthouse Floor. He was sitting on the floor cleaning his pistols on the coffee table. They were disassembled on a copy of The London Times newspaper to protect the mahogany table. She was lying on the couch with Happy curled up next to her. Lady Jane was looking at the photograph of her new Appaloosa colt.

Col. Randal said, "Have you and Bronc filled out the pony's registration papers?"

Lady Jane said, "We have."

"What did you decide to call him?"

"I named him after you – Gallant Commander."

"Really."

"That's not his name though."

"What might that be?"

"Butterfly Boy."

"Good name for a stud."

COLONEL JOHN RANDAL WAS IN A MEETING WITH MAJOR Jack Dance in the VIP section of the hotel lobby which was fast becoming his office. Hiding in plain sight. What looked like socializing was, in fact, classified operational planning – for the most part.

Col. Randal said, "In compliance with Raiding Forces' Rules, I'll keep this short and simple, Major. I'd like you to reconsider your decision not to relocate to Seaborn House for the run-up to D-Day. Not sure how long that'll be but after the invasion if you still want to transfer back to Castelrozzo I'll make that happen."

Maj. Dance said, "What is it you have in mind for me here, sir?"

Col. Randal said, "I have responsibilities that are going to require me to be away from time to time. I've been designated the SHAEF Airborne Advisor. General Patton has tapped me to be his First United States Army Group special operations officer – commander of the 575th Ranger Regiment. FUSAG is a phantom organization but I'll have to travel with the general to keep up the charade. I'm also the Office of Strategic Services, Chief of Operational Group Branch – which means ground ops. I'm getting ready to stand up an Escape & Evasion organization in France – that's classified Need to Know.

"And I intend to continue leading raids."

Maj. Dance said, "Some job description."

Col. Randal said, "What I need is for you to be my deputy commander. Run Raiding Forces' day-to-day operations. On paper you'll be seconded to the Office of Strategic Services as deputy commander of the Operational Group Branch. In that capacity you'll be responsible for coordinating OSS OG Branch operations in Europe – *all* of Europe. A big job.

"Promotion goes with it."

Maj. Dance had already turned down the opportunity of being promoted to stay in Raiding Forces instead of commanding a parachute battalion in one of the airborne divisions, so that was not much of an incentive. As a reserve officer who enlisted for the duration, he had no intention of making the Army a career. In civilian life he was the head football coach of a junior college in Alabama and could not wait to get back to his coaching duties after the war.

That said, the assignment sounded interesting. Maj. Dance was competitive by nature. He liked a challenge.

Still, Castelrozzo was a choice duty station for several reasons.

Raiding Forces' Rule: 4 "Right man, Right job'' was likely the most frequently quoted Raiding Forces' standing order. However, it needed to be applied in tandem with Col. Randal's personal policy of putting "a round peg in a round hole." He believed a good commander did not order an officer or NCO to take an assignment they did not want if there was any way to avoid it.

Unit cohesion on a level that transcended high morale and *esprit de corps* is created when highly qualified people have the posting of their choice and are giving one hundred percent effort.

He was not going to order Maj. Dance to England.

"For what it's worth Major, Lady Jane is upstairs meeting with Stephanie as we speak. She's offering her the job of coordinating Raiding Forces' HQ at Seaborn House and our Rear here at the Bradford. Her quarters will be a suite on the Penthouse Floor."

Maj. Dance and Captain Stephanie Fawcett-Tatum, RM, were dating.

"Now that I think about it, sir, I've always wanted to check out London's swinging nightlife."

"Good call, Colonel."

COL. JOHN RANDAL WAS IN CONFERENCE WITH CAPTAIN Roy Kidd. They first met when Capt. Kidd had been an American officer serving in the 1st Battalion King's Own Royal Regiment stationed at Karachi, India. The 1st KORR was the first British infantry battalion ever to be air-landed directly into a hot combat zone. It flew in to reinforce RAF Habbaniya during the siege. Because of then-Lieutenant Kidd's performance as troop leader – the quintessential quiet professional, he was invited to join Raiding Forces.

Capt. Kidd was a steady officer on operations – absolutely reliable and it was not to be forgotten when he was with King's Own Royal Regiment (KORR) he was seconded to the Provencial Forest Department to track down and kill man-eating tigers.

Col. Randal said, "Raiding Forces has been tasked with covertly standing up an Escape & Evasion program in France. No one is to know about what we're doing with E&E until the fact that it exists eventually comes out and it's too late to stop it. 'No one' includes our Allies in Raiding Forces.

"As you are aware, the British have the Directorate of Military Intelligence, one of which is MI-9. Its unofficial name is 'Escape.' They're responsible for helping Allied airmen who have been shot down and are on the run E&E-ing back to England."

Capt. Kidd said, "I'm aware of MI-9, sir. Veronica Paige heads it up in the Aegean. I've observed her operation."

Col. Randal said, "Our problem here in the UK is the DMI community aggressively opposes any direct U.S. involvement in intelligence work on the Continent. The Brits have a monopoly and intend to keep it. OSS is only marginally allowed to assist British intelligence to include SOE supported guerrilla operations. Usually, by attaching a few token OSS people to a British-led mission.

"Classic inter-Allied rivalry, sir – not to be underestimated." Capt. Kidd said, "I know Mrs. Paige has hard feelings toward MI-9 ever since they tried to replace her with a male officer."

Col. Randal said, "We can expect MI-9 to protect its turf. They don't want OSS competing with them. The other DMI organizations will line up in support.

"So we're not going to tell anyone what we're up to until it's too late to do anything about it."

Capt. Kidd said, "Good idea, Colonel."

Col. Randal said, "I need an officer to run the operation. It's a big assignment – independent command. How would you like the job, Roy – a promotion goes with it?"

"Why me, sir?"

"I know I can depend on you to make it happen – your time in the British Army might be invaluable."

"How do you see this secret E&E organization unfolding, sir?"

"There are thousands of downed USAAF airmen on the run in France. The American public would be less than pleased to learn there's no United States plan to bring them out. We need one."

Capt. Kidd said, "You're saying there's currently not an OSS Escape & Evasion program at this time, sir?"

"Negative."

"Hard to believe, Colonel."

"Yes it is."

"Do I have a choice, sir?"

"Absolutely."

"My preference is to remain a troop commander. I'm not cut out to be a staff officer or administrator, Colonel. I've seen what Mrs. Paige does – a lot of liaising with the Air Force, Navy, logistics..."

Col. Randal said, "Fair enough, Roy. I wanted to give you the opportunity. Can't blame you for sticking with a troop command – that's what I'd do too."

"Appreciate the offer, sir."

Col. Randal said, "In that case I have another assignment for you that's a better fit – evaluating suppressed weapons. Starting with one called the De Lisle Carbine. It's brand new. Jack saw a prototype used by a British officer on a recent raid.

"Gave it a mixed report – possibly because of the way the weapon was utilized."

Capt. Kidd perked up. He was one of Raiding Forces' two go-to firearms experts. The other being Lieutenant General "Geronimo" Joe McKoy. This assignment was putting a round peg in a round hole.

"What is it you require, sir?"

Col. Randal said, "Rate every suppressed weapon in the Allied inventory regardless of country of origin. We're about to launch an intensive program of clandestine small-scale ops targeting the coast of France. We need quiet weapons. I want the best – that'll be your responsibility.

"You'll still be in the rotation for cross-channel missions. I need every troop commander I can get."

"Can do, sir."

"Talk to Jim… one of his duties is to liaise with Special Operations Executive. SOE has a relationship with the Royal Small Arms Factory, Research Department – he can hook you up with them. They should be able to supply you with the British models.

"You'll have to improvise how to acquire the rest."

Capt. Kidd said, "If there's anything I can do to assist with E&E count me in, sir. We need to do everything possible to bring our people home.

"No U.S. escape organization… that's not right, Colonel."

"Roger that."

COLONEL JOHN RANDAL DID WHAT HE ALWAYS DID WHEN faced with a military problem he was not sure how to move forward on. He consulted with Lieutenant General "Geronimo" Joe McKoy. Waldo Treywick sat in. Both of them were aware of the subject to be discussed but not the details. The three were in the VIP section with their tall-backed chairs pulled close.

Waldo passed out his custom rolled panatela's, which they stuck in their teeth… unlit. Cigar smoking was prohibited in the hotel lobby.

Col. Randal laid out the E&E situation in bullet points which was how Lt. Gen. McKoy liked to hear a problem. He wanted to know all the key elements out front and center. That way he had them in mind while discussing an issue without the conversation having to stop and backtrack so he could be filled in on a detail.

When Col. Randal finished, Lt. Gen. McKoy ticked the main points off back to him to make sure he had not missed anything. The two had worked through a lot of problems this way. Around Abyssinian campfires, in desert RONs, aboard boats and various RFHQs in different remote parts of the world.

Lt. Gen. McKoy said, "We need to set up an American E&E operation in France because we don't have one right now. If they find out before we can get it up and goin', British intelligence will oppose us on general principle protectin' their turf – they want a monopoly.

"Not even our British personnel in Raidin' Forces can know what we're doin' so we're gonna be short on manpower to work with. You're plannin' to use Preston Butterfield to organize the escape line on the French side, him havin' lived in Paris and sold jewelry to all those French show girls at the *Follies Bergere*.

"And you can't go to OSS for direct assistance or to let 'em know what you're up to until you're ready to pass E&E off to London Station to take over once it's too late for the Brits to stop us.

"Why? Because you know the Outfit leaks like a sieve when it comes to its boys talkin' to their opposite numbers in British intelligence. MI-6'll get word what we're up to and they'll pass it on to MI-9 – then the catfight commences.

"I leave anythin' out?"

Col. Randal said, "Only that we need someone to run it who is skilled in the art of bribing local officials, knows how to set up secure hiding places and transport precious cargo out of enemy territory."

Lt. Gen. McKoy said, "How're you plannin' to bring your escapees back across the Channel?"

Col. Randal said, "PT boat – if there's a high-value evader we should be able to request a plane to fly in and conduct an extraction off a clandestine strip. Pretty sure Bronc will assist with that."

Lt. Gen. McKoy said, "So, what's the hard part?"

Col. Randal said, "Finding the right person to plan, organize and coordinate E&E's activities."

Waldo said, "The problem is the solution."

Lt. Gen. McKoy said, "You don't even have to say the words out loud this time, John."

Waldo said, "Jumps right out at ya."

Col. Randal said, "You might want to elaborate on that, General."

Lt. Gen. McKoy said, "Waldo's spent more time sneakin' into places he ain't supposed to be and spiritin' out poached ivory and other misplaced items a' value across international borders and bodies a' water than any man I ever knowed of.

"I'm law enforcement – before the war I headed the U.S. Marshal's Fugitive Warrants Squad. Handpicked manhunters down to the ground – stone cold professionals.

"The kind a' crooks my boys chased were on the run in a big way. Some of 'em even tried resortin' to plastic surgery to alter their appearance. Not that it did 'em any good. Once we got on their trail we'd track those perpetrators down nationwide.

"It's fair to say I got a pretty good idea what a getaway plan looks like – the ins and outs, dos and don'ts."

Waldo said, "Clear as a bell."

Lt. Gen. McKoy said, "A no-brainer."

Col. Randal said, "I see."

Which meant he did not have a clue what they were talking about, or in this case, that they might be serious.

Waldo said, "We're your men, Colonel."

Col. Randal said, "Let me get this straight. You two want to run LONG NECK *and* take on Escape & Evasion? Leopoldville is four thousand miles from Paris. How are you planning to carry that off?"

Lt. Gen. McKoy said, "I'll move some people around."

Col. Randal had no idea what that meant. However, he had a policy not on any list – his 'enthusiasm indicator.' If a qualified individual or individuals demonstrated a desire to take on an assignment, he tended to let them do it.

"Make it happen, gentlemen."

COLONEL JOHN RANDAL WAS SITTING ALONE IN THE VIP section of the hotel. He had one of Waldo's long thin panetella cigars in his teeth unlit, watching people stream through the lobby. It was a pleasant way to spend time. Sloan Marlow appeared at the velvet rope gate. The VPW security operator looked over at Col. Randal.

He nodded to let her in.

Col. Randal could not help but notice when S&M moved she was as supple as a leopard stalking its prey – he clicked on.

"Care for a cigar?"

"Never smoked one."

"Mandy and Beverly sneak in the smoking lounge now and then."

"Afraid I am not Mandy or Beverly."

"I can see that."

Sloan said, "We have not had the opportunity to meet. Jack holds you in such high regard I wanted to stop by and introduce myself properly."

Col. Randal said, "Good."

"Do you mind if I ask you a personal question?"

"Okay."

"Aside from the obvious, what attracted you to Lady Jane?"

Col. Randal said, "I'm a social climber."

Sloan laughed, "Something Jack would say."

Col. Randal said, "Other than the fact he's a gentleman and a scholar what about him interested you?"

Sloan said, "The very first thing Jack said to me was a total lie. He knew I would know and did it anyway. In the circles I move in it is rare to meet a man who does not at least attempt a pick-up line – not our hero."

Col. Randal said, "Jack does tend to let his guns do the talking."

A King's Messenger arrived at the velvet rope. Even though by now this particular courier had delivered several KM messages, he produced his Silver Greyhound identification badge. Then he made Col. Randal go through the routine of taking out his photo ID card. Once they had both satisfactorily completed the ritual of identifying themselves to each other he passed over a sealed envelope and had him sign for it.

When the KM departed, Col. Randal stuck the dispatch in the inside pocket of his Class A blouse. Then he sat back down and continued his conversation with S&M as if nothing had happened.

Sloan was a highly skilled MI-5 counterintelligence operative whose assignment was to draw out officers who talked too much. "Loose Lips Sink Ships" was more than just a catchy slogan in Section B-1B. Her job was to put a stop to security violators.

She was aware the communiques King's Messengers carried were of the utmost importance… rarely conveyed to individuals, usually to ministries, agencies or Army-level military formations. If a KM delivered a dispatch to any of the officers Sloan encountered in the normal course of her counterintelligence duties the odds were they would not be able to resist showing off how important they were.

"You are not going to read your message, John?"

By now the two were on a first-name basis.

"I'd rather talk to you."

"Very good answer. I asked a personal question. Do you have anything you would like to ask me?"

"Yeah, what's the date set for D-Day?"

Sloan laughed, "I am supposed to be the one asking that kind of question."

Col. Randal said, "Well, I can't get anybody to tell me."

Sloan said, "That's priceless. Let me be the first to know if you ever do. I can see you shall be a challenge – we should probably be friends."

Col. Randal said, "Friends are good."

Sloan said, "You are not at all what I imagined."

Col. Randal said, "Is that a good thing or a bad thing?"

Sloan laughed, "Based on the stories Jack has told me I rather expected a semi-deranged fire-breathing berserker."

Col. Randal said, "What makes you think I'm not?"

Beverly walked in the front door of the hotel returning from her meeting with the XX-Committee. She saw Col. Randal and S&M sitting together. If looks could kill they would both be dead.

Her eyes were spitting tracers.

LIEUTENANT COLONEL THOMAS ARGYLL "TAR" ROBERTSON arrived at the Bradford Hotel. Lieutenant Colonel Robin "Tin Eye" Stephens, the Commandant, Camp 020 (MI5 Interrogation Centre), had conducted a ruthlessly efficient interview of Major Hanns von Reisen. He was able to determine that the major had, in fact, forwarded his concerns up the chain-of-command through the Paris station to Abwehr Headquarters (Berlin). However, there was nothing unusual or alarming about the fact he was worried some of Germany's spies in England may have been turned and were secretly working for the Allies.

Maj. von Reisen was an Abteilung III Counterintelligence officer. He was supposed to suspect everyone of collaborating with the Allies until proven otherwise. Suspicion was his job description.

Berlin had not responded to his reservations.

Lt. Col. Robertson was at the hotel to link up with Mandy Paige, Beverly Blackwell and Rikke Runborg. Rocky was about to transmit an agent report to the brand new Army Group B, Commander-in-Chief, Field Marshal Erwin Rommel. This would be Rocky's first controlled deception transmission since notifying FM Rommel she was now in England under the "protection" of Lieutenant General "Geronimo" Joe McKoy.

Mandy was Rocky's handler. Beverly was understudying her. Lt. Col. Robertson was there to observe, as was Major the Lady Jane Seaborn who had no other reason to be involved other than to see what her two girls were up to.

The message to be transmitted was short and simple in the best Raiding Forces' tradition.

```
MAJOR HANNS VON REISEN ABWEHR PAS-DE-CALAIS
DEFECTED TO ENGLAND THIS DATE STOP
```

Tomorrow a photo of the major would be on the front page of the *London Times* sitting in the VIP section of Bradford Hotel's lobby holding up a copy of the newspaper with the date on it. The names and photographs of Germans who came over to the Allied side were not normally public information. However, in this case MI-5 decided to make it easy for the Abwehr to understand they could not trust any past reports from Maj. von Reisen.

As Beverly had pointed out to Colonel John Randal – it was MI-5 best practice not to make the Abwehr work too hard to come to the desired conclusion. Why take a chance? The Germans might get it wrong.

In addition, as an added benefit the photo coming out right after the controlled transmission would go a long way toward helping restore FM Rommel's trust in Rocky's bona fides. After all, she had transmitted "spoof" messages on two previous occasions for Brigadier Dudley's A-Force that caused the Desert Fox to be away from his command immediately prior to the start of the Allies launching a major attack.

Rocky was going for a hat trick.

The night before D-Day when it was too late for the Germans to react, she would send another spoof message to FM Rommel to the effect of "nothing to see here." Rocky would claim the landing taking place in Normandy was a feint. The real attack, she would insist – when it came, would take place in Pas-de-Calais.

When it eventually became clear that landing was never taking place Rikki would have completed her obligation to MI-5.

Col. Randal was not cleared to know any of that. Neither was Mandy or Beverly at this stage. Nor was Lt. Col. Robertson. In fact, not even General Dwight D. Eisenhower was aware of the specifics, though he would have been cleared for them had he wanted to get into the details of the deception.

There was a reason for all the secrecy. The problem the Allies faced in protecting classified information was not German spies. It was their own officers boasting to show off how much in the know they were. Failing to exercise individual security discipline was an escalating issue that would only get worse as the SHAEF staff mushroomed in size and composition during the buildup to D-Day.

It was the reason MI-5 kept an army of hush-hush girls like Sloan Marlow on staff.

How did Rocky come to be the centerpiece of the Allied high-stakes D-Day deception gamble? She had spied for the Norwegians, Russians and Germans, though not necessarily in that order. In Cairo, two years previously, Brigadier Dudley Clarke recruited her for A-Force. Then with D-Day looming Brig. Clarke handed her off to Lieutenant Colonel John Henry Bevan in London to use for BODYGUARD/FORTITUDE SOUTH.

Rocky had been working for the Allies with the caveat Col. Randal and Major the Lady Jane Seaborn be her sponsors. She did not trust British intelligence to look out for her best interests.

Rocky's true loyalties – if any – were known only to her.

Lieutenant General "Geronimo" Joe McKoy liked to say, "You don't know what you don't know."

That was why the D-Day deception campaign was so important.

LIEUTENANT WESTLY SLADE ARRIVED AT THE BRADFORD Hotel in from Seaborn House. He reported to Colonel John Randal in the VIP section, per his orders. The colonel was sitting with Major the Lady Jane Seaborn, Mandy Paige and Beverly Blackwell. Lady Jane was giving them a preliminary rundown on the subterranean buildout of the basement floors.

Lt. Slade said, "You wanted to see me, sir?"

Col. Randal said, "Are you prepared to accept a Warning Order?"

There was only one acceptable answer when that by-the-book question was asked.

"Yes, sir!"

"Let's go down to the War Room." A number of different names had been floated for the Raiding Forces' Rear Headquarters. Over time the personnel assigned to it had begun to settle on "War Room."

Lady Jane disappeared in search of the hotel manager to discuss her renovation project. Time was of the essence. She was in a race against the clock. The underground floors needed to be at least partially prepared for occupation before the Luftwaffe launched its second iteration of the London Blitz.

Her problem was because the intelligence of the impending attack was Signals Intelligence (SIGINT), Lady Jane could not explain the reason for her urgency to anyone other than Col. Randal and she was not authorized to tell him.

Like Beverly, she did it anyway, having told some of it to Major General Sam Houston "Bronc" Blackwell – leaving out the part about SIGINT.

The good news for her short fuse project was Lady Jane had Bronc in her corner cracking the whip. He did not care why Lady Jane was in a rush. Maj. Gen. Blackwell wanted a floor for Troop Transport Command Headquarters – and right now.

Mandy and Beverly came along to the War Room with Col. Randal and Lt. Slade. The U.S. Marine/OSS Maritime Unit officer was one of the newer additions to Raiding Forces. Mandy, who liked to date around, was considering going out with him.

Lt. Slade was not aware of that.

When they arrived in the War Room Col. Randal led the way to the giant patchwork of aerial photos, maps and picture postcards that formed, a not fully complete at this stage, mosaic map of the entire French Coast. Captain Penelope "Legs" Honeycutt-Parker joined them. She had been standing by waiting for their arrival.

Col. Randal said, "*Situation*: The Germans are in France. We're in England."

Whenever possible he liked to start his Warning Orders with a statement that lowered the level of tension inherent in receiving orders preparatory to making plans for a high-risk mission.

There was a reason.

Anyone in Raiding Forces, when asked if they were prepared to accept a Warning Order would immediately go on a high state of alert. Nothing unusual about that. Something would be seriously wrong should they not.

However, Col. Randal wanted the people he was briefing to be as relaxed as possible so as to be focused and not miss anything he said. It was important for him to project a calm, casual, business-as-usual demeanor – known in military circles as "command presence." Along the lines of… 'This is what we do in Raiding Forces.'

"Here's what *you're* going to do."

Col. Randal took out the folded dispatch delivered by the King's Messenger the day previous, "There's an unnamed, uninhabited tidal islet we're interested in located 50 degrees 58' 30" N, 1 degree 48' 00" E. That's just west of Calais midway between Sangatte and Cap Blanc-Nez."

Col. Randal tapped the map, "Right about here. Your objective is located approximately eight hundred yards off the mainland. The shore in that region is a rugged stretch of coastline that features tidal flats, sandbanks, high chalk cliffs and outcrops that expose and submerge twice a day with the tide. At low water a shingle causeway links it to the beach. At high tide as the water rises it becomes an island.

"The prominent feature on the objective is a chalk rock slab elevated 20 feet above the flats.

"*Mission:* You will lead a four-man Special Warfare Operator recon patrol to surreptitiously infiltrate the target area under cover of darkness during high tide, confirm the presence and composition of a German LP/OP and/or a light anti-aircraft gun position believed to be found on the elevated rock – then return to base.

"*Execution and Concept of the Operation:* You will travel by PT boat to a position located off the target to be selected by Capt. Honeycutt-Parker. From there you are to infiltrate the islet by rubber assault raft and conduct a reconnaissance of the enemy position suspected of being constructed on the rock feature.

"And return.

"*Administration, Logistics & Command & Signal*: Coordinate with Captain Honeycutt-Parker for transport. This is a quick in and out. Suppressed weapons. No tracer ammunition. However, this is not a covert mission.

"I say again, this is not a covert mission.

"In the event you should encounter enemy personnel, do not initiate contact unless it can be done surreptitiously. I don't want a firefight if it can be avoided. However, when you withdraw you *are* to leave a piece of gear behind with U.S. stenciled on it. The idea is for the Germans to know you've been there.

"Notify me two hours prior to issuing your Operations Order and I'll come down to Seaborn House to sit in.

"What are your questions?"

Lt. Slade said, "Captain Jaxx likes to attach himself to Special Warfare Operator missions…"

Col. Randal said, "I'm pretty sure Jack's going to be tied up tonight."

Beverly said, "S&M."

Mandy said, "Exactly."

LIEUTENANT GENERAL "GERONIMO" JOE MCKOY AND Waldo Treywick were sitting with Colonel John Randal in the VIP section. The two had been working up plans for the Escape & Evasion line for OSS. They had a few questions.

Lt. Gen. McKoy said, "You kinda caught us off guard earlier, John. Me n' Waldo been kickin' around ideas. This E&E deal is gettin' to be real interestin'.

"We got a' few things we need to understand out front."

Col. Randal said, "Like what?"

Lt. Gen. McKoy said, "Where's your exfiltration point gonna be?"

Col. Randal said, "I'm thinking somewhere in the Calais area because of the short distance across the Channel."

Lt. Gen. McKoy said, "Won't that be a dangerous route? It's in the process a' bein' the most heavily militarized area in all a' enemy-occupied France – if it ain't already."

Col. Randal said, "Two reasons Calais might work for us. One, we can support it with our PT boats – won't be dependent on anyone for transport. Two, the Germans won't be expecting us to be carrying out escapes right under their noses.

"It's your call."

Waldo said, "Could work, Colonel. It's always good to be smugglin' your goods through some place nobody expects you to be stupid enough to try."

Col. Randal said, "There's another reason worth thinking about. MI-9 doesn't have an escape line in the Calais area – Hitler's 'Fortress Calais' zone. We won't be stepping on each other."

Waldo said, "Good information."

Lt. Gen. McKoy said, "All civilian movement 'll be tightly controlled. Anyone without proper papers or ration cards 'll face arrest. We'll need us a good forgery team."

Col. Randal said, "I understand OSS has a Documentation Section, R&D Branch here in London."

Lt. Gen. McKoy said, "OSS is a non-starter, John. I already checked. They can do the job but there's a dozen or so British technicians and artists seconded from SOE and MI-9 to OSS London Station to handle the fine detail work. You know what that means."

Col. Randal said, "It means you need to come up with another idea, General."

Lt. Gen. McKoy said, "Doin' this covert limits our options but I got a thought or two."

Waldo said, "Rule a' thumb you might wanna keep in mind, Colonel. When runnin' a smugglin' operation the weak link's always the possibility one a' the crooks workin' for you is workin' for the cops or another criminal organization who's made 'em a better offer."

Lt. Col. Randal said, "Good point, Mr. Treywick. We need to anticipate the Abwehr attempting to penetrate our escape line. Probably using undercover agents posing as shot down aircrew on the run."

Lt. Gen. McKoy said, "That's how I'd do it. Send in some boys who could speak American. Say they're on the run. Get in the escape line, learn all the contacts and safe house locations, then we'd roll it up from the inside."

Col. Randal said, "Veronica's flying in with Captain Butterfield. She can tell us how she handles the problem."

Lt. Gen. McKoy said, "One last question, John. Since we gotta do this covert, how you plannin' to handle Lady Jane – she's MI-6 *and* SOE. I'm just sayin'…"

Col. Randal said, "We had an 'honesty is the best policy' agreement in place – no keeping secrets."

Lt. Gen. McKoy said, "How'd that work out?"

"Lasted about five minutes."

BEVERLY BLACKWELL FLEW COLONEL JOHN RANDAL AND Lieutenant General "Geronimo" Joe McKoy to Seaborn House aboard a Percival Q.6 Petrel aka Percival Petrel. The plane was a short-range air transport provided by her father, Major General Sam Houston "Bronc" Blackwell. It was the smallest twin-engined, six-seat, short takeoff and landing (STOL) aircraft in the Allied inventory.

A Royal Air Force asset, it was still fitted with the luxury cabin interior from when it had been a civilian VIP transport for a major oil company before the war. The RAF loaned the plane to Troop Transport Command on a semi-permanent basis.

Bronc assigned the Percival Petrel to Major the Lady Jane Seaborn. She could use it for her personal travel and to shuttle people back and forth between Seaborn House and the Raiding Forces' Rear Headquarters at the Bradford Hotel.

The specs on the Q.6 were tailor-made for Raiding Forces.

*Seats: 6 including pilot

*Range: 700 miles

*Cruising Speed: 175 mph

*Engines 2 x 205 hp Gypsy Six

*Takeoff/Landing: Grass strip capable

*Primary Role: VIP transport.

It was a good deal for all parties involved. Bigger and faster model VIP transports were in the Royal Air Force system by this time capable of carrying more passengers. The RAF got a plane off their books they did not have much use for while banking a favor from the Commanding General of the United States Army Air Force Troop Transport Command.

Maj. Gen. Blackwell got to return the favor of Lady Jane gifting him prime high-end subterranean real estate in the Bradford for his HQ – trophy property. Now she would not have to take the train or drive the commute to and from Seaborn House. Captain Pamala Plum-Martin and his daughter Beverly would serve as the duty pilots, an assignment both girls loved.

Civilians would be surprised by how much horse trading went on in the Armed Forces.

There was an added benefit to Raiding Forces having a STOL aircraft assigned. If the need arose to land a small team in France or pick one up from a remote clandestine grass landing strip in the dark of night, the twin-engine Percival Petrel was a top choice for the mission. No one realized it at the time Bronc gifted the plane to Lady Jane but the little luxury aircraft was perfect for certain Escape & Evasion missions.

Those would have to be flown by Capt. Plum-Martin. Beverly was restricted from flights over the Continent of Europe. The Texas beauty queen was not happy to learn Raiding Forces would be flying to France by moonlight and landing on improvised clandestine strips and she could not be a part.

Col. Randal said, "Explain to me again how you and Waldo intend to handle LONG NECK and Escape. In addition you're supposed to be one of General Patton's FUSAG corps commanders. You need to be seen in public around London."

Lt. Gen McKoy said, "I'm gonna do some delegatin'."

Beverly touched down on the long drive leading to Seaborn House. As the plane rolled to a stop she said, "Don't forget Johnny, you have to be back at the hotel by 1900 hrs. The promotion party Lady Jane has planned for her godfather is a big deal to her. I'd advise against you deciding at the last minute to tag along with Westly to observe his Special Warfare Operators in action."

"Wilco."

Unknown to Col. Randal, that possibility was the reason Lt. Gen. McKoy was aboard the Percival Petrol this evening. Lady Jane had ordered the general to travel with him and make sure he was back in time for her event.

By force, should that be necessary.

RIDING DOWN IN THE PRIVATE ELEVATOR ON THE WAY TO the promotion celebration, Major the Lady Jane Seaborn had organized for her godfather she said, "I saw you engaged in a conversation with Sloan Marlow."

Col. Randal said, "I was."

Lady Jane said, "What was your impression of her?"

Col. Randal said, "Even better looking up close."

"I meant as a person?"

"Poised, direct eye contact – dry sense of humor, good with men. Interviewed me straight out of the MI-5 handbook. She has a hypnotic effect…"

Lady Jane said, "Beverly is beside herself. She is convinced you and Jack are playing with fire – insists S&M is a black widow."

Col. Randal said, "I don't think so."

"Do you believe there is a possibility Jack may actually fall for her?"

"She likes him."

Lady Jane said, "Oh my, Jack has never been in a serious relationship. I do hope he does not get hurt. This may not end well."

"Jack's fine."

"What did you and Sloan find to talk about?"

Col. Randal said, "She wanted to know what attracted me to you."

"What did you tell her?"

Col. Randal said, "The truth – I felt sorry for you, seemed desperate, big smile…"

Lady Jane laughed, "My recollection is I pursued you relentlessly from the night we met. Finally ran you to ground in the middle of a battle on a mountain in darkest Abyssinia. As you recall."

"I left that part out."

"Love you, John Randal – I took pleasure from the chase except for not being confident you were noticing me."

"I was."

MAJOR THE LADY JANE SEABORN HAD PLANNED A SMALL exclusive party for her godfather, Lieutenant Colonel John Henry

Bevan. He was being promoted to full colonel. The British handled their rank structure in a way that was sometimes difficult for their American counterparts to fully comprehend.

In the U.S. Army, a rigid adherence to the chain of command was in place. While that was also true in the British Army, temporary and even honorary promotions were not uncommon. Jumping several grades – almost unheard of in the U.S. Army – occurred from time to time.

When it came to quasi-military agencies like MI-5, Major General Sir David Petrie, the Security Services Director General, held an honorary rank. Before the war he had been Director of the Intelligence Bureau, Indian Imperial Police. That description of his job may have been a cover. Some said he had never been a policeman.

It was also not uncommon for a British officer-in-charge to hold a rank lower than some of the people in his organization who reported to him. For example, Lt. Col. Bevan was the Allies' top Deception officer. He reported to Prime Minister Churchill. And he passed his deception plans directly to SHAEF Ops B. However, one of his LCS liaison officers outranked him.

Tonight Lt. Col. Bevan was being promoted to full colonel. To the U.S. Army observers' way of thinking, his new rank did not make a lot of sense. For the pivotal influence the London Controlling Section had on the Allied war effort they thought he should have been promoted to Major General – honorary, acting or temporary.

The only possible explanation for not needing the rank was because his power came from access, not rank…a subtle distinction. Lt. Col. Bevan had a direct line to the Prime Minister – weekly private meetings with copious amounts of brandy being consumed and cigars smoked. That was all the standing needed.

He could have performed his job as a private.

The guest list tonight was a who's who of D-Day deception planners: Lieutenant Colonel Harry "Joe" Hollis – Deputy Director, LCS; Major Roger Fleetwood-Hesketh – LCS Planning Officer; Squadron Leader Dennis Wheatly, LCS Deception Advisor; Lieutenant Colonel Sir John Cecil Masterman – Chairman, XX-Committee; Lieutenant Colonel Thomas Argyll "Tar" Robertson aka Passion Pants – MI-5, Section B1-A; Major General Sir Stewart Menzies aka "C" –

Chief of MI-6; Brigadier Claude Dansey – Deputy Chief MI-6; Colonel Peter Wright – MI-6 liaison to LCS; Colonel Benjamin H. "Monk" Dickinson, SHAEF G-2 deception oversight; Lieutenant Colonel Noel Wild – Chief, Ops(B), SHAEF; Lieutenant Colonel David Strangeways, DSO – Chief of Deception, 21 Army Group aka R Force.

Major General William "Wild Bill" Donovan and Major General Sam Houston Blackwell were also invited as were several of Raiding Forces' personnel currently staying at the Bradford.

When it was learned Prime Minister Churchill would be there, both General Dwight D. Eisenhower, SHAEF, and Major General Sir David Petrie – Director General of MI-5, had their offices contact Lady Jane to inquire if they could attend.

Permission granted.

Colonel John Randal went over the guest list with Lady Jane. He had never heard of over half the people on it. Some, like Lt. Col. Wild and Lt. Col. Strangeways, he served with as far back as Oasis X when the two were senior members of Brigadier Dudley Clarke's A-Force. If the rest of the officers he did not know were of the same caliber as those two, the Allied D-Day deception campaign was in capable hands.

One detail caught Col. Randal's attention. Lt. Col. Bevan was Director, London Controlling Section. Lt. Col. Strangeways was Chief of Deception, 21st Army Group – meaning all the Allied ground forces in the upcoming D-Day invasion.

That meant prior to implementation, Lt. Col. Bevan's (after tonight *Colonel* Bevan's) carefully crafted LCS strategic deception directives would be reviewed by Lt. Col. Strangeways. He was an extraordinarily talented officer. A man who marched to his own drum and had, in the course of his A-Force duties, taken charge of a task force during the Tunisian campaign winning the Distinguished Service Order – for battle command, not staff work.

Col. Randal thought there was a good chance Lt. Col. Strangeways would edit or even rewrite some of the LCS cover plans before passing them on to his boss, Field Marshal Bernard Montgomery.

Sparks were likely to fly.

Col. Randal did not mention his thoughts to Lady Jane. That was her godfather's problem. He intended to hide and watch.

Looking at the people invited Col. Randal could not help but notice there was a lot of jockeying for power taking place. From Cairo, Brig. Clarke was seeding SHAEF with handpicked A-Force officers. MI-6 was doing the same. OSS was attempting to as well with some success. He wondered if Gen. Eisenhower was aware of all the friendly spy vs spy intrigue on his staff.

Had the Nazis been able to lay their hands on Lady Jane's guest list it would have been of enormous interest to the Abwehr. Those invited consisted of the top echelon of SHAEF's BODY GUARD/FORTITUDE Deception planners.

Cover Plans, Chain-of-Command, SHAEF, Deception:

1) LCS, (Bevan, Chief of Deception)
2) Ops(B) (Wild, operational planning)
3) Deception G/(S) Ops B (Strangeways, 21 Army Group)
4) Double Cross (Masterman/Robertson XX)
5) B1-A Double Agents (Robertson MI-5)

As they arrived at the reception Lady Jane laughed, "We had to get Uncle promoted so he shall no longer have to salute you, John."

Col. Randal said, "That's too bad."

One of the guests, Lt. Col. Robertson, the consummate counterintelligence officer – Mandy Paige's boss at MI- 5, observed Captain Billy Jack Jaxx walk in with one of MI-5's B-1B's best female operatives. The infamous S&M. A woman of whom it was said possessed the ability to tempt officers to talk themselves into a court-martial as if she cast a spell over them.

Tar wondered what Sloan Marlow being with Capt. Jaxx tonight portended. Nothing was ever as it seemed in the murky world of counterintelligence. Everyone was suspect until proven otherwise.

Was Jack Cool a security risk?

11

NOT HAVING THIS CONVERSATION

LIEUTENANT WESTLY SLADE LAUNCHED HIS TYPE M BOAT, Rubber, Assault over the side of Captain Penelope "Legs" Honeycutt-Parker's PT boat one mile off his objective. Time to go to work. Lt. Slade's orders were to conduct a reconnaissance. By definition, recon work is clandestine. The stated purpose of the exercise was to determine what enemy activity was taking place at the location provided. However, subsequent instructions incidental to the Warning Order cast doubt on the mission statement – as it related to the actual purpose of the exercise. Leaving behind a piece of gear marked 'U.S.' was not clandestine.

Aerial photos indicated the Germans were constructing something on a large flat chalk rock slab in the center of the islet above the high tide mark. It was believed they were constructing – or had already constructed – a listening post, observation post (LP/OP). There was the possibility of a light anti-aircraft gun having been emplaced. It was not believed the position was occupied during the nightly12-hour high tide period.

Not that it seemed like nighttime. There was a full moon out. Almost bright enough to read by.

Initially the plan called for four OSS Special Warfare Operators to paddle ashore. However, when Colonel John Randal flew in to observe the

Operations Order, Lt. Slade requested permission to add two additional Frogs to the party. The two men would stay with the assault boat to secure the ERP while the other four operators carried out the reconnaissance.

Col. Randal agreed to the request. It was his long-standing policy to grant the mission commander wide latitude in making adjustments to the composition of his team provided he cleared it first. On operations of this nature Raiding Forces had few hard fast rules as long as security was never compromised.

In a number of ways the Office of Strategic Services Maritime Unit training program was superior to the U.S. Navy's Underwater Demolition Teams. The Underwater Demolition Team's (UDT) mission typically stopped at the water's edge though they were capable of landing ashore and clearing beach obstacles a short distance inland.

The Maritime Units (MU) were masters of all UDT capabilities: offshore surveys, demolitions, shallow water clearance, etc. plus covert beach work, coastal infiltration skills, maritime sabotage, intelligence gathering, land/or amphibious raiding techniques and also conducting ambushes and prisoner snatches short distances ashore.

After the OSS Maritime Unit was assigned to Raiding Forces, their infantry skills were honed to perfection through an intensive unit assessment program and a series of live fire on-the-job training (OJT) missions against actual targets in the Aegean. Then the Special Warfare Operators were packed off to the Commando Training Center at Achnacarry, Scotland to put the final polish on their small unit raiding skills.

Now Lt. Slade's team was cocked and locked. Good to go. Ready to put all that hard training and no small number of actual missions run out of Castelrozzo to use.

The problem facing the Frogs was the water. In the Aegean it was warm. Here in England it was cold. So much so the British, who had pioneered special naval commando operations, stood most of their units down in the UK and transferred them to warmer climate in the China, Burma, India Theatre of Operations.

Lt. Slade and his people would not be swimming ashore with a knife in their teeth tonight – not in that frigid water. The Frogs would paddle to the islet and dismount like Commandos, not go in like combat swimmers.

Tonight Lt. Slade was acting as the stern man. That meant he steered the rubber boat by the use of paddle strokes that acted as the rudder to keep the assault raft on course. In that role he was going to be constantly adjusting for crosswinds, tide, and drift.

Lt. Slade would also be determining how far the boat traveled by the use of ancient mariners' "dead reckoning" using speed, time, distance and stroke count. This is more complicated than it sounds. Working practical math problems while approaching an enemy shore under cover of darkness is not something taught in most public schools.

For the navigator knowing your boat team is a must. There is a known stroke count for a specific crew. The desired measurement being the number of paddle strokes per 100 yards. Determining it requires hours and hours of practice in all weather conditions, day or night.

Learning how to estimate the distance your boat typically travels in a given period of time is a specialty skill. Stronger crews take longer, more powerful strokes which results in greater distance traveled per stroke. All the Special Warfare Operators were strong paddlers which helped Lt. Slade with his calculations.

A fully loaded boat sits lower in the water which produces more drag and that equals shorter distance traveled per stroke. The state of the weather and sea are both factors. Paddling against the current translates into more strokes. If there is a crosswind, stroke production is uneven on different sides of the boat.

Tonight Lt. Slade also assumed the responsibility for being the boat crew's compass man. Meaning he was responsible for staying on azimuth while paddling. While estimating distance traveled.

There was no way to overemphasize the importance of the compass man's task. Stray off even slightly and the Frogs would find themselves landing on the mainland – the most heavily fortified territory in enemy-occupied France.

As navigator he would constantly be checking and rechecking his luminous, liquid-filled, wrist compass manufactured for OSS by the Taylor Instrument Company, Rochester, New York. Lt. Slade knew an inherent design flaw produced a 3° error in the compasses.

It had to be factored in.

Not everyone has what it takes to be a small boat navigator. Dead reckoning is an art as well as a skill set. And tonight to make things interesting the enemy's mainland coast was in sight. The rubber raft would be closing the distance to 800 yards – a long rifle shot, which gave the Frogs something to think about.

Lt. Slade was going to be mentally juggling critical factors, numbers and conditions while steering the boat in addition to being the team leader responsible for all tactical decisions.

Once the Special Warfare Operators were settled aboard, Lt. Slade ordered under his breath, "Give way together."

In sync, acting as one, all paddlers began stroking in unison. The rubber assault raft surged forward. It could carry seven men. However, tonight there were only six on board.

Originally the plan was for a team of four the extra Frogs were a precaution. The last thing Recon Team wanted was to come back to find a surprise waiting when it was time for the patrol to exfil the target area. Why take a chance?

Lt. Slade had no plans to.

The Special Warfare Operators were keyed up. Tonight, as briefed, the mission was almost like an operation scripted off a page taken out of one of their old stateside training evolutions. The Frogs were tough, disciplined men who had invested blood, sweat, tears and a lot of time perfecting their amphibious and ground warfare skills. Now they were focused on performing their individual tasks to the absolute best of their ability.

No matter what.

Missions like tonight's quick reaction recon were the reason Col. Randal had gone to such lengths to fold the OSS Maritime Unit into Raiding Forces even though at first the MUs did not seem like a good fit. This mission was the purest form of reconnaissance. Slip in, gather intelligence, slip out undetected – or maybe not so undetected.

They were planning to leave evidence behind revealing the patrol had been there.

Tonight's mission called for stealth, tactics executed with absolute precision and impeccable timing. It was nothing like the raids out of Castelrozzo where the Frogs went in hot behind Captain Billy Jack Jaxx and shot everyone wearing a different uniform than they were.

Not that they had anything against *that.*

On reaching the islet they pulled the Type M, Boat, Rubber, Assault up on the beach a few yards inland – it marked the ERP. As per the plan, Lt. Slade left two Frogs to secure the ERP. Then his four-man Recon Team went to the prone and listened.

For five minutes.

No one had any idea what they were listening for. But what the Special Warfare Operators wanted to hear was nothing. Total silence would be perfect. Intelligence had reported the island was not believed to be occupied during the night high tide period. Military Intelligence being, in Lt. Slade's experience, an oxymoron, he and his team of Frogs would not be taking that information at face value.

They listened for the full five minutes. It seemed like an eternity on a small island 800 yards off enemy-occupied France that might or might not have German soldiers stationed on it who had spotted them coming, lying in wait.

Clouds were drifting in, obscuring the bright full moon except on occasion when a gap in the cloud cover allowed it to shine through briefly. Time to move out. From this point on, no verbal commands would be issued. All communications were by hand signal.

The islet was tiny – approximately an acre in size. In the brief moments when the moon was back out the Special Warfare Operators could see water for a full 360°. No sign of enemy personnel. That did not mean there were not any. The Germans could be in defilade.

This mission had a different feel from those they had gone on in the Aegean. The Wehrmacht 15th Army, the heaviest enemy troop concentration in enemy-occupied France, was less than a half mile away from where the Special Warfare Operators were standing. Knowing the Germans in such large numbers were right over there felt spooky strange.

Not an emotion the hard-as-nails Frogmen would have cared to admit to – though it was a bit of a rush. Not many people had pulled a recon mission quite like this one.

Lt. Slade gave the signal to move out. He took the point. The patrol stepped off silently, carefully placing every foot down in exaggerated slow motion before putting their full weight on it. Not a sound was to be heard except for the lapping of the waves.

The order of march was Lt. Slade, the slack man – meaning the operator directly behind him in the column providing cover as he worked the compass, followed by another operator, then last in the column came the rear security man who walked backward from time to time. Walking backward in the dark of night on patrol is its own specialty skill set.

Every member of Recon Team was armed with a suppressed 9mm M-3 Grease Gun – a weapon so utilitarian it entered service without an official name – only the numeral designator. "Grease Gun," as the weapon was universally called, was an unofficial nickname so widely in use it might as well have been official.

Suppressed, for close-in clandestine ops, the stubby little SMG looked like it had been bolted together out of a box of spare parts. Cost per weapon – $20. It was designed to be thrown away if one broke down.

While not perfect, the standard issue M3 Grease Gun was close enough. The suppressed OSS 9mm model was outstanding for close-in covert work. It was very quiet.

Moving slowly, only slightly faster than what civilian deer hunters called 'still hunting,' the patrol worked its way toward the chalk rock base where the LP/OP, a possible anti-aircraft gun position, was reported to be. The white chalk rock was plainly visible reflecting the moonlight when it was not covered by clouds.

Land navigation was not a problem. The islet was so small there was no need for a pace count. The only reason Lt. Slade even bothered watching his compass was for the return trip. He wanted to be able to establish a back azimuth that would lead him straight to the ERP.

"Not for the weak or fainthearted" was heard frequently around Raiding Forces. Leading a patrol in close proximity to the heaviest concentration of German troops in enemy-occupied France – with the mental checklist that had to be worked through, while making the constant stream of life and death tactical decisions required to accomplish the mission, and bring your men home – pretty much captured the essence of the creed.

Patrol leaders, regardless of rank, were highly respected.

The terrain on the tiny islet was no walk in the park. It was deceptively uneven consisting of broken rock, hard chalk ledges and jagged shelves. When the moon peeked through the cloud cover, the chalk reflected it, creating dark silhouettes making walking precarious.

The winds blowing in off the Channel were relentless which caused the vegetation to be stunted. It was mostly short salt-grass, maritime scrub and occasional patches of sea lavender, whatever that was. Lt. Slade had no idea. It was mentioned in a copy of Baedeker's Northern France travel guide he found in the Seaborn House library when searching for information on his objective. There was a chapter titled "Islands" that covered flora and fauna.

While the low scrub was not like pushing through the jungle the Frogs had trained for, anticipating duty in the Pacific, nevertheless, it made for hard going. The short, bushy, extremely tough vegetation combined with the broken rock underfoot made it necessary for care to be taken not to trip or turn an ankle. The team moved forward in bounds, only a single man traveling at a time.

Lt. Slade advanced ten yards, then froze in place to allow the trailing Frogs to catch up one by one. It was slow, tedious, exacting movement. The idea was to arrive at some place in the dark of night, where, if there was an enemy present, they were not expecting you. The Frogs simply appeared. One second, they were not there – the next, they were.

It was clear to Lt. Slade if there was a German fixed position on the island it would be on the flat white chalk rock. It was the only place smooth enough to set up permanently. And it was believed to be the only location that remained above the waterline at high tide.

Lt. Slade reached the edge of the white slab. The rock took up about a quarter of the entire tidal islet. Up to this point the patrol had not come across any sign of enemy occupation.

Now, out in the center of the slab he could see the faint shadow of what appeared to be a low structure. If that was what it was, the position would have an open-topped firing port facing out toward the Channel. Possibly with a canvas shelter half cover. That meant the patrol needed to circle around to approach it from the land side.

He signaled the patrol to go down on one knee in a tight perimeter pulled in so close their shoulders were touching. Lt. Slade whispered, "We're going to move to leeward before advancing to check it out. Stay frosty boys."

He was not exactly sure what that meant, but it always sounded good when Jack Cool said it.

Moving very, very carefully, the patrol skirted the giant white rock slab. With the wind blowing and never letting up, the fact it was impossible not to break a stem of scrub from time to time by stepping on it was not turning out to be a problem. The sound dissipated in a wind gust almost immediately.

When they reached the leeward side behind the target, Lt. Slade halted the patrol again. The Special Warfare Operators went to the prone in a tight perimeter defensive position facing out. He moved forward alone out onto the slab feeling very exposed.

The wind was blowing, the chalk rock was stable, and without the vegetation he was moving like a ghost. No loose rock, no breaking twigs, no noise. The first sign of enemy presence Lt. Slade came to was a landline running from the LP/OP across the slab toward the tidal flats to the mainline. Most of which were submerged at this time of night. He knelt down and cut the line with his blunt-tipped, sheep-foot blade-style, Western Cutlery Company utility knife. The tool was manufactured to OSS Maritime Unit specifications.

For sentry elimination/ hand-to-hand combat he also carried a Fairbairn Fighting Knife strapped to his canvas-topped raiding boot. The suppressed M3 Grease Gun virtually eliminated any need for knife work. However, Lt. Slade had fully bought into the ethos of Raiding Forces' Rules and its unofficial credos: "Too much ain't enough" and "Ain't no such thing as overkill" being two of his personal favorites.

Raiding Forces was a big believer in redundancy.

The landline led straight to the LP/OP. The islets' small size meant the defensive position would not have been laid in by German combat engineers. The soldiers tasked with manning the site built it. Rocks had been piled up about 4 feet high on three sides to knock down the wind. There was a Wehrmacht grey rain cape stretched over the open-air top.

Lt. Slade carefully eased up to the open back side of the position, M-3 to his shoulder. No noise was coming from the position. It was dark. No light showing. He made out the shadowed silhouettes of two men inside, wrapped up in triangular German Army standard-issue Zeltbahn groundsheets – sound asleep.

His orders were to leave something behind to let the Germans know the Special Warfare Operators had been there.

SSSSS, SSSSS –That should do the trick.

The Grease Gun as normally issued came in .45 caliber – approximately 450 rounds per minute, a very slow cyclic rate which felt like it was pumping out ping-pong balls. OSS had opted for the conversion kit that would convert the M3 to 9mm which was only slightly faster – 500 rounds per minute.

Lt. Slade marveled, as always, at how controllable and quiet the weapon was.

After making sure both Nazis were – as Jack Cool would have said, "Seriously dead," he went back to pick up the rest of the team. Even with the wind blowing in their direction, the Frogs had not heard a sound. They trooped up to the German LP/OP. Lt. Slade let them conduct the search. While nothing much of interest was found in terms of intelligence or war trophy value, from a purely leadership perspective it was a nice move to let the men have what there was.

In compliance with his orders to leave something behind with 'U.S.' stenciled on it, Lt. Slade pitched an empty K-Ration carton inside stamped 'U.S.' brought along for exactly that purpose. To the Nazis it would likely indicate the Americans shot the two men manning the post then sat down to eat a meal.

Not a bad message to send to your enemy.

Lt. Slade was tempted to say, "Let's get the hell out of Dodge," but he restrained himself.

Mission accomplished.

COLONEL JOHN RANDAL SAID, "ARE YOU PREPARED TO ACCEPT a Warning Order?"

Captain Dick Courtney said, "Sir!"

He and Lieutenant Chase Starrett were in the War Room at the Bradford Hotel having been summoned from Seaborn House. They had no idea when they arrived an operation was imminent. Col. Randal liked to see the reaction his officers exhibited when taken off guard by an unexpected assignment.

The mission was on for tonight – another hasty recon.

Col. Randal decided to turn the operation into a live fire training exercise – in anticipation of – if things went according to plan – there not actually being any live fire. Capt. Courtney, his most experienced reconnaissance officer, needed experience leading a patrol larger than four men. Lt. Starrett – a veteran SOG officer and rising star in Raiding Forces – could use more time getting adapted to cross-channel work before being assigned his own independent missions.

The fact there was an actual enemy target to reconnoiter came in dead last on the 'purpose-of-the-exercise' priority list as far as Col. Randal was concerned. Bringing his small unit leaders up to speed as fast as possible was what he cared about. The frequency with which new missions kept turning up indicated the tempo of operations along the French Coast was likely to intensify the closer it came to D-Day.

All Col. Randal knew for sure was the buildup of U.S. troops arriving from the States was gaining momentum. The word was in the first thirty days after D-Day, the Allies would need to have a lodgment in France of over two million men ashore. Best guess was it would take at least another six months before the U.S. share of those troops could arrive in England for the invasion.

Another story making the rounds was that more British Commonwealth troops would be landing on D-Day than American. Then, due to manpower shortages and casualties, the UK would have to start cannibalizing units due to lack of replacements.

At the same time the U.S. buildup would be increasing disproportionately – eventually growing to a three-to-one numbers advantage.

Raiding Forces had the troop strength to carry out a series of small-scale raids for the next six months – barely. What Col. Randal did not have was enough officers to lead the teams Raiding Forces would be operating in. And that was a problem.

With the troop buildup of the line infantry and airborne divisions preparing for the Second Front accelerating, there was no ready pool of junior officers arriving in country to recruit from. The pipeline of regular Army NCOs had dried up. No commander was willing to release any of their men. Unless, of course, it was to get rid of incompetents or troublemakers.

There were plenty of those to be had.

Col. Randal had been taken off guard by how quickly he had been required to commence pre-invasion Raiding Forces' operations. If the tempo of missions held steady, and he expected them to pick up the closer it got to D-Day, Raiding Forces was going to take casualties.

He could expect to suffer an inordinate number of losses in his team leader ranks.

Not only was the steady drumbeat of missions set in motion by the mysterious hand behind the King's Messengers' assignments already starting to pose a strain, but Commander Ian Fleming was asking to have a conversation about the state of his Red Indian program. Which would put an even greater strain on Raiding Forces' thin ranks. And there was the Escape operation to be put in place.

Aware of the Naval Intelligence Division project Major General William "Wild Bill" Donovan had instructed Col. Randal to have a competing program in place for OSS in time for the invasion – to be called "Target Force." Which was going to be hard to do since Wild Bill had not bothered to mention when D-Day was going to take place or where he was to get the people he was going to need.

Raiding Forces was over committed. His troop commanders would be carrying a disproportionate share of the operational burden. And presently there were not enough of them to go around.

This was on Col. Randal's mind as he began his Warning Order.

"*Situation...* Enemy Forces: A German coastal artillery battery is located north of Ambleteuse consisting of four 155mm guns in open concrete emplacements. The position is supported by machine-gun tobruks, a rangefinder tower, surrounded by concertina wire entanglements and mine obstacles. It's manned by an estimated 60 to 100 Heeresküstenartillerie with local infantry support. Night patrols move on fixed routes along tracks around the perimeter wire.

"*Friendly Forces*: Mrs. Brandy Seaborn will provide transport to and from the French coast. There are no other friendly elements operating in the immediate vicinity.

"*Mission*: At a time and place to be designated Raiding Forces' Recon Team "Courtney" will infiltrate the French coast west of Ambleteuse with the intent to reconnoiter the coastal gun battery, confirm layout and defenses and exfiltrate prior to first light.

"*Execution: Concept of the Operation*: A 10-man Recon Team under Captain Courtney consisting of eight Raiding Forces' operators and two Life Boat Service Men, will embark aboard Mrs. Seaborn's PT boat and put to sea from the river dock at Seaborn House at a time to be provided by her. Two miles off the coast of France the team will transfer to an M-1943 Boat, Assault, Inflatable. Land west of the battery and infiltrate through the dunes to establish an Objective Rally Point which will also serve as an Observation Post. You will conduct limited sabotage, cutting communications cables etc. when and where found. This is a clandestine mission. Silence and stealth are paramount.

"*Tasks*: Secure the Initial Rally Point/Exfiltration Rally Point. Move to your ORP/OP. Gather intelligence from the OP. Map searchlight positions. Note any nocturnal enemy activity. Stay ashore no longer than one hour then conduct your exfil. I say again, this is a clandestine operation – sneak and peek.

"*Coordinating Instructions*: Coordinate your departure time with Mrs. Seaborn.

"*Equipment*: Suppressed M3 Grease Guns common to all.

"*Transportation*: PT boat, M-1943, rubber, assault…"

Following the obligatory, "This concludes my Warning Order – what are your questions?" There were no questions. There should have been. The Concept of the Operation did not make a lot of sense.

What could the Recon Team expect to learn about an enemy objective they were ordered not to approach in the dark of night?

Col. Randal said, "You're not going to ask any questions?"

Neither Capt. Courtney or Lt. Starrett responded – they were confused but not enough to request an explanation.

Col. Randal said, "I'm not in the business of sending my troops on fool's errands. There's no intel you can obtain that an aerial photograph wouldn't provide just as well, possibly better. Nothing is to be gained from this mission except for you physically being there – and that serves some greater purpose.

"Just don't ask me what it is because I have no idea."

Capt. Courtney said, "I did wonder about that, sir."

Col. Randal said, "Here's what's about to happen. You're going to land and move to the ORP. Leave an item or two off your web gear clearly marked 'U.S.' or a soft cap for the Germans to find – then exfil.

Lt. Starrett said, "That's it, sir?"

Col. Randal said, "Affirmative – everyone that goes in comes out, is that clear?"

Capt. Courtney and Lt. Starrett looked at each other, "Clear, sir!"

As mud.

COLONEL JOHN RANDAL WAS SITTING WITH MANDY PAIGE IN the VIP Section. They had their chairs pulled close together for privacy. He did not want anyone to have any idea what it was they were talking about. The Vulnerable Points Wing security operator had been alerted no one was to disturb them. Unless, that is, Major the Lady Jane Seaborn appeared.

The relationship between the two of them was hard to quantify. Lady Jane said she was his muse – might be true. Col. Randal sought Mandy out to hear her slant on serious subjects. She had gone from being a brave dispatch horse girl at RAF Habbaniya during the siege to one of his most trusted advisors.

Col. Randal said, “We’re not having this conversation.”

Mandy said, “Yes, we are.”

Col. Randal said, “I need your advice, but if what I am about to ask causes any conflict of interest for you, stop me immediately. Then forget everything I’ve said up to that point.”

“I can do that, John.”

“Your mother is flying in later this afternoon. She’s bringing Captain Butterfield with her. Raiding Forces has been tasked with standing up an OSS Escape & Evasion operation. Preston’s going to handle the French end.

“I plan to ask Veronica’s advice on how to organize it. Then she’s going back to Castelrozzo. How are we doing so far?”

Mandy said, “I am fine.”

Col. Randal said, “Here’s where it starts to get tricky. As you know, British intelligence believes it owns intel gathering in Europe. OSS is being frozen out. Currently there’s no American Escape & Evasion organization in place to assist USAAF aircrew who have been shot down.

MI-9 will get them out if they can, but at the end of the day, it’s a British agency.

“Politics just entered our conversation – we still good?”

Mandy said, “I am aware what you said is true about our intelligence agencies aggressively keeping OSS marginalized – they want a monopoly. Did not know General Donovan does not have an Escape organization. That comes as a shock.”

Col. Randal said, “If MI-9 finds out we’re setting up an E&E operation for OSS they’ll try to intervene. My orders are not to let that happen. I need to get an escape line up and running before our British friends know what's going on.

"Crossing any red lines yet?"

"Negative"

"I have been instructed to keep Escape a standalone U.S. operation. The American public would not be well disposed if they found out their boys were being shot down without any US rescue organization in place."

Mandy said, "Who would blame them, John? What you are telling me is not acceptable. I would call it a national disgrace."

Col. Randal said, "I don't like doing things this way, Mandy – keeping secrets compartmentalized within the unit. And I don't want to put you in a bad spot. What's your thought?"

Mandy said, "Set the E&E program up for OSS. Full speed ahead. Do what you have to do and let the chips fall where they may. I know you always say 'teamwork, teamwork, teamwork,' but this is a unique situation.

"It may be political but there is the morale factor of the United States Army Air Force personnel flying missions – they deserve better, and the American public to consider. The mothers of those boys shot down over enemy territory need to know their country is doing everything in its power to bring them home safely."

Col. Randal said, "So, you're not going to hold it against me when this all comes out and blows up in our face as it inevitably will."

"Absolutely not, John. I speak French and would volunteer to help if you would allow me, but as you know my MI-5 work with Rocky prohibits me from exposing myself to the possibility of capture. Beverly was threatened with the Tower of London for flying your mission to snatch Major von Reisman."

Col. Randal said, "No conflict of interest with MI-5 or risking a post-war job opportunity with the Security Service? Tell me if there is."

Mandy said, "Not on my part. Five may feel differently. It is irrelevant to me if they do."

Col. Randal said, "How do you think Jane's going to react – she's MI-6 *and* SOE."

Mandy laughed, "Now I understand. You have not let Lady Jane in on your secret project yet. You want to know what I believe her reaction shall be."

Col. Randal said, "Roger that."

Mandy said, "After the war, my plan is to go straight to Big Sur as fast as I can and live in the private compound Lady Jane is planning to build on the ranch she bought you. Help raise spotted ponies. Enjoy the finer things."

Col. Randal said, "I see."

Mandy said, "Quit worrying about Lady Jane or me. There is no possibility of any divided sense of loyalty on our part. Go kill Hitler and 'let's get the hell out of Dodge – California or Bust'."

Col. Randal said, "Good to know."

"Feel better now?"

"I do."

A KING'S MESSENGER ARRIVED AT THE VELVET ROPE GATE TO the VIP Section. After the SOP process of identifying himself and requiring Colonel John Randal to do the same, the KM passed over a sealed envelope and departed the Bradford Hotel. Reading the contents it was immediately clear… this was different. Not like anything Raiding Forces had done previously.

Col. Randal was ordered to conduct a hydrographic survey of a beach in the Pas-de-Calais Military District located at the coordinates provided to ascertain if it was suitable to support heavy wheeled and tracked vehicles to include tanks. He knew to invade France it was going to be necessary for the Allies to land all their motor transport over the invasion beaches, move inland, cross the Line of Departure (LD) and drive on Berlin.

Victory would be contingent on the application of simple fundamental military tactics that would be affected at every turn by a complex series of outside forces wind, rain, soil composition, terrain etc. in addition to enemy activity. All of which had to be identified, understood and planned for.

The dispatch specifically stated "…take soil samples, measure water depth and record the speed and strength of the currents." Not the type of reconnaissance Raiding Forces had ever trained for or carried out. Basically it was a geology experiment conducted on an enemy beach under cover of darkness."

Col. Randal realized immediately this dispatch was asking for a sophisticated geological survey that in all probability exceeded the capability of even the highly-trained OSS Special Warfare Operators. No time requirement was stipulated. Was this some sort of a test like the earlier missions?

The stark KM directive did not leave that impression.

Major the Lady Jane Seaborn and Beverly Blackwell were sitting with Major General Sam Houston "Bronc" Blackwell and Brandy Seaborn studying a set of blueprints spread out over a coffee table. They were going over the plans for the Troop Transport Command. Construction was already well underway.

Col. Randal made eye contact with Beverly. She excused herself and proceeded straight over. The King's Messenger had not come and gone unnoticed.

"Yes, sir."

"I need you to fly to Seaborn House, pick up Lieutenant Slade and bring him back here immediately."

"On the way, Johnny."

Seeing Beverly go tearing off like she had been fired out of a cannon, Lady Jane walked over to inquire what was taking place.

Col. Randal handed her the KM dispatch, "Where am I going to find a geologist qualified to go on a reconnaissance mission to France for the purpose of 'carrying out a hydrographic survey of a potential invasion beach'?"

Studying the dispatch, Lady Jane said, "Professor Winthrop has a double PhD – archaeology and geology. The two disciplines are complementary. He taught both subjects at the University of Cairo.

Col. Randal said, "Really?"

Lady Jane said, "I shall see how fast Bronc can arrange to have him here."

After a brief conversation with Maj. Gen. Blackwell, Lady Jane rushed off to send a telex to Dr. Winthrop on Castelrozzo.

Bronc strolled over to speak to Col. Randal. He was a world-class delegator when it came to TTC's daily operations. But the instant the situation demanded, Maj. Gen. Blackwell became a take-charge, hands-on commander capable of leaping tall buildings in a single bound. Wanted to be kept in the loop about Raiding Forces… at all times.

Col. Randal had no objections to that.

"What's going on, Colonel?"

Col. Randal showed him the KM's dispatch.

"I need Dr. Winthrop here as soon as possible, General."

Maj. Gen. Blackwell said, "That's what Lady Jane was telling me. If TTC doesn't have a flight out of Cairo scheduled, we'll expedite one. Looks like you've got yourself a serious mission here, Colonel."

Col. Randal said, "That's the way I read it, sir."

BEVERLY BLACKWELL AND LIEUTENANT WESTLY SLADE arrived at the Bradford Hotel after a whirlwind flight from Seaborn House. The Special Warfare Operator had been preparing for a hasty mission later that night to deliver a geological auger to a beach in the Pas-de-Calais region. He needed to get back as soon as possible.

Colonel John Randal was waiting in the War Room. Captain Billy Jack Jaxx and Beverly sat in, even though they did not have any part in the mission to be discussed. That was fine with Col. Randal. He liked his people taking an active interest in Raiding Forces' operations.

Col. Randal handed the King's Messenger's dispatch to Lt. Slade. He read it silently. Then he passed it to Capt. Jaxx who scanned the contents and handed it to Beverly.

Col. Randal said, "What does that tell you, Lieutenant?"

Lt. Slade said, "SHAEF is initiating a series of hydrographic surveys to determine the feasibility of amphibious landings on certain beaches of interest in France – this is advance work for the big show, sir."

Col. Randal said, "Are your people capable of making such surveys, and if so, what size team is required for the job?"

Lt. Slade said, "Up to a point, sir. My Frogs are trained to conduct beach surveys. However, what is being asked for in this dispatch is going to require someone like a trained geologist for the hydrographic evaluation."

Col. Randal said, "Why might that be?"

Lt.. Slade said, "Beaches that look firm at low tide can liquefy or collapse under weight when wheeled and/or tracked vehicles go ashore. A geologist is needed to identify zones likely to become soft when saturated by tides, rain or shelling. There were problems with the beach surveys in North Africa.

"It takes a specialist to evaluate whether exits off the beaches can be cut by combat engineers – there are shingle ridges and clay cliffs behind some landing sites that will have to be dealt with.

"As for team size, surveys can be done with as few as two operators – the problem is finding the geological specialist."

Col. Randal said, "If I supply one…?"

Lt.. Slade said, "Then my people will handle the surveys, no problem, sir. However, this request has another element that complicates it."

Capt. Jaxx said, "What's the problem, Westly?"

Lt.. Slade said, "Each beach is topographically different with varying geology and gradients. A sandy beach with a gently sloping gradient in the Pacific is different than what we're going to face in France.

"Offshore beach obstacles, minefields and defensive positions will all need to be probed. We can do that. If you have a geologist, he can handle the scientific details – we'll take him ashore, can do.

"But this directive also requires us to go inland to determine where airfields can be constructed during the buildup after the invasion. We've never done anything like that, Colonel."

Beverly said, "Wow – insane!"

Lt.. Slade said, "Special Warfare Operators like to say 'we do the difficult right away – the impossible takes a little longer', but this is a different magnitude of problem, sir."

Capt. Jaxx said, "Glad it's you not me, Westly."

Col. Randal said, "Doctor Winthrop is a geologist. He's en route as we speak. Draw up a list of the equipment you'll need. I'll get clarification on the airfield evaluation."

Lt.. Slade said, "The Doctor's 'Right Man, Right Job', sir – my Frogs will like working with him."

Col. Randal said, "OK then, Beverly fly Lt. Slade back to Seaborn House. He's got work to do."

"Wheels up in twenty, Johnny."

Col. Randal said, "I'll try to get down to see your team off, Lieutenant. In the event I can't make it, good luck. I'll expect a full report on your return."

"Yes, sir."

COLONEL JOHN HENRY BEVAN ARRIVED AT THE BRADFORD Hotel. He saw Colonel John Randal in the VIP section of the lobby talking to Major General Sam Houston "Bronc" Blackwell. He walked over and spoke to the Vulnerable Points Wing security operator manning the rope gate.

The VPW guard proceeded to where Col. Randal was sitting and whispered in his ear. He excused himself and came to the velvet rope where Col. Bevan was waiting. It did not escape his notice that the Controlling Officer, London Controlling Section appeared uncharacteristically tense. Normally Lady Jane's godfather was the epitome of composure.

"Is there some place more private we can talk?"

Col. Randal and Col. Bevan took the private elevator to the Penthouse Floor. They entered the Phone Room after instructing the VPW security operator stationed at the desk outside Major the Lady Jane Seaborn's private wing to post an additional guard at the door outside the room. No one was to be allowed in.

Col. Bevan was well pleased to see Col. Randal acceding to his request for privacy with no questions asked.

"A new security flap has erupted. We have a rather serious breach on our hands. Last night a Combined Operations Pilotage Parties' team conducting a hydrographic survey of a beach somewhere in France accidentally returned to base having left behind a geological auger used to take soil samples. It will be instantly recognizable as a piece of survey gear.

"SHAEF is in full meltdown crisis mode again. General Strong, G2 Intelligence, is using terms like dereliction of duty, gross negligence, unacceptable risk to OVERLORD, etc.

"The printable part of the Naval Intelligence Division's response was "leaving this implement behind constitutes malfeasance of the first order."

Col. Randal's reaction, which he kept to himself, was the COPP party must have been surveying an actual landing site. Raiding Forces had intentionally left something behind on almost every mission to let the Germans know they had been there.

"General Laycock, Chief of Combined Operations, is seeing his life pass in front of his eyes – COPP belongs to COHQ. He already had a spotty run of luck in Africa and on Crete. This scandal might be enough to win him a bowler hat."

It was said the first stop a British Army officer made after being cashiered was his hatters to purchase a civilian bowler hat. Col. Randal had no idea if that was actually true or not. Made a good cautionary tale.

Col. Bevan said, "Leaving the auger behind is being treated as a grave breach. You have proven to be an unconventional thinker. I came by to ask what course of action you would suggest in this situation.

"I need to hear an objective recommendation for a course of action from a reliable special forces officer I can trust – since for all practical purposes, you are part of the family."

Col. Randal said, "Describe the auger."

"A hand-powered sand boring tool. Thin metal shaft 3-4 feet long fitted with a helical screw blade on the lower end designed to be twisted into sand or sediment. The purpose of the exercise is to extract a core sample in order to determine if the beach can support landing craft ramps, tanks, wheeled vehicles, etc."

Col. Randal said, "And why exactly does an auger being left behind have SHAEF, LCS and presumably MI-5 in panic mode?"

Col. Bevan said, "No civilian would have any reason to be at the shore in France with a piece of hydrographic survey equipment – beaches are Restricted Areas. It could only have been left there by an Allied military survey party. The auger is a dead giveaway the beach is being evaluated as an invasion site.

Col. Randal said, "I don't see any problem."

Unable to constrain himself, Col. Bevan said, "Are you stark raving mad? The object of FORTITUDE SOUTH is to confuse the other side about our intentions. Not tell them in advance what we are planning to do."

Col. Randal said, "Are these augers in short supply?"

Col. Bevan said, "Quite common actually."

"Col. Randal said, "Good – round me up all you can lay your hands on. I'll put one ashore on every beach in France. Norway too, if you like. That should give the Germans something to think about."

Col. Beven said, "Bloody genius!"

Col. Randal said, "What are families for?"

COLONEL JOHN HENRY BEVAN ARRIVED AT CHEQUERS – THE Prime Minister's estate 37 miles northwest of London. He had been summoned. His best guess was the PM had learned about the geographical auger being left behind on Gold Beach, SHAEF's code name for one of the British invasion beaches. Tonight was not their regularly scheduled meeting.

Prime Minister Churchill demanded to hear bad news in person.

Col. Bevan was ushered into the study by Detective Inspector Walter Henry Thompson of Scotland Yard – the PM's bodyguard. The air in the room was blue from the smoke of the great man's signature *Romeo y Julieta Churchill* Cuban cigar – named for him. It was said he smoked 8 to 10 per day. PM Churchill was holding a cut-glass brandy balloon in one hand and the blunt in the other.

He did not offer either a cigar or a glass of cognac to Col. Bevan. A sure sign this was a strictly business meeting of short duration. And that the PM was out of sorts.

PM Churchill said, "No need for the details about how a piece of survey equipment came to be left behind on Gold Beach. Just tell me what in the blue blazes you intend to do about it, Colonel. The Admiralty views this matter with the utmost seriousness – claims we have compromised the invasion."

Col. Bevan said, "I discussed the situation with Colonel Randal – Lady Jane's friend."

PM Churchill said, "I met the colonel at your promotion party."

Col. Bevan said, "He proposed a solution I believe should resolve the issue to everyone's satisfaction."

PM Churchill said, "Pray tell, do not keep me in suspense. The Navy is acting as if the sky is falling."

Col. Bevan said, "Colonel Randal offered to place augers on every beach in France. Even volunteered to do the same in Norway if we so desire. In his words that shall, 'Give the Germans something to think about'."

PM Churchill said, "By Jove, a solution worthy of Solomon. The objective of deception is not for us to deceive the enemy. It is for us to make the enemy deceive himself.

"Execute Colonel Randal's plan at once – action this day."

Col. Bevan said, "Already in motion, sir."

PM Churchill said, “Splendid. What prompted you to consult the colonel? I was given to understand you are not particularly enamored of Lady Jane’s paramour.”

Col. Bevan said, “I am warming up to him.”

12

GET BLOODY STUFFED

COLONEL JOHN RANDAL AND JAMES "BALDIE" TAYLOR WERE sitting in the VIP Section of the Bradford Hotel's lobby. Jim had come to see him acting in his capacity as the Raiding Forces' liaison to Special Operations Executive or maybe vice versa – his exact role was not completely clear when it came to SOE. There had not been much flow of information between the two organizations since Col. Randal's arrival in England.

That was in part due to Jim's long-time advice to have as little involvement with SOE as possible due to what he described as their "lack of professionalism." That advice was given early on in Egypt. Now here in the UK, Col. Randal had reasons of his own to have doubts about SOE. His concerns centered on the Country Section Officer, Section F (France). Lieutenant Colonel Maurice Buckmaster.

There were several former bilingual Raiding Forces' officers who had been seconded to SOE over the years because of a high priority need for their language skills. From time to time they dropped by the Bradford Hotel to pay a courtesy call on their former commander. The picture they painted of Lt. Col. Buckmaster's handling of Section F – for France – did not inspire confidence.

There was a distinct gulf between SOE staff who lived in the lap of luxury in London and the intrepid field operatives behind the lines in enemy occupied France who risked their lives twenty-four hours a day, every day.

The consensus of the ex-Raiding Forces' officers was Lt. Col. Buckmaster suffered from "dangerous optimism." They believed he was overconfident and slow to recognize German penetrations of resistance circuits. And worse… he ignored the security checks radio operators were taught to put into their messages to alert SOE they had been captured and were under German control – attributing them to be simple mistakes by the W/T operator.

Inexcusable bad judgment.

Lt. Col. Buckmaster was also ambitious – a workaholic. He was in his office eighteen hours a day. The claim was he set up underground networks without enough time spent laying the groundwork to give them a chance at success. It was said he drove the expansion of Section F to fill in the blank spaces on his map board to impress his boss – who wanted to impress his.

However laudable his work ethic, faulty decision making and ambition in tandem with a dose of over optimism are a deadly combination in a Country Officer. Entire circuits were barely operational before the Germans swept in and rolled them up.

Jim had not modified his advice for Raiding Forces to have as little contact with SOE as possible since Col. Randal's relocation to England and he intended to continue to take it.

Three former Raiding Forces' officers who had been seconded to SOE requested to be returned to the unit. The problem was they were British and might inadvertently reveal details of ongoing Raiding Forces' operations over drinks with their old comrades at SOE. Even the possibility disqualified them for assignment to Seaborn House.

The three were packed off to Castelrozzo to be met with open arms by recently promoted Lieutenant Colonel "Pyro" Percy Stirling, DSO, MC. He was delighted to have them. The officers brought valuable guerrilla warfare experience he could put to good use in the Aegean.

Col. Randal did not like having to consider nationality while reorganizing Raiding Forces (Europe). Inner Allied rivalry, turf wars and now politics were of no interest to him. Nevertheless, he had to acknowledge they presented clear and present complications that were not going away.

And they could not be ignored… not in the climate that prevailed in the intelligence community currently and at SHAEF.

Jim said, "SOE asked me to facilitate a relationship with Raiding Forces now that you have shifted your flag to England."

Col. Randal said, "What type of relationship?"

Jim said, "SOE does not have any sea transport under its own authority. When Baker Street needs to insert or extract its agents by boat they have to submit a formal request to the Admiralty."

Col. Randal said, "How does that work?"

Jim said, "The request originates inside SOE's F Section or at times Operations/Planning Division. The requesting party evaluates the target, cargo to be transported, agents involved, rendezvous point and required craft type prior to sending it up the chain for approval. Next it's forwarded to SOE's Baker Street HQ to be evaluated for feasibility – tide tables, moon phases, reception committees, etc.

"Then a formal indent for an MGB or equivalent craft is drawn up to be sent to the Admiralty. Once there the Naval Staff does their own review of the request. A determination is made to ascertain whether an MGB or other Coastal Forces' unit is available without interfering with ongoing anti-E-boat patrols, convoy escorts, mine laying missions, existing Special Duties operations and so on."

Col. Randal said, "How long does that take?"

Jim said, "Could be weeks, sometimes longer. The Royal Navy absolutely will not sail to France except during certain moon periods. For example, they want a full moon. And the tides have to be right. Getting those two requirements squared up can slow the process down even more. Any lengthy delay requires all the items on the mission's operational checklist to be reevaluated."

Col. Randal said, "So much for lightning-fast Commando strikes across the English Channel."

Jim said, "Sometimes I wonder how we have managed to stay in the war this long with all the rigid protocols, reams of paperwork, miles of red tape and the whims of Mother Nature that have to be adhered to."

Col. Randal said, "You didn't answer my question. What kind of a relationship does SOE want?"

Jim said, "SOE has noticed Raiding Forces is assigned a mission, then same night carries it out. The lads at Baker Street also learned we have our own PT boats. Since we do and they do not, Colonel Buckmaster would like us to provide sea-going transport for Section F's operations on request."

Col. Randal said, "How're you planning to get us out of this, Jim? We can't commit to SOE for additional ops. Our PT boats have skeleton crews. They can barely keep up with the pace of our own missions as it is."

"Jim said, "Being the diplomat I am, I will simply tell Colonel Buckmaster to get bloody stuffed."

Col. Randal said, "Whoever tapped you for your role as liaison officer to practically everyone in the intelligence business must have a real sense of humor."

Jim said, "My exact thoughts, Colonel. I can say Raiding Forces' missions have a higher priority than SOE. We work directly for SHAEF. You are not authorized to divert your assets.

Col. Randal said, "We need to start calling you Mr. Diplomacy."

Jim said, "You might want to hold off on that. MI-6 is interested in us inserting or extracting SIS agents from time to time as well, and Broadway will be far more difficult to brush off."

Col. Randal said, "Enjoying your new liaison duties, Jim?"

"Not one little bit."

It did not escape Col. Randal he had used the word "we or us" at least three times in their conversation. Jim may have been a pre-war professional MI-6 officer, however, he had clearly developed a personal connection to Raiding Forces from long association.

Baldie was one of his closest advisors.

Col. Randal said, "Is that true…we work for SHAEF?"

Jim said, "I do not know who Raiding Forces works for, Colonel, and most likely would be prohibited from telling you even if I did."

They both had things they could not discuss with each other. It was no secret Jim was not telling him everything. He was not telling Jim everything either. The two of them danced around the fact… but there it was, the pink elephant in the room.

Col. Randal had never felt all that great about having to keep Jim out of LONG NECK. Now he would have to insulate him from the E&E program as well. Times like this Col. Randal wished he were back at Oasis X.

His war was simpler then.

COLONEL JOHN RANDAL HELD AN OFFICERS' CALL AT THE Bradford Hotel. Now that he was getting his people around him it was time to put out command guidance. This was going to be his interpretation of their mission. No one had taken the trouble to sit down and explain it to him.

King's Messengers just kept arriving with new orders.

To say the way the missions had been rolled out was disorganized would be an understatement. Most likely this was due to Supreme Headquarters Allied Expeditionary Force being in the process of getting organized. It was also expanding rapidly with new staff pouring in.

Raiding Forces had been thrown into the mix with minimal prior planning.

Col. Randal did not like to operate this way. He wanted his officers and men to have a certain amount of clarity, not be second-guessing why or what. His people needed to have a sense of purpose.

Most commanders would have held one big showy briefing, arrive late after keeping everyone waiting and make a grand entrance with his troops standing at a rigid position of attention.

However, this was not a mission briefing, it was a *change* of mission briefing. Col. Randal preferred to brief his officers here at the Bradford Hotel then allow them to return to Seaborn House and hold their own individual team briefings. In that way his orders flowed from the top down.

He briefed his officers. They briefed their men. That way the troops got the word directly from the individual who would be leading them in action. This was one of Col. Randal's methods of building up his subordinate commanders in the eyes of their troops.

Not all commanding officers did it that way and there were those who would not have agreed with his method. If this were about an individual operation he would be personally leading Col. Randal would brief everyone involved. He liked being in front of troops.

In attendance were Lieutenant Colonel Jack Dance, Captain Billy Jack Jaxx, Captain Roy Kidd, Captain Richard "Dynamite Dick" Coogan, Captain Clint Hays, Captain Dan Bonham, Captain Jake Novak aka "Jake the Snake", Captain Dick Courtney, Captain Dan Morgan, Lieutenant Ricky Mascuch, Lieutenant Chase Starrett and Lieutenant Westly Slade. With the exception of Lt. Slade, who was a relatively new arrival in, these were all long-service Raiding Forces' officers.

The table of organization as it pertained to rank in Raiding Forces was badly skewed, top-heavy. In the typical command pyramid there would be more lieutenants than captains. Each of Col. Randal's captains needed at least one and preferably two lieutenants on his team going forward.

That had never been achieved except for a brief period in the early days when Raiding Forces was initially being formed. Not even the infusion of officers from the 1st Battalion, 575th Parachute Infantry Regiment, (Separate) (Airborne), the 10th Ranger Battalion (Airborne) (Provisional) and the direct commissioning program Captain Mike "Mad Dog" Reupart had been conducting had remedied the deficiency.

The casualty rate of junior officers had always been high due to the intensity of operations starting from the time Raiding Forces was running mule cavalry patrols out of Force N.

The badly misdropped jump on Benevento, Italy had taken a heavy toll on the lieutenants. Junior officers suffered a disproportionate number of losses – leading from the front.

Col. Randal was going to have to address the problem.

The officers' call was held in one of the private rooms in the hotel. Having his officers travel from Seaborn House to London was Col. Randal's way of emphasizing the importance of what they were about to hear. Major General William "Wild Bill" Donovan was observing. Raiding Forces' operations on the French Coast were of paramount importance to the Office of Strategic Services – more than simply being part of the direct action arm of the FORTITUDE SOUTH deception campaign.

Wild Bill needed OSS success stories from the ETO to tell President Roosevelt. He was interested to hear how Col. Randal was planning to frame Raiding Forces new assignment.

Lieutenant General "Geronimo" Joe McKoy and Waldo Treywick were also present.

At the last minute Major the Lady Jane Seaborn slipped in the back.

Col. Randal said, "It's no secret the Allies intend to invade France. Raiding Forces is paving the way. In case you've been wondering that's what we've been doing ever since we deployed to England – we're the sharp end of the stick.

"Our mission is to conduct strategic forward reconnaissance, carry out small-scale raids against selected point-type targets and perform other special tasks upon request for Supreme Headquarters Allied Forces Europe. Primarily, Raiding Forces will be charged with gathering intelligence on potential invasion beaches and conducting raids incidental to keeping the Germans off balance.

"The purpose of the exercise is for SHAEF to better understand the defenses our ground troops will be facing when they land ashore on D-Day. And we're going to put the Germans on notice they're not safe anywhere along the coast of France. Raiding Forces will be coming for them… some dark night.

"Specifically, we have been tasked to:

- Capture German prisoners for follow-up interrogation.
- Gather enemy equipment and documents for intelligence purposes.
- Carry out classified tasks on request.
- Conduct hydrographic surveys of the landing beaches."

The room was dead quiet. This mission statement meant they would be doing something significant. No more operating on the periphery of the main battle area waging a hit and run guerrilla campaign in some remote corner of the war. Raiding Forces was going straight at the Germans.

"Captain Jaxx, how do you spell hydrographic?"

"No idea, sir."

Everyone laughed. Tension ratcheted down even though the officers had just been issued a set of high-risk command directives that would materially affect everyone present far into the foreseeable future. Now they knew what was in front of them – so be it.

One thing was clear… Raiding Forces would be spending a lot of time in harm's way *before* the invasion.

Col. Randal said, "Don't worry people, most of you won't be conducting the geological surveys. Lt. Slade's Special Warfare Operators will be responsible for those. The rest of you will be doing what you do best... taking it to the bad guys. One mission at a time.

"You've been tapped to be the first men in... leading the way.

"This concludes my briefing. What are your questions?"

Col. Randal's briefing style was to keep his marching orders short and simple. His delivery inspired confidence and did not leave much doubt in anyone's mind about what was expected of them. There were no questions.

Capt. Jaxx jumped up and shouted, "Hell yes!"

Uncharacteristically for briefings everyone in the room stood up and applauded. Col. Randal had laid out a mission statement Raiding Forces could get behind. Now it made sense.

Finally Col. Randal said, "We have a couple of administrative details to address. We'll be reorganizing into teams. Effective immediately each captain in Raiding Forces will be required to have at least one and preferably two lieutenants on his team. Go recruit them and make it fast.

"General Donovan has informed me the Office of Strategic Services takes priority for volunteers. Identify who you want and have them volunteer for OSS. We can give direct commissions to worthy NCOs.

"Make it happen, gentlemen. You have important decisions to make – choose wisely. Feel free to talk over your candidates with me.

"I have final say on all selections."

Recruiting their junior officers was a privilege the Raiding Forces' troop commanders could fully appreciate. It gave them the ability to structure their teams as they saw the light to do so – not be assigned a replacement. The harmony and cohesion a high-speed unit demands starts with its small unit leaders.

Selecting the right ones was imperative. It was said in the unit that it was easier to get into Raiding Forces than to stay in it – the Return To Unit (RTU) rate was high. To qualify the new lieutenants would need to have seen action in some other outfit, have a reputation for leading by example, and they had to be a good fit. That last was essential.

Col. Randal said, "Now, Lady Jane, if you will come forward, please. Lieutenant Starrett, Lieutenant Mascuch and Lieutenant Slade front and center. Assume the position, gentlemen."

Surprised, the three moved to the front and snapped to attention.

"By direction of the President, the following-named officers… well, you know the drill. Congratulations. You studs have been promoted to the rank of captain. Now you have to organize your own teams and do some officer recruiting of your own – subject to my approval."

Lady Jane pinned silver bars aka "railroad tracks" on the collars of *her* very surprised new captains. All three were standing braced at a rigid position of attention. They were in total shock experiencing a mild sensation of vertigo.

Chanel #5 may have been a contributing factor.

While Col. Randal did not like surprises himself, he was known for springing good news on people. Everyone in the room stood up again and cheered – Raiding Forces was that kind of outfit.

Col. Randal said, "Captain Slade… General Donovan would like a word with you as soon as we dismiss. See me in my suite when you two are finished – OK, let's do it, gentlemen."

Lt. Gen. McKoy and Mr. Treywick made their way to the front to congratulate Capt. Slade, Capt. Mascuch and Capt. Starrett. Waldo handed each of them a cigar – the traditional promotion gift in the U.S. Army. Now it began to sink in.

When Capt. Slade reported to Maj. Gen. Donovan, the Chief of the Office of Strategic Services said, "Congratulations, Captain. You've certainly made a mark in the short time you have been with Raiding Forces. Now we need to find you two junior officers. I want you to have the best. Leaders you can rely on."

Capt. Slade said, "Thank you, sir."

Maj. Gen. Donovan said, "Is there anyone serving in the Maritime Unit or Navy UDT or any other unit in the entire U.S. Armed Forces you would like to have? OSS can have them transferred in from anywhere – worldwide.

Capt. Slade said, "Yes, sir. I have two in mind."

Maj. Gen. Donovan said, "Provide me their full names to include middle initials. It's imperative OSS make a good showing during the run-up phase to D-Day. I'll be following your exploits, Captain."

"Do my best, sir."

As they were walking out, Lady Jane said, "Jack, who are you planning to select for SOG now that Chase shall be moving onward and upward?"

Capt. Jaxx said, "I'm thinking Horn Dog Hansen could use a direct commission."

Col. Randal said, "That'll be the day."

Lady Jane laughed, "You are incorrigible."

CAPTAIN WESTLY SLADE REPORTED TO COLONEL JOHN RANDAL and Major the Lady Jane Seaborn's suite as ordered. The U.S. Marine had never been there before. It was magnificent – off-white paint, crown molding, crystal chandeliers, thick pile carpet, beautiful Oriental throw rugs in muted colors. Happy greeted him at the door.

Lady Jane was in blue jeans and barefoot.

Col. Randal said, "Come in, Captain."

He and the colonel sat in oversized natural-leather, bat-winged chairs. Lady Jane sprawled out on the couch with Happy next to her on the floor. Beverly Blackwell came in from another room and plopped down on the far end of the divan.

This was the first time Capt. Slade had been with the three of them when they were in their quarters. He felt comfortable being there. Not always the case around senior officers outside normal duty hours.

The Bradford was an exclusive five-star hotel but the impression Capt. Slade had was the atmosphere would have been the same had they been in a General Purpose (GP) tent with canvas camp chairs and bedrolls. These people liked being around each other and so did the dog.

Col. Randal said, "I know you're busy, Captain. This won't take much of your time. Are you prepared to accept a mission?"

It was not a question and it was not what Capt. Slade expected to hear when he walked in. He went on red alert. This day was turning out to be full of surprises.

"Yes, sir."

Col. Randal said, "We have a situation. A COPP team doing a beach survey in the Normandy sector left a geologist's auger behind during its exfil. As you can imagine, a tool like that would only have one purpose on an enemy-held beach."

Capt. Slade said, "Yes, sir. The Germans would immediately realize the location was being analyzed as a possible invasion site."

Col. Randal said, "We've got a major flap on our hands. There's no way to get the auger back. So what we're going to do, meaning teams of Special Warfare Operators under your command – is go to every beach in France and possibly Norway and leave an auger in plain sight."

Capt. Slade said, "That is a brilliant plan, sir."

Col. Randal said, "The idea is to slip in, leave an auger and slip out undetected – totally covert. What's it going to take for your Frogmen to carry that out?"

Capt. Slade said, "We'll insert by two-man Mark II Cockle. Launch a mile or so offshore. Infiltrate unseen and undetected. Once we make the beach we can be in and out in a matter of seconds.

"Not a problem, sir."

Col. Randal said, "What's the hard part?"

Capt. Slade said, "We've trained for two years for exactly this kind of clandestine insertion, sir. My people are fully capable. It's my understanding the French coastline runs for approximately 2,000 miles. The difficulty factor lies in travel to and from all the different target areas.

"How many beaches are we talking about, Colonel?"

Col. Randal said, "The criteria for an invasion beach is a gentle gradient, firm sand or shingle capable of supporting wheeled and tracked vehicles, within fighter cover from England and a few other variables. I'm waiting for an exact number, but the best estimate for France is in the range of 10 to 15 potential sites."

Capt. Slade said, "What about Norway, sir?"

Col. Randal said, "Zero."

Capt. Slade said, "There are *no* beaches in Norway suitable for us to land on, sir?"

Both officers had heard the word, because it was being widely circulated by the London Controlling Section, that Norway, FORTITUDE NORTH, was a prime candidate – if not the actual location of the D-Day invasion.

Col. Randal said, "Negative."

Capt. Slade said, "So much for the rumor mill, sir."

Col. Randal handed him the folded-up copy of a King's Messenger dispatch, "Here's the coordinates for your first mission.

"Coordinate with Mrs. Seaborn. Either she or Captain Honeycutt-Parker will provide the sea transport. We'll be making other arrangements for the remainder of the missions. I want you to delegate them. You can lead the first one to see how it goes. But after that I need you available for the beach survey assignment with Doctor Winthrop we discussed earlier. Is that clear?"

"Understood, sir."

"One other thing. The auger missions are classified Top Secret codeword. No one has the Need to Know, including other Raiding Forces' personnel. We normally don't give our small-scale ops codenames but you need to come up with one we can use as the codeword for this series of missions. They may be ongoing for a while until we can hit all the beaches or we're ordered to stop."

Capt. Slade said, "How about FINDERS KEEPERS, sir?'

Codenames were supposed to be selected at random, neutral, innocuous or sometimes bureaucratic. They were never, according to the book, to be clever or an on-the-money description of the mission. But that's not how Raiding Forces and other units like the Special Air Service or even MI-5 did it on occasion.

Col. Randal said, "Works for me."

COLONEL JOHN HENRY BEVAN WAS AT THE SECURITY DESK ON the Penthouse Floor requesting to be allowed in to see Colonel John Randal. Not a man who liked to be kept waiting, he realized he should have called ahead. Major the Lady Jane Seaborn answered the phone in the suite when the VPW security operator called to inform her Col. Bevan was at his desk.

Lady Jane said, "Colonel Randal is wrapping up a meeting and shall be available momentarily."

She took some small satisfaction from making her godfather wait. Lady Jane had a long memory for slights. He should have stood up at Seaborn House when Col. Randal returned from snatching Major Hanns von Reisen.

When Captain Westly Slade exited the security door separating Lady Jane's private wing from the rest of the Penthouse Floor he said, "Sir, Colonel Randal will see you now."

Col. Bevan was not expecting to find Beverly Blackwell there when he was admitted to the suite. What he had to discuss was classified Need to

Know. However, neither Col. Randal nor Lady Jane seemed inclined to ask her to leave.

The beautiful Texas sorority girl was the OSS liaison to XX-Committee read in on virtually all the Deception classified material – nevertheless…

Lady Jane said, "Is this a social call Uncle?"

Col. Bevan said, "I dropped by to confirm you are to proceed with the plan you presented me about our auger problem."

Col. Randal said, "In progress as we speak. Captain Slade, who you met in the hall, will be the action officer on the project. He's codenamed it FINDERS KEEPERS."

So much for an ambiguous code name.

Col. Bevan said, "Apropos, is there anything in the way of support I can assist with?"

Col. Randal said, "There is – the 15th MGB Squadron is based at Dartmouth. I need two of their boats transferred to Dover on a semi-permanent basis to be on call for FINDERS KEEPERS and other Raiding Forces' assignments. I also want a senior Royal Navy liaison officer stationed with the MGBs who will ensure when my headquarters tasks them with a mission they comply same night – no questions asked, no debating moon, tide data or the state of animal spirits."

Col. Bevan said, "I shall make the arrangements. Anything else?"

Col. Randal said, "You might tell whoever's delivering the geographical augers to step it up. Captain Slade will have a team of his Special Warfare Operators emplacing the first one on the beach located at the coordinates specified by King's Royal Messenger tonight.

"It's the only one we have."

Col. Bevan said, "Outstanding! I shall have the remainder delivered here with a list of every beach you need to visit. Be advised, the PM is personally monitoring the project – quite enthusiastic about it, actually. Informed me I should have come up with the idea of placing one of the augers on every potential landing beach as part of my original FORTITUDE SOUTH cover plan.

"Your turn of phrase, 'Give the Germans something to think about' struck a chord. Quite likely the Prime Minister shall appropriate the quote for himself at the first opportunity."

Beverly said, "Johnny's pretty good at turning a lemon into lemonade."

Lady Jane said, "Yes he is."

COLONEL JOHN RANDAL AND BEVERLY BLACKWELL WERE sitting in the VIP section people watching. Major the Lady Jane Seaborn had been back and forth for the last hour looking at plans with the hotel's manager and talking over details about the buildout with the construction manager. The clock was ticking. Major General Sam Houston "Bronc" Blackwell was there as well to assist her and to inspect the work.

And to motivate the construction crews to work faster.

The Luftwaffe was preparing to launch a second Blitz on London. It was the reason for Lady Jane's rush. It was imperative the floor designated as the Air Raid Shelter be ready and stocked for the hotel's guests – to include the Aid Station, before the Luftwaffe air assault commenced. There was even a small kitchen being constructed to prepare light meals and snacks.

Lady Jane was hoping to have her ballroom 'Secrets' completed in time as well. Hotel guests could dance the night away as the bombs rained down. That was better than having to sleep in the Tube as several hundred thousand of the citizenry in London were going to be forced to do once the air raids started.

Lady Jane's concept of taking care of her troops extended to the lodgers in her hotel. Her plan was to make the German attack as bearable as possible. There was nothing she could do for the rest of the Londoners sheltering in the subway.

Beverly said, "Do you know the difference between escapers and evaders, Johnny?"

Col. Randal said, "Why don't you tell me?"

Beverly said, "To be an evader all you have to do is be on the run from the Nazis. Escapers – well, first you have to be captured, get away, and that makes you an escaper… who's evading."

Sloan Marlow walked through the front door of the hotel.

Beverly said, "Uh-oh, here comes trouble with a capital T. I can't do anything about that idiot Jack but I want you to stay away from her, Johnny.

No more cozy conversations between you two on this couch while I'm away saving the world from the evil Nazi peril."

Sloan saw them and waved.

Beverly said, "She's relentless – I hate her."

Col. Randal said, "No you don't."

"She's going to get you in trouble."

Sloan walked over to the velvet rope gate and the Vulnerable Points Wing operator opened it for her. No questions asked.

"Thank you, Wilson."

Col. Randal said, "See… she's gone to the trouble to learn the names of our security personnel."

Beverly said, "Brother, give me a…"

Sloan came over, "Beverly, I have been hoping for us to have a chance to talk. You are always in and out of MI-5 so fast I can never catch you."

Col. Randal said, "Do you ladies need privacy?"

Sloan said, "Oh no, I merely want to recruit Beverly. Work with me evenings when she's free – I could use a wingman."

Col. Randal had never seen the ex-beauty queen at a loss for words. He had been having a pleasant conversation with her before S&M arrived. Now he was really enjoying himself.

"You two would make a deadly duo."

Beverly said, "I'll have to…"

Col. Randal said, "What are you talking about Beverly, Stand To – duty calls!"

Beverly said, "I'd probably need a lot of training."

Sloan laughed, "All we do is go club hopping – talk to men. I doubt you need training for that. With your looks you shall be a natural 'flirtation agent'."

Col. Randal said, "The sacrifices we make for our countries."

Sloan said, "I discussed the idea with Lady Jane. She has a vast wardrobe in storage here at the hotel. Offered to allow us to raid it."

Beverly said, "I won't sleep with any of the men."

Sloan laughed, "You do not even have to hold their hand – I never do."

Beverly said, "Might be fun… maybe."

Col. Randal said, "Can I come watch?"

CAPTAIN DICK COURTNEY, CAPTAIN CHASE STARRETT, THREE Raiding Forces' troopers from the 1/575th "Rangers" Parachute Infantry Battalion and a Lifeboat Service Man boarded Captain Penelope "Legs" Honeycutt-Parker's PT boat. The sleek craft was sporting a new ultra dark 5-N Navy Blue/5-D Dark Gray camouflage paint job. They were the most effective combination of colors for night operations in the English Channel. Especially when combined with a Measure 31 Dazzle Scheme to distort the boat's silhouette.

Capt. Courtney would have thought flat black to be the best choice of color for night work. Capt. Honeycutt-Parker explained if there was any moon out, a solid black boat looked like a hole in the water – a dead giveaway.

Even though the paint job was sharp and crisp, it looked like it had been painted by a drunken sailor. Long, straight black stripes not unlike the American flag ran from bow to stern on the beam sides. Only the lines were broken up by radical 45° angular bands of stripes shooting up abruptly and then just as suddenly diving down a few feet later before continuing on their way.

The paint scheme looked like abstract modern Cubist or Futurist-style geometric art. Measure 31 Dazzle Scheme stripes were aggressive, angular, illogical bands. The result was a crazy zebra pattern that did not make any sense but that was the purpose of the exercise. The idea was to "break the hull's visual logic by creating optical chaos."

At first glance Capt. Honeycutt-Parker's PT boat gave the impression it was going backwards.

In addition to the paint job, a complete overhaul of sound and visual suppression devices had been carried out with heavy emphasis placed on the exhaust system – exhaust arrestors, water injection, exhaust cooling and extended exhaust trunks designed to discharge closer to the waterline.

Hooded blackout navigation lights were mounted, as were removable navigation light covers. Instrument lighting was subdued by fitting low-intensity red and blue bulbs. Some gauge faces were painted over, a light shroud made of canvas was placed over the bridge chart table and a non-reflective matte coating was applied to all the fittings above deck.

The engines had been tuned for quiet running at low RPM and silenced auxiliary generators were installed. Rubber isolation mounts were placed on the engines and machines. Padded covers went over any equipment that might rattle.

To reduce wake and visual water signature, like bubbles around the blades, low cavitation propellers were fitted and the angle of the propeller blades was re-pitched to improve performance at low speed and reduce phosphorescent glow trail.

When ghosting into an enemy shore on a clandestine mission under cover of darkness a glowing wake following your boat in was officially "not good."

The PT boat was not armed. The decision had been made to wring every possible knot of speed from it. An extra 2 knots was gained by leaving the weapons off. According to some schools of thought the 2 knots were worth more than guns if they were spotted by an E-boat.

Brandy Seaborn and Capt. Honeycutt-Parker were not convinced by the wisdom of the decision. Both skippers wanted weapons. This subject would likely be revisited. The only defensive armament the PT carried was six smoke-making float canisters stored on the stern in the event of contact with a Kriegsmarine patrol. Additional floats could also be put over the side to create a smoke screen to cover their escape – with any luck.

Thanks to the herculean efforts of the Royal Navy Coastal Forces engineering workshops and marine artificers at HMS Wasp, the shore establishment administering Dover's naval facilities every effort had been made to turn the two Raiding Forces' PT boats into low visibility, silent running, close inshore special operations craft. It was possible Maj. Gen. Donovan and SHAEF had also been involved in expediting the work order.

Capt. Courtney assembled his team around him. He went over the plan one more time. Tonight he was operating without Vanish and X-Ray. This was a scratch team consisting of a long-service LBSM, three Raiding Forces' operators in from Castelrozzo pulling their first mission to France, and Capt. Starrett.

Capt. Courtney wondered if the former Small Operations Group (SOG) officer was along tonight to step in if he got things wrong.

While the initial briefing given by Colonel John Randal was to carry out a reconnaissance of an enemy shore battery immediately following his Warning Order, the colonel modified the Actions on the Objective. Now the mission was a simple in and out. Not to be ashore more than a handful of minutes.

It was a curious assignment.

Because the sector in the Pas-de-Calais District where Capt. Courtney's team was landing was heavily occupied by German forces, the PT boat was not going to approach closer than a mile to shore. The grid coordinates where the team was assigned to land was in a section that consisted of heavily broken terrain not suitable as an invasion site. It was not the type of place where the enemy was going to be patrolling – other than a narrow shale shelf, there was no beach.

The target was the perfect setup for what Col. Randal had ordered Capt. Courtney to do. Go in covertly. Drop something easily identifiable as U.S. equipment for the Germans to find hopefully. Then come out.

While hope was famously "not a course of action," there were some tactics that when executed… it was hoped they would work.

As the PT was making the approach to the French Coast, Capt. Honeycutt-Parker kept gradually reducing speed in small increments. Now the boat was purring on one engine at low RPM. Finally, she quietly gave the command, "All engines stop."

Capt. Courtney led his team of Rangers forward while two sailors lowered the Folding Boat, Rubber, Assault over the side being careful not to make noise. Sound carries across open water. No one wanted any Germans who might happen to be manning a gun position on the coast to hear them preparing to launch a dinghy preparatory to paddling ashore.

Capt. Honeycutt-Parker's crew consisted of former Sea Rover Scouts who had served out of Seaborn House since the start of the war, before they were old enough to enlist – some might still be pushing the age limit. Now they were veteran sailors at home in small boat service. The former Scouts were highly disciplined.

Even though this was a sneak and peek of short duration, tension mounted as Capt. Courtney's Rangers went over the side into the raft. Once everyone was settled in he gave the command, "Give way together."

The LBSM was stern man responsible for steering. Capt. Courtney was compass man in the bow. Tonight did not require pinpoint navigation. They merely had to land on the shale shelf.

While he was still in his twenties, Capt. Courtney had grown up in Africa, worked as a professional white hunter guiding clients on big game safaris and served in the Gold Coast Border Police before Col. Randal recruited him. He was at home on operations, day or night and could navigate by the stars if need be.

The three highly experienced Raiding Forces' operators in from Castelrozzo had never met Capt. Courtney previously. They were well satisfied by the ease with which he was handling the team. On command, the paddlers dug in causing the rubber raft to surge toward the shore. In the distance a thin black shadow was barely visible.

The sight carried an undertone of menace even for the veteran Rangers.

Forty minutes later they came in to shore. The rubber raft made a whispering sound as it slid up on the shale. The flat rocks were slick – shining faintly in the moonlight. The team dismounted the boat one at a time, moving tactically taking care not to slip and fall.

After dragging the raft up on the shelf, the LBSM and one of the Rangers dropped to the prone with their suppressed 9mm M3 Grease Guns pointed inland. This was the dual purpose Initial Rally Point (IRP)/ Extraction Rally Point (ERP). Capt. Courtney silently led Capt. Starrett and the other two Rangers through a rough belt of large angular rocks that created a barrier between the Channel and the coastal plain farther inland.

There would not be any amphibious landing here. Wheeled and/or tracked vehicles would never be able to get through this natural defensive system. It was a thin-skinned and armor death trap.

From this point on, all instructions would be given by hand signal. The going for the first twenty-five yards was challenging because of the broken terrain but the team worked its way through. When they came out of the rocks onto level ground, Capt. Courtney signaled the two Raiding Forces' operators to remain in place establishing a Rally Point (RP). Then he and Capt. Starrett advanced another fifty yards until they came to a wide sandy patch of ground bordering a well-worn path running parallel to the coastline. The perfect place for what they had come to do.

The two stomped around leaving as many boot prints as possible as fast as they could. The tread pattern on their canvas-topped raiding boots was unique. Sooner or later German intelligence would come to recognize the design as belonging to Raiding Forces – if they had not already by now.

Three of Waldo Treywick's cigars were 'accidentally' dropped on the ground in a spot that ensured they would be found. The smokes were wrapped in a fake 'smoking hot' love letter Beverly Blackwell authored to her 'boyfriend' for the mission.

She signed off with a luscious red lipstick kiss next to her signature and the initials SWAK. The Germans were not going to have much trouble determining a U.S. Army reconnaissance team had come calling – "*Dumm Amis*."

Once that was done Capt. Courtney and Capt. Starrett retraced their steps, rolling up the men at the Rally Point as they went. The team worked its way back through the rocks, loaded onto the raft and were away in less than the fifteen minutes allotted to be ashore. With adrenaline kicking in hard, the men made the paddle back to the PT boat at a rate of speed that would have impressed even Captain Westly Slade's Special Warfare Operators.

Mission accomplished.

13

FINDERS KEEPERS

VERONICA PAIGE, CAPTAIN PRESTON BUTTERFIELD, DR. LAYTON Winthrop and Dr. Stephen Milam arrived at the Bradford Hotel. Major the Lady Jane Seaborn was waiting with an army of porters to whisk them off to their rooms. Space was at a premium in the private section of the Penthouse Floor. Veronica could stay with her daughter, Mandy Paige. Dr. Winthrop was going to bunk with Lieutenant General "Geronimo" Joe McKoy who would be flying out to the Congo, Capt. Butterfield would be sharing a room with Captain Roy Kidd and Dr. Milam would be in with Waldo Treywick, also departing for the Congo.

These arrangements were only temporary.

Colonel John Randal spoke to Veronica, Capt. Butterfield, Dr. Winthrop and Dr. Milam as they were waiting for the private elevator up to the Penthouse Floor. "Get settled in then meetings are set up for all of you – things are moving fast here in England with the buildup for D-Day underway.

"Veronica, you'll be going back to Castelrozzo as soon as you help General McKoy with a project.

"Doctor Winthrop, you'll be transferring to London until after the invasion. Your talents are needed here for the next six months or so. Make arrangements for your Number Two to take over your duties in the Aegean temporarily.

"Captain Butterfield, there's a classified mission tailor-made for you in your future. I want you to link up with General McKoy and Mrs. Paige to discuss it. Sergeant Major Beckwith will be taking over your anti-smuggling duties. You'll need to brief him on what he's in for. Unfortunately, time does not permit the two of you to go back to Cairo so he can observe your operation for a couple of weeks.

"Dr. Milam, Lady Jane has been dying to show you around your new Aid Station built into the bomb shelter."

Lady Jane laughed, "Yes, I have been. We need your input, Doctor. I want a state-of-the-art surgery unit here at the hotel.

Dr. Milam said, "Looking forward to it."

Col. Randal said, "Veronica, I need to get with you, Captain Butterfield and General McKoy first."

MAJOR GENERAL SAM HOUSTON "BRONC" BLACKWELL AND Major the Lady Jane Seaborn were down in the subterranean level of the Brandford Hotel that was being turned into the Troop Carrier Command Headquarters inspecting progress. Work was advancing at breakneck speed. Lady Jane was escorting him around all five floors under construction. Bronc was interested in her entire project, not just TTC's part of it.

Maj. Gen. Blackwell said, "I want you to know how good it makes me feel when I walk into your hotel and see the colonel in the VIP Section with my daughter. I taught Beverly how to sit a horse, fly an airplane and shoot a gun but you two have given her the confidence to mature into an amazing young woman – don't think it's gone unnoticed.

"Veronica tells me she feels the same about Mandy."

Lady Jane said, "We love Beverly."

Maj. Gen. Blackwell said, "Can't claim I was much of a father. But when I see her talking to the colonel as busy as he is and he's dialed in on her every word – that's a nice feeling for a parent."

Lady Jane said, "Beverly is family."

Maj. Gen. Blackwell said, "Now with me seeing your cousin..."

Lady Jane laughed, "You're part of the family too, General, with or without Brandy. Do try to be gentle with her. She is rather special to me."

"You have my word – Brandy's pretty special to me too."

MAJOR GENERAL SAM HOUSTON "BRONC" BLACKWELL WAS talking to James "Baldie" Taylor in the VIP Section of the Bradford Hotel. While Jim did not represent Bronc in any of his liaison assignments the two regularly kept in touch to share notes. Both men were in a position to help the other from time to time.

Maj. Gen. Blackwell said, "I'm thinking about forming a Special Operations Squadron. TTC may be in the people and freight hauling business, but I'm not about to let this war pass us by without a little active involvement."

Jim said, "That is an excellent idea, General. The RAF has a couple of Lysander squadrons dedicated to Special Operations but their heart is not in anything other than fighters and bombers. The Air Ministry is under the impression it can bomb Germany into submission."

Maj. Gen. Blackwell said, "The USAAF has the same idea – I don't believe it's true."

Jim said, "What is your plan?"

Maj. Gen. Blackwell said, "I thought maybe you could help me with that."

Jim said, "MI-6 is always in need of STOL aircraft to insert or extract agents. SOE requires transports to drop weapons and explosives to their underground resistance groups as well as inserting and or pulling their agents. Political Warfare Executive needs aircraft for propaganda leaflet drops as well. All three of those agencies have to indent for pilots and planes which are not always forthcoming in the requesting agency's preferred time window – not high-priority RAF missions.

"You will never lack for customers, General. And you will make a lot of important people in the intelligence services indebted. The kind you can call on to repay your favors later."

Maj. Gen. Blackwell said, "Can I count on you to be my go-between – official or unofficial?"

Jim said, "Absolutely."

Maj. Gen. Blackwell said, "Any way we can set this up so it looks like Colonel Randal is the conduit to TTC – you'd be fronting him?"

Jim said, "You want it to appear as if the colonel is providing this USAAF Special Duties service in the spirit of inner-Allied cooperation?"

Maj. Gen. Blackwell said, "Affirmative, something like that. You tell me which works best – going through OSS Operational Group Branch or Raiding Forces direct?"

Jim said, "No British intelligence organization will want to be dependent on OSS. Even for air transport which they need. Politics is at play, General."

Maj. Gen. Blackwell said, "What kind of politics?"

Jim said, "MI-6 will claim its afraid if OSS supplied them aircraft it might compromise its agents or copy SIS tradecraft. What Broadway is really worried about, but will never admit, is the very real concern OSS will supplant SIS in Europe post war.

"As for SOE, they will be afraid accepting air support from OSS would provide General Donovan leverage in other areas it does not want him to have."

Maj. Gen. Blackwell said, "That's an ugly picture, Jim – we're supposed to be on the same side."

Jim said, "I believe there is a workaround. London Controlling Section occasionally has need of aircraft for deception purposes. Bevan has already vetted Randal. I know because I did the vetting.

"He is well aware Raiding Forces operate outside normal channels carrying out tasks no one wants to explain later. Its missions are often not entered into official logs, its personnel not listed on establishment returns and many of its operations are conducted without formal titles, written orders or after-action reports.

"LCS will have no problem working with Raiding Forces – it has no post-war or even, as far as I am aware, post D-Day ambitions. Bevan does not care who he does business with. He simply wants the job done and right now. Once Deception starts utilizing TTC's Special Duties Squadron the other services will not have any trouble coming on board and doing so as well."

Maj. Gen. Blackwell said, "Exactly why I asked your advice, Jim."

Jim said, "Downplay the OSS connection as much as possible – it's the kiss of death for the British Intelligence Services. We spooks cannot help ourselves. Intrigue is in our blood and we do not play well with others."

Maj. Gen. Blackwell said, "Anyone asks, I want to be able to claim you recommended the TTC Special Operations Squadron locate its headquarters in the Raiding Forces' Tactical Operations Center here at the hotel – that a problem for you?"

Jim said, "Feel free, General."

Maj. Gen. Blackwell said, "Now what kind of TO&E do you think…"

CAPTAIN WESTLY SLADE AND LANCE CORPORAL RAY "TANK" Karlsson boarded HMS *Seraph* (P219), a Royal Navy S-class submarine with a history of special operations support. A two-man Mark II Cockle was already loaded. The cockle was commonly called a canoe but in reality the Mark II was a two-man kayak, perfect for covert insertions. This was the first time Raiding Forces had conducted more than one mission on the French Coast on the same night.

While the two OSS Special Warfare Operators had spent a great many hours training aboard U.S. submarines, this was their first trip on a British sub. The primary difference noted was Royal Navy etiquette was more formal and the submarine a lot more cramped. The crew was only half the size found on a U.S. Navy boat.

There were at least five beaches along the approximately 80-100-mile coastline in the Pas-de-Calais District that were suitable for the D-Day landings. Hitler believed the Allies would come ashore on at least one of them – possibly more, when the time came.

It was LCS/Raiding Forces' job to keep him thinking that.

Tonight was the first of the FINDERS KEEPERS missions. There could be as many as fifteen in the series. The mission had one objective: To place a geological auger ashore to cover the mistake a COPP team had made when it accidentally left one behind on a Normandy beach it was surveying. The idea was to confuse the Germans as to the Allies' intent.

If an auger turned up on one beach, that was an indicator the site was being evaluated for the invasion. If augers were found on every beach in France or even most of them, there was nothing to be inferred from finding one.

"Dirty deeds done quick" was something Captain Billy Jack Jaxx liked to say, describing his SOG operations. Tonight was Colonel John Randal's idea of playing mind games with Hitler. In military terms, Raiding Forces was "distorting Hitler's appreciation of the situation" – which the Nazi Leader would likely feel qualified as a dirty deed.

And it was being done quick.

Colonel John Henry Bevan's favorite toast was "Confusion to the enemy" – he loved FINDERS KEEPERS.

Capt. Slade was leading the first one to see first hand how it worked so he would know how best to organize the remainder of them. Following tonight he was under orders to task his Special Warfare Operators for the remainder of the FINDERS KEEPERS missions – but not accompany them.

Col. Randal had other plans for his talents.

The short hop to the target area was uneventful. Which was the reason a submarine had been selected for this first mission. The Dover Strait was heavily patrolled by German naval craft. The most dangerous threat to Raiding Forces' small-scale cross-channel raids was E-boats.

Tonight was a live fire field test. Going in submerged virtually eliminated the danger of small boat surface craft interference – the good news. The bad news was in the dark of night, a surfaced submarine was going to be a difficult target to find on the exfil. No matter how skilled the navigator manning the Mark II Cockle.

Exfiltration was the weak link in the mission. No Plan B. In the narrow confines of the heavily trafficked Dover Strait there would not be any fallback pickup point.

The *Seraph* hove to on the surface a little more than a mile off the beach. The submarine would lie to while Capt. Slade and Tank paddled to shore, dropped off the geological auger and returned. It was estimated that this would take approximately an hour – which was pushing the limit the sub's skipper wanted to remain on station. Starting from the minute Mark II Cockle shoved off a lot of things could go wrong.

The night was cool but Capt. Slade and Tank did not take notice. There was no moon out, which was not what the Royal Navy preferred for Commando operations. But it was the luck of the draw for Raiding Forces – Col. Randal believed in going when ready.

He had received criticism for that policy over the years but stuck to it.

Capt. Slade and Tank were powerful paddlers. It was pitch dark. They pointed the bow of the cockle in the direction of the desired heading and pulled hard for shore with their double-headed paddles. On the way in the closer they got to land, anti-invasion obstacles began to be encountered. The obstructions became thicker the closer the canoe got to the beach. The agile little Mark II Cockle skirted around them easily.

Finally the boat ran through the surf right up onto the beach. Not knowing if and suspecting it probably was mined, Capt. Slade handed the auger to LCpl. Karlsson. He did not intend for them to get out of the boat and march around on the sand if he could help it.

"Give it everything you've got, Tank."

The big lance corporal stood up carefully – putting a boot through the bottom of the canvas canoe being a mission-ender. He stepped out and hurled the auger as far ashore as he could. Then, the Mark II being double-ended, Tank shoved it straight back into the water and climbed in as it floated off. Capt. Slade turned around and transitioned to bow man/compass man. He had the correct azimuth for the link-up with the submarine pre-set on his U.S. Navy, wrist, luminous, UDT compass made by the Superior Magneto Corporation.

Capt. Slade and Tank made good time to the Rendezvous Point (RVP). HMS *Seraph* was not there. The two Frogs were bobbing around in the middle of the night all alone in the most constricted and hotly contested stretch of water in the European Theatre of Operations. With no fallback plan.

Official Raiding Forces' speak for a situation such as this was "not good."

Tank said, "What do we do now, Captain?"

It sounded like a textbook leadership question straight out of the U.S. Navy's V-7 Officer Training syllabus – leadership is not without its vicissitudes.

COLONEL JOHN RANDAL AND MAJOR THE LADY JANE SEABORN were in the private elevator going up to the Phone Room on the Penthouse Floor. Col. Randal was taking her to meet with Lieutenant General "Geronimo" Joe McKoy, Waldo Treywick, Veronica Paige and Captain Preston Butterfield III.

Col. Randal said, "Did Mandy tell you about our conversation?"

Lady Jane said, "Which one?"

"Escape & Evasion."

"No."

Col. Randal said, "I asked her if you two would have a conflict of interest with Raiding Forces setting up an E&E program and keeping it secret from British Intelligence until we can hand the escape line off to OSS."

Lady Jane said, "What made you feel we might have a problem?"

Col. Randal said, "You are both British and have relationships with your country's intelligence services."

"What did Mandy say?"

"She gave me a pep talk. Said she was going to California to help you raise Appaloosas after the war. Claimed the two of you would not have any divided loyalties."

Lady Jane said, "And you were worried, why?"

Col. Randal said, "I didn't want to put you in an uncomfortable situation."

Lady Jane laughed, "How thoughtful. Nothing to be concerned about, babe. I have no interest in inner-service rivalries – especially petty bureaucratic turf wars. Last time I checked OSS was on the Allied side."

Col. Randal said, "Good, because that's where we're headed – to a planning session on how to proceed with setting up an E&E program in France."

Lady Jane said, "Did you dream this idea up all by yourself or did someone put you up to it?"

"That's classified – the originator of the assignment and the reason why is known only to me."

"John…"

"General Eisenhower."

"Amazing… who exactly shall be exercising operational control of Escape?"

"General McKoy and Waldo – they volunteered."

"I was not aware either of them spoke French."

Col. Randal said, "There is that."

Captain Stephanie Fawcett-Tatum, RM, was waiting in the hallway outside the Phone Room when they arrived.

"During the exfil the *Seraph* came under attack by a pair of E-boats. The sub was forced to crash dive. By the time the skipper evaded the Germans and returned to the RV, Captain Slade and Tank were nowhere to be found. A search was conducted – no joy.

"I have tentatively logged them as Missing in Action."

Col. Randal said, "Keep me informed, Stephanie."

There were tears in Lady Jane's eyes. She was fighting hard not to show them. Overt displays of emotion in uniform were "not done."

Col. Randal gave her a moment to compose herself, "Be brave, babe – you can do it."

Lady Jane had her heart attack smile going by the time they walked in.

CAPTAIN ROY KIDD, CAPTAIN BILLY JACK JAXX AND BEVERLY Blackwell were waiting outside the Phone Room when Colonel John Randal and Major the Lady Jane Seaborn came out. The captains were there on business. Beverly had been summoned by Captain Stephanie Fawcett-Tatum, RM, to be on hand to console Lady Jane, not that she was much help. They walked down the hall to her suite – both women crying.

So much for the consoling.

Neither Capt. Jaxx or Capt. Kidd said anything. In an active combat unit the best way to deal with friendly losses is to not talk about them. It does not pay to reflect on things you have no control over. The war never stopped – you had to move on. There was no other option. More Raiding Forces' personnel could be killed, wounded or missing before this day was over – no way to know.

Dealing with losses by not dwelling on them is not the same as forgetting. Nevertheless, moving on was cold-blooded. That was just how it was.

No one was proud of it.

Nevertheless, seeing Lady Jane and Beverly in tears did nothing for the three officers' morale.

Capt. Kidd said, "If you have a minute sir, Jack and I have something in our suite you may be interested in."

They walked down the hall, no one saying anything. Capt. Slade and Tank may have been relatively new to Raiding Forces but they had both made an impression on the unit during the time they were in the unit. Not an easy thing to do.

Inside the suite Capt. Kidd led the way to the small dining alcove. Lying on the table was a strange-looking submachine gun with a folding metal stock extended. While it looked familiar, Col. Randal had never seen one like it before. The barrel was long with grooves down the length of it cut deep to shed heat and weight. It gave the weapon a sculpted look, unlike the stamped metal SMGs beginning to appear in armories around the world at this stage of the war.

Capt. Kidd said, "What we have here, sir, is the 9mm Beretta M38/43 Folding Stock Submachine gun – distinguished by its lack of a perforated barrel shroud, fluted barrel, integral compensator and folding stock."

The 9mm M1938 Beretta was the submachine gun of choice for most Raiding Forces' personnel. Until the suppressed M3 SMGs arrived for close-range covert work, the Beretta M1938 was Col. Randal's primary weapon.

Capt. Kidd said, "The 38/43 is an extremely rare model, sir. Only a short run was produced for the Italian 185th Parachute Division "Folgore." However, before they could be issued to the paratroopers, the 185th was annihilated at El Alamein.

"When we invaded Italy, a British Ordnance team discovered fifty of these in a warehouse and shipped them to England for evaluation, sir. Baldie says he can obtain their release to us if you decide to add them to our inventory of weapons."

Col. Randal said, "You've been working with Jim?"

Capt. Kidd said, "Roger that. He's gone out of his way to be helpful, Colonel."

Baldie and Capt. Kidd had known each other since Habbaniya.

"Good."

Col. Randal liked it when his officers took the initiative to develop their own relationships with individuals like Jim in a position to assist Raiding Forces, "The folding stock on that 38/43 looks like it would be useful for airborne operations or onboard boats – I like the idea of a fluted barrel."

Capt. Jaxx said, "This is a good news/ bad news story, Colonel."

Col. Randal said, "Bad news first."

Capt. Kidd slapped the folding stock into place and folded it down flat against the bottom of the weapon. Then inserted the 20-round magazine. It was a tight fight, leaving no telltale rattle. "Precision workmanship, sir."

The butt of the folding stock fitted *over* the magazine and rested up flat against the magazine well. "The problem, sir, is with a magazine inserted you can't unfold the buttstock – it's locked in place. You have to remove the magazine, unfold the stock and reinsert it. Until then it's a one shot weapon."

Col. Randal glanced at Capt. Jaxx – he just shook his head.

"Stand fast on the good news, Captain. No one in their right mind would carry one of these."

Capt. Kidd said, "A beautifully made weapon with a deadly design flaw – make that a glaring deadly design flaw. I knew you would never go for it, sir."

Col. Randal said, "What could those Beretta small arms designers have been thinking?"

Capt. Jaxx said, "Educated idiots."

CAPTAIN BILLY JACK JAXX WAS TALKING TO COLONEL JOHN Randal, "Sir, I've been thinking about your order to recruit lieutenants for the teams we're organizing. If everyone complies we could have twenty plus new junior officers."

Colonel Randal said, "That is a fact."

Capt. Jaxx said, "I know everyone is going to try to get the best people for their team but…"

Col. Randal said, "Yeah, we're going to need some way to evaluate them. I've been thinking about it too. Any ideas, Jack?"

Capt. Jaxx said, "At the rate we're catching missions we won't have the time or manpower to conduct much of selection course. I'm thinking we could let the British do it for us."

Col. Randal said, "How would we do that?"

Capt. Jaxx said, "They have something called Battle School they run officers and NCOs through – use troops from nearby units stationed in the area for them to lead. That way the officers are leading men they don't know, which in itself is a leadership challenge.

"It wouldn't tie up any of our people."

Col. Randal said. "How long's the course?"

"Three weeks, sir."

"Look into the school and get back to me."

Capt. Jaxx said, "Another thing, Colonel, when we send the lieutenants to the course we can have one of the sergeants from the team they're assigned to go along. We'll say it's an opportunity for them to get a chance to work together. In reality the NCO will report back privately on how his officer performs – pass/fail."

Col. Randal said, "I like it. You have been thinking this through. Let's check out this Battle School."

Capt. Jaxx said, "I'll get on it, sir."

Col. Randal said, "How's your new girlfriend working out, Jack?"

Capt. Jaxx said, "Recruited Beverly to be her partner in crime cruising upscale bars around town. They're on the prowl for security violators. Men don't stand a chance, sir."

"I can see how they wouldn't."

"Good thing I don't know any secrets… I'd tell those two everything I knew, Colonel."

Col. Randal said, "Roger that."

He wondered if Jack Cool realized how effectively Sloan Marlow was infiltrating Raiding Forces.

14

LIBERATORS

COLONEL JOHN RANDAL AND BEVERLY BLACKWELL WERE sitting on the couch in the VIP section of the lobby of the Bradford Hotel. Beverly was briefing him on all the information she was not supposed to be sharing with anyone other than Major General "Wild Bill" Donovan from the morning's XX-Committee meeting.

"Raiding Forces has made a lot of friends in the Double-Cross Gang."

Col. Randal said, "Think so?"

"Do you know what they say about Seaborn House?"

"Negative."

"It's a black site so secret even the transport drivers making deliveries have to be blindfolded for the last mile."

"Someone said that?"

"Twenty is a tough crowd to impress. They'll be calling on you for more assignments… count on it, Johnny. Not sure winning over those people was such a great idea."

"Yeah – you could be right."

Beverly said, "Do you know what the D in D-Day stands for?"

"Actually, I don't.

"It doesn't stand for Decision, Deliverance or Debarkation as is commonly believed."

Col. Randal said, "What does the D stand for?"

Beverly said, "Day."

"D-Day means Day-Day?"

Beverly laughed, "That's what I thought too but didn't ask because per Lady Jane's firm instructions, I *never* ask any questions during the meetings. Turns out the "D" is simply a placeholder for the date of the invasion. It stands for a future day to be determined once SHAEF decides on which one it's going to be."

Col. Randal said, "You *are* going to keep me informed as soon as you find out when that is?"

Beverly said, "You know I never tell you classified information."

Col. Randal would have loved to sit in on one of the weekly briefings Beverly gave Major General "Wild Bill" Donovan when she reported back to him acting in her capacity as the OSS Liaison Officer to the XX-Committee. No telling what she had to say.

It had to be entertaining.

MAJOR THE LADY JANE SEABORN WAS WORKING HER WAY around the lobby of the Bradford Hotel. She had a team of porters with her. They were putting up tripods with large posters showing architectural renderings of the nightclub she was building out – 'Secrets.'

The first underground floor was the hotel's bomb shelter/Aid Station. A diagram of it was on an easel next to the one of the club.

The second level was Secrets.

There was no mention of the next four levels down – they were Off Limits.

The third floor down was the Raiding Forces' London Headquarters Rear aka War Room. The small Troop Transport Command Special Operations Squadron was to be headquartered there as well to be immediately accessible to mission planners. The "War Room" did not require anywhere near a full floor's space – 35,000 square feet. So, acting on Captain Billy Jack Jaxx's suggestion, a long, narrow section the length of the building in the far back was walled off, soundproofed, and turned into a live fire pistol and submachine gun transition range.

And another section was walled off for an indoor Olympic-sized pool where Rikke Runborg could hold yoga, exercise, Indian club training, and swimming classes daily for the female Royal Marines and FANYS.

When Col. Randal teased her about it, Lady Jane said, "Happy misses his yoga class."

The fourth floor down was Major General Sam Houston "Bronc" Blackwell's Troop Transport Command Headquarters. Space being at a premium in wartime London the United States Army Air Force had not been able to provide TTC acceptable alternatives for quarters. Now Bronc was going to have the most prestigious HQ in England to include the Royal Air Force.

The fifth floor down was the Supreme Headquarters Allied Expeditionary Force, London Section Administrative Headquarters and the European Theatre of Operations United States Army (ETOUSA).

SHAEF controlled all Allied Forces: US, British, Canadian, Free French etc. – it was a temporary Allied operational headquarters created to fight the campaign in Northwest Europe until Victory Europe (VE) Day.

ETOUSA was a U.S. Army theater command whose primary role was administration, logistics, replacements and supply for the U.S. Army Forces stationed in the United Kingdom and Iceland. Other countries would be added as the invasion of France took place and Europe was liberated country by country.

General Dwight D. Eisenhower was in command of SHAEF and ETOUSA. However, he was planning to have his SHAEF General Headquarters located 11 miles southwest of the city at Bushy Park in Teddington, Middlesex. The general was delighted with the quarters Lady Jane provided at the Bradford. It was central, it was safe from Luftwaffe bombing attack and it was prestigious.

The bottom floor consisted of 165 small single bedrooms built out like a bachelor officer's quarters (BOQ) for Raiding Forces, TTC and ETOUSA personnel on duty at the Bradford.

Guests and casual visitors to the hotel would not be allowed below the Secrets ballroom floor. Raiding Forces, Troop Transport Command and Supreme Headquarters Allied Expeditionary Force offices were not mentioned on Lady Jane's posters. There were not to be any signs providing directions.

Visitors to the various subterranean headquarters would need to know where they were going to get there. They would be expected or call down to whoever they wanted to meet with and have an escort sent up to the lobby to take them down. Security was tight.

Lady Jane came over to pry Colonel John Randal away from Beverly on the couch in the VIP area. She took him around to show him the posters. Secrets looked like it was going to be a happening place.

Col. Randal said, "There's a question I've been wanting to ask."

"What John?"

"I can't help noticing you have been very accommodating to General Eisenhower. I understand why that might be. What I don't get is the reason you have snubbed the general's driver, Kay Summersby – seems out of character."

Lady Jane said, "As you know, I attended virtually all of the MI-6 and SOE intelligence schools. The purpose behind the extensive training – unknown to me at the time – was to keep me as far away from active service as possible because of my social standing. There is a derogatory term for what was taking place – 'cotton-wooled.'

"Meaning sheltered."

Col. Randal said, "Well, they failed in their mission."

Lady Jane laughed, "Only because you came along and stole me away."

Col. Randal said, "What does that have to do with Kay – seems pleasant enough to me."

Lady Jane said, "On day one of my very first course at MI-6 the instructor said, 'Take a look around at the people in this room. Memorize their faces. In the event you should encounter anyone present here today, at some later date – on the street, in a bar, at a social event, anywhere... under no circumstances acknowledge them – you never met."

Lady Jane did not mention General Eisenhower's driver was a former model, considering that to be information Col. Randal did not need to know. It might affect his estimate of the situation.

Col. Randal said, "I see."

COLONEL JOHN RANDAL MET WITH VERONICA PAIGE privately before going into conference with Lieutenant General "Geronimo" Joe McKoy, Captain Preston Butterfield III and Waldo Treywick.

"I need you to answer a question for me. Tell me the truth, Veronica. If it's the wrong answer, you can spend a week here in London then fly back to Castelrozzo – no harm no foul."

Veronica said, "What happens if I give the right answer?"

Col. Randal said, "In that case, you'll need to spend part of your leave time consulting with General McKoy and Mr. Treywick on a project they're currently working on."

Veronica said, "What is your question?

Col. Randal said, "If I were to tell you Raiding Forces needs to set up an escape line for downed USAAF aircrew on the run in France – would you feel compelled to inform MI-9?"

Veronica said, "You placed me in charge of Escape in the Aegean. The first, and as far as I know, the only woman to have autonomous control of a program of this scale. As soon as we began to enjoy some success MI-9 London tried to replace me with one of its officers.

"You intervened on my behalf. As we have discussed previously, I am personally loyal to you for more reasons than one. Ask me not to disclose anything, anything at all… I shall not do so under any circumstance – on my word."

Col. Randal said, "You just sacrificed part of your R&R."

FOLLOWING THEIR MEETING WITH VERONICA PAIGE, Lieutenant General "Geronimo" Joe McKoy, Colonel John Randal and Waldo Treywick repaired to the Smoking Room to enjoy Waldo's cigars while they went over what had just transpired. Veronica had given them a preliminary outline of the steps needed to set up an Escape & Evasion operation. Her input was invaluable.

She and Captain Preston Butterfield III were in the hotel's main restaurant for a more detailed one-on-one question-and-answer session over lunch.

This was one of Col. Randal's classic meetings after the meeting – he was also known to have meetings *before* the meeting. The idea was to make sure the key players were on the same page, sometimes before and always after a meeting, to be certain they were clear on all of the details and understood the implications of what had been said. It was easy to miss something even when dialed in. And there was always the possibility for there to be more than one take on what was said.

Why take a chance?

Veronica had explained that an escape line running through the Pas-de-Calais district controlled by an officer based in Paris would require compartmented organization, reliable local collaborators, secure communications, forged documents, movement through German checkpoints, and exfiltration by sea or air. They could expect to recover 2 to 3 evaders per month, possibly more after the line had been established.

Not a big operation but complex.

Capt. Butterfield would function as the Paris-based officer-in-charge/controller. Day-to-day handling of the escapers would be compartmentalized down the line locally to limit the effect of Abwehr penetration. His network would be recruited from old Foreign Legion contacts and people he had known when he worked in the jewelry business in Paris prior to the war – a number of them dancers at the Follies Bergère.

Lt. Gen. McKoy said, "Settin' all that up sounds pretty intimidatin' but the fact is once you get it goin' an escape operation ain't all that big a deal, John. Less is better.

"Tighter security that way – security, security, security."

Waldo said, "Loose lips can sink more than ships."

Lt. Gen. McKoy said, "Now you got your 'Command & Control' – that's Butterfield. He'll be the escape line's responsible authority, funding officer, cipher custody man, and in charge a' communication & liaison access. Veronica says he's not to have any contact with the evaders so in the event they get caught, they can't identify him under torture.

"Next you got your 'District Chief, Calais,' which is where you're plannin' to establish the evaders' exfiltration points. He runs the local escape cells. Probably have two or three a' those consistin' a' no more n' 5 individuals each. Cells only report to the District Chief and he reports to Butterfield.

"All communications are in person usin' go-betweens or through secure channels by means a' cut-outs. Butterfield's a mystery man. Nobody meets him. He uses intermediaries or dead drops.

"And lastly you got your 'Escape Cell Structure.' That's three to five men, actin' as handlers, guides and quartermasters. They have a network spread out over the entire countryside to collect escapers & evaders on the run and set 'em up in safe houses until they can be passed on along the line. Cell members 'll only know their local boss for compartmentalization and they won't know the people in the other cells.

"Couriers never meet each end… always go part way then use a third party 'go-between'.

"Security is the main thing. Can't emphasize that enough – like I said, security, security, security.

"Then throw in a little more security."

Waldo said, "Like Joe said, it ain't as complicated as it sounds, Colonel. Me and PJ Pretorious had lines set up to smuggle elephant tusks out a' three different countries at one time or another. Escape's pretty much the same concept 'cept we was smugglin' ivory. Capt'n Butterfield – he's gonna be smugglin' people.

Col. Randal said, "How do you plan to handle the necessary document-tation for the evaders?"

Lt. Gen. McKoy said, "There's a long list a' papers that'll have to be counterfeited, John. Identity Papers, Ration Cards, Work Documentation, Movement & Travel permits, Residence Registration and most likely they'll need Zone Papers. We can't use any British forgery shop to make 'em. And we can't use OSS's London Office either – it's compromised.

"Donovan's boys borrowed SOE and MI-9 artists and engravers to help do their work. They'd report back to their people what was goin' on in a heartbeat. We'd be busted."

Col. Randal said, "So what's your plan, General?"

"I've contacted some friends a' mine in the U.S. Secret Service. They're arrangin' to have five major league white collar counterfeiters released from the Federal Penitentiary as we speak. To wit: "A Master Forger who'll be shop chief, a handwritin' & signature specialist, a Stamp & seal engraver, a paper & agin' specialist, and a Photograph & assembly technician.

"Every perpetrator a top man in his field. We'll have to sign for 'em but they ain't violent offenders. Give us any sass we'll just handcuff 'em to their work stations. Bronc has a plane standin' by to fly 'em here the minute the paperwork clears the warden's desk."

Col. Randal said, "You knew how to work all that out?"

Lt. Gen. McKoy said, "Naw, but the boys at the Secret Service did. They handle counterfittin' cases. Glad to help put it together – even volunteered to send a couple a' agents over to keep an eye on the perps. Thinkin' about takin' 'em up on it – if it's all right with you."

Col. Randal said, "Make yourself happy, General."

Lt. Gen. McKoy said, "Our forgery shop's gonna be so good, once word gets out what we're doin' and there ain't a need for secrecy, MI-6, SOE and MI-9 'll be standin' in line to have us create documents for their people.

"We're gonna be able to leverage this before it's all said and done."

Waldo said, "Like I told you, Colonel – the problem is the solution."

LIEUTENANT GENERAL "GERONIMO" JOE MCKOY AND WALDO Treywick met with Major the Lady Jane Seaborn in her suite. A Vulnerable Points Wing security officer was posted outside the door. This was not a social call.

Lt. Gen. McKoy said, "Colonel Randal told us you were up to speed on the Escape project Waldo and I are workin' on."

Lady Jane said, "I am."

"We're gonna need to set up a forgery shop here in the hotel to counterfeit documents. It needs to be discreet – clandestine. Might be able to do it hidin' in plain sight if we work it right. We'll keep things small, most a' the people currently on the Need to Know list are sittin' in this room right now."

"Understood, General. Do you have any idea what you shall require in the way of space?"

"Yes ma'am, I do." Lt. Gen. McKoy took out a folded piece of paper. "There's gonna be five permanent personnel assigned plus two U.S. Secret Service agents for security. What they need is a main document bench room, don't ask me what that is – 200-250 square feet. A darkroom that's light-tight – 80-100 square feet. A printin'/stamp bench – 80-100 square feet. Secure storage & agin' room – 60-80 square feet.

"Comes to around 500 plus square feet more or less – say 600 to be on the safe side."

"Do you have a list of the supplies and equipment needed? The colonel has tasked me to acquire it."

Lt. Gen. McKoy handed her another folded sheet of paper. "That's my only copy."

Lady Jane looked at the list. It was long and detailed.

"Writing Materials: steel dip pens, nib sets, fountain pens, penmanship guides, slant boards.

"Printing & Stamps: Hand press/platen press for seals & forms. Rubber stamp carving tools, vulcanizer, metal seal dies, ink slabs, rollers/brayers, period inks, iron gall, aniline variants, and registration pins & drying racks.

"Photography: Bellows camera –35mm or 120 mm, tripod, darkroom enlarger or contact frame…

The list went on and on and became more and more specific.

Lady Jane said, "I have no idea what most of this is, General. We cannot simply indent from MI-6 or MI-9's forgery shops for equipment or requisition it through normal supply channels. The people who have this material will get suspicious and report us to the authorities – not going to be easy."

Lt. Gen. McKoy said, "We're dependin' on you, Lady Jane. You're a key player."

Lady Jane said, "When shall you require the room to be set up?"

Lt. Gen. McKoy said, "Bronc's flyin' the forgers in just as soon as their release from the United States Penitentiary, Atlanta, Georgia gets processed. My understandin' is that's happenin' now."

Lady Jane said, "You plan to have five criminals check into *my* hotel for an extended stay?"

"Yes ma'am, that's where this is headin'."

Lady Jane laughed, "Better than any movie."

MAJOR THE LADY JANE SEABORN CALLED A MEETING IN HER suite. Present were Mandy Paige, Beverly Blackwell and Happy. The dog likely knew as much about setting up a forgery section as the women did.

That did not discourage them in any way.

First off, Lady Jane went over the meeting in the Phone Room with Veronica Paige. She covered every last detail without notes. None had been allowed to be taken during the initial E&E briefing.

Then she detailed her conversation with Lieutenant General "Geronimo" Joe McKoy.

Lady Jane said, "We are all three intelligence officers or have been in one capacity or another. We can do this. First we need to decide where to set up a 600 square foot room to produce the fake documents the escapers and evaders shall need to make their way home."

Mandy said, "If we build a 600 square foot office in the back of the War Room everyone in Raiding Forces will eventually realize something secret is taking place in there. No matter how cautious we are about keeping the details hush-hush."

Beverly said, "Same thing if we put it on Daddy's TTC floor."

Mandy said, "Probably not a good idea to wall off a small corner of the SHAEF room even if we put in a private entrance – asking for trouble."

Beverly said, "We should put it in the nightclub. Back of the dance floor. Wall off the space we need. Have a concealed entrance through the kitchen or somewhere – maybe through the cloakroom. Low light, people coming and going, no one will ever suspect a thing."

Lady Jane laughed, "Very good – problem solved."

Mandy said, "You are developing quite a flair for clandestine work."

Beverly said, "It's from hanging out with all those liars on the XX-Committee."

Lady Jane said, "We have a lengthy list of supplies and equipment to obtain for the forgers. None of this works unless we can supply the material they require. Top quality. No cutting corners. Quite a lot of the items on the list we shall have to wait for our counterfeiters to arrive so they can explain to us what it means."

Mandy said, "We shall have to be extremely cautious about our procurement process. It is fun to laugh about MI-5 at times but it is quite excellent and good at knowing what is going on in this country. Security will sniff us out if we are not careful."

Lady Jane said, "Agreed – let's come up with a cover name for the forgery section. Then possibly we can work backwards to develop a strategy on how to go about stocking it without raising eyebrows."

Mandy said, "Needs to be something innocuous and so boring it does not raise any red flags."

Lady Jane said, "I have been giving the subject thought. How about 'Records Reconstruction & Replacement Office'?"

Beverly said, "That's so mind-numbingly dull it makes my teeth ache."

Mandy said, "Exactly."

Lady Jane said, "Some of the items on the list can be explained away as being needed for reconstructing damaged or lost documents. We can buy those supplies here in the city – in small amounts, from different locations to be on the safe side.

"We shall have to find most of the rest of what we require in villages and towns outside of London. The shops in the provinces are less likely to recognize buying patterns like our big city stores and shall not be alarmed enough by the purchases to report our activities.

"Besides, we shall not establish a pattern – no suspicions to be raised."

Beverly said, "This could be fun. Organize a big shopping safari – a covert scavenger hunt. We send out a posse of cutouts – no connection to us. Different people make different purchases in different towns for different reasons."

Mandy said, "Going to require serious organization."

Lady Jane said, "We shall be the only three to know what the materials we are acquiring are to be used for – the lives of escaping aircrew depend on security."

Beverly said, "Our own secret network – cool."

MAJOR THE LADY JANE SEABORN MADE THE DECISION TO appoint Mandy Paige as Logistics Officer for the "Documents Office" as the "Records Reconstruction & Replacement Office" was informally being called.

Beverly had regular XX-Committee meetings, needed to report to Major General William "Wild Bill" Donovan and rotated with Captain Pamala Plum-Martin as the duty pilot for daily flights to Seaborn House. Since Capt. Plum-Martin traveled frequently with King on LONG NECK business. Beverly's available time was somewhat spoken for.

After her meeting with Lieutenant General "Geronimo" Joe McKoy Lady Jane met privately with Veronica Paige. Veronica stressed something that had not come up in the initial discussions about the Raiding Forces' escape line. There had to be a counterintelligence component to the operation. The Abwehr could be expected to try to infiltrate agents into the line disguised as USAAF aircrew who had been shot down.

That could not be allowed to happen.

Lady Jane dispatched Beverly to discreetly interview Lieutenant Colonel Thomas Argyll "Tar" Robertson about the British screening process designed to detect Abwehr infiltrators posing as evaders on the MI-9 escape lines. While not the most experienced intelligence operative, she had the ability to go full-on airhead at the bat of an eyelash.

That always worked with men.

Not that her questions mattered to Tar. Nothing in their conversation was any more classified than everything else that took place at XX Committee meetings. He explained how MI-9's security worked.

Lady Jane said, "Colonel Robertson did not mind answering your questions?"

Beverly said, "I told him Daddy wanted to know for when some of his boys get shot down."

Lady Jane laughed, "Mandy is right, you are developing a knack for this line of work."

Beverly said, "I'm an art and drama major – it's a role."

Lady Jane laughed, "Nevertheless, you never cease to amaze. Playing the part of a secret agent – that is priceless. You are a secret agent.

"What did you learn?"

Beverly said, "Screening has to be conducted in the field by a counterintelligence section Preston needs to set up. Escapers must prove they're who they say they are. Failure to do so means they're taken out and shot – immediately!

"Once an escaper arrives in England they undergo an intensive screening process conducted by MI-5 Security Service agents with RAF Air Intelligence and MI-9 liaison officers assisting. It's serious.

"The threat they're safeguarding against is 'Abwehr penetration' of the line resulting in an enemy agent being infiltrated into the country by our own people unwittingly."

Lady Jane said, "You are right that is serious."

Beverly said, "No matter who you are you have to go through the debriefing – read 'interrogation' – when you return to England. Tar says it's methodical, layered and deliberately stressful.

"On arrival the evader is immediately separated from other personnel, placed under guard – not arrested, but there's no free movement. The aircrewman, officer, or enlisted is denied contact with other returned evaders, people from his old unit, members of the press or any civilians."

"The idea is to prevent enemy plants from passing information to each other or coordinating their stories. Sometimes the evader is held for days… or even weeks until cleared. The returnees are only trusted after their stories survive repetition, demonstrate their technical knowledge of Allied aircraft, dodge traps designed to catch 'em in a lie, and their behavior holds up under pressure."

Lady Jane said, "That sounds brutal for someone who has been shot down, and in some cases escaped from a German POW camp to have to go through when they finally reach England. Not the 'Welcome Home Hero' imagined."

Beverly said, "Tar told me some of the evaders claim convincing MI-5 they were who they said they were was harder than escaping."

Lady Jane said, "What happens to German infiltrators found out on this end?"

Beverly said, "They're turned over to Tar. Work for him as a double agent or they can be stood up against a wall. I hear rationing has put a stop to the traditional last cigarette – oh well."

Lady Jane said, "Most likely we shall have to get your father involved with organizing the screening process. We dare not run the risk of allowing a German infiltrator to slip through our fingers."

Beverly said, "Daddy will love helping."

Changing the subject Lady Jane said, "How are you and Sloan getting on now that you two work together?"

Beverly said, "Sloan's not the evil person she's been portrayed to be. I misjudged her based on her reputation for destroying men. Turns out we have a lot in common."

Lady Jane said, "This is a new development."

Beverly said, "One of the reasons she's called S&M is because the men at MI-5 say she's torturing them – won't go out with anyone she works with. A policy I intend to adopt."

Lady Jane laughed, "Good for her – do you believe you could ask Sloan's advice about how to set up our own hush-hush girl operation for E&E without revealing why?"

Beverly said, "I think we should recruit her. Sloan enjoys hanging out with us here at the Bradford. Really crazy about Jack. Loves talking to Johnny – I think she has a crush on him. Hates working at MI-5."

Lady Jane said, "Why?"

Beverly said, "They don't treat her very nice. She won't date the men and the women are jealous because she's so good-looking. I know that for a fact, they've told me.

"Sloan doesn't believe hanging out in nightclubs every night is contributing much to the war effort – though it really is."

Lady Jane said, "I consider her counterintelligence assignment vital work."

Beverly said, "What we do is known at MI-5 as 'elicitation'. You wouldn't believe what some highly placed officers will volunteer if they imagine it might get them somewhere with us – disgusting.

"We don't have to lure men into revealing classified information by implying we'll sleep with them. No need to. Even senior people love to show off how important they are – lot of big egos in the officer ranks."

Lady Jane said, "Let me think about Sloan. First you distrusted her, I believe the term you used was 'snake in the grass' – now you two are girlfriends. If your change of heart is misplaced our covert, off-the-books, escape line will be blown before it gets started."

Beverly said, "I don't believe I'm wrong about Sloan."

Lady Jane said, "Keep in mind the idea is to set an E&E program up then hand it off to General Donovan – your longtime family friend."

Beverly laughed, "He's Daddy's attorney… I grew up calling him Uncle Bill."

Knowing she would do it anyway, Lady Jane said, "I am authorizing you to brief John about our plans for the Documents Office – tell him everything. Then make sure he is kept in the loop as we move forward.

"Ask his opinion about bringing Sloan onboard – he might voice a concern to you he'd rather not say to me. More than likely unless John objects, I shall rely on your judgment.

Beverly said, "No pressure."

She was not laughing.

COLONEL JOHN RANDAL WAS SITTING IN THE VIP SECTION OF the Bradford Hotel with Beverly Blackwell talking to Lieutenant General "Geronimo" Joe McKoy, Captain Billy Jack Jaxx and Lieutenant Ted Hamilton aka "The Great Teddy". The lieutenant had arrived to pick up his new Jacket, Flying, Type A-2 Major the Lady Jane Seaborn had painted for him.

He had specified he wanted one like Col. Randal's with an oversized 575th Ranger Regiment scroll painted on the front and a pair of regulation-sized silver U.S. Army Jump Wings pinned under it.

Col. Randal said, "Where have you been hiding, Lieutenant?"

Lt. Hamilton said, "General Patton's First United States Army Group, sir. I am his 23rd Headquarters Special Troops officer. I do not believe the general is very impressed with me because of my age. The general can be a little cranky."

Col. Randal said, "You'll grow on him."

FUSAG was a notional unit. That was classified and Col. Randal did not have the Need to Know, but he did – The Great Teddy had told him.

"What does a Special Troops officer do, exactly?"

"We are a deception outfit, sir – "Ghost Army." You will be seeing a lot more of me from now on. I have been ordered to raise an armored division in the vicinity of Seaborn House."

"An armored division, really – you've come a long way from Habbaniya, stud."

"A notional armored division, sir. The tanks are just big balloons. From the air they look like the real thing. When I get everything put in place we should get Pam or Beverly to fly us overhead. You will be impressed."

Lt. Gen. McKoy said, "When me n' Waldo get back from the Congo we'll be wantin' to see that, Lieutenant."

Capt. Jaxx said, "Yeah – me too, Ted."

Lt. Hamilton said, “Before FUSAG I was at SOE Station IX – which used to be called the Inter Allied Research Bureau, helping design Rats, Explosive.”

Col. Randal said, “Rats, Explosive?”

Lt. Hamilton said, “We skinned rats and filled them with Nobel 808 plastic explosive. Then we had a taxidermist sew them back up. The idea was to ship the rats to the Underground in France to use to sabotage the railway system. Operatives were to infiltrate railyards and put a rat or two in the trains' coal bins. Then when the coal was shoveled into the firebox or boiler it would explode and disable the engine.”

Beverly said, “You’ve been skinning dead rats, how awful – who thought that one up?”

She may have grown up on a ranch, but Beverly did not like vermin alive or dead though the thought of a rat exploding was not too bad as long as she did not have to see it.

“Actually, that would be me, Beverly. I’m an illusionist. SOE wanted to make the German-run railway system in France disappear. I came up with a plan… Hey, Presto!”

Col. Randal said, “So, how did that work out, Lieutenant?”

Lt. Hamilton said, “Blew up… in our face, sir – literally. The Nazis intercepted the first shipment of rat bombs. Turned the plan into a counter-intelligence propaganda coup by playing it back against our side.

“Now the Germans are making training aids to include films to teach rail workers to be on the lookout for saboteurs and not throw any dead rats in the boiler.”

Lt. Gen. McKoy said, “Best laid plans a’ rats and young lieutenants…”

Capt. Jaxx said, “Sounded like a good idea to me.”

Lt. Hamilton said, “I brought a new toy you might be interested in, Captain. Show it to Captain Kidd when you have a chance.”

“What kind of toy?”

“FP-45 Liberator, sir – SOE was sent a shipment from the U.S.”

Lt. Hamilton produced a crude stamped metal pistol from his pocket.

Lt. Gen. McKoy said, “Ugliest handgun in the history a’ small arms – looks like a crushed beer can.”

Col. Randal said, “What’s the FP stand for?”

Lt. Hamilton said, "Flare Pistol – a cover name intended to confuse the Nazis, sir."

Capt. Jaxx said, "Looks like a zip gun some juvenile delinquent welded in shop class when the teacher wasn't paying attention."

Lt. Hamilton said, "Stamped steel construction, spot-welded halves, smoothbore barrel, no safety, single shot, no extractor – you push the spent .45 caliber cartridge case out with a wooden dowel shoved down the barrel."

Lt. Gen. McKoy said, "A muzzle *unloader*?"

Lt. Hamilton said, "The U.S. went all in on the Liberator project. It ordered one million FP-45's. And this is not a joke – they could make one faster than you can reload it. One every ten seconds, they timed it at the General Motors factory where they're produced."

Col. Randal said, "Why so many?"

Lt. Hamilton said, "The plan was to provide Liberators to resistance movements around the world. Underground fighters were expected to only fire it one time. Sneak up on a German or a Japanese, shoot him in the back of the head and seize his weapon.

Capt. Jaxx said, "Taking out one million of the opposition has to be a good idea."

Major General Sam Houston "Bronc" Blackwell saw them examining the Liberator and walked over. He had a lifelong interest in firearms. He was a connoisseur of military weapons with a large collection from around the world at his ranch.

"What is that monstrosity?"

Col. Randal said, "Not sure, General. Lieutenant Hamilton brought this in. We've never seen one before."

Maj. Gen. Blackwell said, "Let's hear the story, Lieutenant."

Lt. Hamilton said, "I came across this handgun while working on a project for SOE, sir. It's called a Liberator – a single-shot, .45 caliber, stamped metal pistol made by the Guide Lamp Division of General Motors under contract for the Joint Psychological Warfare Committee in the U.S. One million were manufactured at a cost of $2.50 per pistol.

"The JPWC plan was to drop Liberators to resistance fighters in Europe, CBI and the Pacific. Half – 500,000, were shipped to England. They came with self-explanatory pictographic instructions – a cartoon that did not require written directions to understand. Just numbered steps.

"Special Operations Executive regards itself as the preeminent Allied agency for guerrilla warfare in Europe. It rejected the U.S. plan to indiscriminately drop Liberators *en masse* to just anybody willing to kill a Nazi. They wanted to vet the recipients, control the issue of weapons, and conduct training in order have recovery and accountability…"

Lt. Gen. McKoy said, "You can't cure stupid – that defeats the entire purpose a' the exercise. Can you imagine what the Germans would be thinkin' knowin' half a million Frenchmen were runnin' around with a pistol in their pocket loaded for bear under orders to pop a Nazi first chance they got?"

Capt. Jaxx said, "Licensed to kill – now that's a plan."

Lt. Hamilton said, "When the JPWC heard what the SOE wanted to do it refused to release control of the Liberators. Baker Street lost interest in the project. It essentially died on the vine."

Col. Randal said, "Where are the pistols now?"

Lt. Hamilton said, "Stored in a warehouse, sir."

Lt. Gen. McKoy locked eyes with Col. Randal, "This is too good to pass up, John."

Col. Randal said, "Roger that. It's not necessary to supply all 500,000 Liberators to the Resistance. All we need to do is drop in enough for the Germans to realize what we're doing.

"You want in on this, General Blackwell?"

"My TTC boys help scare the hell out of a bunch 'a Nazis or better yet kill a few – count me in. We'll have to secure the pistols from where they're stored. Then we'll drop 'em wherever you advise us to, Colonel. There's going to be some nervous German supermen in enemy-occupied France before our work is done."

Lt. Hamilton said, "Obtaining the Liberators is not a problem, sir. The warehouse where the weapons are stored is at a U.S. Army supply depot. They are gathering dust and taking up space."

Col. Randal said, "General Blackwell, why don't you advise General Donovan about this development, get his thoughts – we'll make this an OSS Operational Group mission."

Lt. Gen. McKoy said, "That's a good idea, Bronc. Talk to him. Wild Bill's not part a' that JPWC outfit. He might not be up to speed on the FP-45 Liberator 'Flare Pistol'.

"Gotta love that cover name – light us up some Nazis."

Maj. Gen. Blackwell said, "Can do – Bill's gonna like you running it as an OSS Operational Group Branch mission."

Lt. Gen. McKoy said, "Sounds like we stepped into the makin's of another turf battle here. SOE thinks they got a monopoly on guerrilla war in Europe. Don't want OSS hornin' in. What they don't seem to understand is guerrilla warfare is part a' the OSS charter.

"Let's just do this and don't tell anybody."

Maj. Gen. Blackwell said, "I'm getting sick of all the inter-service rivalry. We need to quit stabbing each other in the back and get on with winning the war. All this infighting is having a negative effect."

Lt. Gen. McKoy said, "A friend a' mine in Washington once told me he heard a three-star on the General Staff say, 'We need to hurry up n' get this war over so we can get back to fightin' our real enemy – the Navy'."

Capt. Jaxx said, "Seems like a good idea to have the Germans always looking over their shoulder."

Lt. Gen. McKoy said, "You ain't wrong about that, Jack."

Col. Randal said, "Affirmative."

Maj. Gen. Blackwell said, "We're going to put these Liberators in France where they can do some good."

Beverly said, "Beats Rats, Explosive."

MAJOR THE LADY JANE SEABORN TRAVELED TO WHITE'S TO see her godfather. The limousine pulled up to the curb in front. This visit, Happy got to stay in the car. Lady Jane was not trying to intimidate Colonel John Henry Bevan today.

Women were not allowed inside. Groom, the hall porter, came to the door when she rang the bell. He was expecting her. She had called ahead.

Groom said, "Nice to see you again, Lady Seaborn. The colonel shall be right with you."

He was glad her dog remained in the Rolls-Royce.

While ladies could not go inside White's, protocol allowed for female visitors. The member would come to White's famous bay window. The woman wishing to speak to him remained outside on the sidewalk. They conducted their conversation through the glass.

Col. Bevan was not going to have his goddaughter go through that rigmarole – he came outside.

Lady Jane went straight to the main point, "Uncle, if I were to tell you about an operation we are contemplating that would likely be met with disfavor by SOE would you feel compelled to inform them once you find out about it?"

Col. Bevan said, "Will it have any impact on my work?"

Lady Jane said, "Yes, but only tangentially. I believe you shall like the project. Personally, I believe it to be hilarious."

Col. Bevan said, "In answer to your question – no. I am not compelled to inform SOE of anything not a threat to the national defense.

"You do not want to tell me what this is about?"

Lady Jane said, "I shall let John explain. He and General McKoy came up with the idea. You should drop by for lunch and they can explain the concept of the operation."

Col. Bevan laughed, "You have become rather comfortable using service terminology. Jolly good, Jane. I shall rearrange my schedule – meet you at the hotel."

Lady Jane said, "Perfect."

"You really care for this Randal fellow?"

"With all my heart."

"I have no difficulty with that. Take the matter as settled – until proven otherwise."

Lady Jane said, "Love you, Uncle."

When they met at the hotel, Lieutenant General "Geronimo" Joe McKoy joined Colonel John Randal, Lady Jane and Col. Bevan in one of the small private dining rooms at the Bradford. Col. Randal laid out the story behind the FP-45. Lt. Gen. McKoy removed the pistol Lieutenant Ted Hamilton had brought from his pocket and slid it across the table to the Chief of Deception.

An avid sportsman with a refined taste for bespoke double shotguns from Wesley Richards, Purdey & Sons, and Holland & Holland, Col. Bevan gasped when he saw the crude handgun. "Dreadfully inelegant! Will this pistol actually function?"

Lt. Gen. McKoy said, “It will. But it’s intended to only be fired once even though ten spare rounds are stored in the grip. Assassinate a Nazi – one fat .45ACP round to the back of his head, take his weapon, throw the Liberator away.

“Designed to be disposable.”

Col. Bevan said, “A sound plan. How many units did you say are stored in a warehouse here in the UK?”

Lt. Gen. McKoy said, “Half a million.”

Col. Bevan said, “SOE does not want to drop Liberators to the French Resistance. What do they intend to arm them with?”

Col. Randal said, “Sten guns.”

Col. Bevan said, “Bloody ridiculous, these Liberators can be stuck in a pocket. Best place to hide them, what! What is wrong with SOE? One cannot conceal an assembled Sten gun. Submachine guns are not to be brought out of hiding until just before the invasion when the French Underground rises up.

“So, what is your plan, gentlemen?”

Lt. Gen. McKoy said, “Bronc Blackwell’s gonna drop enough Liberators for the Germans to figger out what’s goin’ on. He’ll make sure some accidentally get misdropped to the Germans. And we’ll be puttin’ a few ashore.

“The idea is for the bad guys to be aware a’ what the weapons are intended to be used for – which is, like I said, shootin’ Nazis in the back a’ the head.”

Col. Bevan said, “What is it you want from me?”

Col. Randal said, “We’d like you to tell the Germans we dropped the entire 500,000 Liberators in the Calais area.”

Col. Bevan said, “Now that is genius. You are spot on Jane. This is hilarious.”

Lady Jane said, “I thought you would see it that way, Uncle.”

Col. Bevan said, “The sole purpose of having a resistance movement in France prior to D-Day is to spread alarm and despondency among the Nazi occupiers – keep them off balance. Imagine being stationed in Calais having to live with the knowledge there are half a million angry civilians walking around armed with a .45 caliber pistol under orders to eliminate the first German soldier they have the opportunity to.

"In the deception business, if you are going to tell a lie – tell a big lie."

Lady Jane said, "You will help with our project then?"

Col. Bevan said, "Try to stop me. Your operation will literally drive the Nazis crazy. I do not get to be a part of doing that often."

Lady Jane said, "You are not simply humoring me?"

Col. Bevan said, "Not at all, Jane. I shall take great pleasure in knowing LCS contributed in a small way to making every German in the 650 square mile area of the Calais District be frightened out of his bloody wits. Because of tin pistols so flimsy they appear likely to explode in your hand should you ever dare fire one."

What Col. Bevan did not say was what Lt. Gen. McKoy and Col. Randal had outlined dovetailed perfectly with LCS intentions for FORTITUDE SOUTH – the deception designed to make the Germans believe the D-Day invasion was going to land in Pas-de-Calais.

Arming the populace would be interpreted by the Abwehr as the Allies preparing the battlefield – a precursor to invasion. Col. Bevan wondered how SOE could have free access to all those weapons and not find a use for them.

Defied belief.

The Raiding Forces' plan was clean and simple. There was no way for the Germans to know how many FP-45s were actually supplied to the Resistance. The Abwehr would have to take the word of their spies in England for how many. And they were all under the control of MI-5 and would say it was 500,000.

The massive number would give the appearance the Allies were serious about focusing their intentions on the Calais district, which was what the LCS was working around the clock to make the Germans believe. And, as icing on the cake, no one on the Allied side would care if every single FP-45 Liberator pistol sent to France was captured – militarily they were worthless.

Except you would not want to get shot with one some dark night.

Col. Bevan said, "I shall instruct Colonel Robertson at B-1A to commence having his double agents inform their Abwehr contacts OSS is in the process of supplying 500,000 assassins' weapons to the French Resistance in and around Calais.

"An absurd number. There are only 250,000 Germans stationed in the entire district. Two FP-45 Liberators for every Nazi.

Lt. Gen. McKoy said, "They'll be sleepin' with one eye open."

Col. Bevan said, "Quite!"

WHEN HE LEFT THE BRADFORD HOTEL COLONEL JOHN HENRY Bevan drove directly to Thames House, the home of the Security Service, MI-5 aka Five. He was not expected. Lieutenant Colonel Thomas Argyll "Tar" Robertson, Chief of Section B1-A, interrupted a meeting he was in with his staff to see him. The Head of the London Controlling Section did not drop by for casual visits.

Col. Bevan gave him a short rundown on the meeting he had just left at the Bradford Hotel. "I want your Double Cross agents to lend full support to this FP-45 Liberator program. You can commence immediately. Have reports begin trickling in '500,000 Liberator assassin's pistols are being prepared to be delivered to the Resistance in the Calais District'."

Lt. Col. Robertson said, "Definitely cause a stir, Colonel. We give the Germans advance warning. Then the Liberators begin showing up. It is the classic textbook Double Cross. Start with telling the Germans something is about to take place, then the event follows. Demonstrates beyond question the quality of the intelligence our turned agents are able to deliver – always valuable for credibility."

Col. Bevan said, "Precisely, we shall make sure a handful of the Liberators are actually recovered by the Nazis – that is crucial. It establishes beyond any doubt the FP-45 Liberator story is credible.

"Coordinate with James Taylor. He shall keep you updated as to the status of weapons delivery. That way you can gauge what and when to have your XX controlled agents report to their Nazi handlers."

Lt. Col. Robertson said, "The Germans in Calais are going to be most distraught over this development."

Col. Bevan said, "That is the idea."

As soon as the Head of LCS departed, Lt. Col. Robertson placed a call to Mandy Paige at the Bradford Hotel.

"Have Rikke Runborg stand by. I shall be at the hotel within the hour."

"See you then, Tar."

Very little of the controlled agent traffic transmitted aroused excitement in the B1-A staff – this did. German soldiers in Pas-de-Calais were going to be petrified by the news about the FP-45 Liberators. Now the occupiers would never be able to let their guard down. War is generally not personal. Knowing the countryside was teeming with armed civilians under orders to blow your head off suddenly made it very much so.

What could be better than that?

THE PHONE RANG. COLONEL JOHN RANDAL WENT FROM SOUND asleep to wide awake before the first ring ended. He moved Major the Lady Jane Seaborn's tawny thigh off his chest – her preferred sleeping position, rolled over and took the phone off the cradle. The luminous hands on his Rolex read 0345 hrs.

"Randal."

"Colonel Randal, this is Major Hawkins, Southern Command, GSO-2 intelligence. We are holding two Americans identifying themselves as Captain Westly Slade, U.S. Marines and an enlisted man, also claiming to be a Marine, known as Tank."

Col. Randal said, "Those are my people. They've been MIA for three days. How did they end up in your hands?"

"A local Home Guard coastal patrol picked them up when they landed. The two men arrived in a canoe wearing black-dyed clothing, armed with a model of submachine gun the Guard troopers had no familiarity with previously. The Patrol erroneously believed them to be Brandenburger Commandos and detained them under Home Guard authority.

Col. Randal said, "What took so long to contact me?"

"Home Guard passed them to the Kent County Constabulary for verification – the men were not carrying any identification. They refused to provide any information other than name, rank and serial number."

Col. Randal said, "That's what they're supposed to do – it was a classified operation."

Maj. Hawkins said, "The two were transferred to Southern Command where they were logged in as suspected enemy infiltrators."

Col. Randal said, "Did you notify MI-5?"

"Affirmative, sir, as soon as it reached my desk. We were instructed to suspend interrogation until their identity could be confirmed. At that point Captain Slade requested you by name. On that basis Southern Command stood down questioning pending confirmation. It was immediately forthcoming.

"Apparently even the MI-5 night duty officer knows you, sir."

Col. Randal said, "Major, I am holding you personally responsible for the men's well-being don't let them out of your sight. Make sure they get a shower, clean clothes and the best meal in the finest restaurant in your AO – is that clear?"

"Sir, eating establishments are closed at this hour."

"Drag one of the owners out of bed and have him start cooking. Make it happen, Hawkins. I'll be flying down immediately to pick my people up – they better be clean, fed and undamaged."

"Sir!"

As Col. Randal was dialing Beverly's room, Lady Jane said drowsily, "Who were you talking to, John?"

"Westly and Tank paddled home on their own power. They were arrested by the Home Guard. Been in custody three days – typical foul up. I'm calling Beverly.

"We need to fly down to Southern Command to pick them up."

Lady Jane said, "Marvelous, I am coming with you."

15

PRE-MISSION DELEGATION

COLONEL JOHN RANDAL MET WITH DOCTOR LAYTON WINTHROP and Captain Westly Slade in his spacious office in the new Raiding Forces' London Headquarters aka War Room. Its build-out was completed in record-breaking time – a testament to what could be accomplished under wartime conditions with no civilian oversight, permits, or city inspections to hold up a project of the magnitude Major the Lady Jane Seaborn had undertaken.

Granted, most of the space in the War Room was an open bay with offices along the walls. It was not a complicated build-out. There had been an army of contractors working around the clock seven days a week. Nevertheless, it was an impressive demonstration of what could be done when it needed to be.

It was a good thing most of the remodeling on the subterranean floors, with the exception of Secrets, was completed. The German Luftwaffe had launched the start of its second Blitz the night before. London was in the crosshairs again. After years of intermittent bombing raids following the original high-intensity Blitz in which over 40,000 Londoners were killed from September 1940 to May 1941, the city's inhabitants were resigned to air raids.

Life went on.

Which was what Lady Jane anticipated when she set out to put in a nightclub on one of the basement floors. Revelers could dine and dance. Safe from aerial bombs.

It was her way of improvising, adapting and overcoming.

Also present in Col. Randal's office was Commander Mark Buffington, RN, Submarine Service (X-Craft). He was there to conduct a briefing on miniature submarines. While not a separate branch of the Royal Navy X-Craft were highly classified special operations boats. Since not much was known about them a senior officer read into the program was required to explain their capabilities, limits and risks.

Typically, miniature submarine beach reconnaissance was a Combined Operations program. However, geologically qualified intelligence officers to conduct the surveys were proving difficult to find. Col. Randal had a resident geologist – Dr. Layton Winthrop, who was a long-time intelligence officer.

Col. Randal also had Special Warfare Operators who were trained in on-site pre-invasion surveys of enemy beaches and they were world-class combat swimmers. Which was why Captain Westly Slade was present.

Recently released from a holding facility aka the "Cage" run by Southern Command – Capt. Slade had been held for three days as a suspected German infiltrator. Not an experience the Frogman would recommend.

The purpose of the exercise today was to determine if X-Craft would be a viable fit for Col. Randal to use to conduct clandestine geophysical reconnaissance of the beaches in and around Pas-de-Calais, France – Raiding Forces' Area of Operations (AO).

Cdr. Buffington was unsure why he was at the Bradford today and not having this meeting at Norfolk House on St. James Square where Combined Operations Headquarters was located. He did not ask. And Col. Randal did not enlighten him.

Cdr. Buffington said, "In short, gentlemen, X-Craft are miniature submarines 51feet in length with a 5.5-foot beam, crew of 4 – skipper, pilot, engineer and diver. They have a diesel engine for surface running at a speed of 6 to 6.5 knots, and an electric motor for submerged operations with a speed of 2 to 3 knots. For long-range missions the subs are frequently towed to a release point by a parent fleet submarine to conserve fuel for longer operating time in the target area.

"X-Craft are developed for covert work in shallow, defended waters. They can operate submerged for extended periods and as I mentioned, be towed to the target area to conserve endurance. For Combined Operations they put swimmers ashore unseen to conduct nocturnal physical reconnaissance of potential invasion beaches – specifically to evaluate gradients, sediment bearing strength, obstacles and tides.

"The subs stand off the beach under cover of darkness to recover the swimmers and their soil samples with the coastal defenses ashore being none the wiser.

"Operationally the boats work at low speed and shallow depth using electric propulsion on the surface when in the immediate target area. Swimmers exit the submerged X-Craft through a diver lockout chamber to swim ashore and take core samples and measurements, then swim back to re-embark. When the swimmers are recovered the sub then withdraws submerged and is recovered by the towing submarine or surface escort once clear of the enemy coastal belt.

"Time ashore is measured in minutes.

"X-Craft operations are tightly controlled by Combined Operations. The exact number of boats is classified but we do not have many of them. They experience a high casualty rate in the 40-plus percent range.

"What are your questions?"

Dr. Winthrop said, "Is an X-Craft capable of transporting an extra swimmer?"

"Negative."

Dr. Winthrop said, "For a short trip under twenty-five miles, would it be possible to eliminate the pilot and substitute another combat swimmer?"

"Possible but not recommended."

Capt. Slade said, "I would think coordinating with the Navy for two submarines is a complicated process. Is it possible for a PT boat to provide the tow?"

Cdr. Buffington said, "They can, but it would be dangerous. PT boats are unsuitable for stealth approaches near defended coasts...."

Col. Randal looked up at that statement but made no comment. The scar on his cheek tightened. Clearly the commander did not know much about PT boat operations. They had electric motors designed for last stage close inshore work. All manner of other modifications to enhance stealth. And tactics for quiet running.

"...retaking the tow close to enemy-defended beaches is hazardous. PT boats lack the submerged rendezvous capability submarines have. Searching for each other in the dark is not what one would describe as an ideal solution for high-traffic contested waters like the Dover Straits.

"All in all, towing by PT boat, while possible, is tactically risky and doctrinally unsound."

Dr. Winthrop said, "What are your thoughts about having a geologist onboard an X-Craft to make observations of target beaches through the sub's periscope during the hours of daylight?"

Cdr. Buffington said, "A periscope survey can be done but it is high risk, inadequate and a misuse of assets. Afraid the Navy would view the intelligence gained as insufficient for assault planning. Possibly a periscope mission could be approved for supplemental confirmation to back up information gathered by a ground survey conducted by swimmers – but it would not be accepted as primary intelligence."

Col. Randal said, "Any other questions? OK then, thank you for your time Commander. Appreciate your professional assessment."

Capt. Slade was sitting in on his first pre-mission fact-finding meeting held with an outside agency since being assigned to Raiding Forces. He noted Col. Randal had not asked a single question. Why?

The Marine would discover that was not unusual.

Col. Randal liked to bring in experts to meet with the officers who would be carrying out an operation. Then he sat back and let his people ask questions. This was an advanced form of leadership – pre-mission delegation. The men who were about to go and do got to ask. His officers took ownership of the operation then and there – *before* being issued a Warning Order.

Most commanding officers had no idea what pre-mission delegation was. The concept was not taught in any military leadership course. It only worked where there was a trust relationship between a CO and his subordinates.

And a commander who wanted to build up his junior officers.

Captain Billy Jack Jaxx was waiting outside the office when the meeting broke up. He had a sixth sense when missions were in the offing. Col. Randal was not surprised to find him there – standing by.

"Anything I need to know, sir?"

"That was Commander Buffington you saw leaving. He was here to brief X-Craft operations. Beach surveys are in our future."

"What's an X-Craft, sir?"

"Midget sub – about 50 feet long, little over 5 feet wide, crew of four."

Capt. Jaxx turned pale, "Isn't that a little cramped, Colonel?"

Col. Randal said, "Approximately 70 feet per man but it's not open deck space so it probably seems like a lot less. I've been told the interior of an X-Craft is a steel tube with a maze of machinery, batteries and pipes crammed in.

"You have to move sideways and never for more than a few feet at a time in a straight line. Barely enough room to sit. Crew has to lie curled on their side – 40% loss rate.

"Sound like something you might be interested in, Jack – being our most experienced submariner?"

Capt. Jaxx said, "Not a snowball's chance in hell you'll get me on a midget sub, sir."

Col. Randal said, "Don't worry, we won't be carrying out any X-Craft missions. Dr. Winthrop might, though. Combined Operations is having trouble finding a qualified intelligence officer with the right background in geology to run their beach survey section."

"Gets my vote for the Medal of Honor if he takes it on, sir."

COLONEL JOHN RANDAL WAS DRIVEN TO WHITE'S BY ONE OF the Bradford Hotel's limousines. The hall porter, Groom, let him in when he rang the doorbell. He was expected, having called ahead.

"Nice to see you again, Colonel Randal. Colonel Bevan asked me to escort you straight back. Would you like me to have a drink brought to you, sir?"

"No thanks, Groom. I won't be here long."

Unlike Major General Sir Stewart Menzies, aka 'C', Chief of MI-6, – whose semi-official office was in the Billiard Room, Colonel John Henry Bevan did not have a permanent place where he conducted business at

White's. When Col. Randal called, he booked one of the small private rooms upstairs away from the main club.

Col. Bevan said, "What can I do for you, Colonel?"

Col. Randal said, "Previously I asked you to have two Motor Gunboats from the 15th MGB Squadron made available to Raiding Forces with a senior Royal Navy officer to act as liaison."

Col. Bevan said, "That is in the works."

Col. Randal said, "I've heard rumors the 15th MGB Squadron is being stood down sometime this year. The reason for the initial request for a couple of their boats was because Brandy and Penelope are running missions several times a week – that pace seems likely to increase.

"Those two have been on almost constant operations with no break for nearly two years – I need them to have some down time."

Col. Bevan said, "I was not aware of the high pace of their sea duties in the Aegean."

Col. Randal said, "Our two PT boats are not going to hold up to the constant pounding they're taking. Which means one or both will be down at times for maintenance. We need a naval dockyard detachment at Seaborn House to service the boats so as not to interrupt the flow of our raiding campaign."

Col. Bevan said, "The last thing we need is to have the missions Raiding Forces is conducting truncated due to crew fatigue or a lack of routine servicing. Calais is our primary. Every one of your operations is vital to making our landing there a success when the time comes."

Col. Randal knew that was not true – at least the part about Pas-de-Calais being the primary, but he was not offended. After all, Col. Bevan was the Chief of Deception. It was his job to make him believe Calais was going to be the site of the invasion in the event he was ever captured and interrogated.

Col. Bevan said, "What do you recommend?"

Col. Randal said, "If the 15th MGB is disbanded the two boats you're planning to have loaned to us may be reassigned somewhere else. I'd like them seconded – OPCON to Raiding Forces at least until after the invasion."

Col. Bevan said, "Once the Navy decides to do a thing, it is difficult if not impossible to put the genie back in the bottle. We cannot afford to take a chance – one of your catch phrases I understand. Those two 15th MGB

Squadron boats could receive movement orders, weigh anchor and sail away before we knew what was taking place."

Col. Randal said, "That is a possibility."

Col. Bevan said, "Time we do not have would be lost replacing them."

Col. Randal said, "That's why I'm here."

Because Brandy was so close to his goddaughter and Captain Penelope Honeycutt-Parker a longtime family friend, Col. Bevan knew Col. Randal could have dispatched Lady Jane to speak to him in an effort to make his case.

It spoke well of him not to go about it that way.

Col. Bevan said, "You were right to bring this to me. I want to get out in front of it. Those two MGBs need to be under Raiding Forces' operational control – permanently. And we shall have the Navy provide a Dockyard Party to keep all four of your patrol boats shipshape as part of the package.

"Speaking for myself, one would not want to find himself in hot water with Jane for overtasking the two skippers you currently have. I need you to ensure Brandy and Penelope are looked after for me. I had no idea…"

Col. Randal said, "If we left it up to those two they'd go out every night."

Col. Bevan said, "In the future when concerns arise, and they shall, do not hesitate to bring them to me straight away. When it comes to you, I have an open-door policy. It may not seem like it at times but what the two of us are involved with is a collective effort. LCS and Raiding Forces are playing a deep game – staking all for our countries on one roll of the dice.

"I would like you to see our relationship that way."

Col. Randal said, "Fair enough… understood."

LIEUTENANT GENERAL "GERONIMO" JOE MCKOY, MAJOR General Sam Houston "Bronc" Blackwell, Colonel John Randal, Major the Lady Jane Seaborn, Brandy Seaborn, Beverly Blackwell and Rikke Runborg were sitting in the VIP Section. They were waiting for the arrival of the five counterfeiters being flown in from the federal penitentiary at Atlanta, Georgia.

While they waited Waldo Treywick was entertaining them with a story about the time he and PJ Pretorious had gone in search of the legendary elephant's graveyard.

Maj. Gen. Blackwell said, "You knew PJ Pretorious?"

Waldo said, “We was pardners right up ’til he got married, settled down and raised a family.”

Maj. Gen. Blackwell said, “I’ve read everything I could get my hands on about PJ going up the Rufiji River after the commerce raider *Konigsberg*. You were in on that?”

“I definitely was.”

“Your name never came up in anything I ever saw, Mr. Treywick.”

Waldo said, “It was them reporters savin’ ink. I was always referred to as PJ’s ‘Number 2’, ‘loyal companion’ or sometimes his ‘trusty sidekick’.”

Maj. Gen. Blackwell said, “Yeah – I read that.”

Waldo said, “Anyways, me ’n PJ got word there was an old village chief we knew who was on his deathbed and he’d sent a runner for us. By the time we got there he was about gone.

“The chief told us he’d make us rich beyond our wildest imagination if we made a promise to take care a’ his tribe with some a’ the money after he was gone. We did, and he trusted me and PJ – so revealed to us the secret location of the elephant graveyard.”

Beverly said, “What’s the elephant's graveyard?”

Waldo said, “It’s a legendary place known only to elephants. No white man has ever found it. It’s a known fact old or dyin’ tuskers leave the herd. Where they go is a mystery and no one ever even finds the skeleton of a dead pachyderm. Story is they head for an undisclosed communal place to die – the elephant graveyard. Sometimes travelin’ a great distance to get there.

“Nobody knows where it is – ’cept maybe a native or two, chief claimed he did.”

Lady Jane said, “My father told me the legend when I was a child.”

Maj. Gen. Blackwell added, “I heard it on safari in Kenya.”

Beverly asked, “Why would dead elephants make you rich, Mr. Treywick?”

Waldo said, “Generations and generations a’ deceased tuskers would create a vast cache a’ ivory just layin’ on the ground waitin’ to be picked up and converted to gold. You have any idea how many millions a’ pool balls gets sold ever year?”

Beverly laughed, “Probably a lot.”

Lady Jane said, “What happened, Mr. Treywick?”

Waldo said, "Me and PJ traveled for over a week. Hard goin' through some bad bush and not all a' the natives was friendly. We was countin' our money ever step a' the way. One big payday – that's all we wanted.

"We came out a' the jungle and there she was. Three hills the old chief had told us marked the spot next to the confluence a' two rivers. Our reference point. Only now the spot was about a five-hunnert-acre lake. Local farmers had dammed up the rivers to create a reservoir for irrigation – dead trees still stickin' up out a' the water.

"If the elephant graveyard ever existed it was out a' reach now."

Maj. Gen. Blackwell said, "That's a pretty good story, Mr. Treywick."

"Not from where me n' PJ was experiencen' it first hand."

Beverly said, "Might still be out there somewhere."

Waldo said, "I ain't goin' lookin' for it."

Two well-dressed, hard-eyed individuals walked into the hotel escorting five middle-aged men wearing cheap federal penitentiary release suits – the ex-cons. Mandy Paige greeted them at the door.

Lady Jane excused herself and joined the group. They walked to the service elevator located in the back of the hotel. A key was required to operate it. Lady Jane and Mandy had keys. The two U.S. Secret Service agents would be issued copies.

The forgers would not. Once downstairs they might as well have been incarcerated. The men would not be allowed topside unless accompanied by an armed escort. Photographs of all five had been distributed to the VPW operators and hotel security posted throughout the hotel and at all doors leading outside.

They were not going anywhere.

The deal made with the felons was simple. If they served their country well, the men would have their sentences reduced to time served. If any one of them violated the conditions of the agreement then all five would be sent back to serve out their full terms. Counterfeiting was a 15-year hitch. None of the five forgers had more than six years in.

The arrangement was good for all parties concerned.

The first project on the agenda was to prepare documents for Captain Preston Butterfield III. He needed to be on his way to Paris as soon as possible. Before work could get started on his papers, Mandy, acting in her capacity as 'Documents Room Procurement Officer', needed to have the list of supplies interpreted in order to know what to go shopping for.

The group sat down at a table in Secrets where construction was still in progress and went over the Stores Requisition List.

Lt. Gen. McKoy would be coming down later to have a heart-to-heart with the ex-cons – "Lawman to perpetrator… let 'em know who it is they're workin' for." Then he and Waldo were flying out to the Belgian Congo.

They had LONG NECK business.

LIEUTENANT COLONEL THOMAS ARGYLL "TAR" ROBERTSON arrived at the Bradford Hotel. Beverly Blackwell and Rikke Runborg were standing by waiting for him. They went up to the Phone Room on the Penthouse Floor. Normally Mandy Paige would be with them since she was Rocky's MI-5 Section B1-A handler. However, because of her commitment downstairs with the counterfeiters, Beverly was filling in.

Since Lt. Col Robertson did not possess a Need to Know about the counterfeit documents section, Beverly said, "Mandy was called away on other business."

It was not much of an explanation but nobody could do "…Short and Simple" and make it sound like an in-depth conversation better than she could.

Today the purpose of the exercise was for Rocky, acting in her capacity as German spy, to send a message to Field Marshal Erwin Rommel. She was going to inform the Desert Fox about the Liberator FP-45 pistols.

Rocky's agent report would soon be confirmed as fact when the weapons began to turn up in Calais.

One of the MI-5, B1-A technicians was waiting with the transmitter set up ready to go when they arrived. Rocky sat down and began to send.

ALLIES PREPARING TO ISSUE 500,000 DISPOSABLE ASSASSIN WEAPONS DESCRIBED AS FP-45 LIBERATOR PISTOLS TO RESISTANCE IN CALAIS DISTRICT STOP PURPOSE ASSESSED AS TARGETED KILLINGS OF COASTAL DEFENSE TROOPS AND DISRUPTION OF REAR AREA COMMAND STOP

A chilling report if you were a Nazi residing anywhere in or around the Pas-de-Calais Military District.

Slapstick comedy if you were an Allied deception planner cleared to know the details of OPERATION REVERSE MUSKET – as the semi-true plan to deliver Liberator pistols to the French Underground was now styled.

BRANDY SEABORN HOVE TO A MILE OFF THE FRENCH COAST. The night was dark. It was barely possible to see the thin shadow of the coastline in the distance. Tonight was a hasty mission.

A truck transporting the first consignment of FP- 45 Liberators arrived at Seaborn House earlier in the afternoon. When Colonel John Randal was notified he immediately initiated an alert for a cross-channel operation. Then he and Captain Billy Jack Jaxx were flown in from the Bradford Hotel by Beverly Blackwell. They were going to carry out the first REVERSE MUSKET mission.

Only this consignment of weapons would not be going to the Resistance. They were intended for the Germans. As Beverly liked to say, "Don't make it too hard for the bad guys to figure out."

Liberator FP-45s came packed in small individual cardboard boxes, placed ten units per in a larger container. Each individually boxed pistol was sealed in waxed paper. Every box contained ten rounds of 45 ACP ammunition, a wooden dowel for ejecting spent cases and a simple pictorial that showed how to load, fire and eject the spent shell casing step-by-step.

Each box also contained French language instructions for the pistol's use. The Liberator was described as, "A single-use, disposable expedient weapon, designed for a guerrilla fighter to use to kill an unsuspecting German at close range in order to secure a superior weapon and ammunition thereby arming himself for further action."

The Nazis would not have to be able to read French to understand the blood-curdling graphic diagram.

Lance Corporal Ray "Tank" Karlsson was alongside the PT boat in the stern of a 6-man cockle with another Special Warfare Operator in the bow. They were waiting as a smaller folding, 2-man boat was being lowered over the side. This was a tricky process. There were three rectangular corrugated cardboard boxes with ten Liberators in each one in the canoe. Care had to be taken so that the boat did not tilt and spill the boxes.

When the 2-man cockle was safely down, Liberator pistols still on board, Col. Randal and Capt. Jaxx went over the side and climbed in – not the easiest of evolutions.

Col. Randal was stern man. He said, "Give way together."

He and Capt. Jaxx started paddling. The larger 6-man cockle pulled in behind and followed as they headed toward the beach. At that point the adrenaline kicked in. No matter how many missions you went on, it always did.

The only difference was now after as many ops as Col. Randal and Capt. Jaxx had under their belts they knew what they were experiencing was a rush of anticipation, not fear. A familiar feeling most people would not understand if they heard the experience explained. It felt good.

That did not seem rational – possibly a little crazy.

Col. Randal and Capt. Jaxx were experienced small boat handlers. But they were nowhere near as skilled as the two Frogmen in the 6-man cockle behind them. Still, they made good time – 35 minutes to the shore. The target beach was not large enough or suitable to support an invasion. There were steep vertical cliffs immediately inland behind it which would prevent wheeled and tracked vehicles from moving inland.

That meant this stretch of the shore would not be defended the same as invasion-capable locations. No matter how many German soldiers were stationed in and around Calais there were not enough to guard every inch of the approximately one hundred-mile coastline in the district. And that was based on a straight line measurement. Considering inlets and coves, there was substantially more waterfront to defend.

Upon arriving in London and realizing Raiding Forces would be operating cross-channel against Calais in the run-up to D-Day, Col. Randal made his own estimate of the situation. Based on experience with then-Major Dudley Clarke at MI(R) early in the war developing the Commando concept, he adapted an old baseball adage for Raiding Forces' pre-Day mission planning.

"Hit 'em where they ain't."

Meaning never carry out a small-scale raid against a hard target on a defended beach if at all possible. That did not mean do not raid German-occupied targets. It meant do not land in front of them to commence your attack. Small units of Commandos taking casualties at the water's edge quickly find themselves rendered combat ineffective before they can make it ashore and get organized for their attack.

Col. Randal helped write the book on small-unit guerrilla tactics. He knew small-scale raids sent in across a beach against enemy-occupied point-type targets eventually led to disaster. Special Operations Executive's Small-Scale Raiding Force (SSRF) – the forerunner of his Raiding Forces, kept being sent after hard targets until the unit's founder and most other senior leaders were all killed and the SSRF disbanded. A magnificent unit misused by SOE again and again until it literally hammered itself apart.

As they were gliding in silently making their final approach Tank's cockle back paddled and stood offshore. Near the beach Capt. Jaxx bailed out in knee-deep water and started walking the boat. Then Col. Randal climbed over the side. Moving along beside the boat they let the waves wash it ashore.

Then they dragged it far enough up on the beach to make sure it would not be washed back out into the Channel when the tide came in…then went back out. That was important. When finally satisfied the cockle was well above the high water mark, they turned it over on one side. Col. Randal unslung the suppressed M3 Grease Gun he had over his shoulder and, firing from the hip, without deploying the telescoping wire stock, emptied half a magazine into it.

Then he took out a half-pint jar from one of the billows' side pockets on his Jump Jacket, M-1942. It contained blood drawn from one of the horses at Seaborn House. Col. Randal unscrewed the lid and poured the contents over the three boxes containing the smaller individual packages of Liberator FP-45s.

Capt. Jaxx whispered, "That'll be enough to confuse the Germans when they conduct their beach patrol at first light, sir. Shot up cockle, blood, pistols, illustrated instructions on how to assassinate an enemy soldier – meaning them…"

Col. Randal whispered, "Let's get the hell out of Dodge, Jack."

"Roger that."

Wading out to climb aboard Tank's cockle, the two were laughing quietly – mission accomplished.

OPERATION REVERSE MUSKET was a go.

APPROXIMATELY FIFTY MILES UP THE COAST FROM WHERE Colonel John Randal and Captain Billy Jack Jaxx were boarding Brandy Seaborn's PT boat for a high-speed run back to Seaborn House, Captain Pamala Plum-Martin and King were flying along a coastal road at treetop level in a Stinson L-5 Sentinel aircraft built by the Vultee Aircraft Company. Major General Sam Houston "Bronc" Blackwell had supplied two of the planes to Raiding Forces for his Special Duties Squadron. The general had them flown in to Seaborn House but he had not assigned duty pilots at this point. He was considering having his Troop Transport Command pilots rotate through short tours in the squadron, as an award for outstanding job performance.

Carry out your duties as a TTC pilot with conspicuous skill, above and beyond – your reward, an unofficial "atta boy" and the opportunity to fly one of the Sentinels on high-risk short takeoff and landing missions behind enemy lines, operating from rough improvised strips or dropping individual parachutists and small cargo packages to the French Resistance. Made perfect sense to Bronc.

The L-5 was the United States Army Air Forces' answer to the Royal Air Force's Lysander.

The RAF aircraft was designed for extreme STOL, featuring slow-speed control. It specialized in single aircraft, moonlit landing ground insertions or parachute drops. The Sentinel was designed for USAAF liaison, courier, daylight and front-line observation & artillery spotting duties.

The L-5 was not purpose-built as a clandestine operations aircraft. Why? Because USAAF special operations doctrine favored parachute insertion from larger transports meaning the C-47 for covert missions. What this meant was the RAF understood air special operations – the USAAF did not.

In a perfect world Capt. Plum-Martin would be piloting a Lysander. The L-5 was what she had. It was a good airplane. Nevertheless, she was compiling a mental inventory of modifications that would make the Sentinel L-5 a much better special operations aircraft.

It was turning out to be a long list starting with "Short & Rough Field Performance."

1. Oversized low-pressure tires – like those used by Alaskan bush pilots.
2. Reinforced gear legs and fittings.
3. Mud scrapers/ debris guards.

Tonight Capt. Plum-Martin and King were looking for the perfect tree. The plan, hastily organized earlier that afternoon, was to drop two containers of ten individually boxed FP-45 Liberator pistols in places a patrol from the Grenadier Regiment 857 of the 346 Infanterie Division would be sure to find. They had been provided with Enemy Order of Battle intelligence on where the regiment operated.

Standard Operating Procedure for occupying troops responsible for coastal defense in Pas-de Calais was to patrol the roads outside their bases every morning at first light. The patrols had to be done early – before traffic erased signs of resistance activities. The Germans were particularly searching for signs of clandestine parachute drops of personnel or supplies. Specifically, silk parachute fragments, harness webbing, container impact marks or drag trails where heavy packages had been recovered.

The idea tonight was for Capt. Plum-Martin and King to give Regiment 857 something to find. Up ahead was an old boundary oak. Part of a long line of English Oak trees running along the road they were flying down. Over time they could grow close to 90 feet tall. There was a tree in sight not quite that big but it was taller than the rest.

King said, "That one works."

To pass directly over it, Capt. Plum-Martin was going to have to gain altitude. She was flying at what observation aircraft pilots called "anteater altitude." King readied a box of the FP-45 Liberators in the open window of the L-5. When the plane swooped up he tossed it out, being careful not to let the container's parachute get caught in the landing gear.

The canopy never had a chance to deploy fully. That was the idea. The bundle hit the oak tree dead center in the middle. The silk caught on a limb but the box kept falling until it dangled down. The chute was going to be hard for anyone on the road to miss.

Capt. Plum-Martin dropped back down low again as they flew past and lined up centered on the roadway. King tossed out another bundle. At that low level the chute failed to deploy properly as well – part of the plan. The box hit the ground, broke open and the individually packaged Liberators spilled out on the road.

The parachute lay there ruffling in the breeze.

Capt. Plum-Martin banked toward the Channel and flew back across it at wave-top level going almost wide open at slightly over 120 mph. The L-5 made landfall and continued on its way to London. Unfortunately, brilliant flashes of bomb blasts could be seen as they approached the city. Suddenly stately white columns sprang up everywhere across the horizon, sweeping back and forth hypnotically – searchlights. And at the far end of their flight path what looked like ten million red tracers started chasing each other as they crisscrossed the sky. London's air defenses were taking on German intruders.

Not about to fly into that blizzard of steel-jacketed anti-aircraft fire, Capt. Plum-Martin diverted to an alternate RAF airfield short of the city. She and King had drinks on the roof of the airfield's Officers' Club watching London burn.

Mission accomplished.

THE BLITZ WAS ON, THOUGH SO FAR THIS BOMBING CAMPAIGN was much reduced from the original version. Londoners were calling it the "Baby Blitz." On average approximately 10 people were killed per night, down from the 70 per night in the 1940 bombing campaign – a clear sign the Luftwaffe was nearly spent.

But the air raid still had teeth.

The 1940 Blitz was made worse because it was widely predicted the Nazis would invade England within two weeks. This time around people who had survived it were encouraged by knowing the Allies were going to win the war.

Now Londoners were reacting to the Baby Blitz as more of an annoyance than a terror campaign. Still, 10 civilians killed a night was significant. And the material damage to buildings in the city proper was appreciable.

The staff at the Bradford Hotel took the air attacks seriously. A loud klaxon went off on every floor as soon as the Air Raid Precautions (ARP) sirens sounded in the city. Generators kicked in. Vulnerable Points Wing operators moved to the roof to take up positions to serve as Air Raid Wardens (ARW) aka "fire spotters."

Air raid warnings were based on radar plots and observer reports – at least that was the official line given to the public. In fact, a substantial amount of early warning was a result of *ULTRA* intercepts of Luftwaffe radio traffic. People were told, and it was confirmed by their experience in the

1940 Blitz, when the sirens went off they had five minutes to get to an air raid shelter.

The problem was many of the residents in the Bradford had lived through that first Blitz. Rich, entitled and long accustomed to exemption from the rules, they resented having to comply with orders. Some chose to stay in their beds.

Major the Lady Jane Seaborn, a member of the "Six Hundred" – the wealthiest families in England, anticipated this was going to happen. She instructed the hotel manager to have the porters designated to be Air Raid Wardens. They were broken down into teams. A team went to every floor. Knocked on every door. They were armed with skeleton keys. If there was no answer the staff went inside to check.

Any lodger who did not immediately go to the Air Raid Shelter or failed to comply with the Air Raid Wardens order to do so, was forcibly removed from their room. Guests repeating the offense a second time were evicted from the hotel same night – as soon as the All Clear was sounded.

After the first dislodgment of a wealthy titled guest that problem went away.

Colonel John Randal said, "Pretty tough, babe."

Lady Jane said, "I do not care who you are – not getting killed on my watch."

"Good for you."

The already intensive efforts to complete Secrets were redoubled with the onset of the air raids. It was going to be the perfect bomb shelter. A bar, live music, dancing and a full-service kitchen for late dinners or snacks.

Col. Randal and Lady Jane were asleep in their suite when the sirens outside, followed immediately by the hotel's internal klaxon, went off. Happy barked to alert them – the dog was a veteran. He knew the drill.

One of the VPW security operators was banging on the door.

Col. Randal was in his pants by the time his feet hit the floor. He grabbed his Colt .38 Super pistols, stepped into a pair of leather moccasins placed next to the bed for just this type emergency – no time for boots, and was headed out into the hall with a tousled Lady Jane looking more glamorous than if she had walked out of a beauty salon. Happy was hard on his heels.

People were coming out of their rooms half-dressed. Headed to the stairs – no using elevators during air raids. Security was posted at them on every floor. There was no panic but everyone was moving with a sense of purpose. Time was of the essence. The Penthouse floor residents in the Raiding Forces' wing were heading to the War Room. They would not be riding out the air attack in the Air Raid shelter with the rest of the guests.

Lady Jane had made special arrangements for them.

Col. Randal ordered the VPW operator at his door, "Go check to see if General Eisenhower is in residence. If he is, escort him to his office downstairs – Lady Jane will check on him there. If he's not come back here and help clear the rooms on this floor."

"Sir!"

"Jane, you go supervise the War Room."

Lady Jane said, "I am staying with you until we clear the floor."

It was her hotel, her private floor and everyone on it *her* people – Col. Randal said, "Stay close then."

The residents in the Raiding Forces' wing were all veterans. That might not be true of some of their guests. Nothing like an air raid to turn the Bradford Hotel into a fishbowl. People were coming out of rooms with their half-dressed overnight guests – some surprises were revealed. Now it dawned on Col. Randal why Lady Jane had chosen to name her nightclub 'Secrets.'

In an incredibly short time, less than a full minute, the private Raiding Forces' wing had cleared out. Everyone was heading to the staircase moving hurriedly. No running. Everyone moved down the stairs.

They had nine floors to go.

When Col. Randal and Lady Jane were satisfied everyone had repaired to the War Room they went down. When they arrived there was a lot of laughter – nervous relief, typical in air raid shelters. People were in various states of undress.

Lady Jane had planned for that happening. Her Royal Marines passed out hotel robes from a prepositioned locker stocked to meet the need. She went around counting noses to make sure everyone was safe.

"John, where's Billy Jack?"

"I have no idea."

Beverly said, "He's up on the roof with Sloan."

Col. Randal ran out of the War Room and raced up the stairs with Happy running along beside him. He could hear the muffled sounds of the air raid in progress outside. It was a long slog but they finally made it to the door that led out onto the roof.

When Col. Randal charged outside, he found an incredible scene. It was like walking into a dark theatre in the middle of a 3-D movie about aliens from outer space invading Earth. Intensive anti-aircraft fire of all calibers, large and small, was going up lacing the sky. Bombs were raining down, detonating all around. Tall white searchlight beams were swaying all across the city as far as the eye could see in every direction.

Enemy bombers droned overhead at low altitude.

The German aircraft were firing their organic 7.92 MG81 machine guns down at the ground as well as dropping what the Luftwaffe called the "English Mixture" – 70% incendiaries and 30% high explosives. The noise was overwhelming. Bombs detonating, pom-pom guns booming – actually they made a sharp flat CRAAAAACK, light and heavy machine guns going *thump-thump-thump-thump*.... In addition, anti-aircraft light machine guns mounted on top of buildings were sending up streams of red tracers that arched into the night.

The sight and sound almost overpowered the senses.

Captain Billy Jack Jaxx was blazing away with one of the heavily modified Raiding Forces .30 caliber M1919 'Stinger' light machine guns firing from the hip. Sloan was acting as his assistant gunner holding the linked ammo to keep the belt straight as the rounds fed into the gun.

Jack Cool was engaging a low-level JU88 bomber about 100 yards away flying straight at the Bradford. The bomber was coming in at a slight angle, 75 feet or so higher than the roof. The aircraft was trapped in the apex of a pyramid of searchlight beams.

Col. Randal knew on low-level bombing runs JU88s typically travel at around 200 miles per hour. This one gave the illusion of standing still and was so close it looked like you could reach out and touch it. The nose gunner was firing at them – or at least the Bradford, with its MG15 machine gun and streams of yellow 7.92 tracer rounds were cracking past.

The Germans used a rainbow of different color tracers – yellow seemed surreal.

Standing on the roof of the hotel put them in the middle of this low-level air battle. The building was over 150 feet high. Everything appeared to be taking place fast in slow motion all around for a full 360 degrees. The 3-D sensation had not gone away – it got worse.

To add to the sensory overload it was all so beautiful.

Capt. Jaxx was standing his ground blazing away, not adhering to the recommended school solution "fire a burst of six" for belt-fed machine guns. He was running the belt on the Stinger. Col. Randal saw his rounds striking the plane. Solid red lines of .30 caliber tracers streamed straight at it as if chasing each other. The lines snuffed out as if swallowed when the rounds struck the plane's fuselage. Hard to believe the belt only contained one tracer every five rounds – Ball, and Armor Piercing (AP) rounds were spaced in between.

BOOOOOM!

The JU88 exploded.

The bomber went from posing a threat as a deadly war machine to being a flash of light. A massive shock wave slammed past. It was a miracle they were not killed, though everyone on the roof to include the ARW spotters were staggered by the blast – momentarily disoriented.

Happy was not happy.

Col. Randal realized he had been firing his Colt .38 Super. He had no conscious memory of drawing it or aiming at the JU88. That was how desperate the situation had been.

Capt. Jaxx said, "Scratch one bad guy."

Sloan said, "You are a fun date, Jack."

Col. Randal shouted, "Let's get the hell out of Dodge."

Now S&M could legitimately claim she had heard him say it.

When they arrived downstairs in the War Room Lady Jane took one look and pulled him aside. "Anything wrong, John?"

Col. Randal said, "We're in the middle of a German air raid. I just ran up nine flights of stairs to the roof thinking Jack had taken S&M up there to watch the fireworks. When I arrived he was firing a .30 caliber Stinger LMG at a Luftwaffe JU88 making a run on the hotel carrying a full bomb load – it blew up in our face.

"Ask Happy how he's feeling."

"I shall."

Col. Randal said, "Miss Marlow has some sense of humor – that, or she's one twisted woman."

Lady Jane laughed, "Let me know when you figure out which it is."

MAJOR THE LADY JANE SEABORN SAID, "DO YOU KNOW WHAT the motto of the Windmill Theatre is?"

Col. John Randal said, "I do not."

"Never Closed, Never Clothed."

"Really?"

"Rita and Lana got fired."

"Why might that be?"

"The rule is 'to move is lewd.' Nude models have to remain perfectly motionless – like Greek statues."

"I heard that."

"Rita and Lana moved."

16

DESIGNED TO FAIL

THE RAIDING FORCES' VIP AREA OF THE BRADFORD HOTEL lobby was not as crowded as it normally was. People still came and went but many of the regulars were away. Nevertheless, Colonel John Randal spent a lot of his time there to be readily accessible for those who had business with him to attend to. He preferred it to sitting in his office in the War Room.

Lieutenant General "Geronimo" Joe McKoy and Waldo Treywick were winging their way to the Belgian Congo to check up on Commander General Frank Polanski. The former U.S. Marine, ex-mercenary, was now back on active duty in the grade of Gunnery Sergeant running LONG NECK diamond interdiction operations along the Congo River. His assignment was to stop Nazi agents from buying diamonds and arranging their transport to the Third Reich. And to seize the ones they had purchased.

By any means necessary.

A vicious little war the Axis diamond buyers had not come prepared to fight was going on around the remote jungle trading posts along the Congo River. The Nazis never stood a chance. Cdr. Gen. Polanski was an old hand at guerrilla warfare from his days as a U.S. Marine Lance Corporal in Haiti and a mercenary in Abyssinia. His orders were to "liquidate" the Axis diamond buyers.

He was being paid a fortune for his services.

Captain Pamala Plum-Martin and King were also traveling… en route to Spanish Morocco. They had cornered the diamond market in the protectorate by entering into a business agreement with the colony's Chief of Police – *Jefe de Policia.* The Spaniard had a predilection for physically fit, tanned, snow-blonde women, like Capt. Plum-Martin but he enjoyed his cut of the profits from their illicit diamond operation even more.

He had no idea who they were, believing them to be international criminals.

Mandy Paige was traveling the English countryside, laying in stores for the Documents Room.

Major General Sam Houston "Bronc" Blackwell was spending more of his time downstairs in his new Troop Transport Command Headquarters. Bronc did not run the day-to-day TTC operations. He had the former President of Trans Texas Airlines to do that. But he loved being in the center of the action surrounded by his pilots.

When Brandy Seaborn was in from Seaborn House he came upstairs to the VIP section to visit with her and people-watch – Maj. Gen. Blackwell was having a good war.

Major the Lady Jane Seaborn and Beverly Blackwell were busy decorating Secrets. Today they were downstairs supervising luminous stars being painted on the ceiling. The nightclub was almost ready to have its Grand Opening.

Captain Westly Slade was supervising two-man teams of Special Warfare Operators tasked with delivering geological augers to beaches the length of France and working with Doctor Layton Winthrop to develop a plan to conduct beach surveys of potential invasion beaches for D-Day. Major General William "Wild Bill" Donovan was having the two officers he requested for his Special Warfare Operators team flown in. Capt. Slade needed them – the auger program required substantial coordination and was going to take a minimum of six to eight weeks to conclude.

Most of the remaining Raiding Forces' officers in the grade of captain were away recruiting small unit leaders for their teams per Col. Randal's orders. They were searching out the best candidates among the junior officer ranks in the ETO. It was not an easy task.

Col. Randal preferred airborne combat veterans. Those were rare. If the right man was found but was not parachute qualified, he could be trained. Direct commissions were available. If a captain was willing to take a reduction in rank to serve in Raiding Forces, that could be arranged.

Captain Roy Kidd was away in Anzio, Italy on a recruiting trip visiting the 1st Special Service Brigade, a joint U.S./Canadian parachute /commando regiment. He knew a lieutenant in the unit who would be a good fit for his team.

Captain Jake Novak aka "Jake the Snake" was also in Italy visiting his old outfit, the battle-hardened 509th Parachute Infantry Battalion. It had recently been attached to the 6615th Ranger Task Force He had a couple of people in mind for his two officers. Exactly the kind of men Col. Randal was looking for – experienced.

Captain Chase Starrett was conducting a three-week Pathfinder Course for the newly arrived in theatre 101st Airborne Division aka "Screaming Eagles." The division had not seen combat yet but it had a number of officers from the veteran 82nd "All-American" Airborne Division who had been transferred in as "stiffeners" for the upcoming D-Day invasion. He was planning to put the word out he was recruiting – some of them might like serving in Raiding Forces better than with a green unit.

Captain Richard "Dynamite Dick" Coogan had an OCS classmate in the 1st Infantry Division "Big Red One" who had won the Silver Star commanding the 16th Regiment's Reconnaissance Platoon. He had seen action in North Africa, Tunisa and Sicily. While not parachute qualified, Mad Dog would have him jumping out of airplanes in no time.

Col. Randal could hardly wait until he began interviewing the volunteers. Infusing new people into Raiding Forces and adjusting his TO&E accordingly when the unit rotated through different theatres of operations was one of the command prerogatives he enjoyed the most.

The new people were going to bring a wide range of differing combat experience when they arrived. And that was always good. Unless they had learned bad habits. A possibility he needed to be alert for. Not everyone volunteering would be accepted. The candidates had to make it past their interview with him first.

Then they had to perform. Col. Randal had one guiding principle when it came to recruiting and retention – not everyone *deserved* to be in Raiding

Forces. Getting in was easier than staying in. Failure to execute at any point was grounds for immediate RTU. That went for everyone. New personnel as well as old hands who had been in the unit for years.

Performance was the single measure for retention – at all times.

As Capt. Jaxx said, "No slack."

Several of the officers being recruited were highly decorated. That could be positive or negative. Col. Randal would not be hiring anyone who believed his own press.

The crazy brave or fake tough need not apply.

SLOAN MARLOW STOPPED BY THE VIP SECTION TO SPEAK TO Colonel John Randal.

"I want to thank you, John."

"For what?"

"Lady Jane invited me for tea. Actually it was a polite job interview. I must have passed thanks in no small part to you."

Col. Randal said, "Interview?"

Sloan said, "She extended an invitation for me to be a part of your new E&E program – vetting the returning escapers. We have to make sure none of them are Abwehr infiltrators. I am sure you are aware of what happened to the Pat O'Leary Line and the Comet Line."

Col. Randal said, "Actually, I'm not."

Sloan said, "The Abwehr, working with the SD – the intelligence service of the SS and Nazi Party, infiltrated the Pat O'Leary line. Identified organizers, contacts and safe houses. Then rolled up the network. The circuit was completely destroyed.

"Same story, slightly different outcome for the Comet Line. German CI agents penetrated sections of it through informers, surveillance, arrests and harsh interrogations – then moved in. While the line is still operating, it's a mere shadow of itself."

Col. Randal said, "So what is it you're going to be doing, exactly?"

"Mandy, Beverly and I shall be conducting discreet security screening of the escapers when they return to England – before they are released to their units. We have a responsibility not to allow Abwehr agents posing as

USAAF airmen to penetrate the circuit, slip through and set up shop here in the UK. The Nazis are definitely going to try."

Col. Randal said, "MI-5 is OK with you doing that for us?"

"The Security Service is never going to know about it."

"And you're thanking me why?"

"Lady Jane said you took up for me. When concerns were first voiced I might be trying to target you and Jack for security violations. That was rather nice, considering…"

"Well, you're the one who said we should be friends."

"Truly, John, the thought of you or Jack being security violators never crossed my mind."

Col. Randal said, "Welcome to Raiding Forces."

"Thank you."

"How do you feel about jumping out of airplanes?"

"Mandy says it's better than sex."

Col. Randal said, "Yes, she does."

Sloan said. "I proposed a name to Lady Jane for your escape line."

Col. Randal said, "What might that be?"

"Dodge City."

CAPTAIN BILLY JACK JAXX ARRIVED IN THE VIP SECTION AS Sloan was departing. Unlike the other captains in Raiding Forces, he did not seem in any great hurry to be recruiting his lieutenants. He should be. SOG did not have any other officers now that Captain Chase Starrett had been promoted.

Capt. Jaxx said, "You hitting on my girlfriend, sir?"

Col. Randal said, "Thinking about it."

"Go ahead, Colonel – you'd be saving me from myself."

Col. Randal asked, "Would you say Sloan's eyes are light gray or pale turquoise?"

Capt. Jaxx said, "How would I know, sir – when I look in them nothing registers."

Col. Randal said, "You're in trouble, Jack."

Capt. Jaxx said, "How long did it take you to realize *you* were sir, with Lady Jane? Word is you and Colonel Stone used to really tear 'em up before she showed up."

Col. Randal said, "Oh, somewhere in the first four or five seconds."

Capt. Jaxx said, "That's what I was afraid you'd say. I'm getting ready to fly out to Italy. Maybe things with S&M will cool off while I'm gone."

Col. Randal said, "What have you got going?"

Capt. Jaxx said, "One of my old teammates on the Texas Longhorns football team is in the 36th 'Texas' Division – they're up on the Rapido River in Italy, sir. The division had a Ranger Company but it was disbanded on orders from Army Ground Forces at the War Department. He will make a great Raiding Forces' officer – landed at Salerno and has been fighting his way up the boot of Italy ever since.

"I'm going to go pick him up, sir."

Col. Randal said, "Good, sounds like what we're looking for."

Capt. Jaxx said, "You'll just promote him to captain so I'm also going to swing by Anzio and recruit a lieutenant I served with at Ft. Benning, sir. A 1st Ranger Battalion man from inception who has recently been reassigned to the 4th Ranger Battalion after his battalion was virtually annihilated at some place called Cisterna – an Achnacarry graduate.

"Want to go, sir?"

Col. Randal said, "Things are moving too fast here for me to leave, Jack. I want a report on the Anzio beachhead when you get back. Not hearing good things about the beachhead."

Capt. Jaxx said, "Can do, sir – change your mind, I'm flying out tomorrow."

"Have a good trip."

Capt. Jaxx said, "One other thing, sir. I found out the 29th Infantry Division stationed here in England had formed a Ranger Company too. It's been disbanded as well. I've told Chase to go recruit it. You might want to give him a hand."

Col. Randal said. "I will – wasn't aware of those divisional Ranger Companies."

Capt. Jaxx said, "When I get back I want to talk to you about an idea I've been kicking around, sir."

Col. Randal said, "What might that be?"

Capt. Jaxx said, "The 1st, 3rd, 9th, 34th and 36th Divisions all had provisional Ranger Companies as well. Some general at the War Department named Leslie McNair ordered them disbanded and the troops dispersed throughout the parent division. I think we ought to make an effort to recruit as many of those Ranger trained personnel as we can get."

Col. Randal said, "News to me – you're in charge of the Ranger recruiting project when you get back."

Capt. Jaxx said, "So, you think I may be in over my head with S&M?"

"I do."

JAMES "BALDIE" TAYLOR CAME TO THE VIP SECTION TO SEE Colonel John Randal shortly after Captain Billy Jack Jaxx departed. He was looking sleek in one of the late Big Five's navy blue pinstriped suits.

Jim said, "Can we go somewhere to talk? You may not be the only person in the hotel who can read lips.

Col. Randal said, "What makes you think I read lips?"

"How else would you always know what everyone in the room is talking about?"

"The Smoking Room's usually empty this time of day."

"That works."

When they arrived, no one was inside. Col. Randal offered Jim one of Waldo's cigars. Erring on the side of caution, the two sat in the far back in case someone came in.

Why take a chance?

They had worked together starting in the Gold Coast from the early dark days of the war when Baldie was presenting himself as a down and out MI-6 agent assigned to a backwater African colony. Nothing could have been farther from the truth. He was there for a specific, highly-classified operation that involved Raiding Forces.

Jim did not play unnecessary cloak and dagger games like a lot of others in the covert world. He was known for no drama. Today's concern about lip readers eavesdropping on their conversation was out of character. Under normal circumstances if Baldy knew Col. Randal could read lips he would have kept that piece of information to himself. How long had he known?

Col. Randal clicked on.

Jim said, "We are not having this conversation, Colonel. I am going to give you opinions – not necessarily facts – that I should not be sharing with anyone. No part of what we discuss is to be repeated – clear?

"Crystal."

"You already know General Blackwell has nominated you to be the SHAEF Airborne Advisor to replace General Gavin who has returned to the 82nd Airborne Division."

"I do."

"What you do not know is that SHAEF is convening something called the Raids & Reconnaissance Committee. It will consist of the highest-ranking officers from the intelligence services and top-tier SHAEF departments to include G-2 Intelligence. The stated purpose of the committee is to approve or disapprove pre-D-Day small-scale cross-channel raids and reconnaissance missions."

Col. Randal said, "Planning raids or reconnaissance missions by committee is a really bad idea."

Jim said, "Maybe not. The committee is going to disapprove virtually every raid or recce job proposed. And *not* bring up for discussion certain operations people in high places actually do desire to have take place – to prevent the possibility of those being rejected."

Col. Randal said, "Lovely."

"Raiding Forces' operations do not fall within the committee's purview. We are outside their remit. That is so highly classified I do not know who has the Need to Know.

"Certainly not you, Colonel."

Col. Randal said, "I see."

Jim said, "You have been proposed as an occasional committee member. Do not ask who made the suggestion or why. I do not know the answer."

Col. Randal said, "What does occasional mean?"

Jim said, "The committee has no fixed membership. No regularly scheduled meetings. It is a 100 percent ad hoc coordinating group. The irony is the Raids & Reconnaissance Committee has no power to actually approve or disapprove operations when it does meet – that part is a gray area. It simply makes recommendations."

Col. Randal said, "How senior are the officers involved?"

Jim said, "Top tier. General Kenneth Strong, SHAEF G2 Intelligence, is the chair but he will almost certainly never attend meetings. Strong will send his deputy, Brigadier Eric Mockler-Ferryman.

"MI-6 will be represented by Colonel Claude Dansey, aka Colonel Z. He's a heavyweight widely disliked and feared by his own people at SIS. Dansey despises SOE – has no use for OSS, General Donovan or Americans in general. He will be a disruptive factor at any meeting he attends.

"SOE will send the head of the French Section, Colonel Maurice Buckmaster. He stays in a constant state of conflict with MI-6 and jealously opposes OSS becoming involved with the Resistance in France wanting to maintain a monopoly on irregular warfare. Buckmaster likes nothing better than a political brawl and his MO is to take his battles up the chain-of-command to uncomfortably high levels for those he is opposing.

"OSS will almost definitely be represented by Colonel David Bruce, the London Station Chief. None of the British officers will want Bruce present. They can be expected to unite in their efforts to marginalize him – the only thing they will ever all agree on.

"Combined Operations will probably be represented by its Deputy Chief of Staff Captain C.E. Lambe, RN. He is probably the most qualified officer to sit on the panel. Lambe is not NID and he does not stand a chance against the intelligence service members. Basically, you can expect him to not be much more than an expert witness on naval matters. He likes or dislikes full moons… I can never remember which it is.

"LCS will probably send Lieutenant Colonel Roger Hesketh, the London Controlling Section's Operations Officer. He will keep his own counsel and never engage in the infighting. Everyone, regardless of rank, will be intimidated by Hesketh being present. It is known that he alone decides what the Chief of LCS, Col. Bevan, sees. And everyone knows he will be reporting directly to his boss about what takes place in the meetings, which makes him a formidable player. Bevan is a man to be reckoned with. Word is he reports directly to the Prime Minister and that is true.

"Last but not least, there will be you, Colonel – unless you decide to make Beverly your proxy and send her in your place. I would pay good money to be a fly on the wall in the event you ever choose that option."

Col. Randal said, "Does that mean you won't be, Jim?"

"Negative, I am officially the liaison to three of the agencies that will have representatives there. Meetings are for members or their representatives only. My role will be to gather verbal after-action reports – notes during the meeting are not permitted."

Col. Randal said, "So let me get this straight. The Raids & Reconnaissance Committee has no charter, no fixed membership, its composition changes from meeting to meeting, there's no directive giving it authority to veto cross-channel operations – but that's its primary purpose… to veto cross-channel ops. And the committee is made up of the most senior officers from intelligence organizations who hate each other."

Jim said, "One way of putting it."

Col. Randal said, "You've described a committee intentionally designed to fail. That many senior officers, even without competing agendas, would never agree on anything."

Jim said, "Why do you think we are sitting in this dark room making sure no one reads our lips? Everything we just discussed is classified to the stratosphere. I'm impressed you figured it out on the first run through."

Col. Randal said, "Why would SHAEF create a top-level coordinating group that has no chance of accomplishing anything?"

Jim said, "Depends on how you define 'accomplish'. Colonel Bevan was the moving force behind establishing the Raids & Reconnaissance Committee. Neither of us nor anybody else possesses the Need-to-Know that tidbit of information."

Col. Randal said, "What's his motive?"

Jim said, "LCS needs to vet every cross-channel op to make sure it conforms to the FORTITUDE SOUTH deception plan. Bevan does not want any written record of him being behind rejecting missions or any other decisions tracing back to Deception. And he does not want to be blamed for the completely justified claims that the US is being excluded from intelligence gathering or irregular operations in France – when OSS proposals are rejected."

Col. Randal said, "What a catfight."

Jim said, "Colonel Bevan is setting up a silent veto that does not leave any fingerprints leading back to LCS even though no raid or recce across the Channel can take place without his approval. That said, you have thrown him a couple of curve balls – claims to be developing gray hair since your arrival in London."

Col. Randal said, "So if I'm ever tasked to sit on the Raids & Reconnaissance Committee, who am I representing?"

Jim said, "That is the beauty of it – nobody."

Col. Randal said, "Oh, that's good – you think the people sitting in on the committee meetings will understand what's going on?"

Jim said, "In a word – no. Most are going to be so impressed at being tasked to take part in what they perceive as a prestigious, high-level conference, they never realize it's all a charade.

"There are a lot of ambitious men with inflated egos to be found in and around SHAEF."

Col. Randal said, "A sham committee. Orchestrated by LCS. To make the top people in multiple Allied intelligence services waste their time. Who would believe that?"

Jim said, "Nobody. And we can never tell."

Col. Randal said, "Why is SHAEF going along with this?"

Jim said, "To diffuse rejection when one of the organizations have their plans for cross-channel operations disapproved – hard to blame a committee. Colonel Bevan does not want people pointing their fingers at LCS – he still has to work with them."

Col. Randal said, "Good thing the average soldier doesn't know about the games being played by the senior officers sending him to invade France."

Jim said, "My guess is the closer we approach D-Day the more vicious the bureaucratic infighting is going to become. Have fun in your dual advisory capacity at SHAEF."

Col. Randal said, "I'm liking your idea of sending Beverly as my proxy better and better."

COLONEL JOHN RANDAL WAS READING AN ADVANCED COPY of a small, dark navy blue book Commander Ian Fleming sent over to the hotel for him. There was no title on the cover. But down in the lower right-hand corner was an embossed Commando insignia – an eagle outstretched over a flat-bottomed anchor with a Thompson submachine gun across the middle. It was said the crest signified airborne audacity, sea-borne raiding and close-quarters violence.

Col. Randal thought if that was true there should have been a pair of parachute wings on the device.

Inside on the flyleaf it said, "*The Official Story of the COMMANDOS*"– No author was attributed, which seemed unusual.

However, there was a Forward written by the former commander of Combined Operations, Vice Admiral Lord Louis "Dickie" Mountbatten, currently the Supreme Allied Commander, South East Asia Command, "A combined operation is a landing operation in which, owing to actual or expected opposition it is essential that the fighting services take part together, in order to strike the enemy with the maximum effect, at the chosen point and at the chosen moment."

Next was an unsigned Preface page, "A combined operation is one in which two or more of the Fighting Services co-operate in order to strike the enemy with the maximum of effect at a chosen place and a chosen moment."

Hmmmmm – 'Fighting Services' was capitalized by whoever wrote the Preface but not capitalized by VAdm. Lord Mountbatten.

Other than that, Col. Randal wondered what the odds were of two different people working separately writing almost identical paragraphs. However, to be fair, on occasion he was known to use a similar phrase, "at a certain place at a certain time"– when the mission profile dictated.

The Official Story of the COMMANDOS looked interesting.

A King's Messenger arrived. Col. Randal put away the book, signed for the envelope and walked to the elevator. He rode down to the War Room scanning the KM's dispatch.

CARRY OUT RECONNAISSANCE AT MAP
REFERENCE SHEET 51B/NE 437612.
CONFIRM ENEMY STRENGTH, WEAPONS
AND DEFENSES. MISSION CONFINED TO
OBSERVE AND REPORT ONLY.

CAPTAIN STEPHANIE FAWCETT-TATUM, RM, CAME OVER WHEN he walked in.

Col. Randal handed her the KM dispatch containing the grid coordinates, "Let's see what we have at this location."

For once there was more than a blank hole in the giant map mosaic on the wall. What they found was an aerial photo of an ordinary-looking rock farmhouse. It was sitting approximately half a mile off the beach at the coordinates specified. A dirt track ran past. No other structures were in the immediate vicinity.

The house was camouflaged.

Capt. Fawcett-Tatum said, "Something of interest is clearly inside the Germans would rather us not see."

Col. Randal said, "If the Germans hadn't tried to camouflage it we probably wouldn't be interested."

On closer examination the farmhouse was actually closer to the beach than originally estimated – approximately 600 yards from the coastline. Not much could be learned from the aerial photo. There were no signs of any defensive positions constructed in or around it.

Col. Randal said, "Stephanie, who do we have that's an Enemy Order of Battle specialist on staff at Seaborn House?"

Capt. Fawcett-Tatum said, "No one, as far as I am aware."

Col. Randal said, "Reach out to Jim. Have him report to me here. He may be in the building."

"Yes, sir."

"Then put Captain Courtney on Standby Ready Alert. If Beverly is available, have her fly to Seaborn House and pick him up. If she's not, run downstairs and see if Bronc will loan us a pilot.

"Put whoever's next on the rotation – Penelope or Brandy, on alert for a mission tonight."

"Anything else, John?"

"We need our own in-house Order of Battle expert on enemy forces in the Calais District. Tell Colonel Dance to start looking for one. Needs to be up to speed on the German Army at the tactical level – we're not interested in grand strategy above 15th Army."

Capt. Fawcett-Tatum said, "Do you have a preference – male or female?"

Col. Randal said, "Most talented."

He might as well have said woman. Capt. Fawcett-Tatum knew Col. Randal did not like having full-time male officers on staff who did not go on operations. In Raiding Forces everyone fought.

There were no cushy rear-echelon jobs.

Capt. Fawcett-Tatum decided to discuss the position with Major the Lady Jane Seaborn. She was on excellent terms with Commandant Mary Baxter Ellis the FANY commander. Instead of taking her boyfriend, Lieutenant Colonel Jack Dance, a staffing problem to resolve, she would bring him a solution.

There was no LD time contained in the dispatch. Nevertheless, missions were always taken on with alacrity. Frequently said around Raiding Forces was, "Don't put off 'til tomorrow what you can do today."

Raiding Forces was never going to be able to develop a solid read on the target in any reasonable amount of time. Not a problem. Reconnaissance missions are by definition designed to gather intelligence. A team would ghost in, recon the target then disappear home.

Col. Randal typically went when ready. If an objective was valuable enough for a King's Messenger to deliver the orders, it was not something to put off until it was convenient.

Whoever was behind the KM dispatches no longer asked if a mission could be done – they just indicated where. The striking arm of Raiding Forces (Seaborn House) was the 575th Ranger Regiment (Airborne). It was developing a reputation as a unit that went and did. There was a reason.

The Rangers went and did.

BEVERLY BLACKWELL CAME RUSHING INTO THE WAR ROOM. "Are you looking for me, Johnny?"

"I need you to fly to Seaborn house to pick up Dick Courtney."

"No need for that. Dick's downstairs talking to Daddy about big game hunting in Kenya. They're planning a safari after the war."

"Go inform Captain Courtney I said Stand By Ready."

"On the way."

Captain Stephanie Fawcett-Tatum walked over, "Brandy is in her suite if you need to speak to her."

"Tell her to meet me here as soon as possible if not sooner."

James "Baldie" Taylor arrived. Colonel John Randal handed him the KM dispatch. He read it and went straight to a phone and placed a call to MI-6, French Section. The SIS maintained updated order of battle intel for their own use – not for general distribution.

By the time Beverly and Captain Dick Courtney arrived, Jim was off the call. He came over to where they were standing, looking at the wall map.

Jim said, "MI-6 reports the 346th Infantry Division continues to occupy the Blanc-Nez-Calais coastal sector. The area in the immediate vicinity of the cape is designated WN109a. It consists of 1 infantry platoon from 5.GR/Grenadier Regiment 858 manning 2 machine gun bunkers, commanded by one Lieutenant Adolf Swartz."

Col. Randal said, "That's pretty specific, Jim."

"It's MI-6 Colonel – what did you expect from the premier intelligence organization on the planet?"

"They give you anything on the 858th?"

"Understrength static division of limited mobility. Predominantly bicycle-mounted. Older soldiers 30s-40s.

"Lieutenant Swartz's platoon command post is billeted in a farmhouse."

Col. Randal tapped the map, "Like this one."

Jim said, "My guess is that would be it. Likely have the two bunkers located forward on the cliff manned by four men each with the rest of the platoon in the vicinity of the house. Platoons have 30-40 men on paper, but in reality generally run closer to 20 all up.

"One other thing, Colonel. The Cap Blanc-Nez cliffs are nearly vertical white chalk – over 400 feet. That's a 40-story building."

Col. Randal said, "Lovely."

Brandy had arrived in the War Room and walked up behind them. "Those cliffs are snow white. There shall be no problem finding the landing point. We should be able to see them from halfway across the Channel."

Col. Randal said, "I'll be going in with Captain Courtney, his two strikers and the Lovats. Except for Ferguson and Fenwick, we're not skilled enough climbers to tackle scaling that cliff."

Major General Sam Houston "Bronc" Blackwell was right behind them. He had come to investigate why Beverly had been in such an uproar to drag Capt. Courtney out of his office. A sure indication Raiding Forces had a mission was in the offing.

Col. Randal said, "I'm going to need to make a VR of that cliff face, sir."

Maj. Gen. Blackwell said, "What are you looking for, Colonel?"

Col. Randal said, "I need to find a way down. We can't go in with 400 feet of rope."

"Go in where?"

"Right there, sir," Col. Randal tapped the map.

"When do you need to lay on this visual reconnaissance flight?"

"Anytime in the next five minutes, General."

"I'll have an L-5 Sentinel standing by as soon as you can get to the airport."

Beverly said, "I'll fly."

Maj. Gen. Blackwell said, "Not a chance. I've been banned from flying over water until after D-Day and that means you are too, baby girl. We both nearly got court-martialed over our last little father-daughter adventure."

Col. Randal said, "Brandy, can you be waiting at the bottom of Cap Blanc-Nez when we extract?"

Brandy said, "I could – only my boat is undergoing an engine overhaul. They say it shall be out of commission for up to three days."

Col. Randal said, "I need you to be off that beach from 0200 hrs tonight – what's your plan?"

Brandy said, "Penelope is at sea delivering one of Captain Slade's FINDERS KEEPERS teams. No way to recall her in that time frame. The two MGBs from the 15th Motor Gunboat Flotilla have not arrived yet. How many people do you plan to have in your party?"

Col. Randal said, "Six."

Brandy said, "In that case we shall take the *Arrow.*"

Maj. Gen. Blackwell said, "*Arrow*, what's that?"

Brandy said, "My yacht. A speedboat. The only craft we had four years ago when Raiding Forces was learning the gentle art of Commandos striking at night."

Maj. Gen. Blackwell said, "That the one you took on the raid called the 'Gunfight at the Blue Duck'? Yeah, I've heard about it. Made the OK Corral shootout sound like a church social."

Brandy laughed, "Whatever you may have heard, Sam, it could not match what took place that night."

Maj. Gen. Blackwell said, "Is it true, Colonel, you walked into a bar full of Germans and ordered a drink – in English?"

Wanting to change the subject, Col. Randal said, "Stephanie, have Fenwick and Ferguson report to the War Room."

Capt. Fawcett-Tatum said, "Already done, John – on the way."

Col. Randal said, "Beverly, can you fly us down to Seaborn House when we get back?"

"Absolutely."

"General Blackwell, I'm going to need a jump aircraft tonight."

"I was afraid you were going to say that."

COLONEL JOHN RANDAL AND CAPTAIN DICK COURTNEY WERE aboard the L-5 Sentinel Major General Sam Houston "Bronc" Blackwell had arranged for their visual reconnaissance of Cap Blanc-Nez.

The pilot said over the headphones, "I'm going to make a single low-level pass down the beach. We may not be picked up by radar but every Nazi in the area with a rifle is going to take a pot shot at us. Bronc ordered me to bring you back alive, Colonel.

"Be advised sir we can't risk a second flyby."

Col. Randal said, "One should be enough."

The L-5 cruised across the Channel with Count Basie blaring 'One O'Clock Jump' in their headphones courtesy of the U.S. Army Signal Corps Armed Forces' Radio Service (AFRS). As Cap Blanc-Nez came into sight the pilot banked hard right as Tommy Dorsey's "Well, Get it!" came on.

Col. Randal was studying the cliff face through his Zeiss 7X50 binoculars captured a few miles from here when he was leading Swamp Fox Force on his first mission in the King's Royal Rifle Corp (KRRC). His war had come full circle. At the time, he would never have believed he would ever be planning to re-invade Pas-de-Calais.

The pilot was not wrong. Light Flak opened on the L-5 almost immediately. Every German soldier grabbed his rifle and blazed away. Red and white tracers crisscrossed the sky. Both sides, Allied and Axis, used red tracers as well as other colors.

Raiding Forces used British green – going to substantial trouble to obtain them. That made it easier to distinguish friend from foe at night during a firefight. Col. Randal always opted for every possible advantage however slight.

The pilot came on the air, "What are we looking for, Colonel?"

Col. Randal said, "Cracks, fissures or clefs in the chalk face we can use to make our way down later tonight."

"You're climbing down *that* cliff tonight – are you crazy, sir?"

"You're not the first to ask."

Col. Randal saw what he was hunting for. A long, thin seam running all the way down the cliff face. He turned and pointed. In the seat directly behind him Capt. Courtney started taking photos with his Leica 35mm camera. The one he had carried to take photos of his safari clients and their trophies before the war.

At slow speed the pilot had informed Col. Randal it would take him slightly less than one minute to fly the length of the beach. The Germans were firing as they flew past. Fortunately, the radar-controlled anti-aircraft, flak guns were not going into action because the pilot had flown in under the radar.

The average German soldier was not trained to hit moving aerial targets. The L-5 was flying at close to 100 mph. So, while it looked big and slow, it was moving along. Nevertheless, from time to time it sounded like handfuls of small stones were thrown against the fuselage of the plane.

The pilot said, "Are we good, Colonel?"

"Roger that."

17

TOUGH DAY AT THE OFFICE

JAMES "BALDIE" TAYLOR WAS STANDING BY AT THE AIRFIELD when the U.S. Army Air Force L-5 Sentinel came in for a landing. Major the Lady Jane Seaborn had provided him one of the Bradford Hotel limousines to race the roll of film Captain Dick Courtney had taken of the cliff face at Cap Blanc-Nez to MI-6. The British Secret Intelligence Service had an in-house photo lab. The 35mm film would be fast-tracked for development – SIS technicians were on standby.

As soon as the film was developed Jim would hand-carry the prints to Colonel John Randal in the War Room.

A second limousine, the Bradford Hotel's Phantom III Rolls-Royce, was also at the airfield. Lady Jane, Beverly Blackwell and Sloan Marlow were waiting to pick up Col. Randal and Capt. Courtney. S&M had been invited along so she could witness firsthand how Raiding Forces operated when a mission was impending – everyone pitched in.

The L-5's pilot was standing beside the plane counting bullet holes as Lady Jane and S&M watched. The aircraft looked like a cheese shredder. He quit at number 37 with more to go when Major General Sam Houston "Bronc" Blackwell arrived and came over to inspect the damage.

"Enjoy your first Special Duties flight, Peterson?"

"Walk in the park, sir."

"Get those holes patched up, Lieutenant."

"Yes, sir."

Maj. Gen. Blackwell walked over to where Col. Randal was preparing to depart for the hotel. "Find a way down that cliff, Colonel?"

"Think so, sir."

"I've got a C-47 and crew lined up for you. Where do you want to stage your departure airfield? Here or Seaborn House?"

Col. Randal said, "Jane?"

Lady Jane said, "This airfield shall be fine, General. After wheels up we can displace to Seaborn House. I want to be there when the team returns."

Maj. Gen. Blackwell said, "My people will organize the marshaling area… all you'll have to do is show up."

Beverly said, "Johnny will be wanting X-chutes – I have to fly down to Seaborn House to pick those up."

Col. Randal said, "Not for this one, Beverly. We'll be jumping USAAF B-8 parachutes. You can coordinate that for us.

Maj. Gen. Blackwell said, "Any other special equipment requirements, Colonel?"

"Negative, sir – we'll be going in light except for a pair of 100-foot rappel lines. "

COLONEL JOHN RANDAL ISSUED HIS FRAG ORDER, MEANING A fragment of a full Operations Order, in the War Room at 1830 hrs. All Raiding Forces personnel to include recently attached FANYs, the new TTC Special Duties Squadron staff, the U.S. Secret Service agents, Captain Mike "Mad Dog" Reupart, MC, Major General Sam Houston "Bronc" Blackwell, James "Baldie" Taylor, Major General William "Wild Bill" Donovan, Major the Lady Jane Seaborn, Beverly Blackwell, Mandy Paige and Sloan Marlow were present.

Lieutenant General Walter Bedell Smith aka "Beetle", Chief of Staff SHAEF stepped in at the last minute with Colonel John Henry Bevan. Lt. Gen. Smith had been in the recently opened SHAEF London HQ when Col. Bevan dropped by to see the new offices. The general mentioned Col. Randal was about to brief a cross-channel raid that would take place later that night.

The two officers decided to repair to the War Room to observe. Only Col. Bevan was aware the purpose of the exercise was to reinforce a London Controlling Section deception. He had orchestrated it.

Col. Randal issued the Frag Order outlining the mission with his usual easy style of delivery. He seemed to be enjoying himself. For a reconnaissance operation, Recon Team was the premier group of people in Raiding Forces, which meant Allied Forces Europe, to accomplish the mission.

Had King been available, the team would have been perfect.

"*Situation*: Raiding Forces has been ordered to conduct a reconnaissance of a point-type target located in the Calais District of France – later tonight.

"*Friendly Forces*: None.

"*Enemy Forces*: Germans of the 346th Infantry Division continue to occupy the Cap Blanc-Nez coastal sector in the Calais region. First Platoon 2nd Battalion, 5th Company, Grenadier Regiment 858 commanded by one Lieutenant Adolf Swartz has its command post situated in a camouflaged house located at grid coordinates 437612 slightly less than one-half mile off the headland at Cap Blanc-Nez sector. In addition to being the lieutenant's CP, the building is suspected of storing coastal defense material.

"Enemy presence is believed to be light. Primarily due to the unsuitability of the location as an invasion site because of the 40-story high cliffs along the shoreline. Infantry platoons in the 346th are currently reported to be running at around half strength.

"*Mission*: A team composed of myself, Captain Courtney, Lovat Scout Fenwick, Lovat Scout Ferguson, Striker X-Ray and Striker Vanish will insert via parachute into this field located approximately here."

Col. Randal tapped the map. Everyone present craned their necks to see the spot, which told them absolutely nothing. It was a wide open space.

"*Execution and Concept of the Operation*: We'll be jumping a C-47 Dakota. Recon Team will drop its chutes, immediately assemble and move out to conduct a reconnaissance of the target house located here," Col.

Randal tapped the map again. "Once completed the team will withdraw to the cliff at Cap Blanc-Nez, move down the face and extract by boat.

"*Scheme of Maneuver*: Order of March will be Striker Vanish, Striker X-Ray, Captain Courtney, me, Scout Fenwick and Scout Ferguson.

"Movement to the target will be in file formation.

"*Actions on the Objective*: Once we arrive at the target, Scouts Fenwick and Furgeson – Exfil Team, will break off and travel to the location where the full Recon Team intends to abseil down to the beach to link up with Mrs. Brandy Seaborn aboard her yacht, the *Arrow*. The Scouts will secure our withdrawal route and inspect the fissure that drops the 40-stories to the beach. Our descent will be made in stages. Parts of it consist of a narrow chimney we can work our way down. Other sections will require rappel lines to be rigged – each of the Scouts will be jumping in with a 100-foot rope for that contingency.

"Best estimate of how long the exfil down the cliff will take is 60 to 90 minutes.

"While the Scouts are securing our primary egress route – there is no secondary alternate, and establishing the ERP the rest of the party… Recon Team(-) will be conducting a reconnaissance of the objective. The Germans have attempted to camouflage the structure. We want to know why.

"This is a sneak and peek. Contact is to be avoided if possible. Our intent is to remain undetected. Only suppressed weapons – 9mm M3s, .22 Colts or High Standards to be carried."

Col. Randal did not mention he had been ordered to leave something behind to indicate Raiding Forces had come calling. While everyone present had a security clearance, all the straphangers in the audience did not possess a Need to Know or had any reason to.

"In the event of enemy contact, Recon Team will avoid becoming decisively engaged and immediately effect a rapid fighting withdrawal to the ERP moving by bounds.

"Once we reach the cliff I will identify our party by three short flashes from my red filtered flashlight. The response will be three long flashes. Any other lights or combination of return flashes and Recon Team will immediately respond with a vigorous assault – I say again, there is no alternate route to the ERP.

"Once down the cliff we will be met by a boat party consisting of Lifeboat Service Men who will row us out to the *Arrow* for return to base at Seaborn House.

"What are your questions?"

Sloan whispered to Beverly, "No alternative route – that means no Plan B?" She had been studying Raiding Forces' Rules.

Beverly agreed, "That's what it means."

Sloan said, "John glossed over the drop to the beach being 400 feet – a long way down."

"Typical," Beverly said.

"How can everyone be so calm?" Sloan wondered out loud.

Beverly said, "It's an act. We aren't. Except for Johnny – he's calm."

Sloan said, "Most people shall never witness anything like this. They have no idea. Parachute behind enemy lines, make a reconnaissance of an enemy position somewhere in France, descend down a *forty-story* cliff, come home – good heavens!"

Beverly said, "Just another day in Raiding Forces."

Which was not exactly true.

RECON TEAM REPAIRED TO THE FIRING RANGE ADJOINING THE back of the War Room. The room was long and narrow. At this time it was restricted to firing suppressed weapons. Later, after the engineers had more time to install soundproofing, unsuppressed handguns and submachine guns could be fired. The range was the length of the hotel – longer than the average engagement on a raid.

Weapons testing was not on for the moment. The team would test-fire later. The purpose of the exercise now was to receive an orientation on the United States Army Air Force B-8 backpack parachute. Not one person on Recon Team had ever jumped the USAAF chute.

The Master Sergeant giving the jump master briefing was a big, tough-looking 82nd Airborne Division paratrooper, sporting two gold combat jump stars on his parachute wings, named Buck Callahan. He was on TDY to Troop Transport Command. Major General Sam Houston "Bronc" Blackwell had brought him in to train his pilots and aircrew on what to do if they ever had to bail out. MSgt. Callahan did not know who these men were – they did not look like USAAF. Had no idea what they were getting ready to do. And did not care – at least that was the image he projected.

MSgt. Callahan may have been slightly intimidated by the fact that Maj. Gen. Blackwell was observing the orientation. That and the fact that Recon Team leader Colonel John Randal was wearing a pair of U.S. Jump Wings with *four* gold combat jump stars. The only decoration on his uniform.

MSgt. Callahan commenced a period of instruction he had memorized word for word. He never varied from the lesson plan. The lecture was delivered in a squared-away military manner with no inflection in his voice seemingly on autopilot – bored.

Recon Team was sitting on the floor with legs crossed, watching closely.

MSgt. Callahan's assistant, acting as his demonstrator, was another 82nd Airborne Division trooper – a corporal who was wearing a backpack model of the USAAF B-8 parachute. He executed each of his movements robotically, exhibiting a blank facial expression that never varied and never said a word.

MSgt. Callahan intoned, "Listen up, men. What we have here is a Parachute, Backpack, USAAF, Type B-8. The configuration you'll be jumping."

The corporal executed a mechanical about-face to show the parachute strapped on his back.

MSgt. Callahan ordered, "Demonstrator recover!"

The corporal performed another about face, returning to the front staring straight ahead at some point in the back of the room, blank-faced – like a man who had a lobotomy.

MSgt. Callahan said, "The Type B-8 employs a flat, circular, silk canopy 24 feet in diameter. It comprises 24 panels, radial seams running from apex to skirt and a reinforced skirt band."

The demonstrator knelt down, picked up a deployed B-8 canopy stretched out on the ground and pointed out each item as MSgt. Callahan ticked them off.

Recon Team was sitting on the floor in a semicircle. Everyone watched the demonstration. It was a sure bet not one of them cared about what was inside the Parachute, USAAF, Type B-8's backpack – as long as the canopy came out and opened up when it was supposed to.

MSgt. Callahan droned on, "The 24-foot suspension lines consist of braided cotton cord, approximately 22-23 feet from canopy skirt to harness risers. Each line is attached to the canopy skirt."

Recon Team watched dutifully as the corporal pointed out each item.

"The B-8 employs an integral parachute harness consisting of two shoulder straps, a chest strap with standard quick-release hardware standard on US T-5 military parachutes, two leg straps and riser attachment points at the shoulders.

MSgt. Callahan continued on in a mind-numbing monotone that sounded like it was coming out of a bullhorn – only now he got Recon Team's attention.

"Operation – the jumper exits the aircraft in a tight tuck position, counts *one* thousand then pulls the ripcord handle."

That did not sound right. Raiding Forces was trained to count – one thousand, two thousand, three thousand, four thousand, then "Check Canopy." No main chute deployed – hit the reserve.

Only they would not have a reserve parachute tonight and no static line to automatically deploy the canopy.

"Demonstrator recover!"

The corporal was up now, standing at a rigid position of attention. He reached up with his right hand, clasped the metal D-ring ripcord handle and ripped it across his chest left to right vigorously in the "approved school solution" for deploying the B-8. The silk canopy spilled out of the parachute pack onto the floor.

Standing at ease for the first time, MSgt. Callahan said, paratrooper to paratrooper, "Give 'er everything you've got, boys – you ain't gonna break it."

No problem.

MSgt. Callahan said, "Take ten – smoke 'em if you've got 'em.

THE DECISION HAD BEEN MADE TO USE THE LONDON AIRSTRIP as the Departure Airfield (DA). That required the C-47 to take off before dark and fly to the RAF fighter field near Seaborn House with Recon Team onboard and stand by. With the Baby Blitz in progress nightly, it was decided to move away from the main metropolitan area prior to nightfall. Why take a chance?

A convoy of limousines from the Bradford Hotel delivered Colonel John Randal, Major the Lady Jane Seaborn, Major General Sam Houston "Bronc" Blackwell, Major General William "Wild Bill" Donovan, James "Baldie" Taylor, Beverly Blackwell, Mandy Paige, Sloan Marlow and the Recon Team to the Marshalling Area. It was a decidedly high-toned way to go to war.

Master Sergeant Buck Callahan and his assistant, the demonstrator, Corporal Roscoe Hailey greeted them when the caravan arrived. As it turned out, Corp. Hailey actually could speak. In fact, it turned out he had a sense of humor.

There was a small briefing tent beside the aircraft hardstand. Maj. Gen. Blackwell and Col. Randal stepped inside while MSgt. Callahan and Cpl. Hailey took Capt. Courtney and Recon Team to inspect the C-47.

The pilot, Captain Donald Breedlove, gave Col. Randal a short briefing on the flight plan.

"Our mission profile calls for us to attach ourselves to the RAF bomber stream en route to Germany. We'll be flying at 20,000 feet when we cross the Channel into France. That way we blend in with the bombers on radar and it puts us at an altitude beyond the range of light anti-aircraft fire.

"Once across the coastline we'll stay with the RAF for thirty minutes. Then break away, bank around, descend to 2,000 feet – as if the plane is a damaged bomber turning back for England. We'll fly directly to your drop zone.

"I've been advised lower altitude is better tonight. You do not want to jump a B-8 parachute from less than 2,000 feet – 3,000 is safer.

"You tell me what you need, Colonel."

Col. Randal said, "800 feet – my team has to land on the DZ in a tight formation, ready to assemble and move on the objective – fast."

Capt. Breedlove said, "800 feet… General?"

Maj. Gen. Blackwell said, "Give Colonel Randal what he's asking for – his people are experienced jumpers."

Capt. Breedlove said, "Eight hundred it is. Understand, sir, the B-8 has a different opening sequence than the static line parachutes you've been used to jumping. Pull the ripcord, a pilot chute pops out – it deploys the canopy.

"B-8s take longer to open."

Col. Randal said, "Master Sergeant Callahan made that clear."

"In that case, sir, I'll put you down TOT."

Time Over Target.

MASTER SERGEANT HANK CALLAHAN AND COLONEL JOHN Randal were talking on the side of the parking apron. Recon Team's walkthrough inspection of the C-47 was completed. Now everyone was standing around waiting to board the plane for the flight to the auxiliary fighter air strip located on Seaborn House's sprawling estate.

MSgt. Callahan said, "Colonel, you might want to mention to your boys the B-8's canopy is the same size as our standard issue T-5 – they won't be coming in hot because of a small chute."

Col. Randal said, "I will."

MSgt. Callahan said, "C-47 cabins are not pressurized to fly above 12,000 feet without supplemental oxygen. Your boys are going to need oxygen.

Col. Randal said, "General Blackwell is making arrangements for Type A6 Walk-around bottles."

MSgt. Callahan said, "You might want to reemphasize when they yank the ripcord's handle it's designed to come off in their hand – it's supposed to."

Col. Randal said, "Roger."

MSgt. Callahan said, "And tell 'em if they can remember – go ahead and drop the D-ring. People jumping B-8s for the first time tend to forget that. Something about seeing that handle in your hand and no canopy coming out yet tends to make you want to hang on to it."

Col. Randal said, "I can see how it might."

MSgt. Callahan said, "One last thing, sir. Make sure you emphasize the jumper has to count 'one thousand' before pulling the ripcord. That keeps the lines from getting entangled in the tail of the aircraft. Might happen if they pull too soon."

Col. Randal said, "I'll make a point of it, Sergeant."

MSgt. Callahan said, "General Blackwell suggested I offer my services to be your jump master."

Col. Randal said, "I jump master my teams. You're welcome to be my static assistant jump master. Handle chuting up and the pre-boarding inspection. Straphang the drop if you want."

MSgt. Callahan said, "I'd like that, Colonel."

Col. Randal said, "You're going to get shot at."

MSgt. Callahan said, "Won't be the first time, sir."

Col. Randal said, "In that case, Sergeant Callahan, take charge of the stick until I give the ten-minute warning."

The plan for Major the Lady Jane Seaborn and her party changed with the decision to reposition the C-47. Now she would fly down with Recon Team in the C-47. Mandy Paige, Beverly Blackwell and Sloan Marlow were scheduled to go bar hopping on "hush-hush" patrol for MI-5.

The girls would hit the town, carry out their "elicitation" duties then Beverly would fly the three of them down to Seaborn House in the Percival Petrel to link up with Lady Jane to be there when Recon Team returned from France.

Sloan said, "This all seems so unreal."

Beverly said, "Always does."

Major General Sam Houston "Bronc" Blackwell came over to speak to Col. Randal, "I'll catch you at the Bradford for breakfast if that works for you, Colonel."

"Roger that, sir."

"Good luck, then."

Col. Randal said, "I'm down a senior NCO, sir. You mind if I talk to Sergeant Callahan about the job?"

Maj. Gen. Blackwell said, "Be my guest. You won't be poaching him from me. He's Eighty-Second Airborne TDY to Troop Transport Command."

Col. Randal said, "See you in the morning, General."

The C-47 whined, the blades on the left engine turned over in slow motion, backfired, wheezed, there was a burst of smoke and flame from the exhaust, the engine ran unevenly like a giant Harley Davidson motorcycle and then leveled off. The process was repeated with the right engine.

No matter how many times you had heard it, and knew it was going to smooth out, the Pratt & Whitney R-1830 Twin Wasp radial engines' startup sequence was never reassuring.

Recon Team started boarding the aircraft.

Major General William "Wild Bill" Donovan said, "Good luck, Colonel."

Lady Jane walked over. She and Col. Randal boarded last. Now the Dakota's engines had settled into a steady roar.

The C-47 rolled down the tarmac and lumbered into the air.

Lady Jane curled up on the starboard side canvas bench seat. With such a small team on board there was plenty of space in the troop compartment. She watched Col. Randal down on one knee in the aisle with Recon Team gathered around. MSgt. Callahan and Cpl. Hailey were listening intently as he walked the men through every step of the mission from the moment they exited the aircraft over France until they boarded the *Arrow*.

One more time.

He reminded them to drop the metal ripcord handle.

UNLIKE THE UNITED STATES ARMY AIR FORCE THE ROYAL AIR Force's Bomber Command aircraft did not assemble in a single large formation circling over England then turn and wing their way toward their target on the Continent. Each bomber took off individually from its airfield, climbed to a specified altitude and heading, then joined the long procession of bombers headed east on a planned route called the "Bomber Stream." The idea was to overwhelm the Freya and Wurzburg tracking radar.

Instead of the German operators seeing a series of dots on their radar screens indicating individual aircraft, the returns blended together creating what appeared to be a relentless river of enemy aircraft – 80 to 120 miles long. Aimed at the heart of Germany.

Tonight was a double first for Captain Donald Breedlove. He was a Troop Transport Command pilot handpicked for the night's mission by Major General Sam Houston "Bronc" Blackwell, not a bomber pilot. And he had never flown in a Bomber Stream.

Crossing the English Coast near Dover Capt. Breedlove flew toward a coastal radio beacon checkpoint. His navigator got a final navigation fix and relayed the information to him in the cockpit. Capt. Breedlove then turned onto the main flight path and continued climbing to 20,000 feet. In the troop compartment everyone was breathing out of an oxygen bottle.

Crossing the French Coast, Capt. Breedlove turned off his navigation lights. This was an unsettling experience with so many planes in the air – tonight there were 700 bombers. The majority were Avro Lancasters carrying up to 14,000 pounds of bombs. He did not want to collide with one.

Luckily tonight it was only necessary to stay in the Bomber Stream for thirty minutes before turning back toward Recon Team's Drop Zone. The Pas-de-Calais coast was one of the most heavily defended air defense zones in enemy-occupied Europe. Primarily there were two types of anti-aircraft batteries in the first belt they would fly over – 88mm guns effective up to 36,000 feet backed up by 20mm and 37mm cannon only effective against low flying planes.

The German 88 was one of the most feared weapons of the war, air or land.

Before the C-47 crossed the French Coast, the coastal batteries opened on the onslaught of bombers. They were firing preplanned barrage patterns with their fuses timed for the Bomber Stream's altitude band. Fortunately for Recon Team, flak caused fewer losses than German night fighters. Capt. Breedlove would be turning back before passing through the last belt of coastal anti-aircraft batteries to where the night fighters would be waiting to pounce – blue on blue friendly fire shoot downs were a significant threat for the German pilots.

The USAAF loadmaster was linked into the aircraft's comms system. He pointed at Colonel John Randal and nodded. It was time.

Col. Randal was sitting on a port canvas bench next to the open door at the rear of the C-47. He could hear the anti-aircraft guns booming, see searchlight beams sweeping back and forth and the burst of 88mm rounds outside. Flak was so heavy it did not seem possible all the planes in the Bomber Stream were not immediately shot down.

Out the door in the distance he could see a burning Lancaster. That was discouraging. Long yellow flames were trailing the airplane.

Then it exploded.

Col. Randal gave the command, "TEN MINUTES!"

There was no drama. Recon Team was composed of professionals. This was their commute to work.

The C-47 continued flying with the Bomber Stream for a few more minutes. Then it banked hard, coming around until it was heading back toward the Channel giving up altitude. Capt. Breedlove nosed the Dakota over into a steep glide attitude exactly the way a cripple running for home would do. He was headed straight toward the Drop Zone. The captain had dropped a lot of paratroopers – two combat jumps and more training jumps than he could remember.

The loadmaster made eye contact with Col. Randal, nodded vigorously and gave a thumbs-up.

Col. Randal began the jump commands. Tonight these were heavily modified. There was no static line to hook up to or check.

"STAND UP!"

Recon Team got up off the canvas bench seat.

"CHECK YOUR EQUIPMENT!"

Master Sergeant Hank Callahan and Corporal Roscoe Hailey moved into the aisle to stand beside the stick to be available in case anyone needed help with the unfamiliar B-8 parachute or lost their balance without a static line cupped in their hand to hang onto.

Col. Randal shuffled to the exit door. He braced his raiding boots on both sides of the frame, locked his fingers in the rim that ran around it and arched himself outside. Around the C-47 in all directions the whole world was blowing up, but Capt. Breedlove was diving fast to get below the barrage.

The C-47 was still too far away to see the target. Above him in the night sky the battle raged. Col. Randal swung back inside.

"SOUND OFF FOR EQUIPMENT CHECK!"

"OKAY, OKAY, OKAY, OKAY, OKAY!"

Recon Team was good to go.

Col. Randal shuffled back to the door, never taking his boots off the deck – the "Airborne Shuffle" designed to prevent tripping when moving around inside the aircraft. He arched outside the door. Up ahead was the Drop Zone. The wind whipped his Jacket, Parachutist, M-1942.

It was still too far away to see in the dark. Overhead the blazing anti-aircraft artillery had not abated. If it were not so deadly – men were fighting and dying, it would have been a spectacular show. Normally at this stage in a drop, Col. Randal was making a safety check outside the aircraft.

Not tonight. He was just looking around. An armed tourist.

When Col. Randal swung back inside, the loadmaster raised one finger and gave him a knowing nod. The veteran TTC loadmaster had dropped a lot of paratroopers. None of those jumps were like anything compared to tonight.

Col. Randal faced the stick. Recon Team was standing, bent-kneed, riding with the aircraft's buffeting. Maintaining balance was a lot harder on this jump because of the absence of a static line.

"ONE MINUTE!"

Col. Randal turned back to make a last check out the door. This was entirely unnecessary. It was a matter of habit – muscle memory. The pilot was going to initiate the green light. A jump master has the option to GO or NOT GO on the light based on what he can see on the ground. Usually there are checkpoints. Not tonight.

He was going on green.

"CLOSE ON THE DOOR!"

Col. Randal needed to keep the Jump Light over the door in his peripheral vision. It was glowing bright red. That was getting ready to change.

The stick inched forward, at risk of shoving Col. Randal out. With adrenaline pumping it could happen. Recon Team was ready to get on the ground. MSgt. Callahan had one arm across his chest, bracing him since he didn't have anything to hold on to and the stick was pressing up tight. The light flashed green.

It happened fast.

Col. Randal shouted, "Let's go!"

Then he was out the door with Recon Team thundering after him. The prop blast spun him around as if an invisible giant hand had reached out. A voice in his head screamed, "ONE THOUSAND!"

Col. Randal ripped the D-ring on the B-8's ripcord as violently as he had ever pulled anything in his life. It tore across his chest. Then horrifyingly, the handle came off in his hand with a metal cable dangling.

And nothing happened.

The tail of the C-47 flew past in slow motion. Everything had gone silent. Then the drone chute popped out. The B-8's canopy deployed. If there was an opening shock Col. Randal never felt it.

Once the realization he was not dead – at least not yet, the night being still young, Col. Randal tried to spot the farmhouse. In the flat pastureland the only terrain feature he had to go on was the dirt road that ran past it.

Finally he ID 'd the building. He had been scanning the horizon. It was close below slightly behind him – if he craned his neck he could see it between his raiding boots. Approximately two hundred yards from where Recon Team was going to land.

Capt. Breedlove had overachieved.

As Col. Randal was studying the ground below, 4-gun batteries of 88mm, 105 mm and a few 128mm anti-aircraft guns were booming. Cap Blanc Nez was six miles southwest of Calais. The Drop Zone was in the most concentrated anti-aircraft zone in enemy-occupied France. Possibly anywhere in Europe outside of Berlin.

The batteries were firing preplanned barrages at a given altitude rather than aiming at individual aircraft. Searchlights were probing the sky from scattered positions along the coast and layered in light batteries staggered inland 1-3 miles apart. The muzzle flashes from the guns, while brief, were dazzling bright yellow/orange in color. The batteries were also spaced 1-3 miles apart. The muzzle blasts were making quite a light show.

There were deep concussive booms when the guns fired. The projectile from a 7.92 Mauser round weighs .45 oz. When a bullet passes by it is supersonic – meaning it breaks the sound barrier. You hear a *CRAAAAACK behind* you – which always seems strange.

It is an evil sound.

A German 88 anti-aircraft projectile weighs 19.8 pounds. It too is supersonic. The difference is the cannon shell is 700 times the weight of the standard rifle bullet. The sound the 88mm projectiles coming past now were making was too terrifying to describe in words that would do the experience justice. Nothing had prepared Col. Randal for anything like this.

As different batteries fired, the effect was of rolling thunder. While the barrage was not continuous, the echo effect made it sound like it was. Four flashes together indicated a battery firing. There were batteries everywhere. Col. Randal felt like he was parachuting into Dante's Inferno.

Col. Randal was a tactician, which is an acquired mindset. He thought tactically. And he saw things through a tactician's eyes. From 500 feet over the DZ as his parachute came in several items of interest became clear to him.

First the Bomber Stream operated three or more nights per week. Second, a large mass of bombers would take 90 to 120 minutes to pass over a single point due to the waves of aircraft in the stream not being a solid mass. Third, Raiding Forces' raids were of short duration. Tonight Recon Team was not planning on being on the objective more than a few minutes before heading for the ERP which should take less than fifteen minutes.

The Bomber Stream would be passing overhead the entire time.

Col. Randal realized an RAF air armada up above created the perfect cover for a small-scale Raiding Forces-type operation.

The Germans manning defensive positions along the coast and farther back inland would have their attention distracted by the three-dimensional battle taking place – focusing on the bombers overhead. The anti-aircraft crews' night vision would be destroyed by the gun blasts, as would the search light operators and any infantry operating in the immediate vicinity of either one.

And everyone's hearing for miles in all directions would be affected to some degree by the deafening thunder of the barrages.

Why none of these tactical advantages had been pointed out to him when the King's Messengers first started arriving was a mystery. Col. Randal wondered – could it be the benefits of conducting a raid while a Bomber Stream was passing over had never occurred to anyone? It was crystal clear to him.

To be fair few officers dropping behind enemy lines would likely be planning future operations while still airborne in their parachute harness having just exited an aircraft in the middle of an aerial battle.

Col. Randal had his feet and knees together, elbows in tight on his chest, chin down hard on his chest, forearms touching. He rocked his legs to make sure his knees were not locked. Checked again to make sure his elbows were in – that was important, and when the ground seemed to blur below, came in backwards then swiveled the instant the toes of his canvas-topped raiding boots touched down. He came in completely limp, hit all of his 5- points of contact, light as a feather – jumped to his feet and dropped his chute.

Nothing to it.

The five jumpers behind him glided in silently, one after the other. As soon as they bounded up from their PLF everyone popped the quick release on their parachute harness. The same system as the releases Raiding Forces had installed on the harness of their British Parachute, Personnel, Type X. Recon Team did not bother recovering the chutes.

Bomber crews bailing out from shot-up aircraft never hung around long enough to recover theirs. The Germans in the area would not find anything out of the ordinary about six type B-8 parachutes lying on the ground. Not after shooting at the Bomber Stream the night before.

Captain Dick Courtney formed up the patrol. Recon Team moved out in the designated order of march. Overhead the battle was raging. It was a dark night but lit up by stark white flashes as the anti-aircraft batteries continued firing on the RAF bombers like the rapid fire popping of flash bulbs on the red carpet at the Academy Awards.

Recon Team shook itself out and moved straight toward their target. They could see the shadow of the farmhouse in the distance. The bombers droning, anti-aircraft guns booming and brilliant muzzle flashes made the movement to the objective seem like an out-of-body experience.

Capt. Courtney and his two strikers, X-Ray and Vanish, who composed the point element, were moving at a fast clip. No one was better at moving across terrain at night than the three of them, having worked together in Africa for years before the war.

In minutes Capt. Courtney was calling a halt. The patrol had arrived at the dirt road. The house was straight ahead across the road and up a short drive. It was dark.

Col. Randal had the patrol pull into a tight perimeter.

"Take charge of the point element, Captain, and recon the house. I'll take up a position where the drive meets the road to provide security."

Capt. Courtney whispered, "Yes, sir."

"Ferguson, you and Fenwick prepare to move out. See you at the ERP. Give me the verbal challenge and response."

Scout Ferguson whispered, "Challenge – Drop Dead."

Scout Fenwick whispered, "Countersign – Gorgeous."

"Light signal?"

Scout Ferguson whispered, "You give three quick flashes – red filter."

Scout Fenwick whispered, "We reply with three long flashes – red filter."

Col. Randal whispered, "Move out."

Then… poof, like one of The Great Teddy's magic tricks, they were gone. "Hey Presto!" He was all alone. Col. Randal walked across the dirt road and stood ready with his suppressed 9mm M3. Tonight, he was the weak link on the team. Capt. Courtney, X-Ray and Vanish were better at reconnaissance work than he was. And the Lovat Scouts were superior mountaineers.

Raiding Forces Rule #4 "Right Man, Right Job" was in full force and effect.

Capt. Courtney led what was now Recon Team(-) toward the objective at a 45° angle. They were moving like the big cats they had guided safari hunters after in days past. There was no need for the stealth. The house did not have any external security in place. Maybe it was because of the 400-foot cliffs, which pretty much eliminated the possibility of a Commando raid in the vicinity. Or maybe Lieutenant Swartz was an incompetent officer.

Either way, there were no sentries posted.

Vanish moved off to go around back. Capt. Courtney gave him two minutes to get into place – not a lot of time but the clock was ticking on this mission. Then he and X-Ray slipped up to the door. A thin line of light was showing around the edges of the blackout curtain covering the front window. Chances were someone was inside.

Orders were to avoid contact. They were to covertly find out why the house had been camouflaged. Then withdraw.

Both of those directives could not occur.

Capt. Courtney tried the doorknob. It was unlocked. These Germans were clearly not concerned about their personal security, surrounded as they were by all the anti-aircraft positions in the immediate area.

They were basically on vacation.

Capt. Courtney stepped inside with X-Ray so close behind he was brushing up against him. They had their suppressed M3s to their shoulders. Lieutenant Swartz, a Feldwebel – likely his platoon sergeant, and a radio operator were sitting at a table playing Skat.

The rest of the platoon's troops were manning MG 42 positions at the cliff or possibly on a patrol. Capt. Courtney and X-Ray commenced fire instantly. Sheer panic ensued. Cards flew. The Nazis tried to run… but where? A swarm of steel-jacketed 9mm rounds chopped them down.

Capt. Courtney posted X-Ray at the door. Then he walked around inspecting the interior of the house with his Leica camera in hand. The building was cram-packed with wooden ammunition crates stenciled "8.8cm Flak." He knew 88s were packed two rounds per container facing in opposite directions to prevent the fuses from striking each other during transit. After reaching four hundred containers he quit counting.

There was more than enough ammunition for a four-gun battery to fire on a busy night. Capt. Courtney decided that this was a case where he needed to "Improvise, Adapt and Overcome." He placed a block of C-3 plastic explosives with a 15-minute fuse in a large stack of ammo boxes. His intent was to cause a sympathetic explosion that would set off all the 88mm cannon shells.

However, Raiding Forces lived by the axiom "Why take a chance?"

Capt. Courtney took X-Ray's one-pound block of C-3 and placed it in the stack of ammo crates in another room. Then he took one last look around before going back to pull the rings on the two igniter assemblies to start the fuses – he knew they were lit because after the small initial crack each of them made a brief sizzling sound.

Outside Capt. Courtney clapped his hands three times. Usually the signal was made by slapping the stock of his 9mm Beretta 38. However, the M3 Grease Gun did not have a wooden stock.

Vanish appeared from around behind the house.

Col. Randal was in position at the dirt road. He heard the three claps and knew Capt. Courtney and his strikers would be linking up momentarily. At that exact moment the unmistakable whisper of tires on the dirt road and the light clink of kit – bicycles approaching, came from his left.

He knew it was common practice for the Germans to send out bicycle patrols at night. They might encounter downed RAF airmen or the occasional French Resistance fighter. The patrols could be any size, but according to Enemy Order of Battle (OOB) intel reports, they were typically three to five men.

The bicycles were coming fast – the riders racing each other to get home.

Colonel Randal stepped out into the middle of the dirt road. He had his suppressed 9mm M3 submachine gun to his shoulder. By the time he could see the outline of Germans they were on him, pedaling hard.

SSSSSS,SSSSS,SSSSS

The first three riders tumbled off, shot at point-blank range. The second two Nazis in the patrol, standing on their pedals with their heads down, crashed into the tangle of bicycles. They were thrown to the ground shouting.

SSSSS,SSSSS

Col. Randal walked around and put an additional three-round burst into each Nazi. *SSS,SSS,SSS,SSS,SSS*

Then he reached into his pocket and took out a FP-45 Liberator pistol and tossed it down beside one of the dead bicycle riders. Tomorrow the Germans were not going to believe they had been shot with it. But they might think the patrol had captured the pistol and then been ambushed or something like that. Either way, the opposition would be confused.

And that was the purpose of the exercise – confusion to the enemy.

Captain Courtney said, “We need to move out smartly, sir. That house is packed full of 88 rounds. I set explosives to go off in about another twelve minutes – more or less.”

Col. Randal said, “Follow me.”

He had the azimuth to the ERP preset on his US Army issue Taylor Instrument Companies M-1938 lensatic compass. Easy enough to do prior to or during pre-mission planning since they had the grid coordinates of the target and the fissure at Cap Blanc-Nez. Capt. Courtney might be the better cross-country operator but no one could follow a bearing at night like Col. Randal. Recon Team(-) shook out in a file formation behind him and they struck for the coast.

Movement to the ERP was not a complicated land navigation problem. The measured distance on the map was slightly over six hundred yards. Col. Randal knew 117 of his paces equaled one hundred yards – he had that drilled into him at Achnacarry. However, when leading a patrol he preferred someone else in the column to do the pace count. He delegated the task to Capt. Courtney who was directly behind him in the file formation.

There was just one problem. There was a gun battery between where they were and where they were going. He had seen it from the air coming down. The battery had been firing ever since Recon Team dropped in.

Col. Randal knew from his observations during the ride down under his parachute that the anti-aircraft gun batteries consisted of four guns deployed in a diamond-shaped pattern. They were set up with the major diagonal facing the Channel approximately 50 yards apart. In the dark after a fire mission or two, the gunners would be practically blind – their night vision degraded to nearly zero by the muzzle blasts. Not a problem for the air defense artillery gun layers. They were concentrating on instruments, not aiming at individual aircraft.

Recon Team(-) made good time, being highly motivated to get as far away from the farmhouse as possible before it went up. Straight ahead the battery fired a staggered burst like a string of falling dominoes. There were reasons for not firing all four guns at once. The noise from a single 88 was mind-numbingly violent and the white muzzle flash seared the eyes. Firing all four guns simultaneously would incapacitate the gun crew and might interfere with neighboring batteries.

As Recon Team(-) approached the 88mm battery position, directly to their front was the right-hand gun. The patrol could have tiptoed around it and continued to march. With their night vision destroyed, the gunners could not see 6 feet away.

And they could not hear either. The 88mm Flak gun has a sharp muzzle blast, more of a giant flat crack up close than a boom. It was only possible for shouted commands to be heard when screamed right in the artillerymen's faces. Ear protection was limited to ineffective rubber plugs that were not always worn because the crew had to hear the shouted commands. Gunners were likely permanently deafened.

The Germans were not going to see or hear Recon Team(-).

The azimuth ran straight through the right-hand 88. If the Lovat Scouts had been there and the team was moving to the coast as a single unit they could have skirted around the gun position and continued on their way unobserved and undetected without breaking stride – the smart move.

But the Scouts were not there, they were at the ERP, and Col. Randal did not feel like going around. Having already shot up a 5-man patrol of cyclists, his blood might have been running hot. He knew German gun teams typically consisted of ten men. At least on paper. This being over four years into the war there might be one or two less. It was unlikely to be more.

He signaled for the patrol to halt. The men circled around in a tight perimeter. Pulled in close.

Col. Randal whispered, "We're going to come on line five-feet spacing. Close on the target. And when the gun to our immediate front fires – that's our signal. We'll go in with our suppressed M3s. Assault straight through the position, keep moving and continue out the far side. The ERP is about one hundred yards or so straight ahead."

Capt. Courtney thought Col. Randal might be joking. That was quickly dispelled when he whispered, "Dick, you're on my right, X-Ray and Vanish on my left – let's do this."

The patrol inched up until they were within ten yards of the gun position. The crew was going about their gun drill oblivious to everything not right in front of them. The Germans were battered, somewhat disoriented and suffering sensory overload caused by the sound and fury of the cannon blasts.

The far left-hand gun in the battery, approximately a hundred fifty yards away, fired, followed by the number two gun at the center point of the diamond. Next was the number three gun directly behind it and then the 88 to their immediate front went *CRAAAAACK WHAAAAAM*! Sharp and violent.

The muzzle blast was scorching and the blast created an instant migraine – full body slam pain starting at the roots of Col. Randal's hair that worked its way all the way down.

Recon Team(-) went in with their suppressed M3s stuttering. As was SOP for covert missions their SMG's magazines were intentionally loaded without tracers. Not only were the weapons suppressed but lack of glowing rounds converging down range did not give away the fact the battery was under attack.

Except to those individuals in their direct line of fire.

The assault was dreamlike. Anti-aircraft guns firing in other batteries created the effect of giant flashbulbs popping off rapid fire. It made the assault line appear as if the Rangers were moving in jerky black-and-white stop-motion – no color was visible.

The bombers droning overhead and the searchlights swaying back and forth in all directions probing the Bomber Stream added to the otherworldly effect. Not that being in an assault line, wading into an enemy position, and squeezing off a short burst every time your left foot hit the ground ever felt normal under the best of circumstances.

When Recon Team(-) went in, there were eleven German artillerymen working the gun. They were stationed around the cruciform mount so they could keep up a steady rhythm of teamwork. At this stage in the fight, the Germans were staggering as they went about their duties. That was due to their equilibrium being affected by the constant violence of the unrelenting muzzle blasts.

The German artillerymen were tightly focused on their tasks and having to struggle to execute them. In the brilliant flashes they seemed to be moving in the same stop-motion as the assault line. The Nazis never realized Recon Team(-) was there until it was at the gun, mowing down the crew.

Col. Randal was in the center of the assault line. The team was guiding on him. Everyone had been affected by the single 88 blast going off practically in their face. Their ears were ringing and they all had splitting headaches. At this point Recon Team(-) night vision was not all that great.

Nevertheless, the assault line was on the Germans fast. Col. Randal led the way, never slowing. He shifted from target to target as he kept moving forward. Raiding Forces practiced shooting on the move extensively.

Every member of the German 88mm gun team was down as Recon Team(-) swept past, out the far side of the gun position and was gone in the dark.

The patrol shook itself out again with Col. Randal back on point. At precisely that moment, the demolitions in the French farmhouse blew. While the blast was a gigantic sympathetic explosion, additional detonations continued to reverberate as individual rounds cooked off inside the fireball that went nearly 500 feet high in the sky.

Recon Team(-) glanced back in awe. They were impressed. Then the patrol moved on, heading for the ERP.

When he had moved an additional 117 paces Col. Randal flashed his red filtered light three times. Directly to their front, Scout Fenwick responded with three long flashes. Recon Team(-) had hit the ERP right on the money – though only a short distance, it was a remarkable piece of land navigation.

"Drop Dead."

"Gorgeous."

Scout Fenwick said, "Rappel lines in place, sir. We can free-climb parts of the way down easy enough but there are three places we have to use the ropes. Lionel is standing by the first rappel line about a hundred feet down."

Col. Randal walked to the edge of the white chalk cliff and looked over. Four hundred feet straight down – forty stories. The height made him dizzy. If there was any angle to the drop to the water's edge he was not able to see it.

Suddenly the loud irregular sounds of engines screaming was heard. A Lancaster bomber engulfed in flames was coming down heading straight toward the ERP.

Scout Fenwick shouted, "Over the edge!"

Then he jumped off the cliff.

Col. Randal thought, *this is a really bad idea.*

Then he followed the Scout over, pretty sure he was committing suicide. The rest of the team came right behind. They only fell a few feet. A narrow shelf ran just below the edge of the cliff.

The Lancaster flashed overhead barely making it past without crashing. The plane flew on for a second or two then slammed into the English Channel. There was a sickening hollow-sounding *CRUUUUUP* followed by a white column of water that rose up over 200 feet. All 14,000 pounds of its bomb load going off at once. The effect was bizarre because the light was all wrong for a normal explosion. There was a flash at water level followed by a ghostly column of white spray, vapor and blown mist that shot up. Not the expected orange fireball.

Not much about this night had been normal.

Capt. Courtney said, "Let's hope that plane didn't hit Mrs. Seaborn's boat."

Col. Randal said, "Roger that."

The route down to the beach was hard dangerous work. While it was not a technically difficult descent, a mistake could – and likely would – be fatal. Major the Lady Jane Seaborn had told Col. Randal Cap Blanc-Nez meant "White Nose Cape." It was white chalk and very unstable for climbing – up or down.

Chalk cliffs weather into vertical fissures, narrow chimneys, and broken ledges where water has cut seams through the rock. Recon Team had to move slowly. And be careful.

Below the shelf where they had taken refuge the cliff face had broken into a web of deep vertical fissures running from the top down to the Channel. In the dark they looked like black lines chiseled in the rock.

With Scout Fenwick leading the way, they slid into one of the larger fissures and started working their way down. Being inside the fissure was technically called in the 'chimney'. It was barely wide enough to brace their boots against one side and their shoulders against the other. Every move sent powdery chalk and gravel down the shaft which did not do much for anyone's spirits.

After about 100 feet the chimney steepened abruptly, plunging straight down.

Scout Ferguson was waiting with the first rappel line. Having been working bare-handed up to this point, the team put on their leather gloves. They were going down the rope in a "body rappel" meaning without the benefit of a snap-link rappel seat.

Scout Ferguson went first and perched on the shelf down below to help the team dismount the rope when they came down.

Col. Randal was next. He slung the M3 Grease Gun over his shoulder onto his back. Then he placed the rope across his back running left to right over the SMG then around his right side to the front where he grasped it with his right-brake hand.

He bent his knees, pushed off from the cliff face into space, pointed his right hand at the ground, the 300 or so feet remaining below, relaxed his grip and dropped – sliding down the rope. Travel was by bounds. When Col. Randal swung back in toward the cliff he bent his knees to cushion the landing, tightened his gloves on the rope that was playing out and jerked it up against his chest to stop the descent and let him recover.

The rappel line being across the M3 was important. The running rope burned against the metal as it paid out. Not his back.

This was Commando-style rappelling as taught at Achnacarry. It was for when other equipment was not available or unable to be carried on a mission. In Raiding Forces it was commonly said, "Don't try this at home."

The rappel down the sheer section of the cliff was not all that difficult but it took time. Once down the sheer drop the descent continued through another series of tight chimneys and small shelves. At times, the men were only able to lower themselves a few yards at a time. In some places the fissure narrowed to the point the men had to turn sideways and wedge down – boots pressing against one side, back against the other. All the while staring out at the Channel – what looked like a mile or maybe more below. The trick was to focus on what was immediately in front of you. No looking around and definitely not down.

Toward the bottom came the last section of vertical drop. Scout Ferguson was ready with the line. Col. Randal went over the edge, eager to get to the beach. He made it in three bounds – almost. The rope dangled about 15 feet above the shingles.

He dropped, instinctively performing a PLF that ended with him landing at Brandy's feet. She had brought the *Arrow* across the Channel to below the towering Cap Blanc-Nez and nosed in to the beach – which was not part of the plan. Then she had her crew cover the yacht with camouflage netting as was common practice in the Aegean.

Once that was done Brandy disembarked and waited for Recon Team, walking back and forth impatiently. Up top the anti-aircraft guns, with the exception of the one 88 Recon Team(-) had taken out, were still booming. Being this close to what sounded like the entire German 15th Army doing battle with the Royal Air Force's Bomber Command was not her usual clandestine small boat exfiltration experience.

Col. Randal was covered in snow white chalk dust from the four hundred foot decent – it had been a long night.

Brandy laughed, "Tough day at the office, handsome?"

It was not really a question.

Col. Randal said, "I'm ready to get the hell out of Dodge."

***THE WAR ISN'T OVER*!**

Continue following Col. John Randal and the men of Raiding Forces as they embark on their next dangerous mission in…

– ***NIGHT JUMP*** –

BOOK XX IN THE RAIDING FORCES SERIES
Coming soon

The Raiding Forces series continues all the way to VE Day.

Be the first to get updates and know about upcoming releases. To be on our notification list, scan the QR below and sign up.

Visit the Raiding Forces series Facebook page at https://www.facebook.com/raidingforces

phil@philward.com

ABBREVIATIONS
ORDERS & AWARDS

Bt	Baronet
CB	Companion of the Bath
CMG	Companion of the Order of St. Michael & St. George
DCM	Distinguished Conduct Medal
DFC	Distinguished Flying Cross
DSC	Distinguished Service Cross
DSM	Distinguished Service Medal
DSO	Distinguished Service Order
GC	George Cross
GCB	Grand Cross in the Order of the Bath
GM	George Medal
KBE	Knight Commander of the Most Excellent Order of the British Empire
KCVO	Knight Commander of the Royal Victorian Order
LG	Lady Companion of the Order of the Garter
MC	Military Cross
MM	Military Medal
MVO	Member of the Royal Victorian Order
OBE	Order of the British Empire
SS	Silver Star Medal
VC	Victoria Cross

ACRONYMS

AB – Able Body
ABC – (RFHQ) Advanced Base Castelrozzo
AFRS – U.S. Army Signal Corps Armed Forces Radio Service
AO – Area of Operation
AOC – Air Officer Commanding
AP – Armor Piercing
ARP – Air Raid Precautions
ARW – Air Raid Wardens

BBC – British Broadcasting Corporation
BDST – British Double Summer Time
BIGOT – a highly classified security designation
BMNT – Begin Morning Nautical Twilight
BOQ – Bachelor Officer's Quarters

CAS – Chief of the Air Staff
CI – Counterintelligence
CIU – Central Interpretation Unit
CO – Commanding Officer
COPP – Combined Operations Pilotage Parties
CP – Command Post

DA – Departure Airfield
DF – Direction Finding
DMI – Directorate of Military Intelligence
DZ – Drop Zone
DZST – Drop Zone Support Team

E&E – Escape and Evasion
ERP – Extraction Rally Point
ETO – European Theatre of Operations
ETOUSA – European Theater of Operations United States Army

FANY – Field Auxiliary Nursing Yeomanry
FUSAG – First United States Army Group

GC&CS – Government Code & Cypher School (Code Name Station X)
GIB – Glider Infantry Battalion
GMT – Greenwich Mean Time
GP – General Purpose

HF/DF – High-Frequency Direction Finding

IB – Incendiary Bomb
IAS – Indicated Airspeed

Cont...

IP – Initial Point
IPF – Inshore Patrol Flotilla

JIC – Joint Intelligence Committee
JPWC – Joint Psychological Warfare Committee
KM – King's Messenger
KORR – King's Own Royal Regiment

LBSM – Life Boat Service Men
LCS – London Controlling Section
LD – Line of Departure
LP – listening posts
LP/OP – Listening Post / Observation Post

MI – Military Intelligence
MI-5 Counterintelligence (SS) London address "58 St. James Street."
- B1-A – A section of MI-5 that handles Double Cross agents

MI(R) Military Intelligence (Research)
MI-6 Secret Intelligence Service (SIS)
MI-9 Escape
MO – Method of Operation
MP – Military Police
MSS – Most Secret Source
MU – Maritime Unit (OSS)

NID – Naval Intelligence Division

OCS – Infantry Officers Candidate School
OJT – On-the-Job Training
OOB – Order of Battle
OOI – Operational Order of Intercept
OP – Operations
OP – Observation Post
OPCON – operational control
ORP – Objective Rally Point
OSS – Office of Strategic Services (The Outfit)
OG – Operational Group Branch (Europe)
R&D Branch – Research and Development
Special Warfare Operators (the Frogs)
X-2 – Counter Espionage Branch
XX – Double Cross Committee, -"The Club"
XX Committee; known to insiders as *Twenty*
PGS – Pigeon Guidance Section (of the National Pigeon Service)
PLF – Parachute Landing Fall
PM – Prime Minister
PRU – Photographic Reconnaissance Unit
PT – Patrol Torpedo (boat)
PWE – Political Warfare Executive

Cont…

R&R – Rest and Relaxation
RAF – Royal Air Force
RF/D – Range Finding/Direction Finding
RIBA – Royal Institute of British Architects
RON – Remain Overnight Position
RP – Rally Point
RPM – Revolutions Per Minute
RTU – Returned to Unit
RVP – rendezvous point

SBU Small Bomb Unit
SD – *Sicherheitsdienst* ("Security Service")
The intelligence branch of the SS and the Nazi Party
SHAEF – Supreme Headquarters Allied Expeditionary Forces
SIGNIT – Signals Intelligence
SIS – Secret Intelligence Service (*aka* MI-6)
SLU – Special Liaison Unit
SSRC – Small Scale Raiding Company
SMG – submachine gun
SOE – Special Operations Executive
Country Section Officer, Section F (France)
SOG – Small Operations Group
SOP – Standard Operating Procedure
SS – *Schutzstaffel* "Protection Squadron"
SSRF – Small-Scale Raiding Force
SSRG – Small Scale Raiding Group
STOL – short takeoff and landing

TAS – True Air Speed
TOC – Tactical Operations Center
TO&E – table of organization and equipment
TOT – Time Over Target
TTC– Troop Transport Command
UDT – Underwater Demolition Team
ULTRA – MOST SECRET/TOP SECRET
USAAF – United States Army Air Force

VE – Victory Europe
VPW – Vulnerable Points Wing
VR – Visual Reconnaissance

W/T – Wireless Telegraphy telephone equipment
WEP – War Emergency Power
WRNS/WRENS – Women's Royal Navy Service

LIST OF CHARACTERS

ACM Sir Arthur Harris
ACM Sir Charles Portal
ACM Sir Trafford Leigh-Mallory
AVM Norman Bottomley
AVM Ralph Cochrane
Beverly Blackwell, SS, DFC
Brandy Seaborn, GC
Brig. Claude Dansey
Brig. Dudley Clarke
Brig. Norman Crockatt
Brig. Gen. James J. O'Connor
Capt. Billy Jack Jaxx
Capt. Chase Starrett
Capt. Clint Hays
Capt. Dan Bonham
Capt. Dick Courtney
Capt. Donald Breedlove
Capt. Jake Novak, *aka* Jake the Snake
Capt. Malcom Chatterhorn
Capt. Pamala Plum-Martin, DSO, OBE, DFC, RM
Capt. Penelope "Legs" Honeycutt-Parker, OBE, GM, RM
Capt. Preston Butterfield III
Capt. Richard "Dynamite Dick" Coogan
Capt. Ricky Mascuch
Capt. Roy Kidd
Capt. Stephanie Fawcett-Tatum, RM
Capt. Westly Slade
Capt. Dan Morgan
Capt. Mike "Mad Dog" Reupart
Cdr. Ian Fleming, RNVR
Cdr. Mark Buffington, RN
Col. Benjamin H. "Monk" Dickinson
Col. David Bruce
Col. John Henry Bevan, MC
Col. John Randal
Col. Peter Wright
Col. Valentine Patrick Vivian
Col. William S. "Billy" Harris
Corp. Roscoe Hailey

Cont...

CWO Hank W. Rawlston
CWO Warren G. Davidson
Dr. Layton Winthrop
Dr. Stephen Milam, Chief-of-Surgery
Flt. Lt. Trevor Roper
Gen. Dwight D. Eisenhower
Gen. Erwin Rommel
Gen. Sir Hastings Ismay
Gp. Capt. W.B. Murray
Happy
Inspector Walter Henry Thompson
King
Lady Barbara Bevan
LCpl. Ray "Tank" Karlsson
Lt. Ted "The Great Teddy" Hamilton, OBE
Lt. Col John Cecil (J.C.) Masterman
Lt. Col. "Pyro" Percy Stirling, DSO, MC
Lt. Col. David Strangeways, DSO
Lt. Col. Elbridge G. Chapman,
Lt. Col. Harry "Joe" Hollis
Lt. Col. Jack Dance
Lt. Col. Maurice Buckmaster
Lt. Col. Noel Wild
Lt. Col. Robin "Tin Eye" Stephens
Lt. Col. Sir Terry "Zorro" Stone, KBE, DSO, MC
Lt. Col. Thomas Argyll "Tar" Robertson
Lt. Gen. "Geronimo" Joe McKoy
Lt. Gen. J.C.H. Lee
Lt. Gen. *aka* "Beetle" Walter Bedell Smith
Maj. The Lady Jane Seaborn, LG, OBE, RM
Maj. Hawkins
Maj. Hanns von Reisen
Maj. Peter Wilkinson
Maj. Roger Fleetwood-Hesketh
Maj. Gen. Cecil R. Moore
Maj. Gen. Harold R. "Pinky" Bull
Maj. Gen. James "Baldie" Taylor, OBE
Maj. Gen. Sam Houston "Bronc" Blackwell
Maj. Gen. Sir David Petrie, KCB, OBE

Cont...

Maj. Gen. Sir Kenneth Strong
Maj. Gen. Sir Stewart Menzies, DSO, MC *aka* "C"
Maj. Gen. Walter Bedell Smith
Maj. Gen. William "Wild Bill" Donovan
Mr. Smith
Mr. Guy Liddell
MSgt. Buck Callahan
MSgt. Mack Beckwith
PFC James "Wildman" Terrell
PFC Norvel Hansen *aka* "Horn Dog"
PM Winston Churchill
Rikke (Rocky) Runborg
Scout Lionel Fenwick
Scout Munro Ferguson
Sloan Marlow *aka* S&M
Sqn. Ldr. Dennis Wheatly
Sub-Lt. Jeffery Macomber
VAdm. Sir Randolph "Razor" Ransom, VC, KCB, DSO, OBE, DSC, RN
Vanish
Veronica Paige, OBE
Waldo Treywick
Wg. Cdr. A.M. Murphy, DSO, DSC *aka* "Sticky"
Wg. Cdr. Alastair "Mac" Macrae, DFC
Wg. Cdr. Leonard Cheshire, VC, DSO, DFC
WO George E. May
X-Ray

ABOUT THE AUTHOR

Phil Ward is a highly decorated combat veteran commissioned when he was nineteen. He served as an instructor at the Army Ranger School. Nowadays Phil lives on a mountain overlooking Lake Austin.

~ ~

OTHER BOOKS IN THE RAIDING FORCES SERIES:

Those Who Dare
Dead Eagles
Blood Wings
Roman Candle
Guerrilla Command
Necessary Force
Desert Patrol
Private Army
Africa 1941
The Sharp End
Raiding Rommel
Strategic Services
The TIP of the Sword
Always So Few
The War That Never Was
Economy of Force
The Magnificent Mission
Military Deception

www.ingramcontent.com/pod-product-compliance
Lightning Source LLC
LaVergne TN
LVHW091341110826
845155LV00050B/26/J